World War When

Elliot Thorpe

World War When
Published in 2022 by
AG Books
agbooks.uk

AG Books is an imprint of
Andrews UK Limited
andrewsuk.com

Cover designed by A E Abbottson

Acknowledgements

Thanks go to my family and to A E Abbottson, Barnaby Eaton-Jones, Kent Edens, Del Fuller, Dan Griffiths, Sarah Leitch, Avi Elyse McCullah and Heather Roulo for their input and support. Thanks also to Paul Andrews, Joe Larkins and the team at Andrews, and most of all to Kenton Hall, my editor and brilliant encourager, for making this far and above better than I had ever envisaged.

World War When

Prelude: 1918

Padua, Italy

Second Lieutenant Alexander Flood was seventeen and had never been outside of his home village of Filby before, let alone England itself.

While he was struggling with the temperature, so far, he had been spared the distress of combat, instead poring over maps and data that his colleagues in the field brought back. He smoked, heavily, partly to combat the September chill, partly from habit but mainly to keep himself awake on his night watch.

In the distance, ack-ack fire rang out, but it was difficult to determine if it was the Allies defending against the Central Powers or vice versa. Guns sounded the same whoever built them and conjured the same result.

If Alex said a prayer it was silently, but the rosary clutched beneath his khakis told his companion enough.

'You should keep your hands on your weapon, lad,' chided Michael Whiteacre. He was Alex's superior officer, but more relaxed than most when it came to watch standards. He had shed his own faith via landmine, alongside the legs of his best friend, a few weeks into the war. But he wasn't the sort of man to deny a fellow comfort. 'Say your prayers and keep looking at the sky.'

Alex nodded and apologised.

Captain Whiteacre placed a hand on Alex's shoulder. 'You'll be fine.'

'I heard the boys talking. That there are too many of them out there.'

'Doesn't listen to trench talk, Lieutenant.'

Whiteacre offered Alex another cigarette, watching the young man stub out his current one in the mud. Alex took it gladly, coughing slightly as his captain held a lit match to its end.

'It's all over the camp, sir. We're outnumbered.'

'Listen, lad. Soldiers whisper. Always have. It passes the time. You have to focus. Do your job. Don't look left or right. It isn't easy but we should do all we can to *make* it look easy.' Whiteacre joined Alex in a smoke. 'We don't know for sure how many of them are out there. No one knows.'

Which was a lie.

The generals knew. HQ knew. Everyone but those on the ground knew. And that was the way it had to be, to keep morale up. To keep those fighting spirits buoyant.

Whiteacre was not immune to fear. Far from it. His guts churned constantly and, away from the men under his charge, he often threw up as his anxiety overcame him. But he was a Captain, full of Yorkshire pride, and he had the courage to see it through to the bitter end.

More ack-ack fire, this time sounding closer.

Alex gripped his rifle so hard it felt like it would melt into his palms.

The temperature wasn't far off freezing. The wind that whipped across the arable parts of the open country made it feel considerably colder.

He had another hour and forty before the relief watch took over and it couldn't come quickly enough. He had a pounding headache. He took a swig from his hip flask: French brandy (hard to come by at the moment) that warmed him better than the cigarette but too strong to keep him focused. He wasn't a drinker and had only started a few weeks ago at the encouragement of his fellow soldiers. He shuddered as he swallowed.

Without warning, the air around them popped and fizzed. It was unlike anything the ack-ack guns produced and neither was it an explosion. As it continued, Whiteacre wound his field telephone to make a connection. The line was dead but it didn't stop him from trying again. And again.

There was a scream of a biplane descending and the captain pulled Flood down into the mud. The plane swooped over their heads and towards the encampment, its engine spluttering and choking.

'Jeez,' Whiteacre wheezed and got to his feet. He grabbed Flood and darted towards the direction of the plane. But it had banked around, as if trying to find somewhere to land. That suggested an Allied craft. If it *had* been German, less care would have been taken by the pilot. Whiteacre nevertheless headed for the encampment. Whatever markings that aircraft carried, the alarm still wanted raising.

'Lad, wake the Major.'

At Alex's hesitancy, he pushed the young Second Lieutenant towards the temporary huts then dashed into the darkness.

'Captain…' Alex whispered, but Whiteacre had gone.

***

The plane was half-buried in the soft earth, a few hundred yards from the night watch position. In the moonlight, Whiteacre didn't recognise it; any markings were obscured. The pilot had been thrown clear and was lying face up, seemingly unconscious.

Whiteacre performed a quick visual check: no fuel leak and a twisted, smoking propeller. The right wings had disintegrated on impact, the left almost vertical to the ground when the main fuselage had tipped onto its side.

The captain snuck to the pilot and checked if he was breathing. He was. Whiteacre felt gently for broken bones. Nothing. If the pilot had any lacerations, electric light back at the encampment would reveal them; Whiteacre was satisfied that he could be moved without risking further injury.

The pilot's black flight suit was unfamiliar. Like the plane itself, there was no insignia, no markings, nothing to identify his nationality or whose side he was on. His flying helmet was thicker, more padded than Whiteacre was used to, finished off with a pair of unusual goggles. At his hip, the pilot carried a Beretta. Nothing unusual there, but a potential sign of theft. He disarmed the pilot, briefly considering removing the bullets. But a handgun at the moment would be more useful than his cumbersome Lee-Enfield. So he slipped his own rifle onto his back and pocketed the Beretta.

The pilot groaned.

Whiteacre leaned in close.

Suddenly, the pilot lurched forward and threw his weight onto the captain. The unexpected assault toppled Whiteacre and as he fumbled for the pilot's Beretta, the pilot was up and on his feet and heading towards the cockpit.

Whiteacre leapt up, retrieved the Beretta and moved to tackle the pilot. His assailant neatly sidestepped the attempt. Whiteacre crashed to the ground, mud splattering his face. Spitting both dirt and rage he tried again but the pilot had already reached the biplane and spun back, a Luger in his grip and aimed at the captain's torso.

'You're a damn *heinie*,' Whiteacre spat.

'No,' came the reply. 'You need to let me get away from here.'

A perfect English accent! A spy?

'Sure thing, *heinie*,' replied Whiteacre, holding the pilot's Beretta steady. 'There's going to be a whole squad of my chaps here at any moment.'

'I don't want to kill you.'

'You wouldn't dare. Not on a British camp.'

The pilot seemed confused for a moment, as though he wasn't expecting to *be* on a British camp. 'I'm… not a German. I work for the Allies.'

'*Work for*? That's a giveaway. None of us *work for* the Allies. We *serve*. Now drop your weapon before I kill *you*.'

Saint-Mihiel, Meuse

The war began with two shots and it would end with one.

At least that was what Daniel Restarick hoped, waiting in the bombed-out shell of what had been shop, judging by the strewn cans of food.

The US Army had withdrawn some hours ago, successful in pushing the German offensive back towards Metz. But the battle was far from over. The air was thick with death and rain, the town deserted save for himself, some vaguely recognisable human corpses and a few mongrel dogs. Spirals of smoke drifted on the air of the autumn afternoon; devastated buildings forlornly lined either side of the main street. At one end, a Renault FT tank was upended in a crater, having been shelled by enemy artillery. Even at this distance, Restarick could smell the petrol settling in a pool at the bottom of the jagged hole.

He was across the street from the church—one of the few fully standing structures, as if some providence had kept it free from the conceit of humanity. He was tired but focused, the rum from his weekly ration having been spilt during the night. Patience, too, was a prerequisite of a man like him.

'Men become boys at the first taste of fear,' his Regimental Sergeant Major had instilled in him, from day one. It was thought he returned to often, even more so now that he essentially worked alone. Losing focus could lead to fatal mistakes.

At twenty-nine, Restarick was considered a veteran, having seen conflict almost from the moment war broke out. Formerly of the Essex Regiment, he had been hand-picked, during the summer of 1916, by Naval Intelligence—to work in the field for the Factory or, more formally, Room 40, the predominant section in the British Admiralty that handled cryptanalysis. Covert operations had led him here, with the knowledge that vital information and thus advantage was going to be passed to the Central Powers. His mission was simple: prevent this by any means necessary.

If the war ended on this one shot, the euphoria and relief across the world would be his doing. It was a heady thought.

It began to rain again, thunderstorms having relented only yesterday evening, almost concurrently with the exchange of fire. Restarick hated the feeling of the cold water against his back, hated the sight of his rifle becoming obscured, hated the stinging in his eyes. Further, he wore no gloves when using his Mosin-Nagant, his choice of weapon during sniper deployments, so the damp had a habit of making his grip more precarious on the lengthy barrel.

He wanted a cigarette but the smoke would give away his position. It would have to wait.

Wiping the sight, he scanned the rubble-strewn street before him, waiting for his quarry and thinking of his return to England, to Surrey and to what he had already lost.

He and Lita had only been married for five months when she died and they had spent very little time together as a couple, stolen moments while he was on leave. There had been no honeymoon. They'd written, of course, as much as the Army Postal Service allowed, but it was a poor replacement. Still, she had not given any indication of unhappiness or discontent. Although, perhaps that was the role of those left behind. Just as those on the battlefield had to callously dismiss them from their minds. Lita had worked at the Silvertown munitions factory. The previous year, she had survived an accident that had killed over seventy and injured in excess of four hundred more. Survived to perish later, in a fire in their home in Surrey; she'd been trapped as the ceiling above her collapsed, bringing the bedroom down around her. The ARP wardens and the fire brigade had been unable to save her.

Her funeral had been a small affair. She'd left Spain as a young teenager and found her own way in life. Most of the mourners had been from Restarick's side of the family, and a handful of officers with whom he'd served. The memory of the day itself was now obscured by the rage that had consumed him. For the first time, even after all the death and pain he'd seen, he had become disillusioned with the world. He and Lita, however, had shared a passion for freedom, that fragile bloom, and this pushed him on, to fight against those who would crush it underfoot.

Her portrait, folded away in his pocket, served as his constant reminder.

The land surrounding the town was forest with the occasional patterns of farmland, not easily traversable by vehicle. The target, he had to assume, would arrive in the town on foot and, with both the Rue des Chanoines and Eglise Saint-Etienne mentioned in intercepted messages, the church was the most logical choice for the information exchange to take place.

He checked his watch. It was quickly approaching mid-afternoon; he had at least a few hours of daylight left.

In the distance, he heard the world rumble. Not thunder, that was too natural a sound. This was the result of mortar shells, ripping into bodies, into metal and into the earth some miles away. The shelling continued for a good hour or so, during which Restarick pushed his mind away from the devastation.

When all was quiet again, he sensed movement in the street below.

And there was his target, clear as day through his rifle sights. A trench coat, its large collar turned up, obscured any sign of expression or guise, a large grey woollen hat pulled low over the spy's face. Over one shoulder, they held a khaki holdall and it was this, Restarick knew, that held the papers he needed to intercept. On reaching the church door, the figure appeared to look around briefly, before ducking into the building.

Restarick cursed and shuffled forward on his belly, careful not to be seen. He couldn't risk going into the church itself in case the spy wasn't alone, though he suspected the spy would be making the exchange while out of sight. He would need to be damned fast to shoot down whoever came out of there.

He scanned the street again. All was quiet.

He aimed for the bell tower, firing and quickly reloading. The bell tolled deeply and Restarick refocused his sights on the church door.

Sure enough, a few moments later, the spy reappeared, holdall still held tightly in such a way that it was clear the precious documents were still inside.

Then it was no longer the church door in the crosshairs. Now it was the traitor's head.

This was it, the moment that would bring the war to an end.

Restarick quickly checked his watch and smiled to himself. 1700hrs. The Great War, 28 July 1914 to 13 September 1918.

He would be the bringer of peace.

He pulled the rifle into his shoulder, the weapon tight in his arms, and squeezed the trigger.

Crack!

His ears rang and his vision blurred. For a split second, he was unsure what happened, but then he tasted the blood in his mouth, felt it stinging his eyes. His rifle was in pieces, some of them lodged in his right arm.

He frowned and looked back at his target, who, judging from the angle of their head, was looking straight back at him. The shot had not come from the spy's direction, but Restarick had been struck all the same.

The spy, seeming to realise that he had been spared by unknown forces, gripped the holdall as if the future of the world depended on it (which, in innumerable ways, it did) and ran from the church, coat tails flapping bat-like in his wake.

Restarick sagged where he lay, shattered rifle parts surrounding him. The flesh on his right forearm was ripped to the bone. Blood continued to trickle from a head wound he found himself relieved he could not see. He heard the dull thump of the spy's retreat, a number of booted feet following, most likely those of the spy's contacts.

With some difficulty, he reached into his breast pocket: there was Lita, spattered with blood, torn but still present. He kissed her sepia image, hands trembling as shock overtook him. The dawning realisation of his failure was as acute as his wounds.

It was all for nothing.

All the killings, the crippling wounds, the broken minds.

The childless mothers weeping into their aprons forevermore.

Excerpt from 'Mohnblumen: Welle (100 Years of Deutsches Kaiserreich)' by Antoine Malik, Jiraf Books, published London 2018

"A stalemate has *occurred on the Western Front. Our invasion of France has failed and, even after we, in Belgium and in one day, killed over 27,000 French troops, Allied troops have proved unexpectedly resilient. Conversely, the British have been attacking for three months but have made little headway, their assaults unable to wipe out or push back our might. More than 120,000 British soldiers leapt from their trenches and advanced on our lines. Expecting to find obliterated bunkers and massacred troops, they were instead met by superior machine-gun fire, artillery shells, mortars and grenades. Yet similarly, our attempt to destroy Paris resulted in an unacceptable number of casualties. We have lost nearly in excess of 150,000 men.*

This can no longer be tolerated. There is only one way we can break the stalemate: returning to the arena in which we have more demonstrated our supremacy. We must demand of the Kaiser that submarine warfare be resumed. This decision will mean war with the United States, but we are confident that a decisive victory can be attained before they are able mobilise."

Paul von Hindenburg, Chief of the General Staff, was adamant that this revised approach would lead to ultimate victory. His deputy, Erich Ludendorff, concurred and together they convinced the German Emperor Wilhelm II of the same. The civilian government in Berlin objected but, regardless, the campaign went ahead in January 1917.

Von Hindenburg's strategy was sound: over three-quarters of the Allied fleet was sunk over the subsequent months, with America's support hindered by a continuous presence of Central Power vessels in the Atlantic. Eventually moving onto land, the Allies struggled to hold back the onslaught and trench warfare arrived in Britain on 15 December 1917.

Information vital to the success of the Allied cause came so close to being retrieved in September 1918 that it was, and remains, rarely mentioned in any retrospective. The very fact that this information would have secured victory for the Allies has long been a subject of contention.

On 4 November 1918, a shattered France agreed to an armistice, and the devastated Allied nations, troubled by extreme revolutionaries in London and Washington, followed suit on 11 November 1918, ending the war in total victory for the Austro-Hungarian Empire and Germany.

Part 1: 1928

Ceylon

Daniel Restarick was invalided out of the Great War shortly before the surrender. He'd been proud of his military career, following in familial footsteps: grandfather George had been killed in the Crimean and his own father James had served in the Merchant Navy, until his retirement, so it was a dreadful decision, albeit one made for him. His injuries at Saint-Mihiel, his superior officers told him, made him unfit for duty. Restarick was in no position to disagree, reluctantly taking up a position as a clerk for a London solicitor. When the Central Powers brought the Allies to their knees, the law firm, along with many other British companies, closed down. He was one of hundreds who had safely escaped, setting up a new life in Ceylon, where his father had settled some years before. The Central Powers had not been able to gain a foothold here and his recovering injuries were well served by the tropical climate.

His military skills, however, did not go to waste.

Room 40 found him again.

He was occasionally assigned to reconnoitre missions or to trail certain individuals of concern to the Allies. He had just finished one such task in Carnarvon, on the west coast of Australia.

Arriving back to Ceylon by passenger steamer, he left the docks at Colombo and caught the train to Kandy. Restarick always faced the engine. As a child, he'd keenly collected the numbers of all the great locomotives. The countryside passed by the windows, all tea and banana plantations and thick jungle foliage, hills and mountain ranges cutting through, a stark contrast to the burning towns and villages on the flat horizons that he saw so much of during the war. The rhythmic *chugga-chugga-chugga-chugga* of the engine snaking its way through the landscape, the erratic rocking back and forth when at full steam, meant that before long, Restarick nodded off, a copy of the *Daily News* open and crumpled in his lap.

He was awoken by the guard when they pulled into Suduhumpola Train Halt. He walked the remaining few miles to home, his battered brown suitcase in his right grip, his paper folded neatly under his left arm. A white panama hat sat atop his head, protection from the blazing sun.

Low, white bungalows with red-tiled roofs peered out over high walls, oxen wandered the roads, children played in amongst broken brickwork and traders pulled their wares on the back of carts, some by hand, lucky others by horse.

The bunting and flags that proclaim *seig* from every lamp post and from every shop window across Europe were refreshingly absent and so here still felt untouched. The country wasn't neutral, but it felt that way for the moment. He enjoyed the solitude and calm, just the birds in the trees chirping in time with the crickets in the long grasses and was looking forward to working with his hands again, helping manage the plantations up in the hills. The Restarick family lost a lot of the hired help when the war drew the able-bodied to the continent. Many of those who had survived, the ones who did not have history here, never returned, instead finding roots in France or in Britain (the Kaiser had formally removed the 'Great'), closer to the larger towns.

The suitcase felt heavy in Restarick's tight grip. He was anxious about seeing his father again. Yet as he walked past the bungalows and unpaved streets, he felt like he had never been away. Just ahead was the plantation that had been, was, home. He passed by the tea bushes up towards the main house. As he got closer, he was saddened to see the shrubbery unkempt in the few weeks he'd been away. His breath caught as he spied through the tired house with the bamboo that still caused no end of bother, but laughed quietly as he recalled his Mother so fondly tending the plants, as best she could, with her arthritic hands.

Inside was worse. Shocking. Filthy and cluttered. He stepped over broken furniture and rubbish, crossing the dilapidated room, further into the gloom. It looked as if the whole place had been ransacked. He hoped his own room had remained in good condition.

A narrow corridor led through to a tiny, dark room where the heat of the day was kept back by the shadows. There in the equally narrow, single bed, sheets twisted and entangled around his legs—thin and mottled with liver spots—was Restarick's beloved father James. He had aged unnaturally, as if some great and terrible burden had befallen him. It had for everyone, Restarick considered, as he sat on the edge of the bed, a hand on his father's skeletal arm: the damn war had placed the weight of humanity upon the fragile shoulders of the world.

Restarick stayed motionless for a while, in silence and with his thoughts, watching the elder Restarick breathe evenly. A great sadness overcame him. His father's decline was all-encompassing and absolute. The wisps of grey around his wrinkled temples were all that was left of a once full head of thick, black hair. His skin was papery and frail.

The elder man stirred and raised a hand, catching Restarick's fingers weakly.

'Son..?'

'Hello, Father,' Restarick said. 'I've missed you.'

Jim Restarick squinted and smiled. 'You look different, lad.'

'I was thinking the same about you. What happened here?' He helped his father sit up, propping pillows behind his neck, feeling skin and bone through his clothes.

Restarick looked around his father's bedroom. On the stool beside the bed was a picture of Mother. She had died of what could only have been a broken heart when the telegram had reached them that Aubrey, Restarick's younger brother, had been killed during the Cape Helles landing, not even a year into the conflict. Aubrey himself was represented by a sepia picture on the mantelpiece, taken shortly after his enlistment. His own photo sat next to it; they were both in full dress uniform. As for Angela, their older sister, her likeness was leant, further along, against a vase of dead flowers, already beginning to stink. On the wall above them all was an oil painting of his father's old Merchant Navy vessel, *Annunziata*, sunk in a violent storm off the Cape of Good Hope over twenty years back. His father had been the only survivor.

There was thick dust on everything and the acidic tang of the unwashed chamber pot under his father's bed overwhelmed the aroma of tobacco residue and soiled bedding.

'Daniel, you can't go back,' Jim whispered, shaking his head. 'You must not go back.'

Restarick frowned. 'Father, the war is over. I'm home now.'

'No.' He was insistent, gripping his son's forearm with surprising strength. 'You mustn't go back!'

'Father, the war… we lost the war. The Kaiser is in charge now. Don't you remember?' Restarick gently held his father's clenched hand. Was his mind now as ravaged as his body? 'There's nothing to go back *to*, Dad. Nothing. When will Angela be here?'

Daniel Restarick and his sister had never truly seen eye to eye since Aubrey's death. Angela, had she not been exempt from conscription, would have been a conscientious objector and often, while on leave, they had argued the morality of war across the Sunday dinner table. Father would stay silent, either unwilling or unable to take either side of his children's argument.

Angela continued to make her point by always setting places the table for Aubrey and their mother, even pouring out a glass of lemonade for Aubrey that sat there fizzing gently throughout the meal.

'In a couple of days,' Jim said. 'But for now, will you go to the kitchen for me?'

'Yes, what can I get you?' Restarick stood. 'Are you hungry? Thirsty?' He looked around him again. 'We need to clean this place up. Where is Raj?'

'I'm thirsty.' Jim coughed, one hand clutching at his chest as he brought the other to his mouth. He tried to hide the blood spotting onto his knuckles; his son noticed and pretended he hadn't, leaving to go downstairs.

'I sent him away,' his father called out weakly, in answer to his son's final question.

Restarick looked quietly around in the kitchen: the sink was loaded with dirty crockery and utensils. The smell from the cold stale water was sickly, a mixture of Rinso and turned meat. He guessed that it had been there for days. The tropical heat had only made matters worse. Pans dangled from crude hooks above the central kitchen table, clanging slightly in the warm breeze from the open window.

It took him a few minutes to clear the sink and clean some of the cutlery and cups. He'd help Jim before coming back to finish. He was concerned his father looked so weak. The old man had been struggling for a while but not to this extent. Daniel took him some fresh water.

'Have you told Angela?'

'No! You know what she'd say.'

'You should have done. She would have come sooner.'

'I know what you're thinking: that I'm just a forgetful old man.' He looked up at his son and smiled. Restarick sensed something behind his father's eyes, the sense of purpose that had always anchored him to the world. 'I know you detest the Kaiser as much as everybody else. They're clearing away the Old World.'

The Kaiser, Restarick cursed to himself. *A viper nesting in the once-great Britain's shallow grave.* 'But they won't get as far out as here. There's no viability of enforcing the curfews this far away from Europe.' But Restarick knew that wasn't going to last forever. It wouldn't be long before the colonies came under the Kaiser's full control. 'There's no need for this. You don't need to sell up. Where will you go?' Restarick rubbed his temples. He couldn't have his father living with him in England. His work was too sensitive and Jim would be a vulnerable target. 'What about to Angela's? Can't she stay on? Or you go to her?' He sighed in frustration. 'You shouldn't have dismissed Raj.'

Jim shook his head. His once-large frame was swallowed by the bed. 'I didn't dismiss him. I gave him time off.'

'Time off? Raj wouldn't know what to do with time off!'

Restarick feared that his father was dying. He knew it was a fantasy, but Death had followed him closely since he had enlisted, when he was just a boy. He felt it owed him the boon of avoiding his home.

Angela arrived two days later.

She was alone, having left her husband Roy behind at their estate in Kandy and she was irate.

'How long have you been back?' she asked, no indication she was pleased to see her brother. 'Not long enough by the looks of things.'

While Restarick had tidied and made some repairs, much of the exterior of their father's property still needed some attention.

'Dad is unwell.' *Hello, Angela.* 'Did you know?'

'That he's ill? Yes.'

'Didn't you think to tell me?' *It's nice to see you.* 'Is he dying?'

'I don't know.'

'He said he hadn't told you.'

'No, he didn't. But I called the doctor and he told me.'

'What's the prognosis?'

'They think it's consumption. So it's quite likely that yes, he *is* dying.'

Restarick sighed, taken aback by Angela's coldness. Over the years, he had realised that they were more similar than he had once thought. He just hoped he had more compassion than she.

'It's serious, then?'

'Of course it's serious, Danny! But not serious enough to make you stay.' Angela removed her light jacket and sunglasses, her hair latticed behind her head. Restarick always saw their mother in her.

'My job. It's—'

'Vital to the war effort?' she snorted. 'The war is done. Ten years ago, Danny. Why won't any of you grow up and stop playing at soldiers? This is your home, the family business.'

'You really think this is a game?' Restarick responded. 'The curfews, the executions, the walls, no freedom to travel.'

'It doesn't affect us here.'

'It affects us everywhere. Eventually.' Restarick sat down at the kitchen table, folding the duster he'd been using earlier. He lowered his voice. 'There might not be a war now but we still need to fight. What we sacrificed can't be for nothing. Because before you know it, you'll have *kaisersoldaten* on every street corner in every city, town and village in every country. It's happened in North Africa. There are rumblings that India is suffering too. It will happen here.'

'Danny, you've not been here for weeks. You've not written. He hasn't heard from you. No one's heard from you.'

Restarick closed his eyes for a moment, the old feelings of contempt coming back. 'I work away. I can't help it.'

Angela placed the kettle on the stove. 'You *could* have helped it. You could have stayed at home instead of doing whatever the hell it is you do.'

'You mean give up? Accept that our King is still in exile? That the Kaiser took his place? Europe is occupied. Fucking hell, Angie, *England* is occupied!'

'Lita is dead.'

Angela might has well have shot him point blank for the effect that had. 'What?'

'You heard me.'

Restarick felt anger rising from his belly. How dare she have said such a thing! 'What's that got to do with anything? This isn't what this is about!'

'Isn't it? What is it then? What makes you dash around the world being a hero?'

He was offended as much by the insinuation that he'd never asked himself this question as by Angela's opinion on the subject. Restarick's reasons for being part of the underground Secret Service went far beyond heroism, beyond Lita, Aubrey or any fallen comrade. The *Kaiser-Regel* ruled and controlled mainland Europe. There were strict curfews, checkpoints and walls built around many of the major cities. Travel between countries was strictly controlled. Import and export was extremely limited.

'The world has been *enslaved*. It's for Aubrey, for Lita, for *you*, that we're fighting to change that.'

'Tea?'

Restarick shook his head. 'I guess there really a corner of this foreign field that is always England.'

'Life goes on, Danny. It is what it is. If someone said to you that you could go back and change it all, how do you know it would be for the better?' Angela picked up the boiling kettle from the stove, a tea-towel wrapped around its handle and proceeded to make two cups of tea.

'Are you actually saying we're better off like this?'

'Look around you. There aren't any German soldiers here.'

'It's just a matter of time!'

'Time! We lost the war a decade ago. And who is to say this is not the way it should be?' The hot water curled steam into the air between them. 'I don't condone the Central Powers. I didn't want us to lose the war. But we did. Aubrey died because of it. Roy is a bloody cripple because of it. Father has worried himself into his death bed because of it. You spend your time fighting an already declared battle. Because of it. But that's the way it is. I have to accept it. We all do. Biscuits?'

Angela pushed a cup and saucer to her brother.

'I don't want biscuits,' he replied petulantly. 'Why *should* we accept it?' he asked.

'Because changing things won't bring Aubrey home, won't mend Roy's legs and won't suddenly put Lita back in your arms. Dad left you the family business. You're leaving it to go under.'

'Raj manages the plantations. And does so well.'

'But he's not Dad's carer. He's employed to harvest the crops.'

'You don't live here either. Why am I being read the riot act?'

'I can't leave Roy, you know that. But clearly *you* can leave Dad.'

'He wasn't this ill when I left.'

'This place was burgled one day, when Dad was out on the plantation. The shock…' She trailed off with a weary shrug.

'Burgled. Was anything stolen? Did they catch whoever it was?'

Angie offered upraised palms. 'A little money. And no they didn't.'

'Well, what did the Police say?'

'The *Vidane Arachchi*? What do you expect? Nothing.'

Restarick stood and looked around him. 'But they said to leave the place untouched?'

'Yes. Not that it made much difference. Dad hasn't been able to look after it.'

'Alright, well, I'm home now, Angie.'

'Yes, but for how long?'

Daniel Restarick sighed and looked back at his sister. He hated to admit she was right. Maddeningly, she usually was. And he was being a little unfair. She had her own business to run, a chain of hotels in Colombo down the coast, as well as her ailing husband.

'I'm sorry,' he said. 'I'll tell them that Dad's ill and I need to stay. They can make do without me for a while. I'll get this place cleared up.'

Angela frowned, trying to read his expression. She shrugged and sipped her tea. 'Drink up. Dad needs a bath and you need to sort that gate out before next door's goats wander in.'

***

Over the next six months, Restarick worked hard alongside Raj, fixing the border fences, overseeing crops and their cultivations and generally dragging the business back on track. Jim had grown steadily weaker but still offered advice, even orders from his sick bed. One morning, maintenance to be done on the largest of the store houses, Restarick could be found moving heavy sheets of corrugated iron along the roof. Raj called up from the ground.

'Someone in the office to see you, sir,' he said, with a smile.

'Who is it?' Restarick replied, peering over the edge, shielding his eyes from the sun. 'This needs to be fixed before the storm returns. We don't have time for visitors.'

The roof was split and leaking and the unexpected rains during the night had ruined at least a fifth of the tea leaves waiting to be shipped out.

'That's what I told him, sir. But he insisted.'

'Can't you take care of it?'

'He does not want to talk to me, only to the boss, he said.'

Restarick exhaled and wiped his brow. It was only just past eight and already the air was broiling. His shirt clung to his back, sweat running between his shoulder blades. Perhaps it was about the break-in—the Ceylon police were notoriously slow. It had bothered Restarick since he'd cleared up the mess that the perpetrators had obviously been searching for something—and the money they had taken was merely an added bonus. There had been an order to the ransacking, as if they had progressed through the house at a deliberate pace. Angela had disagreed.

'Always suspicious, Danny,' she'd said. 'That's what that bloody war turned you into.' An empty house, an unwell old man, underpaid tea-pickers… *of course* they were opportunists. But Restarick still insisted otherwise.

He hooked the hammer into his belt and clambered down the ladder.

'What does he look like?'

'Like all of you Westerners,' Raj responded, a twinkle in his eye.

Restarick laughed and clapped Raj on his back. 'That bad, eh? Come on, let's see what this fellow wants.'

Raj had been with the company for many years now, Restarick having first met him when he'd arrived in Ceylon following his discharge. He'd checked into Paradise Beach, north of Negombo, before heading inland to Kandy to meet his father; he had been looking for a reliable guide. Raj had been delivering food to a neighbouring bungalow and asked him for directions. Raj had instead driven him by cart to Negombo and requested no payment. Once he'd got to Kandy and settled in, establishing the state of his father's business, Restarick had asked after him back at the hotel, managing to locate his one-room *mati geya*. Raj had been at home with a wife, three children, a couple of aunts and an ageing relative of indeterminate generation.

He offered Raj a job on the spot and paid for him and his entire family to move to Kandy.

Restarick had always been proud of his ability to read people and he knew Raj for a loyal man. Nine years later, he was the senior manager, with his wife Chaturi in charge of the workforce's pay. The two aunts and the grandmother had since passed away but the children were part of the large team of pickers.

The main office of Pilawala Tea was a traditional four-pillared veranda with a coconut palm roof, the trunks sliced into thin lengths. It allowed in far less rain in than the heavy corrugate over the storehouses, but Raj was of the opinion that the extra upkeep offset the benefit and Restarick was slowly coming around to the same conclusion.

Sitting at the large desk, in one of the two visitor seats, was a wiry-looking man in a crumpled white suit, clearly uncomfortable in the heat. He was bespectacled and waved a battered Panama hat in front of his face. He stood as Restarick and Raj approached.

Restarick wiped his palms on his trousers, smiled and offered the man a hand.

The man took it, his grip limp. 'Thank you for meeting with me, Mr…?'

'Restarick.'

'But not Mr Restarick Senior?' He let go the handshake. 'You are the son?'

'Yes, I am. But something tells me you already knew that.' Restarick pulled out a chair and sat opposite the man. Raj moved behind his employer. 'Who do we have the pleasure of today?'

The man twitched at the 'we', giving Raj a brief but disapproving frown.

'My name is Secombe. I'm from the Ministry of Home Affairs.'

'Been in Ceylon, long?' asked Restarick, offering Secombe a cloth napkin.

'A few weeks,' Secombe said, looking intently at Restarick as he wiped the sweat from his forehead.

'You'll acclimatise eventually,' Restarick replied, waving that Secombe could keep the napkin. 'What is it that you wish to talk to us about?'

'I had hoped that it would be your father I would meet with.'

'Well you've got Raj and myself, Mr Secombe.' Restarick clasped his hands together and leant back in the chair, the dry wicker creaking.

'There are concerns about Pilawala Tea.'

'Concerns? I thought you were here about the break-in.'

'Was anything taken?'

'Not that we can see.' Restarick tried to read the man's expression. Secombe didn't seem surprised that there had been people on the plantation. 'So what are these concerns you have? Our export is regular, we pay our taxes. There's a full yield every season. What can Home Affairs *possibly* be concerned about?' Restarick knew exactly what Secombe's response would be.

'Your business is managed in an unorthodox fashion.'

'How I run my business is not your concern. Who my employees are, again, is not your concern.'

'But it is not *your* business. Where is Mr Restarick Senior?

'He is… indisposed. Directorship is fully mine. It has been registered accordingly in Colombo.' Restarick unclasped his fingers and scratched the back of his neck with a finger. The mosquitoes were devils this time of year. 'I take it there have been complaints. From the *Grama Niladhari*, perhaps?'

Secombe went straight to the point. 'You employ a woman to tell the pickers how many rupees they have earned and you have a manager and his family living in your bungalow. *And* they are Sinhalese.'

'Are you Tamil?' asked Restarick.

'Well of course not! I'm from Surrey.'

Then perhaps you should fuck off back to Surrey, Mr Secombe? 'Then perhaps you should leave me to run my father's highly successful business that generates a substantial income for the Ceylon government and return to your cool, air-conditioned office, sir?'

'But…'

Restarick stood. 'I know of the conceit in this country that the locals won't respect us if we treat them like equals. I treat Raj and his family as they deserve to be treated: *with* respect. Raj is my friend and the manager of Pilawala Tea. I have had no cause so far to alter either that opinion or his position. What is the true nature of your visit here, sir? I cannot imagine Home Affairs are that bothered by our methods?'

'We feel that perhaps your talents are better suited elsewhere?'

'You're not from Home Affairs at all, are you?

'I can assure you I am, Mr Restarick.'

'Then are you offering me a job?'

'A job?'

'An employment. Of my, as you say, usefulness.'

'You are known to be away for great lengths of time.'

'I travel.'

'To where?'

'What has this got to do with tea, Mr Secombe?'

'You have generated a level of curiosity.'

Restarick walked around the desk and stood next to Secombe, staring out at the sloping rows of tea bushes above them, the tea pickers dressed in brightly coloured saris moving slowly but resolutely along their symmetrical pattern. Further up the hillside was the house. 'We run an honest business.'

'But your trips...' Secombe pressed.

'Master sells our tea to the Westerners, Mr Secombe,' said Raj.

'You insist we export. We know we must export. Ceylon benefits from foreign money,' added Restarick. 'And it's important to me that I know who our customers are. Face-to-face. Besides, I haven't travelled since March.'

'If you like, we can produce the travel papers?' Raj squinted at Secombe, who pursed his lips for a moment to think about the suggestion.

'No. No, I don't think that would be necessary,' decided Secombe, standing, his hat now swatting more bugs than heat. He too drank in the plantation without. 'I must admit, you have an impressive plantation. One of the best I've visited.'

Restarick quietly motioned to Raj to escort Secombe to the main gates, ignoring the compliment. 'I trust that you will file your report accordingly?'

'My report?' asked Secombe as he realised it was his time to leave, putting his hat on.

'Yes. Surely you will write up this meeting when you get back to Colombo?'

'Ah, yes, of course... my report,' smiled Secombe, putting his own hand out to Restarick, who simply motioned towards the descending pathway. 'Well... yes, thank you, Mr Restarick and Mr... er... yes.'

Raj rolled his eyes behind Secombe's back, Restarick stifling a laugh.

'Pleasant journey, Mr Secombe,' Restarick said and sat back down, breathing out long and hard, as Secombe trotted after Raj. He put his feet up on the desk and closed his eyes for a moment. They soon snapped open again.

That roof wouldn't get done if he sat here on his laurels.

***

That night, once he'd showered and had a small supper of pulses and vegetables, Restarick retired to bed. He tried to continue reading one of his late wife's books, a favourite of hers he knew, but his eyes became too heavy to focus. Lawrence was always a heavy read for him at the best of times and *The Rainbow*, banned and burnt everywhere outside of the USA (long before the Kaiser took control of Europe), was no exception. Angela told him to throw the filth in the hearth but Restarick had no intention of doing so. Lita had always been liberal in her attitudes and he saw much of Ursula, Lawrence's passionate creation, in her.

It was a humid night and he listened to the crickets in the undergrowth and the frogs sitting on the banks of the river that ran along the foot of the plantation edge. It was a sound that he never tired of hearing, and whenever he was away, he found its absence disturbed his sleep. It eluded him now for other reasons; he twisted and turned, the sheets tangling themselves around his bare legs.

There had been something about that man from the ministry—he'd been sizing Restarick up, making mental notes. Restarick had a feeling that there was more to the visit that Secombe had let on. Raj had felt it, too, and not just of because of the visitor's prejudices.

A few more hours and still Restarick lay awake, chewing on his bottom lip. Annoyed, he sat on the end of the bed and rubbed his sore eyes. Checking his pocket watch, on his bedside table before a framed photograph of Lita, he saw it was just before four. Soon the tea pickers would be awake and getting ready to start their day at five at the bushes, the wicker baskets strapped to their arched backs. He stood and padded across the cool wooden floor to the trunk against the wall. Sitting before it, legs crossed, he opened it, the smell of wood polish and incense filling his nostrils.

Within were mementoes, scraps of a life once had, saved from the burning embers of the family home. The more the years went on, the more he feared Lita would truly and finally disappear from his mind's eye. His dreams of her were becoming sporadic. This was the one way he knew to keep his memories fresh.

A pocket photo of Lita: he'd had it with him all the time he was serving in the British Army. It was tattered, torn and darkened by spots of his own blood, dry and brown, so the trunk was the safest place for it now. An emerald dress: one she'd worn when he'd taken her to the Theatre Royal in Drury Lane, on a weekend he'd been on leave. They'd made love in the Royal Box he'd reserved. The play was long forgotten, but rustle of her raised slip, the heat of her olive skin beneath his hands… He lifted the dress to his nostrils now and breathed in deep, savouring the lingering scent of her perfume before placing it neatly back in the trunk. His dress uniform: had he still lived in England, he would have been ordered to burn it or shot for hiding it. Here, in Ceylon where the Kaiser hadn't taken hold (yet), he kept it. He didn't know why. He hated the bloody thing. But it was a symbol now, a reminder that he'd had every right to have worn it, was proud to have worn it, even. That freedom had been worth fighting for, even after its loss. A stack of envelopes, tied with string: the surviving correspondence he'd sent to Lita. He pulled the cord, careful not to fray the already delicate paper, unfolding the top letter and began to read.

Within Arctic Circle
Russian Territorial Waters
May 9th, 1917

My dearest Lita,

I hope you have been getting my letters recently. It's been quite difficult to send anything out from here because we've had a terrific snow blizzard. None of us, not even the captain, had seen anything like it before. But the sun's out now and the snow is disappearing fast from around the ship. I think we might be moving again soon.

Of course I told you before I'm not really enjoying being at sea and the entire crew had a change round so I have a new job now, part of the ship. I enjoy the hard work much better and I'm on deck more now so get to see more of the open waters. We're up at 6 and keep working until 1. The sun reflecting on the snow is so bright and we're all getting tans. Some of the crew caught snow blindness and had to stay below decks for a few days in the dark.

There are ships everywhere and once we're back to Canada, I'm disembarking to work with our friends there.

Did you get the £1-0-0 I remitted? I will send a little more next month or later depending on how long I'm in Canada.

It's a blessed relief to me that you have agreed to go to Kandy. The damn war is creeping closer to Blighty every time those German guns sing out. When you get there, tell Father I shall write to him as soon as I can. He probably wants to know all about the ships! All my love to everyone at home, I think about you all.

I am yours ever,
Daniel

He sighed, fingering the edge of the letter, knowing that was where Lita would have held it as she read, imagining he could feel her fingertips under his. Folding it up carefully, he slipped it back in amongst the others, spying an old diary of his under his uniform. It was worn, the leather cover tattered and the spine barely holding it all together. It fell open as he lifted it, some of the pages fluttering to his feet.

From the diary of Captain Daniel James Restarick
19 October 1917

Fifth day of leave.

A break in the monsoon today which is fortuitous as we left Galle early to head to Father's. Lita still isn't impressed with the Renault Type CB Coupe de Ville I borrowed from Corporal DeWitt—but she was happy enough to share the ride with me! It took a good five or so hours, with a couple of breaks en route. I showed her Kandy and the spice market there. She wasn't overly keen on the buffalo curd we had from a little shack but it was cooling in the sweltering sun. They don't have lassi on the island and trying to explain it to a local still (so far) hasn't resulted in an acceptable version of the drink. It seems that it, for the moment, will remain a delicacy for India's sub-continent.

There was a porcupine tied to a stake at a crossroads and Lita insisted we untie it. I explained it was probably used as an attraction for us Western colonials and someone's livelihood. She looked at me disapprovingly with her beautiful dark eyes, a little shocked I was so accepting of the poor creature's fate. It did seem cruel to leave it captive so I unhooked the thin rope from around its neck—very carefully, I might add, as those spines seemed oppressive. It snuffled for a few seconds then scurried off into the undergrowth.

I suggested to Lita we depart as quick as we could in case its owner returned. She agreed and we eventually reached the family estate mid-afternoon.

The Renault is a great little car and runs much smoother than the Model 'S' I crashed last year. Hopefully, its quality won't sink too soon. I am looking forward to driving it back to Galle but will be saddened to leave it back with its owner! DeWitt is a good man and rose quickly in the ranks. I hope to continue our friendship once this bloody awful war is over.

Lita is like sunshine dancing across a lake. I'm dazzled by her beauty, her capacity to make me laugh. I couldn't wait to introduce her; Father said how much she reminded him of Mother when she was younger.

Angela seemed a little hesitant, mind, and took a bit of warming up to her. It took until dessert for me to make the announcement and Angela nearly choked on her custard.

Lita and I will marry the next time I am on leave. Father will arrange for the banns to be read.

I will be heading back to England soon. Lita will remain in our home in Thornton Heath until we are married. She says she wants to stay there, too, as she has found roots there and she has a valued job in the—.

I'm not that fond of London—too busy, too dirty—but we're far enough out not to let it bother me too much. It's a place she calls home now and she's been looking for 'home' for so long, so who am I to take that away from her?

I've been looking, too—for her, that is—and now that I've found her, I'm not willing to let her go.

The boys back in the regiment laugh at me, telling me I am smitten for that Spanish Lady.

Yes, I am head over heels so why should I hide it? She keeps me going at the most dreadful, lowest points of this damned war.

Without her love, there's little point to any of this hell

A knock came at his door: one of the houseboys, no doubt. To have disturbed him at this hour meant there was problem somewhere.

He quickly repacked the trunk, closing the lid. His work and the equipment relating to his Room 40 assignments he kept in a combination safe under the floorboards beneath the bed. It had been months now since they'd contacted him. Yes, he'd expressed his need to stay in Ceylon but rarely, in his experience, had Room 40 ever considered anyone else's needs.

'What is it?' Restarick said when the knock repeated.

'Master. An intruder.'

London, England

In an apartment in the luxurious Melfort Hotel, Aaron Kaplan sat at the foot of the bed. The woman still beneath the covers shivered in the draught from the open sash window.

'Come back to bed, Aaron,' she murmured. Her long legs reached almost to the foot of the bed. He ignored her request so she stretched to tap his thigh with her toes.

He brushed her away and stood, moving to the bathroom. Running a bath, Aaron remained silent as the woman, Aisling, arranged the silks over her chest. He knew she'd be watching him, his broad shoulders moving beneath the light covering of dark hair across his back. Looking for the scratches on the back of his neck where, the previous night, she had dug in her nails. She had escaped neither tooth nor claw herself.

'Get ready,' he said, not turning around to look at her. 'You need to leave soon.'

His Bavarian accent was strong, something which always seemed to thrill her. He moved to the little sink to begin shaving.

A sharp knock at the door made the woman jump. Kaplan glared at her as he grabbed a dressing gown to answer it, lather forming a white beard across his face. There were mumbled exchanges with whoever was standing out in the corridor and the door shut again. Without a further word, Kaplan finished his shave, had his bath, shut the window and dressed. Then he lifted the telephone and ordered room service.

Afterwards, Aisling claimed his bath water, a luxury not to be wasted. Kaplan came back into the bathroom, urinating freely as though alone, before washing his hands and leaving.

The food arrived and, as Aisling dried herself, Kaplan sat at the small table and enjoyed *das Frühstück*: fresh *Brötchen* with a selection of spreads and some sliced *Bröt* with *Leberwurst* and some butter, washed down with a tepid, sweetened cocoa. He always waited until it cooled before drinking it, the heat masked the flavour. He left none for her.

As he pushed his tray to the middle of the table, he finally returned his gaze to Aisling. He enjoyed seeing her naked, for all his brusqueness. The simplicity of skin aroused him. But his superiors were waiting and there was no time to revisit the glories of the night before.

She dressed and tied her bobbed hair in a short ponytail, hiding it under a picture hat, one that complemented the almond shape of her face and the straight lines of her pale blue dress. She moved to kiss Kaplan goodbye but he simply opened the hotel door, ushering her out.

'See you tonight, *A mhuirnin*,' she said, unfazed, heading off down the corridor to the stairs.

Kaplan waited until her footsteps faded away before shutting the door, then turned to the double bed. He lifted the sheets from the floor and slid a case from beneath the bed. Flipping the catches open, he opened the heavy lid and revealed a gun, disassembled. He checked all the parts were present then counted the cartridges: twenty-two. More than enough.

Closing the case, he pulled a jacket over his shirt and braces, the grey matching his trousers, and placed a trilby on his head. With one last check around him, he left, hailing a taxicab from along Gower Street.

***

The flags atop Buckingham Palace at the end of the Mall displayed with disturbing ease the Kaiser's decade-long rule.

The Emperor had only been here once since the Armistice, on a state visit, but the entire building was kept immaculate and under extensive security all the same. It was one of the few landmarks he had not renamed. It was a starker reminder of the Central Powers' might for it to be forever Buckingham Place occupied.

It had become the core of the *Kaiser-Regel*'s British presence, the arm of the Emperor's government taking up permanent residency.

In one of the many offices, the *Verwaltungsbüro* kept a close administrative control over the entire country but today, a meeting of the senior members of staff had been called.

There were six of them, officious, be-whiskered beneath monocles or spectacles, somewhere between schoolmasters and suited owls. They sat in a line behind a long and heavy mahogany desk.

One single chair sat the other side, occupied by Kaplan, his trilby upon one knee. The heavy case was neatly placed to his right.

'You understand why you are here today?' one of the men asked.

'Sirs, I am honoured you have asked me. And yes, I understand.'

There was a series of nods. One of the men looked down at a folder, thick with papers:

Aaron Kaplan. Born 1901, Merkendorf, Bavaria. Late of the *K.u.K. Seefliegerkorps*. Trained with the Austrian Navy as a sniper and military intelligence agent.

'It says your father was present at the capture of this very building.'

'Yes, sir. He led the squadron.'

'Impressive,' murmured one sitting at the far right. 'And you have since taken on his mantle. You were decorated with *Pour le Mérite*.'

'Yes, sir, I was.'

'Were you worthy to receive such an honour?'

'I am grateful to those who felt I was worthy.'

'And now?'

'Now, sir?'

'What do you do now?'

'I am employed with the unit maintaining London.'

'You still have a vested interest in our occupancy.'

'Naturally.'

'Why? We are established. The British have accepted that. There is no need for the—'

'Sirs, with respect…' Kaplan scanned the six faces staring at him, their eyes boring into his own. To speak out of turn could mean a firing squad and his interruption had already clearly caused consternation, judging from the symphony of disapproving coughs. But inwardly he took a gamble: they asked him here, though they evidently hadn't *wanted* him here. Therefore, they *needed* him here.

'The British will never accept our presence. While our occupancy lasts, so too will their resistance.'

One of the officials raised an eyebrow, leaning to his colleague to whisper. Then the one with the folder asked: 'Do you see our time here to be limited?'

'I intend no disrespect to the Kaiser's strength. Rather I wish to protect it. The unrest is there under the surface, if you know where to look. Remember how the Enemy struggled with revolutionaries in Washington. The bombings in Paris last year alone were indicators that we still need to be mindful.'

'That allowed us to take the advantage,' the previously whispering official commented, nodding. Kaplan felt he recognised him, the angular cheekbones, cruel-looking eyes and a thick, unusual narrow-trimmed moustache under his long nose.

The Austrian.

'The seat of their power, usurped. You feel that this may happen here?'

'I believe it is a danger.'

'And how is this danger to be countered?'

Kaplan drummed fingers against his trilby. 'We should accept that pockets of resistance exist.'

'Do the *Kaisersoldaten* not police our streets as they should? Is the curfew not enough?'

'Yes, indeed, sirs. The general public will not rise. It is not the man in the street we need to be concerned about.' *Surely they know this? They're testing me.* 'The Enemy works in the shadows. We ought to do the same.'

'Indeed. And that, as you understand, is why you are here.' The man with the folder closed it, laying clasped fingers across its manila surface. 'It has come to our attention that one such force is moving against us.'

'If you *are* aware of resistance movements, may I ask why this one is of particular concern?'

A second folder appeared on the desk, placed there by one of the officials who had, until now, not said a word or even looked at Kaplan. He pushed it towards the Bavarian, then sat back as if he had little interest in even being in the room.

Kaplan stood, picked up the folder and returned to his chair, moving his trilby to one side. The folder was red, sealed in the centre with black wax. He looked at the six men as if asking for permission to open it, then slid a finger under the middle flap, crumbling the wax.

Streng geheim—Operation: Geschenk declared the top sheet within, a book of matches tucked in the top left corner.

'Destroy the file once you have read and understood it. Do not take it out of this room. You will report to us in exactly twenty-four hours.'

With that, all six men stood and exited the high-windowed room, leaving Kaplan alone with the documents and the matches and the thoughts rushing through his head. He looked down at the open folder and lifted the first page. The instruction was clear, the task was manageable… but the timescale? It gave him little space to prepare but, professional that he was, it would be of no issue. The target's timetable and whereabouts were fully documented, as were those of the people who would be blamed for the event.

The Kaiser was to be obeyed without question and Kaplan was honoured to have been chosen. Further, the quick implementation meant the Enemy would have no time to intercept and overcome.

He hoped, too, that more tasks like this would come his way. As much as he was dedicated to building permanent monuments the *Kaiser-Regel* was powerful, deep inside him he missed the adrenaline of the kill.

Kaplan lit a match and touched the corner of the file with the flame. It caught and quickly consumed the secret plans, now known only to Kaplan and the six men who had been sitting before him.

Kaisersoldaten Regional HQ, Surrey

'This is the fourth such attack in two months,' said the man in the wheelchair, his eyes squinting as the sun streamed in through the window. 'The Resistance are raising the stakes.'

'How many *heimklasse* were killed?' asked Hartmann, a large man who seemed to struggle to even sit comfortably.

'Too many.' König, wiping his watering eyes with a silk kerchief, nodded towards the newspaper on his lap. 'The press have reduced that number, however.'

'Good. We can't have the populace worried.' Hartmann wheezed as he leant forward to drop ash from his cigar into the tray on the table before him. 'Do we know why they targeted that station? That train?'

'Apparently,' König said, 'they believed that it was a munitions train heading to the continent.'

It had been in fact a commuter train arriving at East Croydon, just south of London, that had been subjected to a terrorist attack, leaving twisted remains of the tender engine across three platforms and multiple injured or dead.

'And how on earth did they reach that conclusion?' Cigar smoke lingered above Hartmann's bald head.

'Because we told them,' came the response from the corner of the room. Lorenz Voigt moved towards the table. He was an imposing figure, dwarfing Hartmann. Clean-shaven and in a suit so sharp it could cut glass, he was the eyes and ears of the Kaiser's inner circle. König and Hartmann weren't scared of him, they weren't even in awe of him, but they were wary of him.

'Told them?' König wheeled around to face his colleagues. 'How so?'

'You yourself said that this is the fourth attack in a short space of time. The more the Resistance end up killing the *Engländer*, the more he will turn to us to protect him.'

'So we feed the Resistance with wrong information,' nodded Hartmann.

'Misinformation is, sometimes, even more deadly than truth,' Voigt purred. 'The Resistance itself is spreading fear wherever it goes. We need to do *nothing*.'

'And this is right,' said König. 'But how can we lower the number of *Heimklasse* being caught up in these attacks?'

'I believe the phrase is collateral damage. We must make sacrifices for his Eminence.'

'Does the Emperor know of these attacks?' asked Hartmann

'He will know when he needs to. He will *not* know of our… interest.'

'What do you think his opinion will be?' questioned König, placing the newspaper on the table, the action wafting Hartmann's cigar smoke.

'We are not expected to have thoughts regarding the Emperor's opinions. His word is Law.' Voigt sat himself in the chair at the head of the table, his back to the door, facing the tall sash windows. He could see Pall Mall and the bustle of London's traffic. Outside, beyond the tall iron railings, *Kaisersoldaten* patrolled, their weapons on display to show the might of those now governing this once-scepter'd isle. Voigt enjoyed the view, finding the armed presence satisfying, even more so the irony that the palace they were in was commissioned by the German royal dynasty of the House of Hanover, less than a hundred years ago. It seemed fitting then that the Emperor had finally been successful in obtaining what was his by divine right. 'And in answer to your question… less *Heimklasse* will be caught up in the violence once the *Engländer* sees that the Resistance is actually more dangerous to him than the Emperor.'

'But it is the Resistance we need to infiltrate, surely?' Hartmann looked at the end of his cigar, watching the flickering orange. 'It is they who are threatening our existence.'

'No!' Voigt's fist thundered down onto the mahogany table. 'We are not under threat, *Herr* Hertmann. You would do well to remember that.'

'I… apologise, *Generaloberst* Voigt,' Hartmann said, exercising his colleague's former military title.

Voigt acknowledged the use. 'Are the trains running now?'

'The timetable is back on schedule,' König confirmed.

Pleased, Voigt stood, moving to the map of Britain on the wall. It displayed the main roadways and all the major railway lines and where the border walls were built or planned. 'Then we need to give more mis-information to the Resistance. We will announce that His Eminence will be attending the Anniversary Celebrations in Hyde Park this year.'

'He is not going to Hamberg as usual?'

'Idiot!' spat Voigt at König's question. 'Of course he is! But we want the Resistance to think otherwise! Have I not explained that? This is our tenth year. It warrants some pomp.'

Hartmann stepped in to save König from any further embarrassment. 'We will inform them of his intentions. Perhaps we can have a decoy present to complete the illusion?'

'He can welcome the crowds. It will be a requirement to enjoy the event,' said Voigt.

'If I may ask…' Hartmann began. 'Will the Resistance set off an explosive at such a public event, knowing that many civilians will be there?'

Voigt considered for a moment, then nodded. 'You are right. *We* will set off the explosive ourselves and the blame will be given to the Resistance. We have the right people to do this, yes?'

'Yes. And our decoy?'

'He will remain unscathed. We want no martyrs here. Who do you have in mind to carry this out?'

Hartmann pulled long on his cigar. 'I would normally appoint a team but we have a man who works best alone. And in case of any failure, he can easily be disposed of.'

'I am concerned that you so easily consider failure possible,' Voigt responded.

'A cautionary stance, nothing else. The man I have in mind is quick of mind and body and does not buckle under pressure.'

Voigt nodded approvingly, having been following with great interest the British public's tabloid hanging of the Irish contingent that were believed to be responsible. 'Call him in.'

London

Kaplan and Aisling, partaking in a drink at the Hippodrome, had found the evening's entertainment lacking in spontaneity. Kaplan was slightly inebriated, cursing himself for lowering his guard. He suggested they return to his hotel room but she refused: she wanted to stay out until the last taxicab.

There was a silence between them for a moment as they finished their sixth bottle of *Emrich-Schönleber*, partly because Kaplan didn't want to be seen to be drunk, but primarily because he hoped Aisling *was* too drunk to speak.

'Why…' she began, staring at him through her wine glass, 'why won't you tell me what you do?'

Kaplan leant back and sighed, tapping the side of his own glass. 'There is nothing more to say other than I work to help keep London safe. Rebuild where necessary, when required.'

'You don't look like a builder,' she hiccupped, stroking the back of his hands. 'Too smooth for that.' She gave a knowing wink.

'I do not do that kind of rebuilding.'

'Well, perhaps you should.' Aisling gulped the last of her wine, shuddered, then said: 'You destroyed it.'

Kaplan pulled his hands away. She was becoming irksome now. 'I am returning to my hotel. Come or stay. In either case, you will ask no more questions.'

Aisling's courage had been fuelled by the wine and a line of cocaine earlier in the evening and she stood, her clutch bag firmly in her grip. 'Goodnight, Aaron.'

Kaplan watched her walk to the bar. She was quickly offered a drink by a woman in uniform, her fingers already caressing the officer's thigh by her hemline. He was disappointed she decided to stay but he shrugged inwardly, throwing a couple of *kaisermarks* onto the table as he left.

It was a balmy night, an hour before the curfew—more than enough time to get back to Gower Street. He decided to walk. The air would clear his head and he had an appointment with an architect in the morning. Most of the people he passed were rushing to get home to avoid the *kaisersoldaten* and a night in the cells but there were a group of young men, English and a couple of Welsh by the sounds of them, who seem to be in no rush at all. As he walked by, they said something to him. Kaplan couldn't help himself. He stopped and turned to them.

'I did not catch that,' he said, laying on thick his Bavarian accent. He was looking for sport now. 'What did you say?'

'You need,' one of the lads said, his own accent indicating he was from London, 'to fuck off back to your own country.' He has emphasised every word. To. Make. His. Point.

Kaplan smiled in response and looked sharp at the five young men. He could take them all on. He may well receive a beating but he would be able to overcome them. He put his hands in his pockets. 'You do realise that your words can lead to your arrest.'

'There ain't no one here,' another piped up. 'So go on. Off you fuck.'

'The *kaisersoldaten* will be on patrol very soon. Do you really wish to risk it?' Kaplan knew that even if he was left unconscious on the streets after the curfew had begun, he himself would still be imprisoned. The *kaisersoldaten* simply accepted no excuses without official sanction, no matter who you were or why you still happened to be out on the streets. And public brawling brought its own repercussions. 'I know that I do not.'

'Come on, let's go,' said one of the more sensible lads.

But the group refused to move on, instead started forming a circle around Kaplan, the hesitant boy holding back.

'I am tired and I wish to go home,' Kaplan said with some weariness.

'Then you should have fucking kept walking, ya Hun bastard.'

There was a flash of steel—the Welshman pulled a blade and lunged towards Kaplan, who parried the attack swiftly. Another assault from behind and Kaplan was pushed forward but spun sideways, hitting the nearby shop window with his shoulder. It gave him purchase and he kicked out, toppling two of the lads. The one with the knife tried again, but Kaplan's hand sent his weapon clattering to the floor. Kaplan went to pick it up but a foot met him in the chest. Winded for a moment, he remained bent over and lashed out at the boy to his right. But he was soon overcome with blows raining down over his back and neck. He stumbled to the floor. The knife was picked up by someone he couldn't see but managed to block it with his hands, the blade slicing at his forearm. Then in the distance, a whistle blew. Booted feet, that of the *kaisersoldaten*, came running towards them all. The boys scattered. Kaplan slumped where he was, blood pouring from both his nose and the gash under his sleeve.

***

'Wilhelm's got the King locked up in the Tower of London.'

With the victory over Europe, King George V had been forced to rename the family house from Windsor to Hohenzollern. The ink wasn't even dry on the document he had forcibly signed before the public announcement had been made (it only seemed like yesterday that the House of Windsor had replaced Saxe-Coburg and Gotha).

As first cousins, George V and Wilhelm II had entered into an uneasy alliance, with Wilhelm using Buckingham Palace as his seat of British operations and the King remaining as a figurehead. Until recently, that was, when he had spoken out against his cousin. The Royal Hohenzollern Cavalry then took their place at the front gates and commanded loyalty from the country's subjects while the King shivered in the dark, clamping down on any rumblings that the armistice was a bad thing.

The Langelaan, a long-established gentleman's club at 116 Pall Mall, took upon itself none of the constraints of the Kaiser's rule, remaining independent and, where possible, neutral.

Sitting behind a broadsheet, just fingers and trousered legs showing, was Cedric Swinton. He often fell asleep where he sat, in his favourite armchair, content that no one knew and blissfully unaware that everyone did. His riotous snoring regularly shattered the expected quiet of the main room. Around him, his fellow members read and smoked, rarely talking to each other but occasionally looking over at Swinton, a disgusted tut or two coming from their pursed lips.

Swinton joined the club before the end of the last century. His family was affluent and he had investments in any number of overseas businesses. The German victory seemed not to have dented his pockets one iota.

Today, he was awake and read aloud from the article in front of his aquiline nose. He wasn't a royalist *per se* but their monarch's imprisonment did shake the British foundations. As he continued, sharing the minute details of Wilhelm's actions, a loud rumbling came from outside. It was some distance but enough to wobble the paintings hanging on the oak-panelled walls. Cedric lowered his paper, peering over his spectacles to a member who is sitting opposite him in his own high-backed chair.

'Sounds like the Kaiser's fallen off his ego. All the fool did was allow the Bolshevik rise to power in Russia and ensure the triumph of fascism in Italy. That ignited colonial revolts in the Middle East and in Southeast Asia and has brought the British Empire to its knees. It's made Germany the driving force across the globe. But what has all that achieved? I'll tell you what. The whole damn world has to put up with cuckoo clocks,' he brooded. But a second rumble, louder than the first, made his flippancy short-lived. 'That was an explosion.'

The Club's fire bell sounded. The members had never moved so fast. But Swinton did not follow them along the required route to safety to the rear courtyard, instead turning away from the giant central staircase to the main door and Pall Mall itself.

Outside, a plume of black smoke hung in the air over the Palace of Westminster. For a moment, Swinton thought the palace had been bombed but considered that he had heard nothing to suggest any such attack had been planned. Certainly there was already hidden, traitorous talk on the streets of the Hun making London in his own image, by bombing landmarks and turning the great city into a wasteland. Swinton scanned the streets around them, taking note of the traffic, of cabbies, traders and shoppers… Some casually glanced at the cloud, some seemed vaguely concerned, some simply kept their heads down.

But there were two men in long coats, one with a suitcase, another with an umbrella, who were standing at the base of the Crimean War Memorial and looking straight back at him. The two men said something to each other and Swinton lost sight of them as a horse-drawn omnibus trundled to a stop at the kerbside.

By the time the bus had pulled away, they were gone.

After a few moments had passed, the staff of the Langelaan Club advised the members that it was safe to return inside.

As Swinton looked forward to a glass of port to relax him after all this excitement, he was beckoned by an usher to follow him.

***

In the private cinema of the Langelaan Club, to the sound of an out-of-tune piano, flickering monochrome images were projected across the square screen. The ruby upholstery with brass adornments looked black in the half-light.

Major Dicky "Bladder" Chard, a veteran of the Great War, was alone and sitting in the centre of the middle row. He was a brusque man with more hair in his nostrils and ears than on his head.

Swinton sat down next to him. 'Did you choose this one on purpose?'

Chard pointed at the screen with his free hand. In the other he held a pipe to his mouth. 'I can't imagine you'd appreciate one of Lloyd's. Watching a film by an Austro-Hungarian seems quite apt, don't you think?

'If this is all we're going to get for the foreseeable future, then that bloody four-eyed patsy you like so much seems like a better prospect.'

'*Foolish Wives* or just German expressionist films in general?' Chard laughed. 'I have a hard time trying to keep my own wife indoors!'

'The undermining of our freedoms. You know that, Bladder,' Swinton sighed. 'And this attack in Croydon is not what we want.'

'We did plan it.'

'We didn't plan to kill potential supporters of our cause!'

Chard nodded solemnly. The number of deaths at the railway station was horrific. Someone was to blame but he wasn't about to be moved on the subject. No matter how hard his companion glared at him in the dark. 'The dust needs to settle. We need to get inside Buckingham Palace, get the information early, not at the last minute. There won't be a repeat of Croydon. That said…' Chard tapped his pipe into the ashtray bolted onto the back of the seat in front of him, packed it with fresh tobacco and re-lit it. 'None of this will probably even matter.'

'What do you mean?' Swinton frowned as one of the film's protagonists downed a glass of oxblood, a stomach-churning opener to the meal the scene displayed.

'Take it from me, Swinton, it might be that you and I won't have ever had this conversation.' Chard raised his eyebrows as he puffed away, plumes of smoke attracting the film's images as if they were fireflies. 'In the meantime, I want the Kaiser to start twitching. Get him bloody-well nervous that just because he declared victory, this war isn't over. Not by a longshot.'

Swinton admired Chard, finding the older man's experience in both the Sikkim expedition and the Yaa Asantewaa War vital to their understanding of the German occupancy of Britain. Swinton himself had commanded in the Balkans up until 1916 when he was captured by a Bulgarian contingent and imprisoned for the rest of the conflict.

'What happened outside a moment ago? Us or them?'

'Intelligence will tell us the details shortly. But I can assure you, Cedric, it wasn't us.'

Their meeting was disturbed briefly by an usher handing Chard a sealed telegram. Chard sliced the envelope with a little finger and *harrumphed* as he silently read the pink note it contained.

> HAR 2365 LANG 3=
> URGENT BAKER MISSING CAIRO
> = GRIFFITHS +

'Get this looked into,' Chard ordered, passing the telegram to Swinton.

This was the last thing Chard needed and it had the potential to throw any plans they had to overthrow the Kaiser out of the window. 'Send our best man to find Baker.'

Swinton acknowledged his instructions and left Chard puffing on his pipe. From the screen, Miss Dupont stared out, locked in the celluloid world.

Kandy, Ceylon

The temperature inside the boiler house took Restarick's breath away. Steam fizzed from all directions and the *thump-thump* of the generator worked its way into his chest. It was dark, the weakest of lights cutting through the haze.

'Whoever you are, I wish you no harm,' Restarick called out, 'but I need to know your business here.' There was no answer. Restarick peered through the gloom and saw a shape at the far end of the chamber. The two houseboys either side of him raised their clubs. Restarick waved them down. 'I'm not here to hurt you or take you in. I'm here to talk...'

Still no reply.

The pressure gauge nears Restarick squealed as the steam increased, making it even more difficult to see. But the shape fluttered by again.

'Tell them to leave,' came a voice. It was gruff and laced with pain.

'They're here to look after me. I'm not going to send them away unl—'

'Tell them to leave!'

'...unless you can assure me you'll not harm me,' finished Restarick. He motioned for the houseboys to stay by the door.

'They must leave!'

'Can you assure me?'

The voice did not reply for a few moments, the hissing steam and the rhythm of the boiler all that came between. Then:

'Yes. Yes, I won't hurt you. I *mustn't* hurt you.'

Restarick told the two boys to leave. They were hesitant at first but Restarick was very insistent. 'Get Raj. Make sure my father is safe.'

He waited until the door was closed.

He was alone with the voice: 'Now, let's talk. Why mustn't you hurt me?'

Carefully, tentatively, like an animal wary of a hunter, a man appeared from out of the steam. He was no taller than Restarick's six-foot stature but slightly hunched, as if it was painful to stand fully upright.

'Captain,' the man said, voice a little softer now. 'Captain...'

Restarick stepped forward. 'Do we know each other?'

The stranger was nervous and paused where he was, looking Restarick up and down. Restarick considered it unlikely that the man before him was capable of harm, but he was cornered and that made all creatures dangerous. There was a wildness to his expression, too: madness could take many forms and once it gripped a person so, there was no way to predict their actions.

'What's your name?'

'Major Carter.'

The name meant nothing to Restarick. 'What can I do for you, sir?'

'I know why you're here.'

'You do?'

'Yes,' Carter replied, nodding his head frantically. 'Yes, I do.'

'And why am I here?'

'You were sent here. To find me.'

'You are on my land.' Clearly the major was confused, Restarick reasoned to himself. 'My staff found you here.'

Carter shook his head. 'You are here in secret.'

'I am?' Restarick replied, wondering if Carter had some insider knowledge about Room 40, or he was simply clutching at straws. 'And why would that be?'

'Chard. Swinton. But it's all wrong… all wrong. Wrong!' Carter clenched his fists then grabbed his stomach.

'Are you in pain, Major?' Restarick moved forward again, alerted by his mention of Chard.

'Stay back! Don't come any closer!'

In the haze, Restarick made out something on Carter's torso, under his left arm. It was bulky and uncomfortable. 'I'm not going to hurt you, Major.'

'I—I—' Carter sagged against the far wall, clearly exhausted.

Restarick raced forward before the man could object. Carter flung his arms across his head and Restarick saw that the object under his arm was a gas mask with an extended attachment to the filter. A design he hadn't seen before, certainly not during the war.

'Where did you get this?'

Carter sighed, his breathing becoming laboured. '*You* gave it… to me.'

'Major, we've never met before.' Or had they? Restarick was trying his damnedest to remember this man, but to no avail. 'I don't know who you are.'

'You sent me here! They didn't believe me! But you sent me here.'

'To the plantation?'

Carter nodded then shook his head. 'No. To here. To now! To tell you!'

'Tell me about what?'

The man gave Restarick the unusual gas mask and turned it over. Inside, across the glass and written in wax, was *Operation: Geschenk*.

'Take it with you,' said Carter. 'Keep it safe. I'm no madman, Daniel. You'll soon understand why *they* believe I am.'

'Who's "they", Major? Who are you talking about? Chard and Swinton? Do they think you mad?'

Restarick looked at the gas mask again. Perhaps it was German, a new design. He was duty-bound to report this to his superiors, but he knew he was needed here, by the business let alone his ailing father.

Carter chewed in his fingers. 'I have something else. Something you said would make you believe me.'

Restarick waited with suspicion as Carter fumbled around his pockets to eventually produce a tattered, stained scrap of yellowing card. When Restarick took it from the major's trembling hands he almost recoiled in disbelief. It was a photograph of Lita.

'Where… where did you get this?' he breathed.

Carter looked at him, looking equally as confused. 'You gave it to me?'

'Gave it…' Restarick frowned. It wasn't just any photograph of Lita… it was *the* photograph, the one he'd kept with him all the time he was in service, and the one he had right now in his trunk. He turned on Carter. 'You stole this from my room!'

'No… no, Captain…' Carter said, shaking his head frantically. 'You gave it to me! You handed it to me!'

'But it's…' *In my room. In the trunk.*

Restarick ordered the police be called and the major was duly taken into custody. No mention was made of the photograph or of the gas mask, Restarick merely telling Captain Wyndham, the local senior officer, that the major had been caught trespassing.

On returning to his bedroom, Restarick was as hesitant as he was eager to check the trunk. It was impossible that the major could have stolen the photograph, but here it was, in Restarick's hand. Nevertheless, the trunk was opened and Restarick slumped back to the wooden floor in utter disbelief.

It wasn't just another, matching photograph of Lita: it was the *same* photograph, right down to the blood stains and the torn edges.

Why would this Major Carter go to all this trouble to exactly duplicate it? And then insist that Restarick himself had given it to the major, to prove he was telling the truth? Whatever this truth was.

Gefängnisgelände 5, London

The prison compound took up Trent Park and almost all of what was once woodland, now bordered on four sides by high walls, narrower at the bottom than the top, adorned with barbed wire. At each corner was a lookout tower, permanently occupied by armed guards and a spotlight. On the outside perimeter, eight patrols (with two dogs to every pair of *kaisersoldaten*) kept a day-and-night vigil. The main gate was heavily armed, too, with a single hut by the red and white striped barrier. Once past the barrier itself, the studded solid iron doors were further overseen by men with rifles. It was completely impossible to escape from and was almost as impossible to get in. There were forty-five of these compounds across the country, specifically built for those who would break the curfew. They were in essence holding areas prior to execution or transfer to the existing prisons for incarceration.

But anyone who passed through those foreboding metal doors were rarely if ever seen again. While they were designed to be an effective method to avoid breaking the law, they were filling up almost on a daily basis and space was becoming a premium.

Kaplan found himself sharing a cell, no more than six feet by four, with three other men, two of whom he had been arrested for brawling with, in Leicester Square. The whole of the block they were in reeked of body odour, piss and shit.

Out their line of sight they heard the main door to the block clunk open with a jangle of keys. The prisoners jeered and shouted as the commandant hollered for quiet and for them to move back away from their cell bars.

The regimented, booted steps of the commandant and his entourage were drowned out by the chanting. He shouted again for quiet. When it didn't come, he motioned for one of the guards to fire a volley from his machine gun, the bullets striking the tall ceiling as the empty shells fell to the floor. Another guard immediately moved to collect them: anything could be used as a weapon by the prisoners, particularly the metal casings of empty bullets.

Finally getting the quiet he'd ordered, the commandant walked slowly and purposefully along the corridor, lined either side with the stinking cells until he reached the one containing Kaplan.

He spun on his heels to face it.

'Inmate 594…' he called.

No one in the cell moved.

'Inmate 594!'

Kaplan shifted to the front of the cell. The commandant held a sheaf of papers in a gloved fist: release orders—unhappy because no one ever left his compound by such method. But these had come from an authority higher than he.

Kaplan's journey to the interview room was laced with a mixture of hisses, boos and cheers from the prisoners. Other than that, no words were spoken until he was seated in the thin metal chair in the large room. It contained no other furniture, had no windows and a single light threw a sickly yellow glow across the dirty walls.

'Aaron Kaplan,' said the man who entered the room via the single door. Kaplan recognised him from the meeting at Buckingham Palace.

'Herr Hertmann,' Kaplan responded, snapping to attention.

'Please,' Hartmann responded, puffing on a cigar. 'Sit down.'

Kaplan did so.

'Am I being released?'

'Of course. Your unfortunate incident in the West End has meant many strings had to be pulled. You have caused quite a consternation with the *Kaiser-Regel*.'

'I can't imagine my actions would be of such import to the Emperor.'

'We control with an iron grip, Kaplan. Normally such endeavours would not be tolerated, no matter who you are.'

'I should be honoured,' Kaplan replied. 'And I cannot wait to get out of these… these things.' He looked down at the blue and white striped trousers and jacket he was wearing.

'Do not take this lightly, Kaplan. You have only been granted release because we have a mission for you.'

Kaplan's mood lightened at that.

Hartmann looked at the lit end of his cigar and pulled a loose length of tobacco from his tongue. 'You are to travel to Jordan. It is believed the Resistance are intending to seriously undermine our authority there.'

'In Jordan?'

A guard entered, carrying a bag and gave it to Kaplan without a word.

'In Jordan,' confirmed Hartmann. To the guard: 'Leave.'

As the man left, Kaplan began to change out of his prison gear and into his own clothes from the bag. He sighed as he noticed the crease in his trilby. 'Jordan poses no threat to us. I do not understand the relevance of that location.'

From his jacket pocket, Hartmann pulled out a rolled leather pouch and gave it to Kaplan once the Bavarian was fully dressed.

'The information I am entrusting you with now you will share with no one.'

'Of course,' Kaplan said. That wasn't unusual.

'It may sound strange and you may doubt the veracity of my words, but our very future depends on it.'

'Go on.'

'Do you know how we defeated the Allies?'

'The greater might of the Central Powers.'

'No,' replied Hartmann. 'By luck. It was not through guns or intelligence or the skill of our leaders. It was through the sheer luck of one of our agents.' He almost sounded obsessed, his eyes widening, squeezing the cigar hard between forefinger and thumb. He offered Kaplan a cigar, who accepted and, for a few moments and in silence, they sat there smoking.

'There is a threat to our existence.'

Kaplan narrowed his eyes. 'I have been charged with rooting out any resistance.'

'Of course. And so far, you have performed your duties perfectly.'

'So far?'

'So far,' nodded Hartmann. 'But nevertheless the Allies can wipe away everything we have done as easily as stubbing out this cigar.'

'Are you saying all our work is for nothing?'

'Potentially, yes.' Hartmann stared at Kaplan. 'They have the means to take from us the science that we intend to use against them.'

'Operation Geschenk?'

'Yes. The "gift". You have read the file and therefore you are valuable to us.'

Kaplan enjoyed the smoothness of the smoke passing out through his nostrils. 'But I am a soldier, not a scientist.'

'But you are also trained in espionage, yes?'

'Yes.'

'And that is why you are valuable. We have intelligence that the Allied Secret Service have mislaid one of their agents.'

He explained that a known Resistance member had been seen with an eminent scientist and that the member had since disappeared, last seen on the road to Jordan. Kaplan was told he was to find the Resistance member and bring them in for interrogation.

'Mislaid?' Kaplan looked at his cigar and then at Hartmann through the smoke. 'Perhaps we intercepted them?'

'No. He has not been seen. Normally a missing Allied agent is a good thing, but they seem to be rather concerned with this one.'

'Then the agent needs to be found.'

'Ideally before the Allies and ideally by us.'

Kandy

'Do you wish to press charges?' Raj handed the note to Restarick. 'The police are asking you to go to the station if you do.'

'I think you should,' said Angela. 'He could have done anything.'

'He wasn't here to cause any harm or damage anything.' Restarick sniffed the dried tea, in the shallow bowl that one of the workers held up to his nose. 'Yes, that's good.'

'But that Mr Secombe...' Angela nodded as she also was offered to test the tea's scent.

'What about him?'

'If he was here making noises about how things are run here, then that other chap appears out of nowhere—'

'You're linking them together?' Restarick folded the note from Captain Wyndham, putting it in his pocket.

'It makes sense, surely?'

Restarick considered. 'It's possible, but there was something about Major Carter. Something that doesn't smack of a conspiracy to shut us down.' He didn't tell Angela about the photograph or the strange gas mask. There was no need to. She would simply get angry that it would be another excuse for him to run off and play soldiers.

'So press charges. Make this Secombe know we're not going to be bullied.'

Raj agreed, his head wobbling from side to side. Restarick looked at him then at his sister.

'Very well. I'll speak to the police.' He stood and moved to the large French doors that opened up onto the veranda. His office overlooked the entire plantation, the distant view of bright saris and wicker baskets moving slowly between the bushes. 'We need to finish the roofing. Raj, see to that before the rains come back. I'll head into town now.'

'I'll come with you,' said Angela, picking up her bag.

'No, stay here. Raj will be too busy managing the repair work. I need to run a few errands while I'm there.'

Angela waited for Raj to leave.

'You're worried, Danny.'

'Of course I am. There was no sign of a break-in. Carter looked positively terrified when Wyndham's officers took him away.'

'And he said nothing to you? No reason why he was in the boiler house?'

'No, not a thing,' Restarick lied. 'He was probably just homeless and looking for somewhere dry to sleep in case the storms returned.'

'I still think it's an odd coincidence him turning up after Secombe's visit. He probably ransacked the house.'

'No, I don't think it was him.'

'Then who?'

'Opportunists, like we said.' Restarick gathered some papers and bid his sister goodbye, taking the family Bentley into town.

It was a leisurely drive and he took his time, drinking in the shimmering landscape, jungle either side of the snaking dirt track, the green and lush rolling hills looming up all around.

Kandy itself was a bustling, humid place, full of crowded markets and Buddhist dagobas. Restarick left the car at the police station, an impressive Colonial building, surrounded on all sides by a wrought iron fence. He wandered into the spice market, seduced by the scents and sounds. The English palette often struggled with Asian food but Jim Restarick, before settling in Ceylon, had often brought home the most wonderful ingredients. He'd concoct dishes that awakened the senses, let alone the taste buds. Restarick had maintained his father's love of cooking as best he could and the chance to stock up the larder while in town couldn't be missed.

He soon loaded his purchases into the boot of the Bentley then asked to speak to Captain Wyndham. Having been told he was away on a case, Restarick met instead with a superintendent, Seneviratne.

The thin-faced young man, black hair slicked to one side, didn't look old enough to wear the uniform, mused Restarick, but seemed capable enough. He was certainly professional, knowing that Restarick wanted to meet with Captain Wyndham and having Major Carter's arrest papers with him.

'Are you sure you don't want him charged?' Seneviratne asked with some surprise, looking at Restarick over his gold-rimmed spectacles.

'As I told your officers when they took him away, he seems a harmless enough fellow.'

'Then why did you ask us to remove him?'

Restarick looked across the desk at Seneviratne. The fan hanging from the ceiling hummed with every steady rotation. A house fly, fat and round, twitched and scurried along the windowsill, then disappeared outside.

'I wasn't sure if he would go without causing a fuss.'

'He was quite subdued when we arrived.'

'Exactly.'

'And nothing was stolen?'

Restarick shook his head. 'But, superintendent, I would ask you for a favour.'

'Mr Restarick?'

'I would like to talk to the Major.'

'We are releasing him. You are free to chat to him at your leisure.'

'I'd like to talk to him while he is still here.'

Seneviratne pursed his lips and drummed his fingers briefly. This was unusual. He knew that Restarick was ex-Army and that his family had been in Ceylon for many years. The Pilawala Tea Company was one of the finest growers and exporters on the island. Captain Wyndham spoke highly of him, so the superintendent made a swift decision in Restarick's favour. With one condition. 'I will be present during your… conversation.'

'I would prefer we are given some privacy.'

'Until Major Carter steps foot onto the street outside, he is our responsibility. It would be remiss of me to allow a member of the public to interview a detainee.'

'I acknowledge your position, but…' Restarick leant forward, offering Seneviratne a cigarette, 'I just want to ask him a few questions. Still being here may make him talk easier… if he believes he is in trouble.'

Seneviratne took it and lit it, while Restarick put the pack back in his pocket, not taking one for himself. 'I do not feel comfortable with this.' He rested his hands on the open file that contained Secombe's arrest papers.

'Major Carter came to me for a reason.'

'As you said, he was probably just looking for a place to sleep at night.'

'But does he look homeless to you? A little ragged, perhaps.'

'He is down on his luck, as you English say.'

Restarick nodded. 'Yes. Down on his luck. How about it?' He peered as nonchalantly as he could at the paperwork. That it was upside down from his angle opposite Seneviratne was of no issue. The arresting officers had sluggishly typed out quotes from Secombe as he was escorted away from the plantation. Restarick read, before Seneviratne closed the file:

I was told to be hwre.
Cairo's foLly is not to be dismissed.
The captain needS to listen to me.

'No. I must insist I am present.'

Restarick knew that the superintendent wasn't going to budge. Wyndham had trained him well. But if this was the only way Carter could be spoken to while still in the station, then so be it.

There were only four cells in the police station, but all were adjacent to each other along a narrow corridor that was itself locked behind a thick-barred door. Seneviratne said Carter was in the third, opening up the first door and leading Restarick along.

As the superintendent selected the correct key for the cell, Restarick wondered if Carter was simply an opportunist or if there really was something to behind the odd gas mask and the photo. Surely the latter was the most obvious—otherwise why would the man have had it with him? It would have been an overly-elaborate scheme just for somewhere to kip. But Restarick wouldn't get the chance to find out because when the cell was opened, Seneviratne pulling the heavy door outwards to clang against the corridor wall, it was completely empty.

Carter had disappeared.

***

Restarick's drive back to the plantation was underpinned by his bubbling anger.

The superintendent had been apologetic, confused, but most of all increasingly panicked for when he had to explain to his superiors where Carter had gone. Restarick had also demanded to know, saying he expected Captain Wyndham to produce a full report to save the matter being notified to the commissioner in Colombo.

Reaching the edge of town, Restarick manoeuvred the 3 litre Bentley onto Sirimalwatta Road, running across the Mahalweli River, swollen by the recent storms. A car pulled onto the bridge behind, Restarick not taking much notice of it until he realised it was following him. It had dropped back a few times then increased its speed whenever Restarick did. No rear-view or wing mirrors meant Restarick had to listen for his pursuer's progress. Turning around to look meant he'd alert whoever it was to the fact that he knew they were there.

The further east he went, the worse the roads were, but to prove to himself he wasn't paranoid, Restarick took a long circuitous route back to Pilawala. Sure enough, his driving companion was never far behind him.

Feeling the suspension (top of the range by 1919 standards, the year his Bentley was made) shudder and shake under him, he pulled over by a shack with the pretence to have a breather. Wrenching the handbrake on, he waited patiently for the car to pass by. He was surprised it was a Maybach, a *boche* car, made by the same bastards who built the Zeppelins. In disgust, Restarick lit a cigarette and got out, stepping onto the dusty road to watch the heavy, lumbering vehicle disappear around a corner.

This was a concern. If the *Kaiser-Regel* had found him here, then they most likely knew of his connections to Room 40. Was Carter a German spy? But why give Restarick the gas mask and the photograph of Lita? Was it to demonstrate that they knew him?

Stubbing his cigarette into the dirt, he jumped back in the Bentley, fired up the engine and raced home. As he saw the perimeter fence of his plantation, he feared for Angela's safety, for his father's, too. There was no reason to think that this pursuers weren't already here and, sure enough, as Restarick threw the Bentley around a corner and to the gates, he brought the car to a skidding, sliding halt, dust and grit billowing into the air around him. The Maybach was blocking the plantation's entrance.

The passenger door of the Maybach opened. Out stepped Secombe, waving the air clear around him with his Panama hat. Restarick gripped his steering wheel tight, weighing up the situation. The truth of the matter was, he had no idea about any situation, so decided to see what Secombe had to say. The driver of the Maybach stayed where he was.

As Restarick walked towards the gates, he heard another car pull up behind him. He was cornered.

'What do you want from me?'

Secombe put his hat on. 'There is a problem.'

'Of course there is. What's it got to do with me?'

'After you'd returned from Australia, you told the Factory you wouldn't come back.'

How did they know this? The *Kaiser-Regel* obviously had people in Room 40. The Factory was an in-house nickname for Room 40 itself, only ever used by those who worked there. Secombe saw the look on Restarick's face, so raised his hands.

'The Maybach helps us move around. We're not the Kaiser's men.'

'How can you prove it?' Restarick glanced back at the second car, and the two heavies who had extracted themselves from it.

'We have a missing agent. We want you to find him.'

'Like you said, I'm not going back. And don't give me all this bullshit about you needing me because you think I'm the best.'

'Far from it,' Secombe smiled. 'There are far better agents than you out there in the field.'

Restarick snorted, shoving his hands in his pockets. 'I'm home. I'm staying at home. My family… I owe it to them.'

'What do you owe to your country?'

'To England? I've given more than enough. England's finished.'

Secombe walked up to Restarick, scanning his face with tired, dust-filled eyes. 'You know that's not true. We may be here out in the wilds—'

'Ceylon is not wild. It may need a little taming but…'

'And you are the one to tame it?'

'Perhaps.'

'It will be safe enough until you return.'

'I'm not going anywhere.'

Secombe circled Restarick, swatting some flies. 'How is your father?'

'My fath—No… you will not bring him into this. He's an old man. He needs looking after. That's why I'm staying here.'

'Don't get so panicked, Daniel. I'm not here to threaten him.'

'Then why mention him?'

Secombe breathed out slowly. 'The missing agent is a Max Baker. You were stationed with him in Passchendaele for a while. He was awarded the VC for bravery in rescuing his fellow wounded soldiers.'

The Victoria Cross wasn't given out lightly and Restarick vaguely recalled one member of the Royal Army Medical Corps going above and beyond in retrieving the fallen from the battlefield. 'But why me?'

'All our agents are on assignments. You're not. You're…' Secombe gestured to the plantation.

'I'm working.'

'What if we offered you support while you're away?'

'You never done so before. My staff, they can manage the business equally as well as me. I told you. I'm staying because of my father.'

'Medicines are hard to come by here.'

'Yes, they are.'

Secombe stepped forward suddenly, a predator sensing weakness in its prey. 'You take this assignment, we will look after your father, offer all the support your sister requires. Inject your business with capital. After all, those roofs aren't going to fix themselves. Once the assignment is complete, you can retire on a full pension and the Factory will never ask anything of you again.'

'And if I refuse?'

The man shrugged. 'Then you are free now to make as many cups of tea as you like.'

'I can feel a "but" coming.'

'Not at all.' Secombe moved back towards the Maybach. 'There are no "buts". There's an "and".'

'That sounds worse.'

'You return to your plantation, you refuse this assignment, and we will close you down. You'll lose everything. No export licence, no staff, no profit.'

Restarick ground his teeth. 'This assignment is that important?'

'Yes, Captain Restarick. Baker was onto something, something that could spell the destruction of the Allies. But if you find him, we could remove the Kaiser once and for all. The freedom of the world rests on you being successful.'

Restarick rubbed his forehead. It might have been the air pressure, the signal that a storm was coming. But it was a sickening sense of *déjà vu*. 'Can I think about it?'

'What is there to think about?'

'Reconnaissance, intelligence gathering… they are relatively straight-forward. Set timescales. Little movement. Looking for an agent? That's a whole different kettle of fish.'

'You first stop will be Versailles.'

'Why there?'

'The gas mask needs to be delivered to this who can examine it, duplicate it.'

'What gas mask?'

'Don't play stupid. We know you had a visitor. We know what he gave you.' Secombe scratched the back of his neck where sweat was collecting. 'You have worked hard for us. We genuinely mean it when we say after this, you can retire. Send your response by telegram to the usual place on Sunday morning, eleven hundred hours.'

'Did you know I would be getting a visitor?'

'We'd been informed that someone had been seen in Negombo. It was clear it was you he was in the country to see. There were rumours that he had some new technology he'd taken from the *Kaiser-Regel*.'

'All that rubbish about working for the government? Why did you not just come out straight and say who you were from the off?' Restarick knew the answer. The Factory occasionally delighted itself in unnecessary deviousness. It was obvious to Restarick too that Secombe had ordered the break-in. Looking for the gas mask, clearly.

'Send your response,' Secombe finished.

Restarick waited until both cars had gone before going to his Bentley. Room 40 had never been so generous before, which made him suspicious, almost as if they knew he wasn't going to return from this. If he did refuse, there was no doubt that Secombe was serious: his life and that of his family's would be over. If he accepted and died in action, his family, his staff and business would be looked after. Conversely, if he survived and came home, he would be looked after, too.

Interestingly, Secombe never once mentioned Carter by name. Perhaps it would come up in the debriefing. Perhaps the Factory had taken him from the police cell.

Damn. Restarick thumped the steering wheel. The debriefing. He was already thinking about that. *Damn Room 40!*

Versailles, France

The wide car chugged into the alleyway adjacent to Rue Ducis, one far too narrow for it to have completely traversed without damage.

It was an unusually cold night and Restarick, his collar up and trilby pulled down—to keep the chill out as much as to disguise his aspect, pulled back on the hand brake. Shuddering, the car came to a stop, a cloud of exhaust pluming up into the dark air. The blackness was alleviated only by the sparse lights coming from *die Konditorei* on the other side of the street.

The permanent curfew in France meant that anyone who was seen out after eight in the evening until six the following morning without Imperial permission would be guillotined in public the next day. Restarick had been warned of this by Room 40 and he noted it was an even harsher punishment here than in England.

Restarick cursed the owner of the shop: the lights could attract the *kaisersoldaten* and he would be hard pressed to justify the rule-breaking without papers additional to the forgeries he had in his coat pocket. He scurried across the road and knocked three times then twice then another three, as per his instructions, on the glass door of the bakery, willing the old boy he could see moving about inside to hurry up to let him in and get those damn lights off.

Soon, but not soon enough in his eyes, Restarick pushed his way in past the shop-keeper and made secure the door from the inside, hissing to cut the lights. The sudden plunge into darkness made hard work in finding his way to the little room at the back of the shop, the man shuffling in front of him.

He was met by three men sitting around a square table, an empty chair waiting for him.

'That was damn stupid,' one of them said, gesturing at the chair, 'coming here by car! That could have brought an entire battalion down upon us!'

'It's a German car,' the shopkeeper pointed out from behind Restarick. He sat in an armchair by the stove and resumed eating a *croque madame*. It had grown cold and he turned his nose up, placing, with a sigh, the remains of the snack back on his plate that was perched on the narrow arm. 'He probably thinks that makes him invisible.'

'None of us are safe if those lights have been spotted,' Restarick hissed and removed his hat. He knew he wasn't overreacting and didn't push the point any further, privately acknowledging that these men were probably right about the Audi 'Type B' he had chosen for the journey down from Calais.

As Restarick took his place, the man who had spoken stood. 'We are all here now, so let's get on with this. Monsieur Restarick, this is Jean-Didier, Georgie and Arthur, who you've just met.' Arthur the shopkeeper waved casually from his armchair.

The fourth man, sitting away from the group and in half-shadow, was silent, watching George, Restarick and Jean-Didier intently.

'Did you bring it?' Jean-Didier asked, leaning forward. He squinted under the single, bare light-bulb hanging above the table in the shop's backroom, the lines in his forehead deep and furrowed. He looked at Restarick, sizing him up.

Restarick nodded and reached into the pouch sewn into the lining of his baggy coat, retrieving the unusual gas mask. Its glass glinted as Restarick placed it on the green baize circle in the centre of the table.

'I've never seen one like it,' said George as he moved in close to it, a magnifying monocle suddenly at his right eye, the man looking for all the world like a jeweller.

'Where did it come from?' asked Jean-Didier. 'Are there any more?'

'It was a Major Carter,' said Restarick.

'You did not mention his name in your communique.'

'I felt it unnecessary.'

'This Major Carter… he made it?'

'No. He gave it to me.'

'So is there any indication as to who made it?' George prised the filter open with a bread knife. 'Look at it! Six layers, six filters.' He stood and removed his monocle. 'I think we can safely assume the Hun is developing more brutal chemical agents.'

'Christ, then don't break it! We need to send it to a lab now,' Jean-Didier decided. The Lab was in a secure site in Orleans, one completely unknown to the Central Powers. 'I miss French brandy. Does anybody have a cigar?' Jean-Didier looked around at his three colleagues expectantly as he sipped his Asbach.

'Sir,' George said to the fourth man, passing Jean-Didier a *Murad*, 'time is against us. I cannot stress enough how any further delays will jeopardise our mission. Jean-Didier is right. This needs to be duplicated now. If the Kaiser has already commissioned the production of these, then we can be damn well sure that the gas that these are protection from also exists.' The fourth man watched Jean-Didier clip and light the Turkish cigar. 'You need to give the order. The Kaiser could use the gas at any time. Here and in London we know what is right. And this,' George continued, gesturing at the room around him but his concerns being more far-reaching than the grimy back room of a pastry shop, 'isn't right. Running around from place to place, hiding from the Kaiser's stormtroopers.'

'The man in Restarick's plantation…' Jean-Didier began.

'I'm not sure that Carter was his true name. He seemed to recognise me.'

Jean-Didier looked at his companions but not Restarick. 'Should we be concerned? Is he a Hun? Are they infiltrating hospitals, schools… anywhere?'

'Good Lord, England is *their* country now. They don't need to infiltrate at all!' Restarick declared, ignoring being ignored.

George agreed, picking up the gas mask and snapping the filter back into place. 'So you're saying that he's not part of this? Isn't involved in developing these chemicals?'

'No, I'm not saying that. But it would be remarkably strange if the Hun had decided to single out an undercover Secret Service agent as far away as Ceylon and present him with new technology.' Restarick looked towards the fourth man who pushed his own chair back and stood, walking to the window to peer through the tiny gap between the tattered blackout blinds to the street outside.

A marching squad of grey-uniformed *kaisersoldaten* were coming around the corner on their nightly patrol, their jackboots a relentless *left-right-left-right* on the Versailles streets. The fourth man watched them pass by, only the slightest expression of distain crossing his moustachioed face. But it spoke a thousand words. Without turning back to the room, he hooked a thumb in a pocket of his waistcoat and finally spoke.

'Can you imagine a world where the Central Powers did not win? Where we do not need to hide in the dark, awaiting word of daylight?'

Restarick nodded. 'This is what we all want. This is the work we've been doing since the Armistice.'

'And we *will* get that. We have to,' added Jean-Didier, puffing like a train on his cigar. 'It may take another ten years.'

'Hell, it may take another war,' agreed Restarick.

The fourth man shook his head. 'No. Not another war. The *same* war.'

Jean-Didier laughed. 'I know many people feel that the war never ended, but my good man, I thought *you* were above such delusions!'

The fourth man sighed. 'You were right to bring us this gas mask, Monsieur Restarick. You were right to tell us.'

I didn't want to but I felt I had to. It seemed related somehow. But I won't tell them about the photo of Lita. It was in his pocket now, just like the original had been during the war.

'Tonight's delivery from Mr Restarick will take us back.'

'To where?' Jean-Didier tapped a stump of ash into the metal dish before him.

George knew what the fourth man meant. 'To before the end of the war itself.'

Jean-Didier laughed nervously, not quite understanding what his rotund companion was saying. Restarick, too, was lost.

'Look, I'm not sure what's going on here. My superiors asked me to deliver this to you here. Room 40 works in cryptanalysis and we seem to be talking in riddles here, too.'

The fourth man's face twitched. Was it a smile? It was hard to tell with his face still to the window.

'Then let me put it plain. The very existence of this gas mask tells me that it will all start again and that all of us, you, Captain Restarick, and our friends here today will go back to before the war ended and fight for our very lives once more. *Nous* écrirons *de nouveau les livres d'histoire.*'

'A fanciful way of putting it,' Restarick responded.

'Perhaps it's the only way you can understand a clear instruction,' Jean-Didier said.

Restarick turned to him. 'I do not know you, sir, yet you have been somewhat hesitant in engaging with me directly. If you have an issue with m—'

'I have indeed an issue, *Captain*.'

'Steady there, old boy…' said George.

'No, no.' Restarick raised his hands. 'Let my colleague speak.'

The fourth man remained silent while Arthur found something of interest under his fingernails.

'Your actions at Saint-Mihiel caused us to lose the conflict,' Jean-Didier growled. '*You* are why we are all here.'

'Do you think that I have not been wrestling with that? That it doesn't play heavily on my conscience? I am aware of what happened that day. I was ambushed by a sniper. They were lying in wait for me, just as was lying in wait for the spy.' Restarick took the drink George poured for him. 'Thank you. Whoever that person was, they knew I was there. I was too well camouflaged to have been seen.'

'Nevertheless,' sneered Jean-Didier, 'you *were* seen. And you say the lunatic in your plantation knew you. And he suddenly disappeared from a locked police cell. Are they investigating that? Should we be investigating *you*, Monsieur Restarick? Perhaps we should be concerned.'

The fourth man raised a hand. In direct and pointed tones, he said, 'Intelligence has told us that it was unexpected, that we had no way of knowing he was being watched in Saint-Mihiel. Captain Restarick is *not* to blame. Room 40 spent many weeks deliberating this and we are grateful for the Captain's continued dedication to our cause. His exoneration is not in question. He has been offered retirement at the end of this episode. Our focus here and now is to set back on the correct path the freedom that is ours to choose, ours by right. If we start to point blame at each other, within our own group, then we will be no better than the cuckoos who consider themselves our masters.'

The consensus in the room qualified the fourth man's statement.

'We can't tolerate this occupancy anymore. Word reached us just last week that a Bavarian contingent stormed a *Mikveh* in Poland. It is outrageous. A violation of such sacred beliefs. The disrespect these people have is without limits,' Jean-Didier seethed.

'An authorised attack…' Restarick shook his head, sickened.

'As far as we know the order didn't come from the *Kaiser-Regel*. The so-called Education and Propaganda Department of the Bavarian *Reichswehr* took it upon themselves to carry out the atrocious act.'

'Who is it run by?' Restarick asked.

George moved to a thick file of papers and thumbed through to near the middle, holding a pince-nez with his spare hand. He read: 'A German General Staff officer, Captain Karl Mayer.'

'Mayer? Wasn't he the one who ordered one of his subordinates to write that infamous letter?'

'The Austrian. The anti-Semite.' Jean-Didier poured himself a glass of French bourbon. 'Yes. An utterly vile man. That same subordinate of his also commanded the intrusion, a decorated *Bildungskommando*. He was awarded the Iron Cross when just a lance-corporal.'

'We need to cut out this cancer. People who consider what they did to that *Mikveh* to be… to be acceptable are… I can't find the words. Perhaps we should add this subordinate's name to our wanted list. The consequences of such a man rising through the ranks of the Imperium are chilling.' The fourth man pulled himself straight. 'However, for now, Captain, you will continue your mission to find Baker. We here will focus our efforts on duplicating this gas mask. We also need to investigate the location of any potential chemical factories. You all have papers that will allow you relatively easy passage across the borders. Be mindful, however. If the *Kaiser-Regel* becomes aware of *our* intelligence, those borders may be closed indefinitely.'

La Celle-Saint-Cloud, France

'Just because I'm American, you think I like bourbon?'

'Don't you?'

'I do, but that ain't the point.'

'Charlie, you've always been hard work.'

'You sound like my mom.'

Restarick had first met Charles Armstrong while stationed in Northern France. They had been born thousands of miles apart but had cemented a bond in the trenches when Armstrong had been injured and found medical help in the British encampments.

Following their respective discharges, Charles had decided to stay in the country, seeing profit could be made working on the black market and out of the sight of the *kaisersoldaten*. His underground life had indeed proved fruitful as he still supplied weary troops with goods that their superiors declined to.

'So you going to drink it or not?' Restarick asked, raising his own glass. The bar was short and there were no other customers in. It was a quiet night for the Café Tabac du Bourg.

Armstrong pulled his drink towards him and sniffed it. The gold nectar caressed the interior of the tumbler. 'How the hell did you find me, kid?'

'I'm here on His Majesty's Secret Service,' Restarick breathed.

'*His Majesty*? Damn, you Brits really need to let go. He ain't no 'majesty' anymore.'

'That's what we're trying to rectify.'

'And how am I involved in this?' Armstrong swigged at his bourbon. 'As you *are* here, I'm kinda guessing that I am?'

'Do you know Max Baker?'

Armstrong sat back and thought about that, pursing his lips and shaking his head, his greased hair not budging an inch. 'Friend of yours?'

'Went missing last month in Cairo.'

'Perhaps you should go to Cairo, then.'

Restarick furrowed his brow and watched a couple arrive and sit down at a nearby table. They were tactile, attentive to each other, hands held tightly. Young lovers? Newly-weds? Certainly the presence of the *kaisersoldaten* on the streets outside didn't make any difference to their states of mind. Restarick wondered if the man in civvies was ex-military. No. Too young. Unless he was invalided out. The woman's hair was bobbed, blonde. They were both very tanned.

'I'm en route. But Baker has been known to frequent some of the Paris suburbs. That's why I'm here.' Restarick leant towards Armstrong. 'Dammit, Charlie, you know everyone around here. A Secret Service operative is, for you, going to stand out like a sore thumb.'

'Unless he's damn good at his job? As good as you?' continued Armstrong. 'Hell, I didn't know *you* were even in France until I got your telegram.'

Restarick laughed gently and lit a cigarette. He smoked occasionally, more regularly when he was required to concentrate. 'Point made.'

'Yeah, but why has he gone missing and why start here? This place ain't exactly on the radar.'

'Charlie, *everywhere* is on the radar…' Restarick's voice trailed off as he felt the lovers look at him. He didn't look back at them but shifted in his seat, giving them more of his back and lowered his voice further. 'Baker might have defected.'

Armstrong stared at the ice melting into the bourbon and squinted at the Rue de Vindé outside and the old man with a bicycle who was arguing with one of the *kaisersoldaten*. The road was narrow, the wall opposite leaning at an uncomfortable angle as if it would topple. 'They must have offered you a shitload of something to get you away from the plantation of yours. Listen, Restarick, I'll be straight with you. Something's happening. Something big.'

'Big?'

Armstrong nodded. 'Across Europe. They're closing borders permanently, shutting off passage. No trade, no supplies, a permanent curfew, all day and all night.'

'That hasn't reached England, yet.'

'Give it time. It's not everywhere, but it will be.'

'It did seem more difficult to get the boat-train to Calais. Triple the number of checks at Dover. Getting out of Versailles took me an age.'

'Exactly. They're planning something. Damned if I know what.'

Restarick looked around him. 'So… Baker.'

'Baker,' said Armstrong. 'Yes, I saw him.'

Restarick rubbed his brow. It had been a bloody long day. Why didn't Armstrong just say he had in the first place? 'Where? When?'

'Two, maybe three weeks ago, I reckon. He was hanging around the Montmartre Steps. They wouldn't let him in.'

'Did you speak to him?'

'No. I watched him for a while until the *kaisersoldaten* moved me on.'

'How do you know him by sight?'

Armstrong pursed his lips, reluctant to say but could feel Restarick's eyes boring into him. He finished his drink and the bartender moved to refill his glass. Armstrong waved his hand in refusal. 'He did some work a couple of years ago that got the attention of the French Resistance. I'd be surprised if the *kaisersoldaten* weren't aware of him and that might explain why he's missing.'

'What work?'

'He was…' Armstrong put a hand to his lips. He looked almost nauseous. 'He was with Leo Stanley,' he whispered.

'Leo Stanley?'

Armstrong almost shuddered. 'Your superiors might know of him. He was Chief Surgeon at San Quentin.'

'Was?'

'He was given the boot due to, let's say, *unethical* medical practices on the prisoners. He went into hiding just before the Armistice.'

'Where did he go?'

'Where do you think?'

'Germany?'

Armstrong nodded. 'Right in the centre of the web. Resurfaced in Berlin in 1919. Word has it that the Kaiser appointed him as CMO. Got himself a nice cushy job. Oversees a team of young *Kaiser-Jünger*, handpicked men and women who remain obsessively loyal to the Imperium. Christ only knows what they get up to.'

Restarick beckoned the bartender back over. '*Une pinte de Spaten, s'il vous plaît. Ajoutez-le à l'onglet de ma chambre.*' He waited until the beer was served and placed before him, the white paper coaster sticking to the glass' base. The bartender moved away. 'Baker *has* defected then. I need to get to Cairo.'

'Good luck to you, kid. I've told you too much already. Anything to do with Stanley and I'm out.' Armstrong, standing, poured the half-melted ice into his mouth and crunched it. 'Thanks for the bourbon. One more thing…'

'What's that?'

'I heard what the Factory put you through after Saint-Mihiel. Was sure sorry to hear it. Watch yourself out there.'

Restarick watched him go, then finished his beer and headed to his room. He was tired now and the ornate clock behind the bar told him it was nearly eight o'clock.

The notion of a British operative directly involved with Berlin was chilling and Restarick wondered how likely it was. He didn't know Baker personally but had it on good authority from Swinton that he was a good man, if a little lazy in his approach to work. It may be such tardiness that had befallen Baker and certainly Swinton gave no indication that there was a defection at play here. He had to see if he could find out more about this Stanley, too. He hoped Cairo would reveal more secrets.

Also playing on his mind were Armstrong's and Jean-Didier's separate comments about his failure at Saint-Mihiel. Room 40 had indeed interrogated him at great length and, using his injuries as evidence, secured a medical discharge. They brought him into their protection, conscious that there may have been some out there who would securely put the blame at his door. The Factory ultimately gave him a new purpose after the war, the chance to make something of a difference, even though Restarick himself took longer to accept the past events.

His train was to leave tomorrow from Paris Gare de Lyon at 0900 prompt for a direct run to Marseille, where he would find passage across the Balearic Sea to Algiers. No tickets had been bought prior to his journey starting. He wanted any trail of his movements to be as short as possible.

The two lovers had been eating a meal, laughing through the main course and focusing now with some seriousness on their dessert. The wine was still flowing and they seemed completely enamoured with each other. The woman looked up at Restarick as he passed by, smiling with her dark eyes. It was then, through that look alone, that he realised that the *amour* was one-sided and her male companion was probably paying by the hour.

'*Bonne chance*,' Restarick said to her and then, '*Bonne nuit, monsieur*.'

***

Restarick's room was small but functional, typically sparse with a wash basin in the corner only a couple of feet away from the single bed (which wasn't particularly comfy).

It had taken him a good while to drift off and he slept now, something he had struggled to do fully since his discharge. Most of his night thoughts were taken up by his wife. He was in the trenches when the news came of her death and his dream took him back there over and over. Always in the dark, the single candle of the dug-out that extinguished itself as he reached the final word of the telegram.

As the pitch black swallows him whole, he looks up and she appears before him, clad in blood-red rags, her hair alight, her olive skin blistering. But there is no heat coming from her blazing form, no smell of roasting flesh. It is his own skin falling from his own bones, his life evaporating in the heat, his nerves seared to the point where there is no more pain.

Then he was awake, sweat soaking the sheets to the extent that he felt as if he had soiled himself like an incontinent old man. His breathing was always laboured at this point, heart pounding under his ribs.

Tonight was no different.

He sat on the edge of the bed, exhausted with the trauma, shivering from the moisture over his bare back. He clasped a glass half-full of water and raised it to his mouth. It felt cool against his lips and he paused before gulping the contents down.

He checked his watch. It was nearly five. He was due to awaken at 0630 and knew he wouldn't get back to sleep.

'Shit.'

He lit a cigarette and stood by the open casement window. He loved French architecture, egotistical and flamboyant, even a window making a statement, just as the Parisienne street signs did and the Guimard designs of the Métro surface-level entrances. He wondered if the Kaiser would eventually recreate his empire's greatest cities in the image of Berlin, wiping away centuries of heritage and culture.

Just then, a shrill whistle rang out from one of the *kaisersoldaten* on night watch, rounding up anyone who had dared to break the curfew. There were running booted feet that increased in volume then suddenly stopped.

Restarick realised they were beneath him, at the entrance to the café.

The door thumped and the soldiers hollered at the owner to be let in. They grew impatient then Restarick heard the bolts slide back and the bell above the opening door jangle.

He decided to get dressed.

He had no reason to suspect they are here for him but, just in case, he didn't want to face the enemy naked.

As he stubbed out his cigarette and walked towards the chair upon which his clothes were resting, his door flew open.

Standing there was the man who had been with the woman eating in the café, a rifle in his hand.

'Get dressed,' he growled, looking him up and down then straight in the eye. 'You have company.'

Restarick complied, hurrying into his trousers, braces up and over the collarless shirt he had first slipped onto his back. 'You here to take me to them?'

'No. I'm here to get you away from them.'

Restarick grabbed the pistol he hid under the mattress, checked it was loaded, and followed his unexpected saviour, shrugging his coat on as he moved. He noticed that the stranger wore black trousers and heavy jacket, army boots and a torch. The rifle that he lifted over his shoulder was American.

'You a friend of Charlie's?'

'No names,' the man replied, accent precise and public-school-boy.

Very sensible. 'Where are we going?'

'Away from here, old boy. Now keep quiet.'

They moved through the upstairs level of the building and out onto the sloping roof via a sash window at the end of a corridor. The sound of the *kaisersoldaten* searching the rooms grew louder—and nearer. In silence, the man motioned for Restarick to leap across to the next building, the roof of which sloped almost to the ground. He did so and the man followed, landing hard. Below them was a small patch of open land with a road to their right. It was difficult in the darkness to see any obstacles but they both risked jumping the short distance.

The man twisted his leg on impact with concrete and cried out, Restarick finding a softer base.

From around the other side of the building the soldiers called to each other, having heard the man's painful descent.

The man stood and dashed across the grass with an agonising gait but did not get far: enemy bullets from another soldier coming from up ahead felled him. Restarick cursed himself for not spotting him sooner.

As the soldier darted to the side of the building, shouting out to his colleagues in German that he had found the Englander, Restarick seized the opportunity to swap IDs with the dead man. He also grabbed the rifle. He then squeezed himself behind a stack of bins and some bushes that sat by the exterior and surrounding walls. He waited for the soldiers to come to the unnamed man who took a bullet that was destined for him.

The soldiers did not delay in searching through the man's clothing. When they found nothing, they dragged him by his lapels out of Restarick's line of sight.

Restarick waited for a few moments then slid himself over the wall and into the woodlands, taking advantage of being awake to head to Paris Gare de Lyon early. He spotted an Army motorcycle on the outskirts of town and considered stealing it. There was no one around and the rider was probably off duty and asleep somewhere, not likely to awaken until dawn. Restarick rolled the motorcycle down the street a few hundred yards, mounted it, kicked it into life and roared off northwards. Hopefully, the distance between him and where he found the bike was enough to keep the rider asleep. By the time the theft was discovered, Restarick hoped he would be safely on the train to Marseille.

***

The German officer, disturbed from his sleep by a dog barking in the street, only noticed his motorcycle had gone when he leant out the window to throw something at the animal. He raised the alarm and the checkpoint at Boulogne-Billancourt was notified.

Restarick had been taking the back streets as best he could but as he neared Paris itself he had no choice but to veer back towards the busier thoroughfares when he saw troops not far from the Paris Observatory. Up ahead, at the pont de Sèvres, the barrier was down and two guards, armed and alert, stood in the middle of the road. There was another barrier on the other side of the bridge. He didn't want to cross the Seine here but it looked like he might not have had much of a choice. In fact, crossing it once would be a challenge: at this point, he'd need to cross it a further two times to get to the Gare de Lyon.

Damn.

The guards saw him.

While he was riding a military-issue vehicle, anyone even in need of spectacles could see he wasn't in uniform, let alone a German one. He had no business being out mid-curfew. He patted his breast pockets: his forged papers were present and correct and he made a split-second decision that he knew could change the next stage of his mission.

To avoid the checkpoints, now that the *kaisersoldaten* had seen him, would be suspicious. They would give chase and cut him off somewhere along the banks of the river. So he slowed, threw the rifle into a ditch, then, pulling back on the throttle, rode casually toward the guards.

They waved him down, asked him to switch off his engine and dismount. They looked him up and down and then at the motorcycle.

One asked him in German for his papers and what business he had.

'I have business at the Government office,' he replied, also in German but with a French accent. 'I must be allowed to pass.'

'You do understand that there is a curfew? Unless you are exempt, there are no excuses. Do you work for the transport infrastructure? For law enforcement?'

'I am on a special mission from London. You will see my papers are in order.'

The guard, the one clearly in charge, nodded as he examined Restarick's papers. He handed them back to him, seemingly satisfied with their authenticity. 'This motorcycle. Where did you obtain it?'

Restarick stroked it with false affection. 'She's been with me since Armistice Day,' he lied. 'A Helios. You like 'bikes?'

The guard raised his eyebrows. 'She is a good looking machine.'

Restarick leant in close to the guard. '*Bayerische Motoren Werke* are merging with *Bayerische Flugzeugwerke* in a matter of weeks, so I'm told. I cannot *wait* to see what they will produce.'

'Merging?' The guard wasn't party to this information, but this Frenchman seemed to be well-informed and sounded quite knowledgeable.

Restarick smiling inwardly that even the smallest intelligence information gathered by Room 40 was always useful. 'Oh, indeed. They will produce beautiful motorbikes I am sure, but I will always have a place in my heart for my Helios. She brought me safely out of Amiens with just a warm bullet in my leg and a hot woman waiting for me in Berlin!' Restarick guffawed and offered the guard a handful of cigarettes, who declined them while on duty. Restarick shrugged and confidently slid them into the man's top pocket. 'For later. Egyptian blend. Smooth.'

The guard pretended not to notice the gift and motioned for his colleague to raise the barrier. He used a short semaphore code to signal the guards at the other end to let Restarick through. Restarick hopped on the 'bike and kicked the engine back into life.

'When I collect my BMW, I will come give you Helios,' he shouted and charged across the bridge in a flurry of exhaust and noise. '*Auf wiedersehen*.'

***

The morning sun cast a warm ochre glow into the carriages as the train snaked its way down through the French southern regions.

Daniel Restarick, formally dressed for breakfast in a suit he had purloined from a passenger's trunk in the baggage car, sat facing the engine, the day breaking on his left. He liked the window seat and, so far, no one had attempted to share his table with him.

The carriage was relatively empty but that could have been because it was still rather early and the curfew lift only applied to specific trades.

Two men were sitting together at another table. Restarick overheard some of their conversation. It seemed to revolve around high value shares in South African stocks, implying they were of wealth. Certainly they were dressed impeccably, hair greased to perfection and their diction, possibly Hungarian or Romanian, was clipped and precise. They were eating smoked salmon and cleansing their pallets with the finest Ayla champagne.

Restarick meanwhile was drinking coffee and reading the paper. He seldom took breakfast but his interrupted start in the early hours had left him hungry. The chef was preparing for him œufs *cocotte à la provençale*.

The identity documents of the man at La Celle-Saint-Cloud were burning a hole in his jacket pocket and, as no one gave him a second glance and he had full view of the carriage with no one to look over his shoulder (he was by the adjoining door), he folded his newspaper neatly before looking at the purloined information.

Hugh Drummond, born Godalming, 4 August 1886. Only a year older than me.

They were likely forgeries, no less real than the ones he carried with him that told whoever reads them that he was Artz Murnau, a Bavarian envoy appointed to the Kaiser's French seat of operations. Room 40 was unfailingly thorough.

But this Drummond, posing as a customer back in the café, was certainly not there by coincidence. Who else knew Restarick was present?

As the connecting door behind him slid back, Restarick quickly put Drummond's papers back in his pocket.

A woman glided into the carriage, a white and gold *minaudière* in her right hand that complemented the black sequined sheath dress that clung to her figure. She wasn't typically slim, the current fashion trend, and Restarick admired the elegant curve of her hips as she moved with determination to a place prepared for her by an attending waiter. She sat with her back to Restarick, her long dark hair cascading across her shoulders.

He pretended to read his paper as she lit a thin cigar, her face angled slightly to view the passing countryside, but was interrupted by the arrival of his breakfast, a side of toast with his eggs and a fresh pot of coffee.

By the time the train had passed by the Sénart Forest, Restarick had finished his meal and could feel the coffee pumping through his system. The next stop would be Lyon where, the train guard had declared, there would be a rest of thirty minutes before continuing uninterrupted to Marseille.

'I won't be able to bear such an awful journey without the company of a gentleman.'

Restarick looked up.

Before him was the woman, a wry smile on her face. He stood and offered her to sit with him at his table. In one movement, she moved in opposite him. As he looked at her dark eyes, he recalled seeing her before today. Her small bag she placed to her left.

'I saw you earlier when you walked in.'

'I know. You tried your best to read your paper.' Her accent was gently laced with French.

Restarick laughed. 'You are very perceptive.'

'It costs me not to be.'

'Costs you?'

She tilted her head and raised a perfectly-maintained eyebrow. 'Occasionally.'

'What is it that keeps you looking…'

'Looking?'

'…looking *contented*?'

'I had a husband.' Her eyes flashed up to catch Restarick's gaze.

'Had?'

'Dead now. Rich, but dead.'

'A widow enjoying her inheritance. I can drink to that.'

Restarick called the waiter over and ordered a scotch for himself and for her, at her polite thank you, a cognac. As they sipped their drinks, the woman watched Restarick dab the base of his tumbler with the white paper coaster.

'Am I expected to pay for my drink?'

'My company will see to that.'

'I see.' She let the cigar smoke drift from slightly parted lips then exhaled gently. 'You are a man kept by his employer.'

'Something like that.'

'And what is it that you do for your employer, Mr…?'

'Drummond, Hugh Drummond,' Restarick replied. 'I work in medicine.'

'A doctor?'

'More in the care system. Ex-POWs, shell-shocked servicemen… that kind of thing.'

'From whose side?'

Restarick leant back in his chair and watched the woman play with her cigarette lighter. 'Does it matter?'

She shrugged. 'I guess not anymore. We are, after all, one big happy Europe. You have business in Marseille, Dr Drummond?'

'What makes you think I'm not getting off at Lyon?'

'Because at the Gare de Lyon you bought a one way ticket to Marseille.'

'Are you spying on me?'

'Does it matter?' she responded, that smile returning to those full lips.

'I guess not anymore,' he laughed. 'Yes, you're quite right. I am going to Marseille and yes, I do have business there. What about you? Going all the way?'

'That depends.'

'On what?'

'If it's worth my while.'

'How will you tell?'

'I'll know.' She swirled her drink and the ice circled in her glass. 'I'm rarely wrong.'

'What if you are?'

'You'll never know.'

A pause.

'What's your name?'

'Olivia Duffy.'

'Pleased to meet you, Mrs Duffy.'

Olivia tapped her cigar into the ashtray the waiter had just brought over. 'Do either of you require anything else from the menu?' he asked.

Restarick motioned to Olivia who shook her head. 'No, thank you,' Restarick replied. 'Are we on time for Lyon?'

'Yes, sir. Will you be alighting from the train during our stop?'

Restarick looked at the waiter then at Olivia, then back at the waiter. 'Yes. For a little while.'

'Very good, sir.'

The waiter left, clearing Restarick's plate and cutlery as he went.

'Shopping?' Olivia asked. 'Lyon has a beautiful haberdashery.'

'Not really my thing, Mrs Duffy. I like to see the sights.'

'Very romantic.'

'Not so much on one's own.'

'Are you asking me to join you?'

'It would be untoward of me.'

'Are you afraid to ask?'

'Not in the least.'

'Then ask me.'

Restarick finished his drink, unfolded then refolded his newspaper and looked at her squarely in the eyes. He stood. 'Sorry, Mrs Duffy. I prefer my own company.'

***

Back in his compartment, Restarick rested on his bed, thinking about her.

Olivia Duffy certainly was beautiful, he mused, as the train clattered over a set of points. He felt cruel for turning her down but had no intention of leaving the train at their next stop. Nevertheless, while he found it easy to talk to women, to enjoy their company, Lita's death still weighed heavy on his heart. Anything more than talk remained purposefully out of his reach.

Before long he began to nod off.

With a loud retort, the locomotive's whistles roused him suddenly; he was annoyed with himself for falling asleep. Rubbing his eyes and immediately alert, he looked out of the window: they were pulling into the newly built Gare de le Pouvoir du Kaiser.

Passengers disembarked and were herded to a line of tables where seated *kaisersoldaten* checked papers and luggage, random searches that made everyone nervous, even if they had nothing to hide. This was Lyon under German rule, positioned to allow all manner of visitors; the Kaiser's fist came down hard here. Behind the station building rose a grey slab, curving away, a wall built to surround the entire jurisdiction. The railway line ran alongside the exterior to re-join the Paris-Lyon-Marseille line that had been cut to make way for the barrier. There were no private cars or public transport allowed inside. Any commuting was managed by military vehicles and at predetermined pick up and drop off points.

Restarick stood at a carriage door and watched the checks being carried out. He sparked a cigarette and leant against the frame. He couldn't imagine Olivia rubbing shoulders on the back of a German truck and couldn't see her amongst the line of people. Perhaps she had decided to stay onboard. A small part of him hoped this was the case.

He looked at his watch. They had arrived on time and would be departing in just under thirty minutes. Restarick threw his cigarette to the floor and reboarded the train. The buffet car was closed so he returned to his compartment but the door seemed to be locked from the inside.

Immediately suspicious, he put an ear to the door. He could hear shuffling. He pulled his pistol from its underarm holster and cocked it as quietly as he could. The wooden flooring creaked slightly as he stepped back, bringing silence to within. With a booted foot he kicked the door open, the brass bolt clattering to the floor. The startled intruder was the waiter from earlier: Restarick's suspicions were confirmed.

'I wondered why waiting staff would be interested if I was staying onboard or not. I didn't think it was because you fancied a jolly into town.' The compartment had been turned over. 'Now what do you want?'

The waiter hurled himself to Restarick who sidestepped. The waiter spun and kicked out, knocking the gun from Restarick's grip. It was a small area to fight in so Restarick recalled his boxing training from school and brought his arms up, jabbing out, blocking, and upper cutting where he could. But the waiter fought dirty, using anything he could get his hands on to stop the blows raining down on him.

A lucky strike across Restarick's brow sent him flying. He was a big man and Restarick could see his arms bulging under his white tunic. Jumping to his feet, Restarick adopted the man's tactics and picked up his own open suitcase, crashing it across the waiter's left ear who stumbled, shaking his head.

They both glanced at Restarick's pistol that had slid part way under the bed and dived for it at the same time. The fight became a wrestle as the men attempted to pull and push the gun free from the grip of the other. It was only seconds into the struggle that it went off, stopping them both for a split-second before resuming the seemingly-check-mated battle.

But Restarick, on his back with the man atop him, saw an advantage: he kicked the retractable bed shut, folding it flush to the wall. It fell open again with little weight, merely grazing the waiter's shoulder. The attempt angered him though and he almost roared in Restarick's face, pulling together some hidden force and head-butting the Secret Service agent full in the face.

Restarick cried out in pain and tried to roll out from under him but to no avail. He could only watch helplessly as the gun barrel edged closer to his bloodied nose. At this close range, his face would be blown away.

Then the man fell unconscious, a dead weight on Restarick's chest.

Over his shoulder, Restarick spied Olivia standing in the doorway, a broken chair she used to clout the waiter with still in her hand.

'Didn't you go shopping for buttons?' he asked, crawling out from under the waiter. 'Thank you.'

'You're welcome,' Olivia purred, entering then closing the door behind her as best she could. She threw the leg to the floor. 'For a medical man, you seem to have determined enemies.'

'Railway staff these days. No respect for the passenger.'

Olivia rolled the waiter onto his back and patted him down. From under his tunic and strapped flush to his back was a thin leather pouch which she removed and placed on the carpeted floor. Then she dragged him to the window and tied him with the curtain cords. 'Just in case.'

Restarick slumped on the bed and breathed a sigh. Olivia turned to him and checked his face.

'Broken?' he asked.

'No. Your nose looks fine. But you're going to have an almighty headache.'

'You seem to have done that before,' he said, nodding towards her handiwork. 'Get much call for tying up waiters?'

'A girl can dream, Dr Drummond.'

She looked up at him as she went back to check on the attacker's bonds and Restarick realised where he had seen her before. 'You. You were the blonde in La Celle-Saint-Cloud.'

'I was.'

'I'm guessing you're not—'

'Really blonde? Or a prostitute?' Olivia laughed. 'No. To both.'

'Your companion… he's dead. I'm sorry.'

'Did you kill him?'

'No.'

'Then why are you sorry?' Olivia straightened and brushed her dress. 'Oh, look, I've dented my purse.'

'I'll buy you another one. About your companion…'

'What about him? If you didn't kill him you must know who did.'

'How so?'

'You're using his identity.'

Restarick sighed. *Of course. Damn stupid.*

As soon as he introduced himself as Hugh Drummond to her, she knew that's who he wasn't. 'My name is Restarick.'

'*Captain* Restarick…' she said, smiling. 'I know who you are, Danny-boy. I've been following you since Versailles.'

Good Lord. Who is *this woman?* 'So will you tell me who you really are?'

'After you snubbed me on a sight-seeing tour? I don't think you deserve to. You're something of a cad.'

'You did save my life. I must have appealed to you in some way.'

She laughed. 'Maybe you did. Maybe you didn't. But I don't mix work with pleasure.'

'It takes work to make things pleasurable.'

'I do believe you're flirting with me. You *are* a cad!' The woman put out a hand. 'Mircalla Richard. A pleasure to meet you.'

Restarick rose from the bed and shook the offered hand. 'Even if not under the most relaxed of circumstances. But at least I know your preferred drink.'

'You do realise that once the train guard sees your compartment in this state, he will have you arrested.'

'Yes, that had occurred to me,' Restarick replied, wincing. His nose hurt. 'I think we should go.'

'And leave our bound man where he is.'

'No. He comes with us.'

'Isn't that going to look suspicious?'

'I'm a doctor, remember,' Restarick said, winking at Mircalla. 'How do you fancy playing nurse?'

'I'm a modern woman. Why don't *you* be the nurse?'

Daniel Restarick laughed and went to untie the waiter who was beginning to stir as Mircalla opened the leather pouch. She blew air through pursed lips. 'You need to see this.'

'Problem?'

There were separate photographs of both him and Mircalla: his taken in his plantations in Kandy earlier in the year, hers while she was buying a pack of slim cigars in Cardiff about three months ago. Four further portraits were nestled amongst a series of orders, written in German.

'Do you know them?' she asked.

'No,' Restarick replied as he slid back in the photo of Charlie Armstrong, knowing what that red line scored across it meant. The fourth was of Baker, the missing man. The fifth he recognised and tried his best to suppress a chill that crawled over him but Mircalla picked up on it. The sixth he genuinely didn't know.

'That guy,' Mircalla began, tapping the last, sixth photograph with a fingernail 'is Doctor Leo Stanley. Nasty character.'

'They are hits. The marked one means he's dead.' Restarick held the sadness inside for Armstrong's killing. But they all knew the risks when they signed up. 'Who's next?'

'You, obviously,' Mircalla said. 'He's an assassin.'

'Well, he's a terrible waiter.' Restarick tried to rouse the man, slapping his cheeks, pushing at his chin. 'Come on, wake up, you bloody bastard.' He looked around them, grabbed a jug of water near the little sink and threw its contents over the drowsy man. 'Who are you?'

After a few short moments, the man stirred and squinted up at Restarick and began laughing, the water still dripping from his hair. 'You are not dead!'

'Clearly. Now tell me… why am I on your hit list?'

The man frowned. 'Hit list? What is hit list?'

He had an accent that Mircalla recognised as Eastern European.

'Russian?' asked Restarick, to which the man shook his head. 'Why are you trying to kill me?'

'You tried to kill me.'

'Don't play games. Who sent you?'

'I work on the locomotives.'

'Don't lie to us,' Mircalla added. 'You fought too well, too trained. I have seen your moves before.' Outside, there were noises that indicated the train was soon to depart. Mircalla poked her head into the corridor and quickly turned back to the two men. 'They're checking the cabins.'

'Train staff?' asked Restarick.

'*Kaisersoldaten*.'

'We need to get off this train now.'

'No,' Mircalla responded firmly. 'We're staying.'

'I need to return to my duty,' said the waiter.

'You are joking? I'm not letting you out of my sight.' Restarick surveyed his little compartment.

'I do not mean to kill you.'

'What about these?' asked Mircalla, waving the leather pouch in his face.

'I found them. I saw this man's photograph in it,' he replied, nodding to Restarick.

'So you wrecked my room?'

'It was like this when I came in.'

'Then why did you attack him?' Mircalla wanted to know.

'I tried to get out but your friend, he is strong. I had to defend myself. Then you hit me,' he added, rubbing his head. 'The papers I found on a seat in the buffet car. When I looked through them and saw your pictures, I wanted to know who you were.'

'What's your name?' she asked.

'Miklos'.

Mircalla gave the pouch to Restarick. 'Well, Miklos, you've got yourself involved.' Then to Restarick: 'Hide it and go to my cabin. Here's the key. We'll imply you didn't re-board. And you, Miklos, our strange secret waiter assassin, get yourself straight.' She ignored Restarick's objections. 'I don't think, even if you're *not* a waiter, that you can afford to *not* be on this train when we depart.'

Berlin, Germany

Buried deep in the ground beneath Charlottenburg Palace was a series of rooms linked by a complex network of corridors. One of the rooms, the largest and best-lit, was entered by crossing a threshold of four thick steel doors, each interconnected by three four-feet by three-feet lobbies. In the first, one was required to strip and leave one's clothes behind. After passing through the second heavy door, one was scrubbed by an attendant covered head to toe in protective clothing, using disinfectant and a soft broom. Dried, one passed through the third door into the last lobby where protective clothing identical to that of the attendant was required to be worn. The fourth door was opened and the room within was tiled from ceiling to floor and across the walls, with one single narrow slit of a window, formed from five separate layers of glass, directly opposite the door and at head height. The room contained thirty beds, evenly spaced and each containing a living person. Some of the people were children, some pensioners, but the majority were in their twenties through to their forties. They had all been infected or poisoned and were at varying stages of dying or suffering. In all cases, the agony was extreme and no treatments were offered or given. Instead, other attendants, all in the same protective suits, observed and took notes. To leave the room, one had to undergo the same process but in reverse, leaving the protective suit in the immediate lobby, decontamination in the middle section and re-dressing in one's own clothes before entering the labyrinthine corridors.

Doctor Leo Stanley, a tall, remarkably thin man with a head of thick white hair set against bushy, black eyebrows, peered into the room through the slit, making copious notes in a worn leather-bound notebook. He was a man of particular habits, uneasy around other people and found it difficult to engage in conversation. He frustrated the *Kaiser-Regel* but they tolerated his peculiarities because of his dedication to his work.

He had never been into that room and had ensured any of his staff he sent in there underwent a handful of days' quarantine, irrespective of the thoroughness of the disinfection process.

Outside of the room, however, was equally stark and clinical. Along one wall was a safe, a large thick door with three combination locks holding at bay any would-be thief or saboteur. Only three people knew the codes that changed daily: Stanley himself, Voigt and Hartmann.

Inside the safe were eight phials, three with concentrated solutions of *B. influenzae*, three with *A*, all cultivated and modified from the subjects inside the sealed room, and two with the anti-virus to both.

A buzzer sounded in Stanley's lab and he glanced up at the red light winking in the corner. He ignored the interruptions but the obtrusive noise sounded again, followed by a tinny voice through the speaker screwed to the wall by the light.

'Doctor Stanley,' rang the voice, in a clipped German accent, 'you are required in the Great Orangery.'

Stanley turned his nose up. What did the German fools want of him now?

His superiors were satisfied that his work was done but they saw in him his desire to keep experimenting, to keep slicing and cutting, to discover new ways of pushing the boundaries of human science. If anything, it would mean that their power in holding the cures for all known diseases, the viruses of a thousand new ones, would make them feared across the world. Europe was under their control; the world would be at their mercy. Blackmail on a global scale.

When he didn't respond, the request became laced with an order.

At this, Stanley slipped the notebook into his jacket pocket and folded his gold-rimmed spectacles, holding them tight. 'I heard ya,' he retorted, knowing that the Germans couldn't abide his American South drawl.

***

The Orangery was elaborate and large, flooded with natural light and space. Extended beyond its original baroque construction, it was exactly the kind of festival room one would have expected of a nation who considered they held the future of the world in those six phials.

It was full of members of the *Kaiser-Regel*, businessmen and even a film star or two. There was a string quartet in one corner playing a movement that Stanley found nauseating, almost as unappetising as the spread of food that had been prepared. He forked at a plate of *hackepeter* that was alleviated by a glass of a herb-infused spirit that he understood was called *akvavit*. A man was trying his utmost to engage him in conversation and all Stanley could think of was slicing the man's fingers off one by one just to see the look on his face.

'…and so it makes sense that we keep the curfews going all day and all night,' he was saying through mouthfuls of meatballs. 'What was it you said you did?'

'I don't believe I did,' Stanley replied. 'Is your food good?'

'Not the best but I believe the *koch* is French, so what can you expect?'

'They remind me,' Doctor Stanley replied, 'of a series of experiments I carried out on the prisoners at San Quentin.'

'How so?' The man continued chewing.

'Replacing the testicles of the criminal set with those of pigs.'

The man looked down at his next spoonful and suddenly decided against it.

'Fascinating results. Would you like to know more?'

Then he was alone, exactly as he preferred, watching the man make his excuses as he was offered more food by an attending waitress.

'Are you frightening our local members of Parliament, Doctor?'

Stanley turned and did not bother to contain the look of disgust as his solace was abruptly halted. But this was Hartmann, a benefactor of his experiments here at Charlottenburg Palace.

'I was simply engaging in light conversation, something I believe you asked of me at the last one of these… these functions.' Stanley sipped at his *akvavit*. 'If you just require me here to make up the numbers, I'd much prefer to be working.'

It had been the belief of the doctor that his experiments would rejuvenate old men, control crime and, importantly, prevent the "unfit" from reproducing. This was an opinion that the *Kaiser-Regel* immediately recognised, hence the American's appointment as senior scientist, but their demands to look into bacterial warfare had taken him away from what he considered vital research.

'I called you here to talk with you. I do not… *enjoy* being in your laboratory.'

'Then why subject me to this awful party?'

'I am away for the next two weeks and I simply need to ask you if we are ready.'

'Ready?'

Hartmann moved away from the spread of food and closer to the quartet, ensuring their conversation could not be overheard.

'You know what I am asking you. Is *das Geschenk* ready?

'Yes. It's ready.'

Hartmann smiled and patted Stanley on the shoulder, the doctor looking down at Hartmann's hand as though it was covered in shit. 'Then we must move at once.'

Stanley, as proud as he was of the microscopic killer he had created, was unsure about this. 'It needs more time to germinate.'

'You said it was ready.'

'For now. But I want to ensure that no cure can be recreated other than what I have formed myself. Only I'll have the key and I'll personally release my cure for your *neue Weltordnung*.'

This unsettled Hartmann and wasn't part of the contract. Did Stanley intend to hold the *Kaiser-Regel* to ransom? 'You are but one scientist. You can be replaced.'

'If that's so,' Stanley leered, waxy breath on Hartmann's face, 'then your Kaiser wouldn't have sought me out so intently or made me your CMO. Any old fucker with a scalpel woulda done, surely? You *need* me.'

Hartmann puffed out his chest. 'You are *not* untouchable, not indispensable.'

'I have in ma pocket, you fat little Kraut, a phial of your so called 'gift'. All I gotta do is throw it into that group of people by the door and… *smash*… you're all fucked.'

'And endanger yourself? I do not think so.'

'In my other pocket, I got me the antidote.' Stanley smiled. He didn't smile very often but this was an occasion that warranted one.

Hartmann's face dropped. 'Then it seems you have the advantage, *Herr* Doctor.'

'I will be present at the delivery of your 'gift'. Now I assume you already have a date in mind?'

Hartmann pulled the doctor towards the exit and lowered his voice. 'You can assure me it will be ready in two days?'

'Yes.'

'Then, Doctor Stanley, we would be honoured to begin a new world together.'

Hartmann led Stanley outside to the gardens, flat grass criss-crossed by right-angled pathways and young trees. He explained that the virus would be released simultaneously at set points across Europe as well as further afield: Moscow and Washington had been targeted, too. Stanley raised his eyebrows in anticipation. This was delightful news. His virus working on a global scale. He would be able to map its route, its effect on humanity: who would be strong enough—and therefore *worthy* enough—to live. His initial hesitancy at being taken away from his life at San Quentin now seemed churlish. *This* was what his career and his studies had been working towards.

London

Summer in Hyde Park always attracted large crowds, even after the Armistice. This year the feast day celebrations for the composer Handel had increased the footfall, with concerts in the hot sun running all day until curfew. It was the first time that the event had been staged outside of Hamburg and some had considered this was a political move to ensure the docility of the British. After all, Handel had settled in England in the 1700s and so there was a sense of ownership between both countries.

Amongst the crowd were *kaisersoldaten* dressed as civilians. They were there to control the crowds before, during and after the presence of the Kaiser. They had not been informed however, that the real Kaiser was still in Germany and this *doppelganger* a decoy target for the Resistance.

Marconi speakers set up around the park crackled and popped into life, bringing all present to a silent standstill.

'His Imperial and Royal Majesty Wilhelm the Second, by the Grace of God, German Emperor and King of Prussia, of France, of Britain, of Russia and of Italy, Margrave of Brandenburg, of Serbia, of Belgium, of Montenegro, of Nejd and Hasa, of Asir, of Portugal, of Romania, of Hejaz, of Greece and of Armenia, Burgrave of Nuremberg, Count of Hohenzollern, Duke of Silesia and of the County of Glatz, Grand Duke of the Lower Rhine and of Posen, Duke of Saxony, of Angria, of Westphalia, of Pomerania and of Lunenburg, Duke of Schleswig, of Holstein and of Crossen, Duke of Magdeburg, of Bremen, of Guelderland and of Jülich, Cleves and Berg, Duke of the Wends and the Kashubians, of Lauenburg and of Mecklenburg, Landgrave of Hesse and in Thuringia, Margrave of Upper and Lower Lusatia, Prince of Orange, of Rugen, of East Friesland, of Paderborn and of Pyrmont, Prince of Halberstadt, of Münster, of Minden, of Osnabrück, of Hildesheim, of Verden, of Kammin, of Fulda, of Nassau and of Moers, Princely Count of Henneberg, Count of the Mark, of Ravensberg, of Hohenstein, of Tecklenburg and of Lingen, Count of Mansfeld, of Sigmaringen and of Veringen, Lord of Frankfurt.'

A fanfare of trumpets cried out, piercing the silence after the announcement had ceased and the Gold State Coach, a familiar sight for the British but now enforcing upon them a different viewpoint, came slowly into the park, pulled by a team of eight black horses, a lone coachman controlling their pace. Within sat a man dressed as the Kaiser, chosen for his similarity to the despot and his ability to keep his mouth shut. His long nose sat above the groomed, upwards-pointing moustache and between his heavy-lidded eyes. At a glance and at a distance he could not be mistaken for anyone else.

Kaplan moved through the crowd, careful not to raise suspicion to the *kaisersoldaten.*

He was yards from the faux-Kaiser's procession but needed to be away from the crowds and on the street within the next few minutes. The bomb he had planted was intended to miss the procession but maim or wipe out many of the public, most of which were Englanders who had been ordered to attend or face detention.

Kaplan saw nothing barbaric in this. It simply reinforced the need for the occupancy. If it was believed that the Resistance were willing to kill their own to overthrow the Kaiser's rule, then before long the people would turn their backs on the Resistance and accept that, for peace, the Kaiser remained in power.

So he snaked through the throng, eventually finding a clear path to Kensington Gore where he could trigger the detonator.

Everyone was oblivious: the *kaisersoldaten*, the public, the man pretending to be His Eminence… and everything was in place. The procession moving towards Round Pond was where it should be.

Then Kaplan released a storm of fire down upon the masses.

Burning, screaming, chaos. Children torn from the breasts of their mothers. Lives torn from the chests of men. Flames leaping, catching, incinerating. So much destruction, so much intensity. So much power.

Kaplan smiled, threw the stub of the cigarette he was smoking to the ground and walked away.

***

5th Bn, King's Royal Rifle Corps (temp), Winchester
March 1918

My dearest Lita,

I am so very sorry to read that you have been so unwell. I hope Angela was able to look after you. Are you better now? I wish I could be there to hold you. How is Father? I wasn't able to read his handwriting so I worry that his fingers are playing him up again. It's been very difficult here what with all the shelling and my worries about you and Father.

We were recently relieved by another division so we could be sent back a few miles for what the RSM called a well-earned rest, which of course was nothing but physical drill and a run before breakfast! The remainder of the morning we did musketry drills and, after lunch, a route march for two hours.

We did that for a good few days before we were dispatched with all possible speed to Ypres, there we went in to support the Canadians (in a different way to when I left the Arctic ship) and spent a dreadful eleven days, during which time we lost hundreds of men. It's quite unnerving to know the enemy trench is there only sixty yards in front, with sudden flashes of their rifles and machine guns. You can feel the thuds on the sandbags, most of the time we're resting against them. Often bullets lodge themselves in the parapet either side of my head leaving inches between me and certain death. I'd made some good friends these last few weeks and nearly all of them were killed or wounded. We had to retire from where we were positioned but luckily the Hun did not find this out until we were safely (more or less) bivouacking in a very pretty woodland. We stayed here for just under two weeks then got to work again, digging reserve trenches just behind the front line, building up the parapets which had been demolished by the enemy. We worked all night, getting what sleep we could during the day. One morning we were disturbed by the most awful racket! We were being bombarded at around twilight and about half an hour later, four of us were ordered to start reinforcements. The ground before us was being swept continually with shells until dawn where, the previous night, just in front of our reserve trenches had been a beautifully green field. The next morning all was left was a mass of blackened craters.

I was on sentry duty for a few hours, from 1am to 4am, and was ordered to keep a sharp lookout. I really did not care for the notion of keeping my head above the trench and looking for beastly Germans, but however it had to be done so I had no choice. There are never any choices in the army.

We are told we are having leave shortly and I'll make sure I come home and see you. After that I'm going to Saint-Mihiel but I don't think many of us are being assigned there. My CO won't tell me why and I know better really than to ask any further.

I am yours ever and with much love,
Daniel.

Orange, France

The train wheezed and groaned down the line, skirting the town to continue its course to Marseille.

Daniel Restarick and Mircalla Richard sat in her compartment, listening for the guard so Restarick could hide away. No knock had so far come but they were both experienced enough not to grow complacent.

Restarick would have preferred not to remain where he was but his own compartment, having been ransacked, was locked and the train staff had reported him as alighting at Lyon. No doubt the *kaisersoldaten* were searching the countryside for him even now.

Mircalla was sipping at a glass of Malbec and watching Restarick as he sat on the floor underneath the window.

Outside, rolling fields and signs of agriculture dominated the landscape.

She gave him a sidelong glance and he smiled back at her. 'Smoke?'

He turned the offer down but lit a match for her. She inhaled and sighed.

Restarick tried to not watch her unfold her long legs as he took the leather pouch she had put on the floor between them. They'd found, sewn into the lining, a map. It was of a place in the Middle East set deep into the country. 'This is really fascinating.'

'I don't mind, you know.'

'What?'

'You looking.'

Restarick tried to shake the creases out of the paper in his hands. 'At the map?'

'At me.' Mircalla laughed and took another pull at her cigarette. 'We're both widowed. We have no ties. You *can* look. *Just* look.'

'I'm...' Restarick shifted uncomfortably. He was not one to stare, especially in the field. Remain professional. At all times. 'I'm working.'

But he had to admit that he had grown to like Mircalla, but his guilt increased whenever she came near: Lita was irreplaceable. It would be a long time before he could look at another woman in that way.

'Are you still embarrassed about me coming to your rescue?' she asked.

'You did save my life, Mircalla.' He asked her for some of her cigarette. As he put it to his lips, he felt a trace of moisture from her own. 'Thanks.'

'For saving your life or for the smoke?' she asked as she took the filter tip back.

'Both.'

'That suits me.'

They sat there silently for a while, the train rocking them.

The rays of sun outside shifted and lengthened as the afternoon headed to early evening.

'How did he die?' asked Restarick. 'Your husband. Or was that "Mrs Duffy's husband?'

'No, that was mine. It's safer to stick to what I know.' She gave a half-smile, then turned it into a slight frown. 'He was shot.'

'I'm sorry.'

'Again, was it you who shot him?' Mircalla laughed, though her grief remained potent. 'He was part of a team sent to assassinate the Kaiser in Berlin. They spent months planning, rehearsing, down to the last detail. Mapping out the Kaiser's cavalcade. It was incredible to watch them work. They had no outside help from anyone, no funding. No support. They knew that killing him would bring the Central Powers to its knees.'

'This was before the war ended? Before the *Kaiser-Regel* was formed?'

Mircalla nodded and continued. 'But, on the day they went to Spa, to the Imperial Army headquarters, they were set up by a band of rebels. Even though they were rebels themselves. François was shot in the back while the rest of the team fled.'

'Did they survive?'

'I don't think they all did. This was the summer of 1918, when there were uprisings across Belgium and other cities. I think they were mistaken for German soldiers. The rebels knew where they were, though.'

'Infiltrators?'

'I would like to imagine not. But it's the only explanation.'

Restarick understood. Especially after the ceasefire and the victory over the Allies, trust was hard to come by. The Kaiser had eyes and ears everywhere. Probably even here in the South of France. 'His intentions were honourable.'

'I often wonder that if he and his colleagues had succeeded, if they'd ended that evil man's life there and then, that the Allies would have raced to victory and we wouldn't be here now.'

Restarick fell silent at her words, his own failure at Saint-Mihiel roiling in his mind.

He'd been told repeatedly by Room 40 that the blame was not his, that his actions were just another cog in a cumbersome war wheel, one that never stopped turning, not even when German stormtroopers took control of both Buckingham Palace and the Houses of Parliament. But if he'd been aware of the spy's cohorts, known that he was a target as much as the spy had been, then the spy would have been dead at the church door, a bullet through their brain and an incendiary device following to burn the papers before anyone else could get to them.

And now he was here, on a train thundering to the Balearic coast, tracing a missing operative, with Europe spending *kaisermarks* and driving Mercedes.

'Is that why you're doing this? Looking to overthrow the Kaiser?'

'For revenge? Perhaps. But I don't want François to have died for nothing. Anyway…'

'The map is marked in a few places…' Restarick beckoned Mircalla to sit with him. Her hair fell onto his shoulder as she leaned it close. 'See? There, there and here.'

'That's a symbol. That's not language, not writing.'

'You're a lexicographer?'

'Graphologist, you mean?'

'Yes.'

'No.'

'Oh.'

Mircalla smiled. 'I trained in palaeography.'

'Pity you weren't trained in cartography.'

'I can't be skilled at *everything*.'

'Then it's fortuitous for the both of us that I am.'

They laughed together and Restarick felt the ease of her company. Mircalla took the map from him.

'So where is this place then, "Mr Mercator"? It doesn't have any names.'

'If I'm not mistaken, this dark area here,' Restarick said, turning it in her hands and indicating a long, intersected strip in the middle of the parchment, 'is the outline of the Dead Sea. Ergo the area marked by the symbol is somewhere in Jordan. Judging by the scale, that makes it about twenty-odd miles from the Israeli border.'

'Are you often mistaken?'

'Not often.'

'Then what's there? What's so important to have this map made?'

Restarick stood and stretched his back. The scar on his arm occasionally pinched a nerve in his shoulder and he could feel some discomfort brewing. Outside, the countryside went swiftly by and in the distance, grey clouds gathered. He turned and perched on the narrow ledge at the base of the window and looked at his unexpected travelling companion.

'What are you thinking?' she asked him, stubbing her cigarette into the silver ash-tray.

Should he tell her what his mission was? Did she already know? She seemed to know something. Importantly, could he trust her? He hoped so. But she clearly was some kind of intelligence operative, as was he, and therefore governed by her mission and her country. He still had no idea why she was following him or how she knew his name. If she was a turncoat, or was already leeching information from him, he'd have no choice but to turn her in or, worst case, kill her. If he stayed with her, she'd have no opportunity to get any details out to her superiors and she could actually be useful to him. She was handy with a weapon, was charming and intelligent: an asset—at least for the moment.

Trust your instincts, Restarick.

He swallowed hard. 'Max Baker is an operative for the British Secret Service. He was reported as missing a couple of weeks ago. I'm assigned to find him, bring him back in.'

She nodded. Did she already know that? 'And this map? It's a link?'

'Possibly.' Restarick pursed his lips and squinted at the map in Mircalla's lap. 'Tentatively. Jordan is a good day's drive from Cairo.'

'But this map got itself to Europe somehow.' She stood and placed her empty wine glass onto the table. 'Did Baker bring it?'

Restarick frowned. 'We don't know who had this map last. I want to know who ransacked my room.'

'Do you believe the waiter?'

'That he didn't do it?' Restarick drummed his fingers on the ledge. 'The boy just wants to play at being a hero.'

'So you genuinely think he found the papers on a seat in the buffet car?'

'It's plausible. More plausible than us playing the Germans at football during the Christmas truce of '14.'

'Reverse propaganda?'

'Had we not lost the war, then perhaps it would have been an image that would have reaffirmed our humanity. And so it's now just an ideal of what could have been. But men playing sport on a battlefield that was covered with shrapnel, bodies and God knows what else just hours before? *That's* implausible. So, if these papers were left behind, the question we should be asking is: were they left there *to* be found?'

'Who by?' As Mircalla went to refill her glass with Malbec she was suddenly and without warning thrown across the compartment, the table and chair flying after her.

Restarick saved himself from being flung to the ground as he grabbed hold of the window blind. Nevertheless, it ripped from its stitching and he put his hands out as he fell headlong towards the bed. Glass, cutlery, anything loose, clattered around them.

The train's brakes had been applied and the great locomotive and her carriages had crunched to an ungainly and violent halt. The engine hissed and smoked indignantly under which could be heard shouting and the unmistakable firing of rifles.

'Are you alright?' Mircalla asked, helping Restarick to his feet.

'Yes. What happened?'

Mircalla pulled the sash window down and leaned out. The train's guards were already on the tracks but up ahead was a troop of horses, their riders' guns raised. Voices yelled in French. One of the riders had dismounted and had the train driver on his knees in the gravel, a pistol pointed at the back of his head. If it wasn't so serious, Mircalla could have easily imagined they'd been transported to the American West tales of Zane Grey and Clarence Mulford.

Restarick looked at his pocket watch that had fallen out from his waistcoat. It had a crack in the glass face and the arms were now stuck at just after three o'clock. He sighed and put it away, saddened that the last gift his younger brother had bought him before he'd been killed was now broken.

Mircalla moved her head back into the compartment. 'We've got company.'

Gower Street, London

Kaplan was engrossed in the evening paper, finding the reports of his handiwork in Hyde Park to be more satisfying at that moment than anything Aisling was doing with her eager tongue.

Nevertheless, he peered around the broadsheet when she stopped to extract a stray hair from her mouth. After a few more minutes, he pushed her away in boredom and pulled up his britches, leaving her sitting on the floor at his feet, wiping saliva from her lips.

The paper he had thrown to the bed remained open on the feature he had been reading, but it was the small column next to it that piqued Aisling's curiosity. 'Are you going to this rally?'

Kaplan hadn't noticed the article. A rally didn't sound like something the *kaisersoldaten* would tolerate, he thought, until Aisling read:

'"The Education and Propaganda Department of the Bavarian *Reichswehr* will be at Buckingham Palace on Saturday at the request of the *Kaiser-Regel* to present to the masses their proposal to encourage domicility and acceptance of the German peoples outside of the Fatherland. The department has the full backing of the Kaiser himself and a large crowd is expected to attend to hear what the *Fuehrer* will say." Do you know who this leader is? This 'Fuehrer'?'

Kaplan stood and picked up the paper, scanning the piece. 'No. I do not. I have not heard of that singular title before in the German army.' It wasn't something that the *Kaiser-Regel* had previously adopted to his knowledge.

Aisling saw the bulge in his trousers and reached out—an offer. He buttoned his shirt up, stepping away. He knew a few faces in Westminster who could tell him more about this leader without raising suspicion. He sat at the writing desk under the window that overlooked Gower Street and began to pen a short note, passing it to Aisling when he was finished. He had written an address on the envelope he had slid it into.

'Deliver this.' Aisling opened her mouth in indignation and was about to object when she noticed he'd hidden a small stack of *kaisermark* notes under the letter. 'Then buy yourself an evening dress and come straight back. We are going to the theatre tonight.'

'Oh, Aaron!'

'Do it.'

'What are we going to see?'

'A play by Sholem Aleichem.'

She frowned, not having heard of him. 'Is it good?'

'It is a Yiddish-language comedy on the difficulty of Jewish-Gentile relationships in the Russian Empire.'

'It sounds… enlightening.' Aisling took the letter from Kaplan and read the neat handwriting: it was addressed to a Mr S Butcon of Garrison Road, Bow.

'It is.'

On hailing a cab in the street, she wondered if he was joking about the play but her thoughts were dissipated by her rough collision with two uniformed men who pushed past her to enter the building.

***

It was a good three hours before Aisling found herself walking back through the foyer of the Melfort Hotel, an assistant from a fashion store in the West End carrying her bags. She gave him a tip as they reached her room and he went on his way, back down the elevator and back to the shop.

She dropped the bags and herself on to the bed, which had been made since, and kicked off her shoes. Toes wiggling, she called out to Kaplan, over the sound of the running taps. There was no reply. She called out again and began to slip out of her clothes.

'You running that for me, sweetheart? I delivered the letter.'

She got as far as her panties and the bathroom doorway before she let out an almighty scream.

In the bath, scalding hot water cascading over his face, was a man, immobile and throat cut. The blood had been watered into a pink torrent, a deeper hue of red all over the black and white tiled floor. Aisling backed out of the room, her knuckles thrust into her open mouth, slipping on the blood and striking her head on the doorframe. She shook the sharp pain away and dashed back to her clothes. Without bothering to dress, she scooped them up and fumbled at the bags before deciding to leave them.

Two military men entered the room, just then—the same ones she collided with earlier on the steps outside in the street.

'*Hinsetzen, Fräulein*,' one of them said, the one she immediately guessed to be in charge. Aisling sat on the bed. 'No. The chair.'

The second man moved the chair into the middle of the room and forced her down into it, pulling her arms straight along the chair's arms and tying them tight. The blood on her feet was already drying and she had left footprints across the luxurious carpet.

'I didn't kill him,' she said, nodding backwards to the bathroom.

'I never assumed you did,' said the first man. He wasn't overly tall but had an air of authority that gave him stature, even with rounded shoulders. He walked with a clipped gait and had a slight twitch in his left eye. His moustache was unusual and did not extend either side of his top lip beyond his nostrils. 'Turn the taps off.'

'*Ja, Mein Fuehrer*,' replied his subordinate and moved to fulfil his order.

'Now, enlighten me as to what an Irish girl from a rich family is doing as the paid whore to a German operative?'

'Are you that man who is holding the rally?'

'You know of me?'

'You're in the newspaper.'

'Answer my question.'

'Aaron looks after me. He's kind to me. He lets me be me.'

'How very noble.' The man sat on the edge of the bed and looked over the clothes she had bought. It was difficult to tell if he was impressed or not until he removed one of his leather gloves and caressed the silks with a level of unexpected tenderness.

'What do you want?'

'That's what I want to know,' said Kaplan as he entered his hotel room. 'I know you.'

The man addressed as *Fuehrer* stood and put his glove back on before turning to face Kaplan and put out his hand. It was the Austrian from the meeting at Buckingham Palace. He struck Aisling across the cheek as she cried out to Aaron.

'You no longer have my permission to speak,' he said and re-presented his hand to Kaplan who hesitantly took it while looking at the growing welt across Aisling's left cheek. 'My name is Adolf Hitler, *Herr* Kaplan. It is a pleasure to see you again. His Eminence is especially grateful for your efforts in removing Sir Henry Wilson and your recent work in Hyde Park.' As his aide returned from the bathroom, he continued: "I have a new assignment for you, one I believe you have already had some awareness of.'

'It is an honour to know that His Eminence holds me in such high esteem. Surely though such an opinion does not warrant this type of treatment of *Fräulein* Thorley?'

'She should be aware of the risks of associating with such a dangerous man as yourself,' responded Hitler.

His aide suddenly grabbed Aisling from behind and pulled her head back. With a flash of steel, he sliced her throat open and up-ended the chair. She fell backwards, making a hideous gurgling sound, eyes wide with panic and legs kicking. Moments later, still bound by her arms to the chair, she was dead, a pool of blood collecting by her head. The aide wiped his knife on Aisling's silk panties and sheathed the weapon away back under his coat.

In the few seconds it took for Aisling to die, Kaplan never flinched, never moved, feeling Hitler's stare, knowing he was being scrutinised for even the briefest flicker of emotion.

Hitler stepped over her and looked into the bathroom at the man in the tub. 'A pity. He was one of my best men.'

'He came upon me as I was bathing. I did not know he was loyal. He struggled courageously before he died,' said Kaplan, adding with a coldness that didn't seem to suit him: 'Not unlike her.'

'I would offer the role as yours, Kaplan, but I am here to talk about other matters.'

'*Operation: Geschenk*?'

'Very astute. Hartmann has already employed your services for some groundwork. You will now proceed to carry out the main body of the project. You will go to our research laboratory in Berlin. You have permission to travel outside of the curfews. You will meet Hartmann and an American doctor who we have employed. They will present you with the gift. Your instruction is to release it into the drinking water at specific locations.'

'Is it a poison?'

'No. It is a virus. Highly contagious. Highly effective. Just one drop can clean an entire town. Those who do not have access to the vaccine will not survive.'

'And who do not have access to it?'

'Those I have ordained will not see the great *Kaiser-Regel* truly become the new total world order.'

'*You* have ordained?'

'His Eminence trusts me implicitly. I am *Fuehrer*. You will show me respect or I will have you shot. Is that understood?'

So this was the man holding the rally. 'Yes, *Fuehrer*. When do I leave?'

Hitler motioned to his aide who gave him a folder paper. 'This is your clearance across Europe. You will not be questioned by even the most dedicated of the *kaisersoldaten*, even outside of curfew. Leave now. You will not return.'

A one-way mission? Is this virus so powerful that I myself will immediately fall ill?

'I understand, sir.'

Kaplan had no family, no ties. It was the way he preferred it. Too many times had he seen a man torn between duty and family and missions had been compromised as a result. If the Kaiser ordered a mass cull of his enemies and this Adolf Hitler had been charged to see it carried out, then who was Kaplan to question? It was the next step in the continued occupation of Europe. Hitler seemed a cold man, perhaps too cold, and Kaplan wondered if *Fuehrer* had been a title given to him or one self-appointed. He looked to be in his early thirties but presented himself as a seasoned, dedicated officer and wore his Iron Cross with obvious pride. He could be one to be wary of.

Orange

The locomotive clicked and hissed, stationary on the tracks leading south to Marseille.

Mircalla and Restarick crouched under the tender, their hands covered in oil and soot. They watched the riders, some dismounted, pulling German officers off the train and to the bankside, rifles pointed. The train staff were separate, further up the track, and Mircalla noticed Miklos, the waiter who had tussled with them earlier, was amongst those with their hands raised.

'Why exactly are we hiding?' Mircalla asked.

'They look like the Resistance but I don't think we can be too careful,' Restarick replied, pulling her back as a rider walked by. 'The fields are too open. If we run, they'll shoot us for being the enemy.'

'I think we'll be fine.'

'They might not share your outlook.'

'So we're just going to hide under the train? That's your plan? It's a terrible plan.'

'We need to be c—'

Mircalla crawled out onto the other tracks and raised her hands, calling to the rider who by now had reached the front of the locomotive.

'What on earth are you doing? Get back here!' growled Restarick through his teeth. 'You're going to get us killed!'

But Mircalla knew what she was doing. She had recognised one of the riders. Restarick was right: they *were* Resistance.

'Eloise?' the rider said, incredulity lacing his question. 'How the hell did you get here?'

Mircalla dropped her arms and laughed. The two hugged. 'I have a friend with me. Don't shoot him. He's a bit shy. Out you come,' she called to Restarick.

Restarick, face like thunder, revealed himself from under the train, keeping a tight grip on his pistol he had grabbed from his compartment.

'This is Barnabas,' she said, introducing him to the rider.

'*Eloise*?' was Restarick's reply, raising an eyebrow. Mircalla shrugged. 'I'm Hugh. Hugh Drummond. Pleased to meet you.'

'Nice to meet you, Hugh,' said Barnabas, a cheery, rotund man with a beard jutting from his chin. He wore a beret which seemed to clash with the army fatigues he was decked out in.

'You don't need to pretend, Restarick. Barnabas gave 'Hugh' his false papers.'

'Oh.'

'I'm guessing Drummond didn't make it out of La Celle-Saint-Cloud?' Barnabas asked.

Restarick shook his head. 'No, I'm sorry to say he didn't. He was shot by German soldiers.'

'Pity. I really liked him.'

'So did I,' added Mircalla. 'But what is all this? Why have you stopped the train?'

'We're looking for someone.'

'Who?'

'Well…' Barnabas moved away from Restarick, taking Mircalla with him. He lowered his voice. 'Eloise, it's a British agent. Your friend. He's…'

'*Not* a British agent,' she said.

'But he *is* British.'

'Not all British are agents, Barney. And look at him… does he *look* like an agent of the Crown?'

Barnabas looked Restarick up and down. 'No. But he looks like a soldier. Holds that pistol with the air of someone who knows how to use it. How do you know he's not an agent?'

'We've travelled down from Paris together. All we did was eat and drink and talk about life before the occupation. He's a nice gentleman.'

'A "nice gentleman"?' Barnabas chuckled. 'Since when have you been so formal?'

'I can be formal,' Mircalla shot back.

'You… you *like* him!' Barnabas teased. 'You do!'

'Hell, Barney, I'm not a child!' It took a few moments but Mircalla began to laugh, too, and hugged Barnabas again.

'What are you doing on this train? The last time we all saw you, you were on your way to Japan,' said Barnabas.

'A slight detour. That assignment was taken by someone else.'

'Didn't that stuck-up Forbes-Sempill like you, then?'

'Very funny. My flying skills weren't up to par. So I decided to take a break. What's this about this British agent?'

A round of gunfire rang out, followed by some shouting. Barnabas readied his rifle and dashed towards the noise, calling Mircalla to follow. As she did so, she said to Restarick:

'You need to keep your head down. They're Resistance. Friends of mine. I said to Barnabas you're not the British agent they're looking for. But I reckon he thinks you are.'

'You're Resistance?'

'Eloise is. Mircalla isn't.'

'And Olivia?'

Mircalla smiled. 'I'll try to convince Barnabas' seniors that you're someone else. I have a feeling Barnabas actually suspects you, anyway. Now go!'

With that, Mircalla followed Barnabas who had already gone the length of three coaches and Restarick headed the other way.

The 2-8-0 locomotive was huge and dark, brasses glinting in the setting sun. The footplate was almost at Restarick's shoulder and he clambered up once he was sure that no one was aboard. The track ahead had been unblocked, the Resistance were otherwise engaged and Restarick had an idea that he had a terrible feeling he would regret. They were no more than an hour from Marseille and the countryside stretched away, with rolling hills and farmland and grazing sheep in the distance.

Kandy – May 1918

The ewe wasn't cooperating.

She was the last one left, her companions safely in their enclosure, and was refusing to join them. Lita had been running after her for the last fifteen minutes, much to Jim Restarick's amusement as he sat on a cart and watched, a clay pipe in his mouth, his walking cane resting against his knees.

Restarick had been temporarily invalided home from a skirmish in Afghanistan. His left leg strapped and immobile, he was in a wheelchair next to his father.

The sun was hot that day and Restarick was frustrated to be a virtual cripple for the next couple of weeks while his injury healed. He was uncomfortable in his bandages and a flask of water doing nothing to quench his thirst. He wished he could help Lita and felt sorry for her, even though the sight of her running and her face flushed made him smile.

Lita was, though, used to the heat, having been raised in Galicia and on a farm, too, so herding sheep when the men and the dogs had all but given up was almost second nature to her.

'You are lucky you can sit down all day,' she laughed, kissing her husband on his forehead as she darted by. 'Your sheep are rude and ill-tempered. Not like Spanish sheep.'

'My sheep are first class!' responded Jim, puffing smoke out. 'You need to control your wife, son.'

Restarick knew his father was toying with him, for the old man adored his daughter-in-law. Jim waved his stick towards the ewe, as if Lita needed prompting as to where the animal had scampered. It was another ten or so minutes before Lita had safely rounded her up into the pen.

Lita flopped on the dry ground next to her husband, wiping sweat from her brow. 'When your leg is better, corazón, *next time it is you. I prefer your tea plantation to your farm. It is less exhausting.'*

They all ate well that evening back at Pilawala and after Jim had retired for the night, Lita and Restarick sat out on the veranda together, watching shooting stars fly across the sky with the hazy white of the Milky Way stretching over their heads.

Insects chirruped and called in the darkness and the last few drops of wine, now warm, remained untouched in the carafe.

'We need to return to England soon,' said Restarick, breaking the silence after a while.

'Do we have to?'

'Of course. My leg will be better soon and my regiment is expecting me back. And you need to return to work, too. The war effort and all that.'

'The exotic life of a London munitions factory!' Lita leant on Restarick's shoulder. 'It is beautiful here. I wish we could stay.'

'Maybe we can. One day. This old place,' said Restarick, tapping one of the veranda's square supports with his knuckles, 'will fall to my sister and I once Father has gone. He's already considering selling the farm. It's haemorrhaging money that the plantation desperately needs.'

'Will you keep the plantation once it's yours?'

'Angela has her own place along the coast road. She'll sell her half of this to me and then when this damned war is over, you and I…' He looked into his wife's dark eyes. They caught the candlelight and her olive complexion looked positively stunning. 'We'll settle down here and hide away from the world.'

'I would like that very much,' she replied quietly. 'Away from everyone. From nosy people who want to know our business. But for now, I am tired. Shall we go to bed?'

'You go. I'll come in when I'm ready.'

'Will you manage?' she asked, referring to his wheel-chair.

'Raj is around somewhere. He should be able to help me before he locks everything up for the night.'

'Do not be long.' Lita stood, her long legs hidden under her sari, and stroked the back of his neck as she went inside.

'I love you, Lita,' Restarick called after her. 'I love you very much.'

'I know,' came her simple reply

Orange

Barnabas and Mircalla had arrived at the source of the noise.

A German couple had stood up to one of the Resistance and the man had been shot, his wife inconsolable and directing all manner of accusations to the group around her. There was arguing amongst the Resistance and Barnabas shouted for quiet more than once before the furore settled down. The German woman had collapsed and was hugging her dead husband's neck and torso.

'Take her and put her in one of the sleeping compartments. Give her a drink.' Barnabas glared at his companion who had shot the German as the woman was dragged screaming from the body. 'What the hell were you thinking? There was to be no killing. We're looking for the British agent. If this gets back to the *Kaiser-Regel*, they'll have a field day. We're already being blamed for attacks on the British people. If they get wind of us killing "innocent" Germans… Get rid of the corpse and get out of my sight.' The Resistance member gave some mumbled excuse about the German being armed and using threatening language as he heaved the body up the bank. Barnabas turned to Mircalla. 'We're becoming a bunch of guerrillas now, bullish morons with itchy trigger fingers. We are standing for something but all that will soon be lost if people like him are representing us.'

'He's angry. We're all angry,' she said calmly, turning Barnabas to face her, his back now to the front of the train. She'd seen Restarick clamber up onto the footplate and had quickly concluded what he was going to do. 'Let's get onboard and really try to get this British agent found, eh?'

Barnabas nodded and gave the order to the Resistance to board while some stayed to guard those passengers and staff who had already been removed. Mircalla joined them, searching for the man she knew was onboard the locomotive. After a few moments, Barnabas stopped where he was in one of the narrow corridors and touched Mircalla's arm.

'Listen…' he said, head cocked to one side.

Mircalla echoed his stance. 'I can't hear anything.'

In the distance, the slow chug-chug and hiss of the great engine moving into life was unmistakable.

'The train, we're moving!' he hissed and flung open a door and stuck his head out. 'We're...'

'Not moving,' responded Mircalla.

'What the... It's the engine! Someone's uncoupled the engine!' Barnabas cursed in French and spun towards Mircalla. 'Your so-called friend! He is the agent! I knew it!' He jumped from the carriage and landed heavily by the other tracks, firing his rifle into the air. 'Everybody, remount! Follow the engine! The rest of you, don't let these people out of your sight. I'll deal with you later, Eloise.'

With that, the horses and their riders galloped off to chase the fleeing engine and to capture the British agent obviously at its controls.

***

The engine was now going at a steady rate, unfettered by the weight of the twelve carriages behind it. Steam billowed from the funnel, the wheels turning faster and faster. It would be a miracle if the horses could reach it.

'What's going on?' asked Restarick, running up behind Barnabas, who turned, open mouthed and incredulous.

Mircalla quickly caught on. 'The British agent. He's only gone and uncoupled the engine! He's off down the track!'

'Good Lord, has he?' replied Restarick, feigning complete surprise. 'Those horses will never catch him.'

'That's what I was thinking,' she noted.

'I'm... You're...' Barnabas was frowning. Mircalla had never seen him so angry. Or lost for words.

'Did you think it was me?' asked Restarick. 'Driving a train? A boyhood dream, I admit but I wouldn't even know where to start.'

'Can you... can you ride a horse?' Barnabas wanted to know.

'Why, yes. We had a farm as a family that bred—'

Barnabas cut him short. 'Then you've been drafted. I like the way you can handle a gun. If you can handle a horse just as well...'

'Drafted? Oh. I'm no freedom fighter.'

Barnabas pointed his rifle at Restarick's chest. 'This isn't a request. I don't trust half of the men under me and I'm not about to trust you now. But Eloise does and that's good enough for me for the time being. You step out of line and I'll shoot you dead. Understand?'

'Absolutely,' said Restarick, holding firm to the pistol against his thigh. *But you're a moron. You don't even know if I'm the man you're looking for or know Eloise isn't even her real name.*

But then perhaps "Mircalla" was as false as "Eloise"... or "Eloise" *was* her true identity! He doubted now that Mircalla would even enlighten him. He felt a headache forming.

'Let's get going. This way.' Barnabas led them to four horses, the riders of which were standing over the passengers and the three took one each. As Mircalla settled into the saddle, she asked:

'Where are we headed? Restarick's right. We'll never catch the loco now.'

'The ones I sent on already might have a slim chance. The next station is Bédarrides but we'll head across country and see if we can get a message ahead to get some points changed or a barricade put up.'

'I can't imagine this agent fellow would want to be harmed,' Restarick said. 'If he sees a barricade, he might bring the train to a halt himself.'

'That's what I'm counting on!'

Barnabas kicked his horse into action and galloped off down the tracks.

'Bloody hell, Restarick,' Mircalla said. 'You are taking a damned risk. If he realises there's no one on board, then he'll know it was you and that you tricked him.'

'They'll make a barricade.'

'How do you know?'

'Because I've just suggested it to your boyfriend.'

'He's not my… Oh, heavens. The train will smash through the barricade. There's no one aboard to stop it.'

'You're right, there's not. And it will. And it will likely explode, too. It will be such a mangled mess all they'll find will be a charred body.'

'Whose?'

'Doesn't matter. But it will mean I can carry on looking for Baker before your Resistance friends find him.'

Marseille, France

It was nearly midnight before Rémy Thibaut had settled the baby for what seemed like the tenth time that evening.

Back and forth he'd gone to her crib, Polly's colic particularly bad tonight. Her crying had become so chronic that his neighbours in the apartments either side had banged on the walls, adding to his frustration and the shortening of his patience.

He'd heard through the Radiola, betwixt bouts of infantile screaming, that there had been some sort of accident on the southerly outskirts of Bédarrides involving a steam locomotive. *Kaisersoldaten* had been assigned to the incident and—because the Enemy had been spotted—locals were warned to lock their doors and keep strictly to the curfew. He was still nevertheless surprised to find, while ensuring his home was secure, Daniel Restarick hiding in his shrubbery.

Initially, he was worried, for Restarick was bloodied and bruised and cradling a German-issue rifle. Thibaut was a veteran of the war and easily recognised most types of weaponry. Restarick wasn't dressed like a *kaisersoldaten*, though, and it wasn't until he had spoken, when Restarick was laying on the *chaise longue* in Thibaut's apartment, that Thibaut realised the man was English.

He tended Restarick's wounds as best he could and little Polly hadn't stirred so far, which was a relief. He didn't want this stranger knowing there was a baby in the next room, for he didn't know if Restarick would kill her to keep her quiet or take her from him. But it became clear after a couple of hours of looking after his visitor, learning his name and understanding he wasn't dedicated to the Kaiser, Restarick posed no danger to him and Polly apart from the possibility that *kaisersoldaten* may discover his presence.

'Harbouring fugitives is not something I do every day.'

'I promise I will be gone as soon as I have rested. I am sorry to intrude,' replied Restarick.

'Where are you headed?'

'To the port.' Restarick was sitting up now, the gunshot wound in his left arm bandaged. He'd suggested Thibaut burn the bloodied rags in the open grate while keeping the bullet Thibaut had removed. He felt he could trust this solitary man, having noticed a baby's pink flannelette bib under the armchair Thibaut was sitting on. Any man who would help a stranger with a young child present had to be trustworthy. The risk of causing a scene would be too great. It also explained why Thibaut kept giving subtle glances to the doorway: he was obviously listening out for the child stirring. 'I'm looking for passage to Algiers.'

'Do you have papers?'

'No.'

Thibaut had given Restarick some of his own clothes, the ones he had turned up in ripped, bloodied and burnt. His false identity papers, all sets, had been lost and he had no idea where Mircalla had gone. He wondered if she'd been killed. Capture was a possibility and it would take a brave man to interrogate her, he smiled to himself.

'Will you say what happened?' Thibaut asked.

'It is a bit hazy but nevertheless perhaps it is best you don't know. In case...'

Thibaut nodded and retrieved a tobacco pouch from an occasional table. 'Smoke?'

'Please.'

'I try not to indoors. Don't want it to affect-' Thibaut stopped.

'It's fine,' Restarick responded. 'I know you have a child here. I mean neither of you any harm.'

Thibaut seemed to relax and nodded, filling a pipe as he looked around for some thin cigars. 'You understand why I did not want you to know.'

'I understand. You are a brave man.' Restarick lit the proffered cigar from a bulky petrol-filled silver-plated lighter. It had a crest embossed on it that he didn't recognise: it looked like an eagle's claw clutching a human heart. He passed it back to Thibaut.

'Brave?'

'To raise a child!'

'You have children yourself?'

Restarick shook his head, a flash of regret across his face. 'My wife... she died before we could have any.'

'I hope the Lord is looking after her,' Thibaut said, pressing a hand to his chest. Restarick shrugged, never one for religion. 'I am sorry for your loss.'

'It was a long-time ago.'

Sensing his visitor wanted to change the subject, Thibaut spoke at length about his time during the war, how he came to be settled in Marseille and how the next generation would grow up in a world free of slavery and oppression. Eventually the conversation turned to how Restarick planned to leave France without papers. 'The port is crawling with the Kaiser's stormtroopers. You'll be lucky to even take a dip let alone get aboard a ship.'

'I need to send a wire to my people.'

'The post office. It opens early. You could send one there. But then again...'

'Then again what?'

Thibaut puffed on his pipe, thoughtfully. 'They do not know you. You might be asked to prove who you are, what your business is here.'

'That's a good point. But I'll have to take the risk.'

'What if… what if I send the message for you?'

Restarick pursed his lips. That *was* a good idea but trusting this local to tend his wounds was one thing. Asking him to send a coded telegram to Room 40 was something altogether. What if he took his baby with him and informed the authorities? He would easily convince the *kaisersoldaten* that Restarick had forced his way in under the threat of hurting the child but had managed to flee, with child in tow. If Thibaut did, Restarick's mission to find Max Baker would be over and the operation to remove the Kaiser from power would be further out of the reach of the British Secret Service than it currently was. But Restarick going to the post office himself was just as risky.

Thibaut seemed to sense Restarick's conflict.

'I will go alone.'

'Alone?'

'I will leave my child here.'

'With me?'

'With you.'

Good God. The responsibility of a child! That's a more terrifying thought than being on the receiving end of one of the Kaiser's thugs! 'I don't think that's a—'

Thibaut leant in to Restarick. '*Monsieur*, I have no love for the Kaiser. You, I think, are on the side *not* of the Kaiser. If I am wrong, I am guessing you will shoot me now. But I think I am right.'

Restarick smiled and placed a hand on the man's shoulder. 'You *are* right and I have no love for him either!'

'Then I will help you. I will send your message.'

'But your daughter. You don't need to leave her with me.'

'It is trust. I want to help you. This is how you trust me. We will talk again in the morning.'

***

It was gone 3am before Thibaut took himself to bed and Restarick settled himself as best he could on the *chaise longue*, the moonlight shining on his face through a gap in the heavy drapes.

He heard Thibaut get up a couple of times and heat some milk in the kitchen on the stove for the child but other than that all was calm. His arm was sore and would be for a few more days yet but he'd suffered worse on the battlefields. Propping himself up on a pillow, he lit a thin cigar that Thibaut had thoughtfully left for him and looked around the room. The lounge wasn't that small but it was cluttered with ornaments and books. It was also chilly—but that could have been the draft coming through the slightly open window.

Restarick must have finally nodded off because he woke with a start and a tightness in his chest, as though something had been pressing against him as he slept. He breathed out heavily and slumped back into the firmness of the *chaise longue*.

'Bad dream again, *corazón*?'

The voice, with its soft Spanish lilt, came from behind Restarick and he sat bolt upright, not daring to turn around. He was still dreaming, he thought. He must have been. But the perfume was… unmistakable and clearly real. As was the voice that came again:

'*Corazón*, why do you ignore me?'

From the corner of his eye, Lita walked around to the window, pulled the drape back slightly, looked out, then turned to Restarick.

'You're…' His voice caught in his throat. For a moment, he even forgot to breathe. But she was there… standing before him. She *was* there. Her thick black hair tied loosely in a pony-tail, her fringe falling across her forehead just as he loved. Her white blouse, the curve of the low neck-line revealing just a hint of cleavage, her olive skin pure and alluring. She wore a long wide layered red dress to her ankles, typically Spanish, and her feet were bare.

'I am lonely, Daniel. Will you stay with me?'

He did not answer. He kept his gaze fixed on her as she moved towards him. His heart was pounding behind his ribs and his throat was dry, his tongue growing thick in his mouth. She stopped at the makeshift bed and knelt, placing a hand upon his legs that were under a woollen blanket. Her dark eyes rested on his wounded arm then she met his gaze.

'You are hurt. My poor *corazón*. Let me make it better.'

Restarick couldn't resist reaching out to her, his hands trembling, the ache of his gunshot wound fading into nothing. He smiled and caressed her face, her chin, her lush, inviting lips… He wanted her. He'd missed her. He still so desperately loved her. *Desperately.*

Under his finger-tips her skin felt warm. Then it became warmer still.

Her beautiful smile with her perfect teeth suddenly became a grimace, then a guttural sound came from deep within her. Her skin darkened in blotches, pustules forming in the corners of her mouth, foam dribbling out from between her lips that now were cracked and dry. Her hair dried, like masses of pencil-thin twigs.

Restarick gasped in horror, tears welling in his eyes.

She looked panicked, terrified, scared beyond all measure.

She looked for all the world like she had succumbed to some disease, a pox that was turning her into something hideous.

She looked like death.

Then without any warning, she spontaneously combusted. Hair, skin, eyes… all alight with such force and speed that within seconds her agonising scream became silent.

And Daniel Restarick awoke from his nightmare, covered in sweat and breathing hard and fast, sobbing into his pillow so loudly that Thibaut came to see if he was alright.

Berlin

Kaplan had crossed the Channel and into mainland Europe without any issue, just as the Austrian had said. His papers were good and some of the checkpoint guards had even seemed fearful of him, such was the influence of the signature they contained. His new superior was indeed a powerful man and the perfect tool for the Kaiser to tighten his grip on his new empire. Kaplan wondered too if it would mean progression for his own career: Hitler exuded influence, so Kaplan could go far.

He sat now in a small room, not unlike an interview suite in a suburban police station. One chair and one table, the latter on which was a collection of six maps, a bulb hanging from the centre of the room, its pointed lamp shade restricting the light to above the table only. The first map, a red "1" scrawled in a corner, was of Kraków, marked in two places, Kazimierz and its surroundings, the second marking indicating some sort of man-made barricade blocking entry and exit into the suburb. Kaplan looked through the five remaining maps, all sequentially numbered and of specific parts of Austria-Hungary. They were marked in similar fashion and as the place names revealed themselves one by one to Kaplan, the colour drained from his face.

These were the locations that the "gift" was to be released and every single one, without exception, was inhabited predominantly by Jews.

He had believed in the superiority of the German ideology, that Europe had long needed their betterment, that the Kaiser was rightly positioned as the omnipotent emperor. He had killed, he had followed orders, he had known it was for the greater cause. He was aware, too, that the Resistance were growing stronger month on month and knew that the *Kaiser-Regel* silently feared that their strength could become a serious threat to the occupancy. He was willing to follow the Kaiser wherever he was required, to enforce the doctrines that made Europe a better place, a unified place.

But this… this *gift* was the first step along a path about which he was conflicted. It was tantamount to genocide, to the systematic killing of his own people.

He sank back in the chair, crucially aware that the mirror high up in the wall was a one-way window and therefore a viewing area for whoever was in another adjoining room. He gave no emotion on his face as best he could but his mind began to race with all manner of thoughts, none of which made sense.

If he carried out his orders, he would be striking the first major blow against his fellow Jews by *das Fuehrer*. If he refused, he would be shot and the orders carried out by someone else. The outcome for his people would be the same. Could he somehow warn his people? He could still carry out his mission but they would be safely ensconced elsewhere. It was a tall order, but one his heart knew he had to complete.

The betrayal of his superior officers, in an Army that had protected him and where he had found a purpose, or the betrayal of his own people. The impossible choice sat heavy in his heart for many hours afterwards, as he rested in the meagre quarters assigned to him.

Transport would be supplied to take him to Frankfurt, then once he was across the border, he was to make his way to Kraków by motorcycle. He had been assured of a clear run. This he put down to the fact that he'd be carrying a concentrated form of a highly contagious bacteria. But first he had to collect the samples from an American man who appeared to be painfully gaunt, very tall and oddly jealous that he himself wouldn't be releasing the virus.

'Keep the temperature of the phials as constant as you can,' Dr Stanley said coldly, moving towards a large safe. Voigt and Hartmann, known to Kaplan, were also present. Between the three of them, they had the combinations to the trinity of locks. Each moved to a dial, clicked them back and forth for a few revolutions and together they cranked the adjacent handles. The thick door opened in silence. 'And sure don't break them or you'll suffer an *agonisin'* death. Only break the seals when you're at the designated spots. Then you got to retreat immediately to a quarantine area.'

Kaplan wondered if these three men knew the targets and how they had been selected. He looked at each of them in turn: the scientist (obvious by his manner of dress) and the two military types, all dedicated to the Kaiser, all subservient to the Fuehrer. But were they genocidal? Was Stanley blinded by his creation of these viruses? He wondered, too, where one of these quarantine areas were, for they certainly hadn't made him aware that they even existed. It was likely he was expendable: Hitler did say he would not return!

As soon as that safe door opened and he saw the six phials in their cradles, Kaplan realised that any morality these three men may have had had been left on the battlefields in 1918. His own, he prayed to *HaShem*, was still intact.

But Stanley, Voigt and Hartmann all looked at each other, a look of accusation on the latter two's faces. Stanley was the first to speak:

'I can't explain it,' he drawled, knowing the two Germans immediately suspected foul play. 'I have no access to this safe on my own. The three of us here, we are all in the same position.'

'Then where are they?' Hartmann asked, his jawline twitching as he began to grind his teeth in anger. 'You have had daily access. You must have removed them somehow before the safe was closed.'

'It is the only explanation,' added Voigt. 'Hartmann, call the guards. The Doctor will be interro—'

'Sirs,' interrupted Kaplan. 'With respect, please can you explain what has happened? I see nothing untoward here. The phials look secure.'

Hartmann and Voight glanced at each other, then Hartmann said: 'There are two phials missing.'

'Missing?' echoed Kaplan. 'Then that means…'

'That means that the virus is not contained,' said Stanley.

'A ruse? Blackmail?' accused Voigt.

'I… I wouldn't have any need to… to blackmail you,' stammered Stanley. 'Where the damn hell would it get me? You would shoot me.'

'Perhaps passing it to your Ally comrades?' Voigt shook his head. 'Guards! Guards!'

'Hell, you damn Hun! I wouldn't pass shit to them.'

Kaplan saw the sheer surprise on Stanley's face. He may have been the mastermind behind this virus but he did seem like a liar. So where had they gone?

'Who else has access to the phials before they get locked away?'

It was a simple question from Kaplan but one that seemed to make perfect sense to the three other men.

Stanley's eyes widened and he removed his glasses. 'Baker!'

Hartmann began to laugh, probably due to the awfulness of the situation more than anything. 'Of course! Max Baker. Your missing assistant, Dr Stanley…'

'Unless you are in this together,' said Hartmann. 'The two of you. One pretending the other has stolen them when in fact you *gave* them to him, perhaps?'

Two guards entered the room, both looking nervous at the open vault itself. Voigt waved their concerns aside. 'You are quite safe. But take Stanley away. He is under arrest for being a traitor to the cause.'

'I sure ain't!' cried Stanley as the guards immediately handcuffed him. 'You are makin' a grave mistake! It was Baker. He took 'em. He must've done!'

Leo Stanley was still protesting as he was led away. Voight turned to Kaplan.

'This does not alter *das Fuehrer*'s orders. You will take the remaining… *gifts*… and begin at once.'

'But how will they be released across all the locations if we only have four plus the two anti-viruses? We need all six of the viruses!' Hartmann rubbed the bridge of his nose. This had suddenly become very complicated.

'Leave that to me,' Voigt replied. 'We will need to explain to *das Fuehrer* there will be a delay in the last two deliveries. I will say that Dr Stanley wants to understand the effects on a wider scope before the entire stocks are depleted.'

'A good idea,' Kaplan said, then, thinking quickly, 'perhaps I may be permitted to accompany you, sir?

'You?' Voigt frowned and looked up at Kaplan.

'He does know of me and I believe he knows of my loyalty, too. It may enforce your position.'

Hartmann blew air through his lips. 'He might be right. We are aware of *das Fuehrer*'s temper.'

Voigt was willing to bend the truth a little but not to listen to scurrilous gossip. 'I will pretend I did not hear that. But nevertheless…'

Kaplan edged towards the phials. 'Once we have had the audience, I can immediately get on my way.'

'Very well, Kaplan. I know *das Fuehrer* speaks well of you. It is why you have been entrusted with this important step in our continued occupancy.'

***

Adolf Hitler's office was situated deep within the Reich Chancellery.

Kaplan had left his pistol and rifle at the main entrance but his canvas satchel had not been searched, something he was relieved about. He only had one chance at this and he needed to get it right. He held the bag against his hip, feeling the strap pulling at the opposite shoulder. As he and Voigt walked the length of the last corridor, the heavy door set far at the end, his heartbeat pounded in his throat. Nerves were never something that overcame him and he wasn't about to let them do so now, but he knew that the fate of his entire people rested on the next few moments. He may not survive himself but he would make sure that thousands of others would.

The door was upon them and Kaplan took a sidelong glance at Voigt who was nervously fiddling with the buttons on his uniform. The guard outside the office rapped once and hard, waited for the somewhat muffled *eintreten* from behind the heavy oak door and opened up *das Fuehrer*'s private sanctuary.

It was a large room, a mahogany desk almost in its centre, a tall-backed chair behind it. Behind that, staring out the tall window, stood Hitler himself. Kaplan and Voigt entered and stood on the thick Russian rug where directed by the guard, who left and closed the door firmly shut. Kaplan had made a mental note that he had been standing to the right when they entered, meaning he'd be on the left when the time came to leave. There had been only a handful of guards and officers on their walk here, probably about twelve in all. Twelve, while not a large number especially when spread out across the route, would still be a challenge to get through if any alarm was raised. There were more still throughout the rest of the building.

Hitler did not turn around for some minutes, giving time for Kaplan to look at the paintings on the walls, the most dominant one being Solari's circa 1520 copy of *The Last Supper*. Busts of Roman generals were dotted around on wooden plinths and on a wall opposite Solari's work was a startling mural of what Kaplan immediately recognised as the Ark of the Covenant. When Hitler did eventually turn around, he caught Kaplan looking at it.

'Impressive, is it not?' the Austrian said in clipped, economical tones. 'I one day will embark upon its discovery.'

'A Hebrew icon, *mein Fuehrer*,' Kaplan replied calmly, bile forming in his throat. *How dare this anti-Semitic cunt display such a beautiful and important vessel!*

'It is telling,' Hitler continued. 'that your ancestors hid it so well. I wonder if their God will tell me where?'

You intend to assassinate swathes of His people to make sure He does? 'I would not know of such unearthly powers. I am here to carry out your will and only yours.' Kaplan nearly threw that bile up on the maroon rug.

'And so you shall, Aaron Kaplan.'

Voigt spoke then, a sentence forcing its way from his nerve-wracked bones. '*Mein Fuehrer*,' he began. 'We come before you to explain to you our intentions regarding the gift.'

Hitler narrowed his eyes. 'Intentions?'

'Before we do that,' said Kaplan suddenly, adding to Voigt already frayed nerves, 'may I ask *mein Fuehrer* a question?'

Hitler casually waved a hand, giving permission.

'Can this not wait, Kaplan?' whispered Voigt, but Hitler still heard.

'I have allowed him to speak. You dare allow otherwise?'

Voight looked at the rug and his booted feet sinking into it. 'Please forgive me, *mein Fuehrer*.'

A wave again.

'*Herr* Hitler,' Kaplan began, not even bothering now to use his superior's title, because he certainly did not now acknowledge it. 'I must ask you why you have chosen me to carry out this… this mission.' *This atrocity.*

'You question my judgement?'

'Not at all. I am simply curious.'

Hitler lifted his arms to his chest and crossed them, elbows clutched by bony hands, fingers drumming. He admired this Kaplan. He was not afraid to speak his mind. Not like the sycophantic wretch to his right. 'I need to be sure of your loyalty.'

'I understood my loyalty was never in question.'

'Yet you have doubts? You do not wish to carry out my orders? To strengthen the Kaiser's imperial might?'

Kaplan, as he and Voigt had been walking to this meeting, had slipped a phial from out of his bag and into his pocket. It now sat in the grip of his palm. A tube of glass the only protection from a microscopic killer. He raised it between forefinger and thumb. Hitler's left eye twitched, the only reaction Kaplan could detect. 'You clearly know what this is.'

'What are you doing, Kaplan?' gasped Voigt.

'Quiet,' Kaplan hissed.

'I know what it is,' Hitler replied, even, measured.

'Then you know that sending a Jew to kill Jews is… is…' Kaplan couldn't finish. He so wanted to squeeze the phial, to shatter it, even at the cost of his own life.

'Unorthodox?' Hitler laughed at his own joke. 'Surely the greatest test of your loyalty. Why do you think I chose you for this most glorious honour?'

Kaplan could see himself launching over the desk, pinning the man to the floor, thrusting the phial into his sneering mouth and forcing his jaws shut, the glass cracking over his tongue, blood and bacteria mixing. Then the virus would take hold and the Austrian, the so-called Fuehrer, would die an agonising and suffocating death, his very organs rotting from the inside out.

But the phial remained in Kaplan's grasp and his booted feet remained on the Russian carpet.

'For the Fatherland,' Kaplan said and slid the glass tube into his pocket. There was an air of resignation about him, one that he tried his best not to convey. He was disappointed in himself, his own betrayal of his people heading into a mass culling.

'Now, what were you saying?' asked Hitler, walking around his desk and towards Voigt.

Voigt swallowed hard. 'Dr Stanley prefers to examine the effect of the initial releases before we cover the entire six locations.'

'Do you agree?'

Kaplan looked straight ahead. 'I am not qualified to answer that.'

'Yet you are qualified to question my motives for selecting you,' Hitler said.

'That was a personal understanding.'

'There is no "personal understanding". You are part of the *Kaiser-Regel* and have no life outside of it. You have no right to question. If you disobey my orders, you will be shot.' Hitler's voice was rising in pitch now, becoming agitated. 'You will answer my question! Do you agree?'

Kaplan did not blink but turned to his superior. 'No. I do not.'

Voigt looked like he had been struck. Hitler spun.

'*Herr Doktor* Stanley is currently incarcerated at your order,' Hitler seethed, close now to Voigt's face. 'How is it that he has expressed his desires regarding the gift when you have had him arrested?'

'How did y—'

'I know everything, I see everything. Nothing escapes me.' Hitler stormed to his chair and sat down heavily, back arched as he leant on his desk, a fist gesturing. 'Kaplan, leave immediately. Carry out my orders. Do not fail.'

Kaplan nodded once and exited the toxic room as quickly as he could.

As he shut the heavy door behind him, he leant against it for a moment, the long corridor ahead of him. He was angry with himself that he hadn't fulfilled his own goal, the opportunity to release the virus into Hitler's face now gone for good.

He pulled his brown leather hip-length coat straight and shifted the bag over his shoulder, nodded to the guard and walked with purpose away from the screaming coming from the office. Voigt would no doubt be suffering in there for having lied to Hitler so blatantly and Kaplan could hear the Austrian screaming and ranting, demanding Stanley be released to continue his important work.

Fuck them. Fuck them all.

Coming towards him was a figure in a short white coat, pushing a trolley of food covered by a silver domed lid. As they passed each other, Kaplan stopped him.

'Where are you taking that?' he demanded to know.

'This is for *mein Fuehrer*, sir,' the boy from the kitchens replied.

'Has it been tested for poisons?'

'Of course, sir, thoroughly.'

Kaplan squinted at the boy. He was young, no older than fifteen with round-rimmed glasses atop a stubby nose. 'I have just come from a meeting with *das Fuehrer*. He has expressed his disappointment in the security in the kitchens.'

This is it! This is my chance!

'I am not aware of that, sir. I do not cook it. I only deliver it. I have been assured that the chef tastes it just as it leaves the kitchens.'

'Taste it yourself.'

'Sir?'

'Do not question me! Taste it!'

The boy gingerly lifted a spoon from the trolley and raised the domed lid from the tray. Under was a bowl that contained some sort of broth. It was hot and in the split-second the boy closed his eyes as the food burned his mouth, Kaplan had opened up the phial he'd quietly removed from his pocket and poured its entire contents into the carafe of chilled water next to the bowl.

'It tastes acceptable, sir.'

'Stir it! Taste it again!'

The boy did. 'It tastes acceptable, sir,' he said again.

'No different?'

'No, sir,' replied the boy, somewhat bemused.

'Very good.' Kaplan replaced the silver dome and waved the boy on his way. 'Delay no further in giving our beloved leader his lunch.'

Kaplan hurried on as quickly as he could, the empty phial back in his pocket, hearing the occasional squeak of the trolley's wheels grow quieter the further away the boy got from him—the closer he got to delivering the last meal Adolf Hitler would ever eat.

Kaplan broke into a grin, then a chuckle, then a laugh as he found his way back to the main entrance. He was never stopped, never questioned and the guards at the main entrance released his weapons back to him without hesitation.

The army truck was waiting for him, and the border was, too.

But he had no intention of going to Poland.

Marseille

A week into his respite and Daniel Restarick's injury was healing nicely. The bullet hadn't travelled too deeply so the wound was more superficial than anything.

Thibaut had gone away for a few days to give Restarick time to rest and now the veteran of the Great War knew it was time to get up from his sick bed and continue his mission. Staying too long in one place was dangerous and even though he'd not stepped foot outside of the apartment in just under seven days, he slept lightly and always listened out for footsteps on the communal stairwell outside. The heavy army boots of the *kaisersoldaten* could not easily be mistaken for anything else but paranoia had grown in him and he needed to be on his way. Restarick had found a pistol and some bullets under Thibaut's sink unit and had carefully hid them under his makeshift bed.

On the Sunday following his arrival, Thibaut finally returned home, but without Polly.

'I have some errands to run,' he'd explained to Restarick. 'It is easier she stays with family until they're done.'

He'd offered to go to the post office to send Restarick's message, but Restarick had refused, sensing something wasn't quite right. He hadn't expressed his concerns and hadn't enquired as to what these "errands" were. Thibaut had merely shrugged and disappeared into the kitchen. He'd remarked on his way out however that Restarick was looking much better and that he imagined he'd be on his way soon. When Restarick had said he planned on leaving this very night, Thibaut seemed anxious and made noises about having to go out to get some things for the larder. He'd left not long after.

Restarick was dressing his wound now, ensuring the scabbing blood wouldn't come away if he found himself in a compromising struggle. The pistol, now loaded, was tucked in his belt at his back. Thibaut had previously lent him an overcoat (as well as some clothes) that he put on as he heard the apartment door open. He thought Thibaut had come back too quickly to have gone to the local shop.

'Are you up?' called Thibaut. Now that *was* strange. He had never found it necessary to call out before to get Restarick's attention from within a small apartment.

Restarick kept quiet, his hand on the pistol's grip. He listened intently and knew that Thibaut was walking too quietly in his own home. The man, then, wasn't alone.

A shadow fell across the room as Restarick hid behind the kitchen door.

There was a gentle click of a rifle's safety catch being released. Restarick pulled his claimed pistol out. Thibaut spoke again, loudly for the benefit of others who weren't his temporary lodger.

'I've got some nice vegetables to make a stew. You said you missed *cawl* from your time in Carmarthen. I thought I'd try and make us some.' He pronounced with his French tongue, the "then" of Carmarthen as "ten". But his theatrics weren't fooling Restarick, who was kicking himself for not getting out of the apartment sooner.

Restarick's only exit was the main door. The window had a small balcony that he could potentially get to the one below on, but with his arm bandaged up, he wouldn't get far. There was only one thing for it. He quietly cocked his own weapon then, raising his injured arm out and straight, gun pointing, stepped into the lounge. Standing at the foot of the *chaise longue* were Thibaut with three armed *kaisersoldaten*.

The French double-crossing bastard has bloody-well gone and shopped me. 'Get out of my way or I will shoot all four of you.'

'Is that my gun?' Thibaut asked, slight nervousness edging his voice.

'Yes,' replied Restarick.

'Then you won't be *able* to shoot all four of us with just three bullets.'

Restarick's eyes flicked to the tall window and the balcony without.

'You won't make it,' one of the *kaisersoldaten* uttered, moving to block his path. 'You need to come with us.'

Restarick pointed the pistol at each of them in turn, settling finally on Thibaut. 'Why?'

'I had to do what is necessary.'

'You took my rifle.'

'Yes,' Thibaut nodded, hands splayed, 'yes, I did. I didn't want you over-reacting. I admit though I forgot about my gun.'

'Overreacting?' Restarick's arm was already beginning to tire but he kept it level as best he could. 'I should have never trusted you. So which one of you is it going to be?'

'You shoot,' the talkative *kaisersoldaten* said, 'and we will kill you here and now.'

Restarick knew he was right but wondered what the alternative would be. Torture? Attempts to prise out of him information he knew or, worse, didn't know? He'd come this far but he'd let his guard down to get himself better following him being shot in the arm. He'd lost the map, had no idea what had happened to Mircalla and now had no way of contacting Room 40. In any direction, in any outcome, he was dead.

'Shit,' he said, and returned the pistol back to its safety setting and turned it around.

One of the *kaisersoldaten* took it from him and grabbed Restarick's left arm, leading him to the door and the stairwell. Restarick had a brief thought of fleeing but again, he wouldn't get far and there was no guarantee that these three soldiers didn't have comrades outside. They must have, Restarick concluded, because he couldn't imagine he'd be marched on foot to the local HQ.

And he was right: a truck with the German cross icon emblazoned across it and three more *kaisersoldaten* waiting, keeping a vigil on their surroundings, with two in the cab: a driver and another guard. They weren't taking any chances.

Restarick was helped into the back, up the dropped tailgate, raised and bolted fast once all were onboard. All except Thibaut who stayed behind and waited as the lorry growled and wheezed out of the square.

Restarick locked eyes with him, angry he was both betrayed and at himself for allowing him to be betrayed. Thibaut would regret it, he thought, the suburban district giving way to a tree-lined country road, is vision hindered by the rectangular frame of the vehicle's canvas tarpaulin-covered canopy.

***

Marseille was always busy, even during the Great War and even with the subsequent curfew.

In a cafe in the shadow of Notre Dame de la Garde, Mircalla Richard hid behind a pair of round tortoise-shell sunglasses and a cup of strong Greek coffee. The sun-drenched street was bustling but still quiet enough that she had to keep her head down, for the German navy had a permanent presence in the port town.

A group of sailors was at the next table, vying for her attention. She deftly batted their advances away and they soon moved on to another patron.

Mircalla's guest arrived, dressed sharply with a new trilby at an angle atop his head. His pin-striped suit, dark grey, was buttoned. She peered over her sunglasses at him, maintaining her cool facade. She noticed the bruise on his forehead just below his hat brim. His eyes looked sunken, as though he hadn't slept in days and his cheeks were flushed. He sat down across from her at the little table, its red and yellow glass mosaic top catching the afternoon sun.

'Aaron Kaplan,' Mircalla breathed quietly and sipped from her colada. 'You look like shit.'

'You never do.'

'I didn't think you'd show.' Mircalla placed her glass back on the table and brushed her damp fingers together. 'What is it you've done?'

'What makes you think I have done anything?'

'Aaron, you only ever contact me when you've done something. Remember the Gold Coast?'

Kaplan glanced furtively around, uneasy at the mention of the place. 'That was a long time ago, Eloise. I assume that *is* the name you're going by at the moment?'

Now it was Mircalla's turn to look uncomfortable. 'Not so loud.'

'I take it you're someone else these days, then?'

'Mircalla Richard,' she replied, nodding one. 'Can I offer you a smoke?'

'Mircalla? But that's the name of—'

'Yes, yes,' she quickly interjected. 'What do you want? I *am* right in saying you've done something wrong, aren't I?' She looked at his thighs hidden under his dark trousers, his knuckles on his hands. 'God, you've lost weight.'

'I've lost my appetite. But I'm not here to talk about my eating habits.' As a waiter from the cafe emerged, Kaplan called him over. 'A glass of water please. Just water. Lots of ice.'

'Then don't keep me in suspense. I'm a busy girl.' A thin cigar appeared in her hand, was lit and began to curl smoke above her head in the gentle breeze.

'I need...' Kaplan leant forward. 'I need to get out of Europe.'

'Got the daughter of someone important pregnant?'

'Don't mock me. Do not fucking mock me,' he wheezed.

Mircalla tensed. This was a side of Kaplan she hadn't seen for a long time. Even when they were regularly getting themselves into all manner of scrapes, he had always retained the stance of a man in control. Groomed, proud. Today, in the bright, glorious South of France sun, he seemed desperate. He took off his trilby and Mircalla saw the state of his hair: matted and unwashed. Oily. There was black under his fingernails, dirt on his neck by his collar. He really *did* look like shit.

'What the hell has happened to you?' She watched him down the water the waiter brought to him. He didn't stop for breath, then gasped finally as he placed the glass down. 'God. You're on the run.'

He nodded. 'Yes. I think I have killed someone.'

'Think?' she said, squinting as she removed her glasses. 'Aaron Kaplan *knows* when he has killed someone. He is an expert. A marksman. And he rarely feels remorse.'

Kaplan raised an eyebrow. 'Aaron Kaplan usually kills an *appointed* target.'

'You've killed a civilian?'

He shook his head. '*Liebchen*, it's worse than that.'

Kaplan hadn't called her that in months. Their relationship was long finished and he was never one to linger. It was why she still liked him so much. He simply got on with things. Refreshing.

'Worse how?'

He shuffled his chair around to her side and leaned in close, an arm around her back. He looked around again. 'The Kaiser has appointed a senior military advisor.'

'This *Fuehrer* I've been reading about?'

'Yes.'

'He is always in the papers. Look...' Mircalla leant over to another table to pick up a discarded broadsheet and indeed there on the front cover was a photograph of Adolf Hitler in all his military finery. He was beneath the headline:

KAISER-AIDE SERIOUSLY ILL: HITLER
QUARANTINED WITH MYSTERY ILLNESS

Kaplan took the paper from her and began to read the accompanying article. It mentioned that under a week ago, Hitler had been found in his private apartment feverish and suffering from some unknown lung infection. Pneumonia was considered but it had transpired that it was some variation of flu that his doctors had never seen before. A boy from his kitchens had been found dead outside the guard room and it was believed that this boy had somehow enabled the virus to get as far as Hitler himself. There was no mention of anyone else contracting it, which wasn't to say anyone else hadn't.

'Bloody hell,' Mircalla said, looking over his shoulder. 'Bloody *hell*.'

'I guess he's dead now.'

'Hitler? From this illness? But what has that got to do with you? Oh! You poisoned him!'

'Yes. I had to.'

'You had to? Well, you've killed the Kaiser's goon!' Mircalla looked for the waiter. 'This calls for a celebration. Waiter!'

But Kaplan waved her quiet. 'No. If they find out it's me, I am a dead man. I'm meant to be on an assignment for him.'

'For Hitler?'

'Yes.'

'But you decided to kill him instead. Infect him or whatever.' Mircalla pursed her lips, the lips Kaplan would never admit to missing. 'Where will you go?'

'I don't know. That's why I need your help.'

'You need to get out of Europe. Somewhere neutral.' She raised the newspaper to her face, pretending to read it. She had seen a handful of *kaisersoldaten* further up the street. They appeared to be searching for someone. It could have been Kaplan. It could have been a coincidence. Mircalla didn't believe in coincidences. On the other side of the road, coming from the other direction, was another group. 'They're on the hunt. I think we should get away from here.'

Kaplan stood as she did, motioning for the arriving waiter to go away. Mircalla grabbed Kaplan's hand and led him from the cafe but the soldiers on the opposite side of the road suddenly began to cross right before them.

Merde. This is getting close. Mircalla ducked into a little store that had a number of large, coloured glass bottles on display in it curved windows either side of its central door. Kaplan went with her.

Inside it was cool and dark and a handful of customers sat at a cluster of bistro tables, sipping at small shot glasses, poured from smaller, thinner versions of the display bottles.

Immediately, Mircalla let go of Kaplan's hand and pretended not to know him as a young salesman scooted towards her, hair greased flat forming a centre parting, his shirt sleeves rolled up, a long white apron touching the ends of his patent leather shoes.

'Mademoiselle,' he began, a smile launching across his clean-cut face. 'It is not often we get such beauty here. Perfection is usually only found in our bottles.' He gestured to the rows of absinthe behind the counter. 'Have you a preference or do you wish to taste?'

Mircalla scanned the shop and its clientele a second time, briefly and effectively so as not to arouse suspicion. She smiled at the oily little man. 'I wish to taste. I have heard of your produce,' she lied.

'Your accent.'

'I am from Paris.' A half-truth.

'Paris! *Incredible, n'est-ce pas?* That our little shop has found fame in the City of Love.'

'What is your name?'

'Pierre. Pierre Ricard.'

'Then, *Monsieur* Ricard, please select for me the finest you have to offer.'

Mircalla glanced at Kaplan who began himself browsing. It took him mere moments to acknowledge that he would be ignored all the while she was being attended to. Hopefully, the guards outside would only give a cursory glance within.

'We have no individual tables for your privacy, mademoiselle,' said Ricard.

'Oh, that is quite alright. I am happy to share with this fine looking officer,' Mircalla responded, having clocked the uniformed German as soon as they entered.

Kaplan did his best to not look concerned, but what the hell was she thinking?

Ricard approached the stern-looking German cautiously. As soon as the officer looked up, Mircalla oozing with charm next to him, Ricard had no fears in upsetting the customer. The officer got to his feet and proffered the empty seat opposite him.

'This is cosy,' Mircalla said, smiling, her tongue just visible between parted teeth. 'Please do not stand on my account. We are all customers here at Monsieur Ricard's fine establishment. But whose company do I have the pleasure of?'

'*Hafenführer* Stein, *Fraulein*. And you?'

Mircalla looked at Stein. He was swarthy and his chin featured a scar that looked the sort to start itching when it got wet or when he sweated. One of his big hands clamped around a shot glass brimming with green liquid. 'I am Lorelie. Lorelie van Houten.' She raised her hand so Stein could kiss the back of it, the scent of absinthe from his breath lingering on her skin.

'What brings you to Marseille, *Fraulein* van Houten?' Stein asked, the alcohol adding a growl to his voice.

'Here,' Mircalla replied, raising her eyes to the bottles around them, the tables at which others sat. 'I like to consider myself a connoisseur. By the way that you imbibe, I think you are too, yes?'

Stein chuckled and threw the contents of the little glass down his throat. 'A weakness of mine.'

'Have you others?' she asked, pulling herself upright in the wooden chair and breathing out.

Stein looked at her chest, at her curves, at her décolletage as it swept gracefully into her jawline. He leant in and moved a length of red hair from her left shoulder with his free hand (the other wasn't letting go of the shot glass). 'Not many. Maybe a couple more.'

Mircalla glanced down at his hand as it stayed at her shoulder. She could feel the warmth from him through her silk blouse. Her eyes moved to the table and at the notebook before Stein. It was closed but some of the leaves were loose and at an angle. She could make out pencil drawings. The pencil itself sat next to the notebook. 'Drawing is one,' she purred. 'Can I see?'

Before Stein could answer, she slid it towards her and flipped it open. Within were remarkably good sketches of men and women, flowers and animals. She was surprised that his ungainly hands could produce such detail. The look she gave told the German that she was genuinely impressed.

'Do you draw?' Stein asked, his pupils dilating, a mixture of the 92 per cent proof booze and his growing fascination with this voluptuous redhead.

'I have not sketched for a while. I never seem to find the time.'

As Ricard offered Mircalla a choice of four types of absinthe and refilled Stein's glass, the officer swallowed hard and said, 'You would make a good subject, *Fraulein*.'

She feigned shyness. 'Do you think, Herr Stein? I couldn't possibly agree.'

'Will you allow me to draw you?'

'Here?' Mircalla giggled and tried the black absinthe. The aniseed was strong and she dabbed her ruby lips with a napkin.

'No, at my studio.'

'As the port supervisor, surely you are too busy?'

Kaplan meanwhile took his seat at a table behind Stein as soon as it had been vacated by other customers. He had his back to the German, to the outside.

'As the port supervisor, I can make time. The shipping can wait if I so desire it,' Stein said, watching Mircalla down a second then a third glass.

'You have that power?' Mircalla said, the absinthe racing into her heart.

Just then, the shop door opened and three *kaisersoldaten* barged in, disturbing the peace. Kaplan tensed ever so slightly but stayed firm, facing away from the new arrivals. Mircalla never flinched, her eyes fixed on Stein's.

'What is the meaning of this?' Stein barked. As the soldiers tried to explain their rationale and that they were searching for an escaped Jew, he waved them away. 'There are no Jews here. Go. I have my own ways of finding them if there are ever some in my port.'

The *kaisersoldaten* excused themselves and left as abruptly as they had arrived.

Kaplan relaxed.

'An escaped Jew?' asked Mircalla, frowning.

Stein waved his refilled shot glass nonchalantly. 'It is a new directive coming from the Reich Chancellery itself. We are to prepare ourselves for the uprising of the Jew.'

'They pose a threat greater than the Resistance?'

Stein finished his shot and squinted at her. 'I do not think this is something that concerns you, *Fraulein*.'

Mircalla detected his suspicion so changed the subject, slyly undoing a button on her blouse. 'Perhaps you should show me how talented you are with that big German pencil,' she said, touching his arm with her fingertips, such a delicate brushing that she considered was probably completely wasted because of the numbing effect of the absinthe. But nevertheless, Stein looked at her hand, lingered his gaze at the slight reveal of skin by her collar bone and called for the bill.

They were interrupted again by the door opening, this time by a lieutenant known to Stein. The subordinate glanced at Mircalla, leant towards Stein and whispered something in his ear.

Hafenführer Stein seemed to sober up almost immediately and grabbed his cap that had slid to the floor. He stood, face flushed and glistening with moisture, and grabbed Mircalla's hand again, kissing it but with more saliva involved this time. 'My dear *Fraulein* van Houten, I must leave you. Urgent business.'

Mircalla pretended to look disappointed. 'But will I see you again?'

'Do you wish to?'

'Yes, *Herr* Stein. I do wish to. Where can I find you?'

'*Die Inseln*,' he said and nodded to her, heels of his jackboots clicking together. '*Auf wiedersehen*.'

With that, he and his lieutenant departed.

Mircalla tapped Kaplan on the shoulder. 'Come on, let's go.'

'Aren't you going to pay for your drinks?' he asked.

'My new friend will take care of that, I'm sure,' she replied, smiling.

Ricard moved forward and nodded. '*Herr* Stein is a good customer. His office always settles up.'

'Then let's be thankful for his generosity, *Mademoiselle* "van Houten",' Kaplan agreed. 'But this still doesn't help me out here.'

'Why not?' Mircalla led them out into the street. The warm sun and the absinthe affected her momentarily, but she still had her wits about her. She could drink people like Stein under the table every night of the week if she had to. 'It was serendipitous we bumped into him in there. He's the man that controls what comes in and out of this port. And who.'

Kaplan wanted to smile, wanted to see that there was hope for him for that moment, but he was as cautious as Mircalla was confident. 'You think you can convince him to give me passage out of France?'

'*Us*, Aaron. Us. I've got business in the Africas, too.'

***

The truck pulled up to the side of the road, the big wheels forcing the vehicle to sit at an awkward angle in the soft verge.

They had been driving for nearly an hour and Restarick was desperate to stretch his legs. He'd not been in the back of one of these wheezing, chugging monsters since the end of the war but had not forgotten how uncomfortable they were. While he was relieved they'd stopped and that the conversation outside between a couple of his captors indicated he was to be unloaded, he wondered where they were and what was to become of him. He'd seen only the sky and the overhang of some passing trees from his sideways position at gunpoint. No one had spoken to him and nothing made him determine what was coming next.

The tail-gate dropped and the *kaisersoldaten* barked at him to climb down.

The ground was firm under Restarick's boots as he landed. It was a warm day and it had been hot under the truck's tarpaulin. Clouds of dry earth billowed up as the truck, belching black fumes, did a U-turn and headed back the way they had come, down the country road lined on both sides by high hedgerows.

They were adjacent to a stable yard and he spotted a farmhouse behind the stables themselves.

The point of a rifle dug into his back as the guard ordered him to move. As they passed the stables, Restarick noticed not all of them contained horses and some seemed to be in disrepair, doors hanging off or missing altogether. A large barn, locked and bolted Restarick noted, was on the dusty track that led up to the house. A couple of horses whinnied and Restarick answered them under his breath.

'You and me both.'

'Silence!' the guard hissed and shoved his captive towards the barn.

Another guard further up the track called to them, motioning to head to the house.

Soon, Restarick and the two guards were standing at the door to the large building and from within, excited talking and raised voices could be heard. Restarick could make out some Dutch in there as well as French, even a couple of retorts in English. Before one of the *kaisersoldaten* could knock on the narrow grey door, it opened and Restarick was ushered in.

To Restarick's surprise, Barnabas was sitting at the heavy wooden table cleaning a rifle. He looked at Restarick and smiled. 'Glad you made it. You had us searching all over for you after that train crash.'

'What the damned hell are you doing here?' Restarick looked at the two *kaisersoldaten* either side of him and only noticed, for the first time, non-regulation undershirts just visible at the collars of their black jackets. 'You're not real soldiers, are you?'

'Oh, they're real enough, Restarick. They just report to me not the Kaiser.' Barnabas motioned for Restarick to sit. 'Quite the run-around you gave us. By chance you took up refuge at Thibaut's. He was very proud he'd found you. Surely as a Secret Serviceman, you should not chat so much to your host.'

'That's how you know who I am,' Restarick said. 'Why didn't you just ask me to come here?'

'We couldn't guarantee your cooperation.'

'Cooperation in what?' Restarick nodded a thank you as he was handed a mug of coffee.

'Well, we *are* the Resistance, so join the dots.'

'Why me?'

'You're headed to Cairo. To find your missing agent.'

'Thanks for the reminder.'

Barnabas spent the next few moments reassembling his rifle. Placing it on the table, he lit a cigarette. 'We will assist you in your mission. We are looking for Baker, too, and Eloise has confirmed you are not him.'

'I don't believe I report to you.' The coffee was nice. 'I can't accept any help.'

'Your missing agent remains exactly that. He isn't in Cairo.'

Restarick sat up, his relaxed slouch in the chair no longer an appropriate position. 'What do you know? Why is he important to you?'

Barnabas put the map on the table, the very same map that had been lost in the train crash. 'We've deciphered this. We know where it represents.'

'And how do you know the missing agent isn't in Cairo?' Restarick looked at the map, hoping he could somehow reclaim it. How had it got into the Resistance's hands? When the train had ploughed into the siding, he'd lost sight of Mircalla. Perhaps she had taken it. But why? She had various identities, one of which, Eloise, was a Resistance member. Then he remembered: it had been on his person in the couple of days it had taken him to find sanctuary at Thibault's. Thibault had cleaned his clothes for him, given him new ones. He would have found the map in his pocket. And there was the man himself, entering the room from another within the farmhouse. 'Why didn't you just say you are with the Resistance, Thibaut? We're on the same damn side.'

'Just as Barnabas couldn't guarantee your cooperation, I had to be sure you weren't a German infiltrator,' Thibault replied.

'And now?'

'You're Factory. They verified your description.'

Restarick was aghast. There was no way that Room 40 would have even admitted he was one of them, let alone willingly communicate at their level with a group of rebels. Unless…

Mircalla Richard came through the same door as Thibaut and sat next to Barnabas.

'You bitch.'

Mircalla did not seem fazed at Restarick's anger. She'd been in the company of men far worse than any of them in that farmhouse could imagine.

'Eloise is our closest confident outside of the Resistance itself,' Barnabas said. 'She joined us just before the Armistice. Her connections with Room 40 are… valuable to us.'

'And has *Eloise* told you that she is known to me as Mircalla Richard?'

'In these dark times, there are many secrets and very few surprises,' Barnabas replied. 'I had a feeling you were the man we had been looking for when I first saw you with her. I understand her reasons for keeping your identity, other than your name, from us. She is protecting her own. Something, I might add, that is very rare in these—'

'In these dark times,' interrupted Restarick. 'Yes, I get it.' He looked at Mircalla. 'So you're Factory, too?'

'Not exactly,' Mircalla replied. 'I did work *with* them, rather than *for* them, towards the end of the war. My role is, you could say, honorary.'

'And the missing agent, the one who *isn't* in Cairo?'

'Max Baker,' said Barnabas. 'He was seen in Jordan.'

Restarick nodded. That made sense if the map was anything to go by. 'By who?'

'By me,' said Thibault.

'Don't you have a daughter to look after?'

Thibault looked serious. 'I never said she was my daughter. My niece. I was minding her for a few days while her father buried her mother, my sister. She was killed by *kaisersoldaten* in her own backyard.'

'I'm… I'm sorry,' breathed Restarick, the weight of familial loss heavy in his own heart.

'She was hanging out her baby's clothes she had just spent time cleaning. It was just after eight. The curfew. *The fucking curfew.*'

'Oh my God.'

'Killing a mother for hanging out washing after eight in the evening. So you see, I have no love for the Kaiser. None of us do here.'

Barnabas stood and placed a hand on Thibault's shoulder. 'Thibault has been part of the Resistance for many years. We believe the *Kaiser-Regel* know that and that is why his sister was shot. To warn him. To warn us.'

The work of Room 40 seemed at that moment to get a whole lot more complicated. The Kaiser ordering executions of civilians could lead to such unrest that a second Great War might be inevitable. Restarick felt sorry for Thibault: he'd come to know him over the days he'd spent as his guest, even going so far as enjoying getting to know him.

'Mircalla, does the Factory know you're here?'

Mircalla looked at Barnabas as if concerned about her reply to Restarick. She pulled her red hair into a ponytail and sighed. 'Yes.'

'But they haven't instructed you to work with the Resistance directly?'

'We're on the same side, as you noted, Daniel, but we can't be seen to be working with them.'

'So you're "Eloise" while you're here?'

Mircalla smiled and nodded.

Barnabas looked at Restarick, then Mircalla then Thibault, the latter shrugging. Barnabas took a sharp intake of breath. 'Come this way, Captain Restarick… with some words of caution.' The bearded man looked Restarick directly in the eye. 'Your superiors gave a specific mission to Eloise, just as they gave one to you. We are assisting her as we now hope to assist you, as you both assist *us*. I do not believe the Factory could forsee how involved your missing man would become in Mircalla's own assignment and that of the Resistance. What we are about to share with you is top secret and one of those surprises. Please…'

Barnabas beckoned for Restarick to step through into the other room.

Along one wall was a map of the world, pinned in place with little flags that bore the Kaiser's crest. It indicated the extent of the Germanic Empire. A cluster of flags, larger, plain black, were within the Austria-Hungary borders. On the table, four gas masks of the same design that Carter had given Restarick, were in pieces.

'What is this telling us?' Restarick spun to face Barnabas.

'We got those gas masks from the area with the black flags. The Kaiser is planning something,' responded Thibault instead.

'The Kaiser usually is.'

'How is your German, Restarick?'

Restarick looked at the far wall where newspaper clippings, photographs and notes were being displayed. 'I get by.'

'*Operation: Geschenk.* Do you know what that means?' Barnabas perched on the edge of the table, poking at the gas masks.

'Operation: Gift.' Restarick walked over to take a closer look at the masks. 'The Kaiser is planning to do what? Use chemical warfare?' He wanted to gauge how much Barnabas and his team were aware.

'We understand that he asked instructed his top scientists to develop a virus.'

'And these black flags?'

'That's where we believe the virus is to be released, hence the gas masks.'

Restarick turned over a filter in his hands. Room 40 were on the same wavelength.

'How can you be sure?'

Mircalla sighed and moved forward. 'I was approached by an old acquaintance. He had been instructed by his superiors to deliver the virus… the 'gift.''

'*Had* been? Meaning what, Mircalla?' Restarick rubbed his forehead. 'He has already delivered it?'

'In a way.'

'I can't imagine the Kaiser taking kindly to his orders being altered. Is your acquaintance still alive?'

Mircalla nodded. 'Barely.'

'Barely,' breathed Restarick.

'Our doctors believe he has days to live, unless his metabolism is stronger than they think.'

'What happened to him?'

'They think he was poisoned.'

Restarick started laughing.

Mircalla frowned. 'And that's amusing, why?'

Putting the filter down, Restarick spread his arms. 'He wasn't poisoned! It's obvious he wasn't!'

'Obvious?' Barnabas stood, suspicion flashing across his face.

'If he was sent to deliver this gift, he was obviously infected with it! He has the virus!'

'He's a carrier?' Mircalla put a hand to her mouth. 'That's…'

'…barbaric!' finished Barnabas.

'So he could spread it wherever he goes!' Restarick finished. Then he gasped. 'Where did you meet him?'

'In Marseille.' It dawned on Mircalla what Restarick was saying.

'He's a plant. Sent here to infect you! If he knows you, he'd know you'd be willing to meet with him!'

'That explains this, too.' Barnabas returned to the other room and they followed. He picked up a newspaper, today's edition that declared Hitler's mystery illness. He threw it to Restarick who read the report with interest.

'He said he'd killed a man…' Mircalla breathed. 'They ordered him to spread a virus but instead he gave it to one of their top men…'

'I'm beginning to like this acquaintance of yours,' Restarick said, raising an eyebrow to her. He put the newspaper down 'Where is he now?'

'In one of the outhouses,' Barnabas said.

'Is he safe to speak to?'

'We put up a make-shift bed in there.'

'You need to quarantine him. Now.' Restarick turned to Mircalla. 'Did you touch him at all? Held his hand? Kissed him?'

'What kind of girl do you t—'

'Mircalla! This isn't time for faux-coyness. Did you or did you not physically touch him?'

'Well… no. I didn't. I don't think I touched him.' Mircalla began to look worried.

'You need to be sure. If you say you didn't, I'll believe you.' Restarick pursed his lips, mind racing.

'Okay, no. I didn't. I'm definite.'

'That's good enough for me, Mircalla. I need to get to Cairo and I'd like you to still come with me.'

Barnabas looked between Mircalla and Restarick, trying to read both their expressions. Restarick was a professional, clearly putting himself in control here. But he knew Mircalla well and was aware she rarely responded to masculine displays of power. That said, she was content to accept Restarick's role.

'I must ask a question,' he asked as Mircalla was about to leave the farmhouse after Restarick. They both turned. 'To you, Captain…'

Mircalla stepped back as Restarick stopped in the doorway, the light framing his outline. 'By all means.'

'Why Cairo?'

'I don't understand.'

'Captain Restarick, we have told you that your missing agent is in Jordan. Why are you still intent on going to Egypt?'

Restarick raised his palms. 'I've always wanted to see the pyramids,' he said, then left.

Mircalla stifled and smile and followed, leaving Barnabas to wonder how Restarick suddenly appeared to be in charge.

***

Restarick sat on a low wall and lit a cigarette. His last one. He offered to share it with Mircalla but she said no. The sun was bright. It glinted on the windows of the farmhouse.

'Barnabas has a point.' She sat next to him.

'Does he?'

'If you know that's where Baker isn't why are you going anyway? And dragging me along?'

Restarick inhaled a lungful of smoke and watched it dissipate into the warm air as he breathed out. 'I had an intruder on my plantation back home. He never said anything of great value to me but to the arresting officers he said something peculiar. They noted it down as "Cairo's folly is not to be dismissed".'

'And you're basing this trip on the ramblings of a mad man?'

'I never said he was mad. I never said that he rambled, either.'

'But you had him arrested. A man like you can take care of himself, more so on your home ground. If you didn't think him mad, you would have dealt with him without involving the police. And as for what he said, have you any idea what he meant?'

'None. But those gas masks you have in there,' Restarick nodded towards the farmhouse, 'he gave me one exactly the same.'

'Do you think he was with the Resistance? Warning you? "Cairo's folly is not to be dismissed" sounds like a warning!'

'He was too… undisciplined to be from any underground movement.'

'So where would he have gotten a gas mask from? Especially one of a new design. Perhaps he's part of the *Kaiser-Regel*.'

'Again, too undisciplined. And yes, that does leave the unanswered question about the gas mask. He knew it was important that he gave it to me.'

'So where is it now?'

'I had orders to hand it to some fellow operatives in Versailles. Like Barnabas, the Factory fears this is a plot. We're investigating the possibility of chemical factories being constructed.'

'With the Kaiser occupying all of Europe, that's a pretty large area to search. Do you really think Cairo is where we should start?'

Restarick raised an eyebrow at her, stubbing the end of his cigarette into the dirt at his feet.

***

'Where am I?' Kaplan wheezed, seeing a surgical mask leering down at him. Green eyes glittered above it, framed by neatly styled blonde hair.

His fever had broken but Barnabas still ensured he was kept isolated from anyone else. Looking beyond the obscured face, he saw he was in a tiny brick room. It looked like a stable. Initially panicking, a muffled voice assured him his health was improving.

'Are you a doctor? I thought the virus was deadly.' Between bouts of coughing, he explained to the nodding woman what he had been told.

'You told Eloise that you hadn't handled the virus nor ingested or inhaled it. We believe you caught a mild strain. You have been very lucky.'

'Then why are you wearing a gas mask?'

'We can't be too careful. I'm Doctor Thurman.' Thurman took Kaplan's blood pressure, his aching body wincing at the touch. 'You have influenza. A couple more days rest and you'll be up and about.'

'How long have I been here?' He opened his mouth as the doctor slid a thermometer under his tongue.

'Nearly two weeks. Eloise brought you in. You were in a terrible state.'

'Ish she shtill 'ere?'

'Don't talk with the thermometer in your mouth.'

Kaplan took it out and said again: 'Is she still here?'

'Don't take the thermometer out,' Thurman chided, pointing.

Kaplan sighed and replaced it.

'Yes, she's still here. She is well, before you ask. You haven't infected anybody else. She's preparing to leave with the British agent.' Thurman removed the thermometer, satisfied with its reading.

'Leave? Where?'

Thurman shrugged. 'Not for me to know. I just patch everyone back up if they ever return. You'll need to speak to Barney. Drink plenty of water. I'll be back later to check on you.'

Kaplan nodded and sank back in his pillow as Thurman left him alone, feeling like he had just woken with the worse hangover imaginable. The taste in his mouth was vile. The bare bulb hanging above his bed swayed gently with the draft coming from the thin glass window.

If he'd caught influenza from just opening the phial, how rampant was this virus? He wondered too if Hitler had survived, relieved that he'd been given that split second chance to try again. That poor kid, though, who'd delivered the "gift" to his *Fuehrer*.

Hitler's plan to wipe out whole swathes of the Jewish community made Kaplan's blood boil in his veins, and he was lying here unable to do anything. Word would have got out that Hitler's order had failed, so it was highly likely that someone else had been tasked to complete the mission. Kaplan knew he was a wanted man know, but better that than a puppet used to carry out genocide. Nevertheless, incapacitated he was a sitting target and there was no reason to assume that the Central Powers didn't have spies in the Resistance, just as the Resistance had spies in Berlin.

His thoughts turned to Aisling. He'd had no love for the woman but he had been fond of her, so it was a shame he would not have her sliding into bed with him ever again. He wasn't about to swear revenge for her death—Hitler hopefully choking on his own collapsed lungs would see to that—but there had to be a point for someone to be killed. Aisling had been slaughtered unnecessarily and painfully.

He had to save his people. But he was just one man. Who would believe him that the Kaiser was advocating such slaughter? Perhaps this Barney would listen.

Nodding to himself, ignoring the aches going down to his very core, he sat up and swung his legs over the edge of the bed. He saw his clothes in a neat pile in a chair over in the corner so slipped out of the nightgown he'd been dressed in and padded over. The floor was cold but the sun coming through the window warmed his back.

***

Mircalla puckered her lips in the mirror, the red lipstick more than ostentatious to capture the leering attention of *Hafenführer* Stein.

Overbearing, sweaty, groping men were not her ideal companions at the best of times, but Stein was malleable and narcissistic—an easy conclusion from just those few minutes in his company. A few cooing words in his ear and a massaging of his ego would no doubt give her a free pass and passage to Algiers. She just needed to convince him to add an extra one for Restarick.

A commotion outside the farmhouse and she slipped into her shoes to dash outside. A handful of guards were shouting at a man who had a pistol raised and was shouting back. It took a few moments for her to realise it was Kaplan.

'Wait! Wait! Lower your weapons!' she called, entering the stable yard.

'What's going on?' Barnaby was immediately behind her, buckling a holster around his waist.

'It's Aaron.'

'What the hell is he doing out here?'

Kaplan saw Mircalla in her striking red dress. 'Tell them! I'm not a spy! I'm not ill!'

'You need to rest,' she replied.

'I need to talk to Barney. Which one of you is he?' Kaplan spun around, keenly eyeing all the Resistance members who had come out to see what was going on.

'Everybody… inside! Dr Thurman!' Barnabas motioned for Mircalla to step back. 'I'm Barnabas. I know you're not a spy. You're a friend of Eloise's. She bought you here so we could help you get better.'

Thurman came running to Barnabas' side. 'He's no longer contagious,' she whispered.

Barnabas nodded. 'Dr Thurman has confirmed you're fine. You just need to rest, like Eloise says. What do you want to talk to me about?'

The guards slowly dispersed, leaving Mircalla, Thurman and Barnabas with Kaplan, who had slumped to the ground, exhausted.

'You are Resistance,' Kaplan breathed.

'You can go in, too, doctor.' Barnabas crouched down. 'Come on, let's help you up.'

Kaplan gritted his teeth, still proud but not foolish, allowing himself to be helped to the farmhouse.

***

They all sat at the heavy table and closed the door. Barnabas called for Restarick to join them as he gave Kaplan a glass of water.

'Daniel, this is Aaron Kaplan.'

Restarick nodded curtly. 'I hear you tried to assassinate of the Kaiser's generals.'

Kaplan squinted. 'Tried? I was not successful?'

'No,' confirmed Barnabas. 'Reports came in yesterday that he is recovering from a severe form of influenza.'

Kaplan sighed. 'Then it is important that you listen to what I have to say.'

'Of course. Are you defecting?' Restarick held his stare, looking for any doubt in Kaplan's expression.

'I am Central Powers. Loyal to the Kaiser. The very idea of a Resistance is sickening to me.'

'We won't hold it against you, Aaron,' Mircalla said.

'Is that what you wanted to speak to me about?' asked Barnabas.

Kaplan shook his head. 'I know what the Kaiser is planning.'

'Germ warfare,' said Restarick.

Kaplan shook his head. 'Worse than that. This is to control the population.'

'Why is that an issue for you? This is what the Fatherland wants. You just said you are loyal.' Restarick drummed his fingers briefly on the table top.

'I believed in the cause. That we should be a united Europe.'

'In peacetime that could work. But the curfews, the walls. Executions without hearings. No freedom of movement. That's not the way we want to live.' Barnabas leant back in his chair. 'That's why we resist. Why your change of heart?'

'Because the Kaiser has changed the way he wishes to control. No one is safe. We are all at risk.'

Kaplan saw the look of horror on everyone's faces as he continued to reveal what Hitler had told him, about the subjugation of the Jewish community to trial the virus, the eventual roll-out to the entire population.

Restarick motioned to the gas masks on the bench behind them. 'And these are to be given out to a select few?'

'Those who are considered righteous enough to live. There is also a vaccine. Not everyone will be allowed to have it.

'But the very fact that you and Hitler survived,' observed Restarick, 'indicates that the severity of infection is random.'

'How does Baker fit into all this?' Barnabas wondered. 'How well do you know him, Restarick?'

'I don't know him at all.'

'So we have no way of knowing if he has gone over to the Kaiser.'

'The Factory won't admit if he has defected or not,' Mircalla said.

'We were told he had,' Barnabas said. 'That's why we're looking for him.'

'The Factory knows you can get your hands dirty. You can be blamed if any incursion goes awry.'

'On more thing,' Kaplan said. 'It's believed this agent Baker has stolen some of the phials containing the virus directly from the man who created it.'

'Doctor Stanley…' breathed Restarick. 'What the damn hell is Baker planning to do with it?'

'Perhaps he intends to take it to our superiors, to show them what the Kaiser intends?'

'No. Baker has disappeared. There's every reason to assume he's gone rogue. Those phials need to be found.'

Barnabas clasped his hands together, agreeing with Restarick. 'Eloise, get to the port. Get those passes. If Cairo is where he is, we have no more time to lose.'

They all stood, Kaplan slower than the others. 'I want to go, too.'

Barnabas looked between Restarick and Mircalla. 'You?'

Mircalla considered. 'Are you strong enough?'

'I am capable.'

'This isn't a revenge mission, Kaplan. If you're coming with us, you need to *be* with us. I don't know either of you—any of you—that well, but I'm willing to trust Mircalla… Eloise.'

'*I* trust Aaron. I know he is Central Powers but he *can* be trusted. If he is with us, then he will not betray us.'

'He's betraying his Fatherland,' Barnabas pointed out. Suspicion was part of the daily thought processes in the Resistance. He already felt that they had shared too much with him, but Kaplan was open about his feelings towards the Kaiser's plan.

'I'll make him my responsibility, Barney,' said Mircalla, Barnabas reluctantly agreeing. 'Now… you boys get your stuff together. I have a date with a soldier.'

***

From the diary of Captain Daniel James Restarick
2 June 1917

The last 6 months have been a whirlwind, a flurry of emotion and drama and I've not had the chance to keep these entries up to date.

Other than being called away every day it feel to somewhere new, there is another reason and her name is Lita.

We met (of all places!) in a butcher's shop in Waltham Abbey, not far from where she had lodgings. I was stationed there for a couple of months while waiting for orders.

Her dark eyes glittered at me over the meat loaves and I couldn't help but ask her name as we left at the same time. She asked me what I did. I said I couldn't tell her, of course, but that didn't seem to bother her. She said that so many of the boys back from 'over there' only want one thing and that it was a pleasure to talk to a soldier who actually took an interest in her. Why wouldn't I? She appeared bright and self-assured. She is Spanish and has been in Blighty for some time—although never really had anywhere she calls home.

Our first date was Jan. 15th. I took her to a little café I knew managed by an old acquaintance. Frankie he was called but was sadly killed a week or so after when an incendiary device went off nearby. His wife, Bernice, was devastated. Lita really looked after her, selflessly giving up any spare time she had after work. It naturally made any time I could spend with her limited—how selfish does that make me sound! But all the same, we did find those moments, fleeting at first, until she told me Bernice had gone to live with some relatives in Filby.

I must confess I have not had too many romances so cannot attest to being any sort of Douglas Fairbanks, but Lita makes me swoon whenever I see her. Her Latino looks and her accent, her intelligence and wit. Our conversations range from the correct colour of cheese, how not to cook paella, how to fix a motor car engine to involved political debates. In the months I have known her, through our written exchanges, too, my love for her grows.

When I asked her to marry me, just a mere six months since we met, she said yes immediately. The ring I gave her overwhelmed her. She had never been given such a gift before, she said.

One weekend we were in Llanelli. Its beach is sand and rocks—she screamed with utter despair, saying her engagement ring had slipped from her finger. I looked high and low in the stones and shingle, only to see her giggling like a child, a mischievous look upon her beautiful face, the ring glinting and safe in her open palm. She has a wicked sense of humour.

Lying together on the sand until the sun set, the world seemed filled with peace.

To quote her favourite poet: "All heaven and earth are still, though not in sleep, but breathless, as we grow when feeling most."

But I knew on the continent my colleagues and peers were dying in their thousands under the fire of the Hun bullets. It would be a matter of time when I had to go back.

Lita and I cannot bear to be apart. Whenever I am away from her, the ache in my chest is as real as any. Love hurts, they say, and it's true. I've never known anything like it.

We plan to marry on 15 January next year. She found that so romantic, one year to the day after we met. I know this is the right thing to do. She is my soul mate. We laugh together, cry together, we're silly together. It's like I cannot function when we are apart. But I have a job to do and an important one at that. And so does she.

The war stretches far beyond the trenches of the western front. Her own support of the war effort alongside all the brave girls in Waltham Abbey is unmistakeable—that's another reason why I'm so smitten with her. She cares unlike anyone else I know. I only hope that my ability to care for her is as great.

Berlin

'*Fraulein* Bachman to see you, *Generaloberst* Voigt.'

Voigt did not look up from the paperwork before him, partly out of dismissiveness of the clerk under him, mainly at the moment to disguise the fact that his face was bruised from where his *Fuehrer* had struck him repeatedly. He grunted an acknowledgement.

Before his visitor could stand before him, he stood and looked out of the window behind his desk, emulating the position his superior often took in similar situations. It further hid his face.

'*Heil* Kaiser,' he heard Bachman say. Voigt did not turn around.

'What do you know of Aaron Kaplan?'

Bachman stood rock still before Voigt, eyes dead ahead, arms straight down by her sides. She was a handsome woman, tall, lithe, close-cropped blonde hair, angular, chiselled features and pale eyes. Every bit an inductee to *Herrenrasse* that Hitler seemed to be growing increasingly obsessed with. 'We served together before the Allies fell.'

'And your opinion?'

'Dedicated, ruthless.'

'A traitor?' Voigt turned around.

Bachman' expression twitched ever so slightly. Voight wondered if it was sight of his swollen eye or the idea that someone as seemingly unshakeable as Kaplan could turn against the Kaiser.

'He showed no… previous leanings towards the Enemy, *Generaloberst* Voigt.'

'He attempted to assassinate a high-ranking official of the *Kaiser-Regel*. He is on the run. He is to be brought into custody.'

'Sir,' Bachman said, 'at what cost?'

'The *Fuehrer* does not want him killed, do you understand? That pleasure is to be his alone.' Voigt tossed a manila file towards Bachman. 'This documents his last known whereabouts.'

Bachman took the file and slid it under her arm.

'Look at it, woman!'

'Of course, sir. My apologies.' Bachman pulled the file open. Her blue eyes scanned it, looking at the map of Marseille and where it was marked in places. With it was a series of photographs of a couple at a bistro table. 'The woman…'

'We believe she is a spy working for the Allies.'

'She is Kaplan's former lover.' Bachman returned her gaze to straight ahead. 'We met when he brought her to Captain Hardenberg's retreat in the mountains, just after the war.'

'Then that would explain his defection.'

'To follow her?' Bachman shook her head. 'He is sympathetic neither to a woman's needs nor her interests.'

'You sound almost disappointed,' Voigt sneered.

'Not at all. Kaplan is—*was*—a comrade. If he is no longer that, then he nothing to me.'

'So you have no compunction about bringing him in?'

'None.' Bachman shifted her line of sight to look directly at Voigt. His face was indeed a painful mess as the rumours in the barracks attested to.

Voigt sat down, clasping his hands together. 'Your record demonstrates commitment to the highest degree. Personal assistant to Heinrich Hoffman. Bodyguard to Miss Braun. Impressive indeed.' There was envy in Voigt's tone. Very few had access to Hitler's inner circle and Bachman was uniquely placed.

The trust put in Kaplan had angered the *Fuehrer* and he had taken that anger out on Voigt. Assigning Bachman to replace Kaplan was intended to prevent a second misplaced step. Bachman was not the kind of individual to be swayed. Voight leant back. This mission would succeed.

'They are intending to cross to the Africas,' Bachman deduced. 'That is the only reason they have headed south.'

'That is our belief also. You will be flown into Marseille tonight.'

'Why not now? Why the delay?'

Voight looked at his watch and considered. 'I welcome the fact that you are eager to begin. But there is no delay. No ships will depart the port until sunrise. You have plenty of time to apprehend them as they sleep.'

'Who is the port commander?'

Voigt checked his notes, wincing as he squinted at the handwritten information he had been given by his clerk. '*Hafenführer* Stein.'

Bachman hadn't met Stein but knew he did not wield the unquestionable power he thought he did. There had been a number of reports from the man's time as a captain on the Western Front of a lack of dedication from his men. This was the problem with the old soldiers holding positions of power in the new order: complacency in the face of perceived unalloyed command. Many of the younger officers coming up through the ranks were blocked by the immovability of their seniors.

A new order meant new blood. Bachman considered herself one such person and welcomed the *Fuehrer*'s exhilarating approach. Create something new, literally the new order the Kaiser so passionately spoke about in his victory speech ten years ago now.

She looked at the top of Voigt's bald head, with its chronic liver spots dotted between the new bruises and welts. He was still an imposing figure, she had to agree, and dressed impeccably he was one of the few of the older generation to perhaps warrant that respect. She wondered though what he would make of the secret plans the *Fuehrer* was making to succeed the Kaiser.

People like Kaplan, highly trained and highly skilled, were dangerous to the new order. Whatever the reasons for his defection, she knew Hitler had made the right decision in sending her to get him. What she didn't think was the best course of action though was to let him live for any longer. Kill him where she found him and be done with it. But her orders were not to be countermanded. If she thought they were negotiable then she would be no better than the scum she was to retrieve.

Kraków, Poland

The six great machines lumbered—with surprising ease for their bulk and weight—into the centre of Rynek Glówny, taking up positions where the market square had its exits.

The tanks' great turrets swung around, covering those who had gathered, many of whom had stopped by on their way home from the synagogue south of the square.

A staff car roared up, dwarfed by the tanks, the driver little interested there were groups of families, young and old, that had to scurry to get out of the way. Even before the engine had been shut off, the general stepped purposefully out from the rear seats, straightened his cap and uniform and raised a megaphone to his lips.

'By order of His Imperial and Royal Majesty Wilhelm the Second, by the Grace of God, your Emperor and King, you are hereby notified to gather in your nearest synagogues and churches. Do not return to your homes. Do not return to the homes of your loved ones. They too are required to gather in their closest places of worship. Do so now without noise or objection. Resist and you will be punished. Run and you will be shot.' The general returned to his seat and closed the door. His lieutenant next to him took the megaphone. 'Look at them, pathetic creatures.'

The people had bowed their heads, gathered up their children and were filing silently out of the square. *Kaisersoldaten* had lined up around, ushering all along. One man, forced towards a church, protested he needed to be in a synagogue. The answer came swiftly: a strike to his temple, blood splashing to the cobbles, dragged by his collar back to his feet and pushed into line. The Jew had no choice but to follow the group of Catholics he had inadvertently joined. A woman, the general couldn't tell if she was also a Jew or not, struggled against the force of a soldier's hands, and was shot where she stood, falling dead at her daughter's feet. The child, who must have only been six or so, burst into tears, screaming for her mother. A man picked her up and hurried away with the others, trying his best to soothe the inconsolable girl.

Once everyone was in the churches and synagogues, the doors and windows were sealed from the outside, save for one carefully broken window in each. The people were no longer quiet, the squad commanders had trained their men well to ignore the pleading and the wailing from inside. The rabbis and the priests did their best to calm the forced congregations across Kraków but even they did not know why they had all been locked in the places they called sanctuary. Nor could they foresee what the general's next order would be.

The squad commanders ordered a retreat as figures dressed in white boiler suits with a gas mask underneath sealed hoods approached every strategically broken pane of glass. They threw within a porcelain egg that shattered on impact with the floor. Then they too retreated. The tanks moved slowly out of the square, the staff car having departed before the boiler suits had given the gift.

Five hours later, the boiler suits returned and quietly unlocked the doors. Again, they retreated.

Sometime after, as the sun was beginning to set, those trapped within realised they were trapped no longer. Carefully, quietly, fearfully, they began to emerge into the dusk, bringing with them their trepidation and terror, and the virus they had all been breathing in.

Marseille

Mircalla slumped down in the little armchair, kicking off her stilettoes. Sighing, she rubbed her heels.

'Pour me a drink, Daniel. That man was utterly ghastly.'

'Were you successful?' Kaplan asked as Daniel prepared a whiskey each for them all. There was a collection of dusty crockery and tin mugs in a cupboard next to the stove.

Mircalla smiled and pulled an envelope from her cleavage. 'Three passes and three tickets to Algiers.'

Daniel had found a room for the night, positioning the three of them as members of the Berlin news service. A trio travelling together ought to have aroused suspicion but the landlord was more than keen to accept a week's worth of rent in advance and so no questions were asked. However the world changed, money always retained a voice. It would be likely he'd report them to the authorities once he'd realised they'd left by the next morning, however, but then they would be halfway across the Balearic.

'What time do we sail?'

'*El Morakeb* is scheduled to depart 0715. She's a transport vessel taking supplies to the troops stationed in Algiers. Once we're out of the city's jurisdiction, we're relatively free to travel.'

'Last reports stated the Kaiser was unable to find a foothold any further in,' added Restarick. 'Is that the case, Aaron?'

Kaplan looked at the amber liquid in his mug. 'We have found the Algerians to be a stubborn race.'

'We?' Mircalla finished her drink and placed the mug on the floor. She looked at the two single beds in the room. 'We'll take turns in keeping watch. We need to be at the port by 0630.'

'You two sleep first,' Restarick suggested, knowing Kaplan was still weakened from the virus. 'Does anyone mind if I smoke?'

'No,' Kaplan shrugged, 'just don't stray too close to the window.'

'Of course…' Restarick breathed in sharply.

'What is it?' Mircalla stood, the look of confusion then over the Englishman's face causing concern.

'Did you… can you hear that?'

'I didn't hear anything,' Kaplan replied, tensing.

'Someone called out… out there.' Restarick held tight to the pack of cigarettes.

'Probably *kaisersoldaten* rounding up drunkards breaking the curfew.'

Restarick peered through the grubby curtains. The street below was empty, not even a cat straying out.

'I said get back! You don't know who is watching!'

'What did they say?' Mircalla looked at Kaplan, frowning. Kaplan raised his eyebrows.

'It was a woman.' Restarick hesitated, verging on a moment of disbelief. 'She said…'

'*Corazón…*'

Restarick spun towards the door. Standing by the sink was…

'Daniel? What's the matter with you?'

He shrugged off Mircalla's grip, forgetting she was even right next to him.

'Lita. My beautiful Lita.'

The room around him shrank into darkness as Lita stepped forward, smiling.

'I knew I would find you.'

Restarick held out a hand to her and she eagerly took it, flinging her arms around him. 'How did you get here? I thought you were… were…' He pressed his face into her neck, her thick dark hair smelling so sweet.

'Do not say it, *Corazón*.' She pulled away, placing a finger to his lips. 'I am here now. We can be together.'

'I have to… I have to go to…' Restarick drank in her beauty. She hadn't changed a day in ten years.

'Have to what? Have to go?' Lita shook her head. 'It is all over now. You do not need to go anywhere except home.'

'Will you stay?'

'Yes.' Lita grabbed him tight again and Restarick gasped in relief. She felt so good in his arms as they spun around, the darkness falling away as the plantation came into his line of sight over her shoulder.

'We're…'

Lita nodded, knowingly, grabbed his hand and laughed, pulling him up the hill to the house. The Ceylon sun was scorching on his head but it did not matter. The whole world could be alight for all he cared. As long as Lita was with him again.

She turned to look at him, throwing her head back to laugh again, revealing the olive skin at her throat. Her hair tumbled around her shoulders as the flow of her red dress caught in the breeze. She was barefoot. 'We are together now, *Corazón*.'

Then Lita stopped where she was, turning full to face him. Restarick's loving gaze, with a smile that made his cheeks hurt, turned into a look of horror as immediately she burst into flames before him. He reeled back with the heat and screamed out, the flames leaping from her bubbling skin into his mouth and down his throat. He tried to scream again in agony but no sound came. But in his own head, all he could hear was the roar of her burning body and the rush of his own boiling blood.

'Daniel… Daniel! Wake up!'

With a gasp as though he had all the air knocked from him, Restarick sat bolt upright on the rickety bed to see Mircalla kneeling by him, holding shoulders.

'Lita…'

'You were having a nightmare.'

'Enough noise to wake the while damn building,' Kaplan growled, standing at the foot of the bed.

Restarick was confused for the moment, then reached out to his cigarettes on the floor, took one out, lit it, inhaled and laid back in the bed. 'I'm sorry… What time is it?'

'Just gone six am. What were you dreaming about?'

'It's nothing.' Restarick shrugged it off, instead sitting on the edge of the bed, the sheet damp with his sweat. He watched Mircalla move to the bathroom. What could he tell them? Who would trust a haunted man? 'Did you serve in the war, Aaron?'

'I was thirteen when war was declared. I wanted to enlist, to follow my father. Mother had other ideas.'

'Poor Aaron had to sit it out until he was old enough. But you made up for lost time!' Mircalla called out.

Kaplan smiled. 'Mircalla and I have known each other for a while now. Always on the opposing sides but we never discussed business.'

That alarmed Restarick. Mircalla, a Room 40 operative, fraternising with the enemy. He wondered if she was a double agent after all. It was always hard to tell which was, naturally, the point. 'But now you're on the same side.'

'I guess you could say that.'

'I won him over!' Mircalla said, returning to the room. *Sans* make-up now, she was in trousers and a white blouse, hair in a pony-tail. Sitting back in armchair she pulled boots over socked feet.

'You served, I think,' Kaplan queried, seeing the pain behind Restarick's eyes. 'Your nightmare. Not a one-off.'

Restarick dragged long on the cigarette before answering. 'I served. I saw Passchendaele, Ypres. Then the British High Command gave me other duties.'

'The Factory,' nodded Kaplan. 'But you did not know Mircalla until now?'

'No.'

'These dreams you have…'

'Not of the war. Of my… wife. She died in an accident.'

Kaplan pursed his lips. 'That's tough luck.'

Restarick stubbed out the cigarette in an empty mug. 'Yes, tough luck indeed.'

'Was she waiting for you when you returned home from the front?'

'The accident was in England, while I was serving. A fire at home. No one knew how it started. They found her… body… amongst the ruins. Ten years ago now, but I remember the day I was told like it was yesterday.' Restarick rubbed his temples.

'Ten years. You must have loved her very much.' Kaplan considered.

'I did. I don't think I'll ever stop.'

'I have not loved anyone like that.'

'Apart from maybe yourself, Aaron,' chuckled Mircalla. 'No one has caught your eye since, Daniel?'

'No. I don't want it to be caught. I realised the hard way that I will never love anyone as much or as intense as I did my wife. It would be unfair on all parties to pretend otherwise.'

'So you do this,' Kaplan said, indicating the room around them.

Restarick knew he meant their undercover life the three of them had in common. 'Not through choice. I *had* hoped to retire. Family business in Ceylon.'

'One last mission, eh?' Mircalla tightened the leather belt around her waist.

'Something like that.'

'Then we'd better make it a good one for you,' Kaplan said, standing and heading to the bathroom, his turn now to freshen up before they headed to the port.

Berlin

'It is done.'

Hitler gripped the telephone receiver with sweaty hands, nodding with pleasure at the news.

'You have done well, general,' he said. 'This will earn you many favours in the days to come.'

'Thank you, *Fuehrer*,' the tinny voice said.

Hitler ended the call and sat back in his chair. He smiled and buzzed his intercom, ordering Stanley to be brought to him. A few minutes and the rap at the door preceded the American's entry to Hitler's private office.

'*Herr Doktor*.'

Leo Stanley swaggered towards the desk and sat in the leather chair facing Hitler. 'I thought I was gon' be witnessin' the administerin'?'

Hitler's temple twitched at the man's audacity in sitting before he was told to. 'I changed my mind. The gift could wait no longer. Now we sit back and watch.'

'It's sure gon' be an inneressin time.'

'It will be a pleasure to watch it unfold.' Hitler had considered alternative methods to cull the unwanted segments of the Kaiser's empire but was concerned that they would have been rejected. Even the Kaiser with his despotic outlook would likely have balked at the mass executions Hitler preferred. When Stanley had created the virus, Hitler knew that was the way forward instead: there would be no direct blame attributed to him. Rather, the Jew would have infected himself and his ilk. Who could possibly accuse the Kaiser? A microscopic ally more virulent than mustard gas which was reliant on a good breeze and fair weather. The virus latest longer and spread further and didn't care if it was raining or not. 'Are you sure that you hold the vaccine?'

'I do. I heard you were given a dose.'

'My doctors told me it weakened the virus I had been given. Your science saved my life, *Herr Doktor*, just as it is now taking away the lives of those in Kraków. That I will not forget.'

'You got the would-be assassin?'

'Not yet. But Kaplan will be brought to me soon enough. The gift has been delivered, far more successfully that the traitor would have managed. Perhaps his failure was meant to be. There would have been a good chance that death from infection would have followed had it been done the way that was originally intended. Kaplan is still alive to see for himself the effect the virus has on the Jews. Then I will execute him personally.'

Stanley raised a finger. 'I have a far better suggestion.'

Hitler frowned. 'Speak.'

'Let him witness the agonies inflicted, then hand him on over to me. He ain't gon' know anythin' else *but* agony.'

'You want to keep him alive?'

'Oh, sure. Don't you want him to pay for try'na kill ya? I've had prisoners back in San Quentin taking part in my research for *months*. They got so used to it the results started to become redundant. But this Kaplan guy, I'll keep him alive for you, *Fuehrer*, for as long as *you* want and in so much pain he'll think he's in goddamn Hell.'

Marseille

Already the streets were crowded. Restarick, Mircalla and Kaplan found a short cut to the port by way of a market, but it was as equally as bustling. Everywhere was choked with hustlers and traders, in amongst the homeless, having been ejected from their overnight digs for the day.

A shapeless bundle of rags moved and Mircalla realised it was a man with one leg and a twisted arm, begging for money. Emaciated limbs stretched out from both sides of the narrow path through the stalls, hands grasping for even the smallest piece of loose change or a morsel of food. A mortally thin woman with an empty eye socket offered Kaplan a good time but he waved back to the wall she had been leaning against.

'We should have gone the long way 'round,' Kaplan murmured.

This was the side of the glorious *Kaiser-Regel* that no one admitted to, certainly not the Kaiser himself. The war-wounded, vagabonds, cripples and prostitutes, more disease that even the *Fuehrer* could order up in a petri dish.

'I just hope us overthrowing the Kaiser will bring an end to this suffering,' Mircalla whispered.

'You really think it will?' Kaplan sighed.

'It has to make some difference. At least people in authority will start to care.'

'I wouldn't be so sure,' Restarick mused. 'Yes, we can bring the walls down, get rid of the curfews, open up the borders… but those in their ivory towers, whether they be *kaiser* or king, they don't want to see this.'

'Then what is the point of us fighting against the *Kaiser-Regel* if the subsequent leaders would still turn a blind eye?'

'Because we would be *allowed* to help them,' said Restarick to Mircalla. 'Relief work cannot co-exist alongside a dictatorship. In a democracy, charity is someone else's responsibility. That responsibility is ours. I fought for these people's freedom. I failed. I won't let them down again.'

Kaplan clapped Restarick firmly once on the shoulder. 'My people are suffering, too. The bastards in Berlin will pay for all of this.'

Mircalla agreed, urging them on. It was coming up to 0630 and they still had to get through port checks before lining up to board. They split up as they joined the queue, pulling into a convoluted affair of their passes being checked and quadrupled-checked, conversations with multiple officials. Having no baggage to speak of seemed to bother the authorities. Mircalla said she had been mugged in the market a couple of days ago while the men separately said they naturally travel light.

They met up back onboard *El Morakeb*, watching with relief as the port of Marseille slipped away. There were a handful of people back on land interested in the ship's departure, port authorities and family and friends of the passengers and crew. Among them was one who was calmly angry that her target had boarded just as she was about to apprehend him.

Bachman turned away, shielding her eyes from the morning sun, considering now how she could reach Kaplan before he reached Algiers.

Amiens, France – August 1918

The British First Army were rejoicing. Even the stink of sweat, mould and open wounds couldn't dampen their spirits. Cheers and laughter, the sound of singing coursing through the trenches, any echo deadened by the mud and water.

The men hadn't been this buoyant in months. The general retreat ordered by Ludendorff gave a sense of hope, finally, to the Allies. Was this it? Was the Central Powers beginning to lose its nerve?

'Calm it, lads,' came the gruff retort from the sergeant. 'The bloody Hun *still has ears.'*

'Come on, sarge, they're running like rats.'

The sergeant let out a half-smile. He had to agree with the men. This was a momentous occasion but his experience told him this was a mere respite. It would be likely that the Germans would be preparing for an onslaught to overcome this brief failure.

'Let them have their few moments, Wilson,' Restarick said, nodding to the men as they filed into the dug-outs, some remaining in the trenches to start a night watch. They had been stationed here for so long now that the gloom, pierced occasionally by lanterns, did not slow their movements. It was second nature to them, finding their way.

Restarick wondered if that was a blessing or a curse. So settled where they that many of the men had almost forgotten about life anywhere else. If this was the beginning of the end, what would they all do next? Where would they go? Wives and sweethearts were waiting for some of them, but could the average Tommy adapt back to civvie life? He watched the faces of the troops, some barely eighteen, all glassy-eyed, caught up in the reverie but all too exhausted to fully understand that this perhaps wasn't it, that there were more hardships to come. They were plastered with filth and dirt, unshaven and bedraggled.

Restarick pulled himself straight and smiled and patted the men on their weary shoulders as they sidled along. Keep their spirits up. Don't let them see you be in any doubt. They're brave and loyal. You need to show them you are, too. *It was damn cold down here, even though it had been a hot day, the first in a long time. He rubbed his hands together.*

Once the soldiers had dissipated, the sergeant brought out a pouch of tobacco and followed Restarick to the officers' quarters. It was a meagre space: three narrow bunks, a table and two chairs, a radio set and a gramophone. A single lightbulb dangling from a cable running back out into the dank mud-lined corridors couldn't penetrate the shadows in every corner.

'Ciggie, sir?'

Lighting up outside was banned. If the enemy saw even the slightest wisps of smoke, they would likely send a grenade over. So the already-putrid air in the dug-outs was often thick with fumes. Restarick declined the offer, lying on one of the bunks. Tobacco was a rare commodity here and he only partook if he really needed to, not to just socially pass the time.

'It's nearly midnight. We should rest as best we can before dawn.'

The sergeant nodded and saluted. 'I'll bid you goodnight, then, sir.'

He ducked out of the hole as Captain Letts entered.

He was older than Restarick by a couple of years and had seen more action, been in service longer. He had a passionate approach to life, something that Restarick occasionally found a little tiring. But in the right circumstances, it was a breath of fresh air.

'Evening, old boy.'

'Barry,' replied Restarick. 'Good result tonight, eh?'

'Bloody good, Dan. The old boche *deserved all he got.'*

'I think we'll have orders to go again tomorrow.'

'Damn well hope so. Need to keep him on his toes. We stop now he'll think we're being smug.'

Restarick smiled, dovetailing his fingers over his chest as he looked at the planking making up the low ceiling. 'You're right. The generals are meant to be gathering now.'

'Bungo needs to give them orders sharpish.'

'You're right. No time to delay.' Restarick swung his legs back out to the floor and sat up. 'Over the top, I wouldn't be surprised.'

'You here to join us?' Letts made himself a coffee, checking the boiled water for mites.

'Meant to be passing through. This was only a social call.' Room 40 had told him to not engage while he was in Amiens. 'But I couldn't bally well sit in here while the boys sat under that barrage of the last few days.'

'Yes, don't blame you But what-ho, you're here now so get stuck in when we go over the top!'

A young boy came rushing into the room, red-faced and panting. 'Sirs…'

'What the bloody hell do you want? Don't you know to knock and wait before entering an officer's quarters?' Letts sat down. 'Speak up, lad!'

The boy looked between the two captains, clearly trying to work out who was who as he pulled a sealed envelope from his satchel. 'I have a letter for a Captain Restarick.'

'That's me…' Restarick took the muddy note from the messenger, dismissed him with a curt thank you and tore it open. 'Who the devil knows I'm here?'

'Apart from your CO?' Letts sipped his coffee.

Restarick shrugged and began to read, squinting in the gloom. His squint turned to a puzzled frown, then a look of horror. He clamped a hand over his mouth to stop him from crying out.

'You alright, old boy? Bit of bad news?'

Restarick turned away, breathed in deeply then pulled himself upright. He turned back to Letts. 'My wife...'

'Run off with the newspaper boy back home? Those lonely wives! Ha! Get yourself a bit of local totty while you're out here. I think my old todger is developing a French accent!'

'She's dead.'

Letts lowered his mug and pursed his lips. 'Shit. Bad luck, old boy. So sorry and all that.' He didn't know what else to say.

'Hmm... thanks...' Restarick's mind was reeling. He looked at the letter again, looking for any sign that it was a hoax. Someone playing a sick practical joke on him back at HQ. The envelope wasn't marked and the letter was typed. 'I need to make a call.'

'The comms officer will help you there. He's about a third of a mile westerly.'

Restarick didn't even remember finding his way to the communications room, the utter disbelief taking over any semblance of consciousness. He was offered a telephone, wound it up, and waited.

Getting through to HQ was swift enough. There was always an open line for any Room 40 operative in the field. When he asked for confirmation of the validity of the letter, his heart sank and he began to feel sick. He gently replaced a handset on the cradle, saying thank you to the lieutenant in charge, and went outside to sit in the darkness. The night chill rushed along the trenches like a demon. He didn't care about the mud or the rats at his feet, some as big as cats. He opened up the letter again and began to sob, making sure no one would notice. His tears ran warm down his face. In the distance, flashes and pops of mortar shells broke the darkness beyond the Allied lines. Restarick screwed up the letter, his grief turning to anger. He stood and slogged through the swamp-like mud, his feet damp in his boots. Men were lying along the walls, playing cards, shaving, sleeping. One was praying, the bible trembling in his palms. A few looked up at him, acknowledging his rank with a nod or salute.

He began to have a growing revulsion for everything, the cold, the hunger, the generals sitting comfortably next to their drinks cabinets. The Hun for slowly destroying the free world. The high honour of fighting for King and Country. It was all fucking meaningless. If he died right here, a bullet through his head from his own revolver, the war would still carry on. If a bomb crater replaced this hovel, none of the men would be missed. They would simply be replaced. There was insanity in what they were doing. Insanity in what others were doing to them.

If he by some miracle survived, he no longer had anything to live for. Lita was dead. A week ago now. Burned alive in a fire at their home in England. The letter said the local constabulary and firemen tried to save her but the flames' were too fierce. They found a charred body the next morning, once the fire had surrendered to a thunderstorm. She had been, they said, clasping a locket, the chain oxidised to her flesh. And in the locket, his picture safe in her palm.

It's not Lita. They must have made a mistake, surely?

But Restarick had to shut that thought down. Of course *she was dead. It was hopeless to think otherwise. The locket he'd given her as a birthday present. He'd bought it in New York and promised to take her there when the war was over. He'd returned to duty, knowing his image was always by her heart, just as hers was by his. He took it out now from his breast pocket and stared at it, at the sepia tones that accentuated her dark eyes and dark hair, her mischievous smile and full lips. He touched her cheek so tenderly, closing his eyes to remember how soft her olive skin felt under his fingertips.*

'Corazón.'

Algiers, Algeria

The sun baked the ground hard, no breeze to throw dust clouds. Only the storms from the great Sahara would impact the city from time to time. The road was cluttered with locals, all hurrying to be somewhere, all looking to sell their wares by sunset, ready to start again the next day. A minaret, pointing up high, broke the low rise buildings with their domed roofs.

Kaisersoldaten, whose authority did not extend beyond the port, stood nervously around, fully conscious that they were not welcome here at this French-controlled colony. They were viewed as the invaders they were by the locals as well as the French bureaucracy. Out in the bay, German cruisers loitered, watching the shore, waiting for something that might never happen. They were like tigers behind bars, prowling back and forth, unable to come any closer but still grandiose in demonstrating their power.

Bachman, her blonde hair covered by a hat and scarf, bright eyes hidden behind sunglasses, sat in a small café drinking tea while waiting for the disembarkation of *El Morakeb* to be completed. The vessel had recently docked and she could freely see all comings and goings. It would not be difficult to spot Kaplan as he stepped onto dry land. She had arrived the day before, her superiors irked that she had missed her target at Marseille but still confident in her abilities to bring him in. They had secured her a flight that had brought her in to a landing strip ten kilometres east of Algiers. She dismissed the café owner three times while she was sitting there for at least half an hour.

And there he was at last… looking a little gaunt than the last time they had been face to face, but still powerful enough to be a worthy opponent.

She finished her spiced tea and threw some coins in a dish. In a swift movement she descended the steps to the bay, the pistol snug in the small of her back under her shirt. A quick arrest and Kaplan would be handcuffed and back on board *El Morakeb* for its return journey.

Moving around to come up behind him, she paused as he looked at his watch, scanning the port around him. A truck, an old battered French thing sold off after the war, lumbered by and came to a shuddering stop. Resuming her stealth approach, she pulled her weapon, aiming at the back of his head.

Kaplan tensed as he heard the gun cock.

'Don't make any sudden moves, *Herr* Kaplan. You are ordered to return to Berlin to face charges.'

He raised in hands. 'I know that voice… Where did they dig you up from?' He spun to face her, ignoring her prior demand. He knew she wouldn't kill him if her orders were to take him to Germany.

Bachman stepped back slightly. 'You're coming with me.'

'I think not,' Mircalla whispered in her ear, a small dagger pressed against Bachman's spine. 'Now drop the gun before our soldier friends over there become interested in our little gathering.'

Bachman went to thrust an elbow out into Mircalla's face. Restarick stepped in between them, shaking his head.

'This isn't a very nice welcome,' he said. 'And you have no jurisdiction here. This is still French soil.'

'What do you want with him?' Mircalla asked, relieving Bachman of her weapon.

'My attempt at killing our beloved *Fuehrer*, I would imagine. Nice to see you again, Bachman.'

'You know her?' Restarick moved Bachman around and sat her on a low wall nearby.

'Of course he does. Biblically, I'd imagine. He's slept with half the Central Powers.'

Kaplan glared at Mircalla, a look matched by the one Bachman was giving all of them.

'I know you, too,' Bachman spat. 'You were hanging on his arm at that ball in the mountains.' There was no jealousy there, it was disgust.

Mircalla didn't recall. 'You were obviously part of the furniture,' she shrugged.

'Are these two your personal protectors, Kaplan? You think running to Africa will save you? The Kaiser tightens his grip everywhere. Soon the whole world will be his.'

'And you're cleaning up the place for him, is that it?'

'I am here on the orders of our *Fuehrer*. You are a traitor.'

'I am? He's a traitor to the Central Powers! The Kaiser would never have authorised the genocide of an innocent people!

'Unless you are truly loyal to him, no one is innocent. The *Fuehrer* offers the gift of release, to give those who are guilty of evil the chance to purge the world *of* their evil.'

'Evil?' Restarick snorted. 'This Hitler… He's insane! To be willing to commit genocide!'

'You talk of genocide. He does not,' Bachman replied matter-of-factly. 'He has a solution.'

'How about we take you back to England and you can be instrumental in the downfall of the Kaiser and his goons?' Restarick said.

'Your precious Room 40 is nothing,' Bachman sneered. 'You are playing at spies. Even one of your own has defected. I realise who you are now, you, *Englander* and the French whore. You have been sent on a mission to find him. Oh yes, the defection is known. Max Baker, decorated captain of the British Army, recruited into a weak underground Allied organisation to overthrow the *Kaiser-Regel* through deceit and lies. But he has come over to us. And you want him back. I am surprised Kaplan has been sucked into your pointless endeavour.' She turned to look Kaplan in the eye. 'Release yourself from them. Release me from them. We can return to Berlin together and you can re-offer your loyalty. You were glorious in the early days of the victory. The *Fuehrer* will see that for himself. He will forgive you for your moment of weakness. He is a compassionate man. You can be a great leader in the New Order!' Bachman said it with such conviction that Kaplan realised she genuinely believed it all.

'The *Fuehrer* asked me to murder my own people. I would gladly stand before him so I can get the chance to kill him again!'

'You were not asked to kill anybody. You were just giving them a gift. If they lived or died isn't the *Fuehrer*'s decision.'

'I've had enough of this crap,' Restarick said. 'I consider myself a calm and understanding man, but you—what did you say her name was… Bachman? You should be shot here and now.'

'Then do it,' Bachman shrugged. 'The *kaisersoldaten* will be over here before I hit the ground and you will all be arrested, French soil or not. There are still laws against murder, even in this slum of a country.' She looked at the three of them. 'If you run, if you leave me here, I will call them over and you will be apprehended. I tell them you are *Englander* spies and they will shoot you. So what will it be?'

'You know me of old, Bachman. I know you,' began Kaplan. 'You wouldn't give up the chance to bring me in alive yourself so easily but I feel you didn't expect to catch up with me so quickly. You were hoping for a hunt. This has frustrated you. That said, we seem to be at some sort of an impasse here for the moment.'

Bachman folded her arms. 'What are you suggesting? That we just go our separate ways?'

'Why not?' Mircalla responded. 'I could slit your throat right now and we'd be up the steps and into the city before your *kaisersoldaten* friends would even realise.'

'You can get us killed, all three of us. Or she can kill you,' Restarick confirmed, nodding to Mircalla. 'What's it to be?'

Bachman squinted, the sun glaring off the sea. 'You choose your companions well, Kaplan. They are not stupid.'

'Then leave.' Kaplan stepped back and opened his arms to indicate she was to go. 'Now.'

Cautiously, Bachman stood. 'I will find you. I will kill all three of you. Do not sleep at night.'

'Who can sleep in the world you created?' replied Restarick.

Grinding her teeth she looked at her pistol in Restarick's grip and cursed under her breath. She was expected to report in this evening. This incident she would *not* mention.

As she strode away, her gait determined and quick, Restarick sighed with relief. 'How did you know she would agree?'

'Her family own hunting lodges across Bavaria,' explained Kaplan. 'She was born with a shotgun in her hands. She's too proud. Hunting for sport is in her blood. So we'll *give* her some sport.'

'If she's that good, aren't we at a disadvantage?' Mircalla asked.

Kaplan smiled. 'Then we had better get going ourselves.' His expression turned to surprise as Mircalla clambered up into the cab of the old lorry.

'Best I could do,' she shrugged.

'We've got a couple of rifles, too,' Restarick added, climbing up into the passenger side, Kaplan following.

'Hopefully they're not muskets,' Kaplan breathed, as Mircalla manoeuvred the vehicle past the soldiers, the port staff and the milling locals up the incline to the coast road, heading east.

'Your girlfriend is getting friendly with the *kaisersoldaten*,' she pointed out. 'She'll be on our tail pretty soon.'

'We won't be hard to spot in this thing,' Kaplan replied, checking over the rifles Restarick had stored under the long seat. 'Put your food down. Let's get some distance between us.'

The lorry roared in indignation and thundered on.

Bachman swore, glaring at its retreat. This was the second time Kaplan had slipped through her fingers.

There wouldn't be a third.

London

The billiard balls clacked against each other on the green baize as the usher brought in a telegram, leaving as quietly as he'd entered. Pausing the game for the moment, Swinton puffed on his cigar, waiting for Chard to read the message.

Satisfied with what it said, Chard threw the telegram into the grate, watching it burn to nothing before returning to the table and picking up his cue.

'Where were we?'

'Top left, yellow,' Swinton said.

'And…' Chard struck the white and it sailed across the table, deftly missing the two reds nestled near the last yellow, the latter ball dropping into the pocket with a satisfying clunk. 'There we go. Two games to me.'

'Best to let you win, Bladder, old chap,' Swinton said as Chard put his cue back in the rack and sat in his favourite armchair. A tumbler of whiskey was waiting for him.

'To a good loser,' Chard said, raising his glass. He downed the contents in one mouthful.

Swinton nodded, gesturing with his cigar. 'Thank you. I make losing look easy.'

He moved to the tall sash windows that overlooked Pall Mall. Outside the Langelaan Club it was a bright morning and traffic was growing heavy. A policeman with his arms in white bands directed the trolley buses and cars.

'Our man is in Algiers,' Chard announced.

'That's good, isn't it?'

Chard stared at the empty tumbler, as if willing it to refill itself. Swinton took the hint and moved to assist. 'One of the Resistance fellows saw him last. They say he's with that woman you have a soft spot for.'

'Mircalla Richard? Good God, I thought she was in Japan.'

'Appears not. Wouldn't surprise me if the Chief had sent her out to keep an eye on things.'

'Restarick's no trouble. You did ask me to send our best man out to bring Baker in.'

'Oh, no trouble if you say he's not. No, I think the Chief is getting a tad paranoid in his old age.' Chard took a sip of his fresh whiskey. 'Having one yourself, Swinton?'

'Later, perhaps. Who's this Resistance chap?'

'Barnabas. He went rogue just after the war. Bit of a nuisance. Bloody glad he's on our side, though. He has can act more directly than we at the moment so the Chief is willing to turn a blind eye. What's happening about that gas mask mystery?'

'The Versailles lot have it. They say it's effective against that peculiar virus the Kaiser's aide caught. They're making copies of it. They think the *boche* are up to no good behind the scenes.'

'Damn germ warfare is a dirty way to fight a battle,' sighed Chard, recalling full well the agonies cause on the Western Front by the mustard gas. 'I hope we're wrong about what this Hitler chap is planning.'

'Word has it, Bladder, that something happened in Poland. A bit hush-hush but the *kaisersoldaten* there were seen wearing the new masks.'

'Testing it out, whatever it is.'

'Yes.'

'The quicker your man can bring Baker in the better I'll feel. Interrogation, that's what's needed here. Understand why the hell Baker ran off like that and what Kaiser Bill is up to.'

'It's his aide, this Hitler, that seems to be pulling the strings now.'

Chard nodded, finishing his drink. He coughed slightly as he lit a cigarette. 'The Kaiser's not far off seventy. He is surrounding himself with younger officers to carry on his conquest. That makes the whole situation far more dangerous. These new bloods are radical. They will squash us old men like we're annoying fleas. It's up to the likes of Restarick, Richard and Barnabas to keep fighting. God knows what will happen if we fall off the horse now.'

A knock at the tall oak door and the usher re-entered with another telegram. Silently he handed it to Chard who waved it away.

Swinton took it, opening it as the usher left. 'Good Lord.'

'What?'

'Tanks have entered the grounds at Buckingham Palace.'

Chard leant forward, eyes narrowing. 'The Kaiser? He won't fool us again like he did at Hyde Park!'

'No. The tanks are to be deployed across the capital. They're delivering a gift, apparently.'

'A gift?' tutted Chard. 'What *are* you talking about?'

Swinton shook his head and handed his senior colleague the slip of paper.

HAR 2365 LANG 3=
TANKS IN BUCK PALACE URGNT STOP
DELIVERY OF GIFT TO CAPITAL STOP
TANKS TO BE DEPLOYED TO ASSIST STOP
NEW GAS MSKS NEEDED NOW STOP
= R40 +

'This gift…' began Chard.

'Bladder?'

'It's the bloody virus. It has to be! Why else would the Factory tell us we need the new masks? Hitler intends to wipe us out! Get on to our friends elsewhere. See if the same is happening anywhere else.'

Berlin

Voigt was nervous. He'd been called to the Reich Chancellery, the first time since his humiliation by the *Fuehrer*, and was standing outside his leader's office, breathing shallowly, his hands clasped behind his back to stop them from shaking.

News had swept through the *Kaiser-Regel* of the decision to release the gift at key points across the empire, so what was the *Fuehrer's* need for him this afternoon?

'Enter,' came the call from the other side of the door.

He swallowed hard and entered Hitler's private office. As well as Hitler himself, there were three others present: Heinrich Hoffman, he knew; the American doctor, Leo Stanley; and a pretty, slight woman who could only be Eva Braun, the *Fuehrer*'s mistress.

The room was stuffy. Braun was at Hitler's shoulder while the two men sat across from him. Hitler stood as Voigt strode up to them, raising his right arm straight out at an angle.

'*Heil*, Hitler.'

The salute, insisted upon in recent days by the Fuehrer, was met by the man himself responding similarly with a brief palm-out action at the wrist.

'Voigt. Why is the traitor Kaplan not yet in Berlin?'

'*Fraulein* Bachman has been unable to apprehend him. She was in contact with me only this morning. '

'You advised me she was efficient. Is this another example of your command?'

'With respect, *mein Fuehrer*, Algiers is a French colony and—'

Hitler's eyes widened and his cheek began to twitch. To be reminded that Algeria was still controlled by Allied scum angered him. Braun placed a hand on his arm, and his tension eased. 'Bachman will not be required to go through border controls while there. There are no border controls! Nothing should be slowing her pace.'

'Kaplan is proving to be a very elusive individual. He will be brought in within the week.'

'It is Wednesday now, *Herr* Voigt,' said Hoffman. 'Your week is disappearing fast.'

You're just the Fuehrer's *photographer. I don't appreciate your tone.* 'Thank you, *Herr* Hoffman. I have faith in my operative's abilities.'

'Now,' Hitler said, clapping once the rubbing his hands together, 'let us talk about the gift.'

'I'm surprised you got it out there darn quick,' drawled Stanley. 'What you plannin' on doin' to contain it?'

'We are closing the borders effective immediately. All subjects are ordered to stay in their chosen places of worship to allow the gift to spread amongst those it is intended for. There will be no access to hospitals for them. All *heimklasse* will be required to report to their local *kommandant* in four weeks from the delivery. Your vaccine, *Herr Doktor*, will be given to those who attend. Those who do not will be considered unworthy and left so that nature can take its course.'

'Goddamn survival of the fittest! Ha! Beautiful! You guys sure are somethin' else.'

Hitler narrowed his eyes at the brashness of the American. He couldn't decide if he liked him or not. He could certainly endure him for as long as was required. Once this exercise had been carried out, perhaps the doctor would no longer be needed. Then again, it was always useful to have a man with such passion for human tolerance levels on board.

'You will begin manufacturing the vaccine at once.'

Fatnassa, Tunisia

The great tyres threw up clouds of sand and dust as Mircalla kept her foot to the floor.

They had been driving for a good ten hours, taking it in turns to keep alert. So far, from what they could see behind them, Bachman was not following.

The road ahead was long and straight, the vista of desert never ending. The heat was overbearing but Restarick, used to the swelter of Sri Lanka, found it unpleasant but manageable. He mopped his brow with his sleeve and took a sip of water from a flask.

They had found provisions in a small village some one hundred kilometres back, food, water, some ammunition left over by the Italians during the war. They had haggled hard for a price, not many locals wishing to trade with *kaisermarks.* Mircalla had managed to exchange some for *francs* while still in Algiers, but the response was much the same. *They are worth nothing here! It is like trading with the wind!* Restarick had swapped Bachman's pistol with a Luger, finding the weight and grip better.

Another twenty kilometres and the landscape changed. From out of the shimmering horizon loomed a valley, as bleak and desolate as the rest of the country. The road felt as if it were descending, such was the effect of the rocks rising up either side.

'I need to piss,' Kaplan announced.

'We're not stopping here,' Restarick said. 'We're too enclosed.'

'Just a few seconds,' Kaplan insisted. 'We're not deep into the valley yet, we'll be fine.'

Mircalla sighed and angled the lorry to the side of the rough road. 'We could stretch our legs, then. But quickly. How far to Mellaha?'

Restarick looked at the map they'd brought with them from France. A local shopkeeper in Algiers had been able to mark out some of the missing information for them. 'Five hundred kilometres I'd say. About another six hours drive?'

'Sounds about right.' Kaplan jumped down, followed by Restarick. He moved away from them, unbuttoning his trousers. Mircalla switched off the engine and climbed down. She lit a cigarette and Restarick joined her in a smoke. Kaplan sighed with relief as he urinated over the sandy floor, returning to them, trousers readjusted, dusting his hands. 'Okay, a few minutes.'

The heat was just as brutal in the entrance to the valley road, but there was a scorching breeze that was, at least, preferable to the sun's relentless gaze.

They were headed to *aeroporto militare di Mellaha*, where Mircalla assured them they could charter a plane to Cairo. She had a couple of favours she could call in with its airport commander she'd met while they were both stationed in Rome. Kaplan didn't ask. Restarick didn't want to know.

'From there it's your lead, Daniel. Have you thought anymore about where this folly might be?'

Restarick nodded. 'On the boat over, I managed to get some research in. The captain has quite a surprising library.'

'He must get bored doing that crossing, a day there, a day back,' Kaplan murmured.

'I found something that was potentially invaluable. Heliopolis. An ancient city. It's where a place called *Ayn Shams* now is, to the northeast of Cairo.'

'Why there?' asked Mircalla.

'It's the only reference of a folly in Cairo. It has to be the place.'

'And if your agent isn't there?' shrugged Kaplan.

'Then I've brought the two of you on a wild goose chase.'

'"Goose chase"?' frowned Kaplan.

'English expression. It means a waste of time,' explained Mircalla.

Kaplan laughed gently then stopped. 'There is something on the ridge. Do not turn.'

Restarick was angled to where Kaplan was subtly nodding. He flicked his eyes up without needing to crane his neck. A glint of metal in the sun. It glinted again, then moved slightly. A ricochet of a bullet made the three jump.

'I think she's caught up with us!' growled Restarick. 'Let's go!'

Mircalla and Kaplan needed no further prompting.

But once aboard, the lorry wouldn't start.

More bullets.

'Come on!' hissed Kaplan as Restarick loaded his Luger and shot towards the reflection.

Finally the engine shuddered into life, Mircalla wrenching the gears and ploughing the vehicle on into the valley.

On the crest, Bachman looked past her rifle's sights at the moving lorry, slung the weapon over her shoulder and jumped onto the horse she'd taken from a Bedouin. There was a slope that descended to the road. She urged the beast on, the grey horse whinnying and wheezing in protest. Now she was behind the lorry, dust and debris flying at her from the heavy wheels. If she could just shoot out one of the tires…

Then again, she might make use of the vehicle to take Kaplan back to Algiers. He was still with those two Room 40 operatives. She would dispose of them. Best not to damage the lorry too badly, she decided. Her thighs gripped the horse as she aimed the rifle with both hands. The left wing mirror… gone. Now the right one. Lowering the gun, she reined the horse over to the other side of the track.

Mircalla swung the lorry, almost toppling it as the road dipped to a slight ditch. It was enough to slow Bachman who pulled up hard. The horse skidded to a halt as the lorry careened back onto the road.

'*Scheiße!*'

The gears whined in agony as they dropped into first, then a burst of power forced the lorry on. Mircalla's knuckles were white around the steering wheel. 'Where is she? Is she still with us?'

Restarick looked out of the window, devoid of glass, in the rear of the cab behind their heads. The tarpaulin covering behind was flapping and snapping with the velocity. Through the dust, he could make out Bachman on her circling horse. The animal seemed reluctant to continue the chase, but a sharp dig in either side of its flanks from her boot heels and it was off again, churning up the ground with its hooves, making little flurries.

'She's not giving up!' he called.

Kaplan thumped the dashboard. 'There… Up there!' He pointed to a slope that carried the road off in a fork up the side of the valley.

Mircalla obliged and move through the gears, guiding the lorry up the incline. 'I hope she follows. Then I can ram the bitch off down the side.' But Bachman ignored the slope and carried on along the road, the horse snorting and breathing hard. 'Where the hell is she going?'

Restarick leaned out and peered over the edge. He looked ahead. On the other side of the track was another incline. 'She's headed for the other side of the ridge.'

'What the hell for?' Kaplan wheezed. He grabbed a rifle and thrust it in Restarick's hands. 'Use this instead of that fucking pop gun.'

Within seconds, Restarick had Bachman in the rifle sights. It had been a while, but the old disciplines came back quickly enough. The rocking of the truck made no difference. This was what he had been trained for. Squeezing the trigger, he fired. His aim was true, even through the billowing dust.

In a moment of clarity, where the sand tumbled and curled, on the opposite ridge they saw the horse was riderless, but nevertheless still galloping of its own volition.

'Good shot,' Kaplan said, Restarick sitting back, the warm rifle between his legs.

'Let's get off this ridge and back on the road,' Mircalla said, finding a descending path. The lorry rocked and swayed then levelled up to resume its course on the flatter surface. Kaplan passed around a flask of water as Mircalla eased off the gas and brought the speed down to a more comfortable pace.

But their reverie was short-lived.

A thump above and behind them. Restarick saw nothing from the remaining wing mirror. Kaplan twisted around to see the great blade of a Bowie knife slicing through the tarpaulin then disappear. Two hands ripped the slit wide. Bachman drop down, feet first, into the rear of the lorry.

Eyes blazing in fury, she dashed towards the cab's opening and grabbed at Kaplan's hair. His face struck the edge of the pane, creating a ruby welt under his right eye. Mircalla veered the truck to topple their passenger, but it only made her grip tighter to Kaplan's scalp.

So she braked, and hard.

It worked!

Bachman let go, sliding straight into the back of the cab. Kaplan reacted immediately and dived through the gap as Mircalla sped off again.

He rained a series of blows upon her shoulders and neck, but Bachman parried them all, rolling out from under him. She kicked out and he fell onto his backside, unable to stand as the lorry bumped and swayed. Instead, he used the momentum to grab at Bachman's legs, rolling her with him, not unlike how an alligator envelops its prey—but she was the animal here and her knife flashed out and pierced Kaplan's thigh. He cried out and clutched at the wound, allowing Bachman to wriggle out from under him. She stood, holding onto the lorry's metal frame, the Bowie knife still drawn in her other hand. She snapped her head forward as the lorry came to a stop, brakes squealing, pneumatics hissing. She realised she was outnumbered again, and this time there were no *kaisersoldaten* to call upon.

She heard the cab's doors open and close. In a flash, her knife was re-sheathed and she dived through the little window as Mircalla and Restarick crept alongside the lorry to the rear. The stupid French whore had left the engine running!

Rifles raised and pointed into the tarpaulin, Restarick and Mircalla looked on in dawning realisation. The vehicle suddenly burst into movement.

'Fuck!' Restarick dived forward, grabbing the tailgate. But he couldn't hold on and stumbled to the ground.

Mircalla jumped over him, lighter, more agile, throwing herself at the lorry, using her elbows to hook onto the back. She clambered up, checking Kaplan over with a cursory glance. In the driver's seat, Bachman glanced back and cursed, pulling on the steering wheel. Mircalla stumbled. She had to get to Bachman… but how?

The torn opening in the roof!

She hopped forward, pulled herself up and onto the top of the tarpaulin. The wind was tremendous and nearly knocked her off more than once as she crawled, spider-like, along towards the cab. Holding on to the frame just behind the cab on the driver's side, she thrust herself over and around, legs through the driver's window, knocking Bachman clean out of her seat.

The lorry swerved violently and struck the valley wall, the right wing mirror crushed and the canvas ripped to shreds.

Bachman grabbed onto the wheel, dodging Mircalla's flying kicks, bringing the vehicle back to the centre of the track. Mircalla wriggled in through and punched Bachman in the jaw, sliding to where she had been sitting, wrestling the wheel from her.

A series of punches, elbowing and a head-butt (the latter from Mircalla), the lorry kept going. Roaring in indignation, Bachman's knife was out again, slashing and stabbing, catching Mircalla's forearms. In response, Mircalla grabbed the back of Bachman's head and thrust her face forward, to meet her knee coming in the other direction. Bachman lolled, dazed and bloodied, her nose smashed across her face. Mircalla kicked her along the seat, once, twice, a third time. The passenger door swung open and Bachman tumbled out, a flurry of arms, legs and blood, to hit the ground hard.

Mircalla looked behind her to see Restarick haring up the track. Of Bachman she could see no sign. She pulled the lorry to a stop and switched off the engine, resting her forehead against the steering wheel for a moment.

'You alright back there?' she asked turning to peer at Kaplan.

'Like I'm in a cocktail shaker,' Kaplan gasped. 'You?'

'That woman's face must be made of stone. I think I broke my kneecap on it,' she sighed, wincing as she moved her legs. 'She was like a machi—'

'Watch out!' cried Kaplan as Bachman's shattered aspect appeared at Mircalla's left shoulder. The German wrenched open the door, grabbing at her arm. Kaplan was scrambling to the tailgate to jump down.

Startled, Mircalla tried to dodge out of Bachman's way but found herself on the ground, rocks and shingle digging into her back. Bachman was on top of her, knife raised, its terrifying blade flashing in the sun. In a blur, Kaplan's boot met with Bachman's chin and she crashed to the floor. Kaplan followed, intending to pin her down but he gasped suddenly, the air sucked from his lungs. He looked down in surprise to see the Bowie knife protruding from his chest. He collapsed back, his head hitting the lorry's front wheel, as Mircalla heard Restarick's Luger opening fire, shooting Bachman dead between the eyes.

'Are you badly hurt?'

Mircalla shook her head, gesturing to Kaplan. 'Is he—?'

'No. He's still alive,' Restarick confirmed, sliding to Kaplan and placing a hand on his shoulder. 'You'll be okay, Aaron. I need to find something to staunch the blood.'

Restarick looked at the canvas but, as ripped as it already was, it was too coarse for a bandage. Instead, he tore the sleeves of his own shirt. Kaplan cried out as pressure was applied to the wound, Restarick ignoring his attempts to say no.

Mircalla shuffled over to them. 'Daniel, he's not going to make it. We're too far from anywhere and he's losing a lot of blood.' It was pouring into Kaplan's lap.

'We can't leave him here!' Restarick never left a man out in the field alone. He took Kaplan's hand and placed it over the sodden material, then stood, bringing

Mircalla with him. Lowering his voice, he said, 'Even if the chances of survival are slim, getting a fallen comrade back to base is something I will *never* dismiss. He came this far with us. He tried to assassinate his own superior. I know the Factory can be an icy club, but some of us do still have a little bit of compassion left.'

'I'll…' Kaplan said, weakly. 'I'll make the decision easy for you…'

They both turned to look at him in horror. Kaplan had the handle of the Bowie knife in both hands. With an effort that literally took the air from him, he wrenched the blade out, dropping it to the dusty ground. Restarick rushed to him, Mircalla alongside.

'What the bloody hell…?'

'She's right. I won't even… last getting into the back of the lorry,' he gasped. 'You have your mission to complete. I failed at mine. Catch your tame goose…'

'Don't be a damn martyr!' Restarick hissed, angry at Kaplan's decision to quicken the end, angry at himself for letting Bachman through. Yet he knew that there was nothing they could do to help him. Mircalla was right. She wasn't unfeeling. She was well-trained. He wondered if he was finally getting too soft for this life. Room 40 had promised him retirement after this. He'd long assumed he'd wanted to give it all up before the offer, but there had always been a hankering, an itch he couldn't scratch. Guilt for not shooting the spy ten years ago; guilt over his beautiful Lita, dead in his absence, over his father struggling to cope on the plantation… Perhaps Angela was right. Perhaps he was still playing at soldiers instead of focusing on the here and now. Running away seemed the safest place to be.

He stepped back from Kaplan as the life left him.

Mircalla turned her face away, biting her bottom lip.

'I'm… sorry,' he whispered.

She turned back and looked Restarick straight in the eye, her expression blank. 'Don't be. He wouldn't be. He wouldn't shed a tear for us.'

Restarick looked down at Kaplan. He hadn't had any time to get to know the man, even on the slow crossing to Algiers. His manner around other had always indicated a lack of trust. Only Mircalla's presence had let him relax more. Certainly the betrayal of his superiors to his people weighed heavily on him. Perhaps Kaplan being here was him running away, too. Perhaps they were *all* running from something.

'We need to bury him.'

Mircalla pursed her lips. 'I don't know the whole process but I know that *k'vod hamet* needs to take place.'

'That's a Jewish thing?'

'It's honouring the dead.'

'Then we need to take him with us. Perhaps someone at the airbase can find a rabbi.' Restarick moved over to Bachman, grabbing her rifle and the bag of ammunition over her shoulder.

'*She* can rot for all I fucking care,' spat Mircalla, glaring at her prone corpse.

'You want to leave her here?'

'Do your sensibilities include dragging your dead enemies along wherever you go?'

'No. They don't.'

As the wind howled through the valley, the hot sun unrelenting, Restarick used the Bowie knife to cut some of the canvas, putting together a make-shift shroud for Kaplan. Carefully and in silence, for it seemed inappropriate to say anymore, Mircalla helped place him onto the back of the lorry.

London

Trafalgar Square, St. Paul's Cathedral, Westminster Bridge… the list went on. It was like a tourist's inventory, except the tourists each weighed five tonnes and were not stopping for ice-cream.

The tanks, six in each location, accompanied a staff car, in which a *Kaiser-Regel* general, beneath the fluttering standards of the Kaiser himself, announced by electric tannoy the instruction the people were to follow as the virus was released.

Paris, France

The Champs-Élysées trembled as the tanks moved slowly and menacingly out across the suburbs, echoing their counterparts across the channel. More instructions, more demands, no negotiations.

Aberystwyth, Wales

No one could agree on which city had the honour of being the country's capital. When the *Kaiser-Regel* razed Cardiff to the ground, no one in Aberystwyth raised an objection. That was, until the tanks moved in via the bridge over the river Rheidol, the attending generals proclaiming that all right to freedom of movement had been suspended and that everyone was to go to the handful of churches and stay within until commanded otherwise.

Edinburgh, Scotland

The Scots had had more than their fair share of invaders over the centuries and the Kaiser and his *Sassenachs* were simply another in a long line. Resistance, however apparently futile, was an everyday occurrence and the townspeople had no qualms about attacking the local *kaisersoldaten* headquarters or blatantly ignoring curfews. Many a time had the city and surrounding villages been put into lockdown, but it made little difference. There had even been talk that the *Kaiser-Regel* would rebuild Emperor Hadrian's ancient defence. Some Scots had encouraged the thought: the Kaiser would be better off walled *out* of the country than being in it with them.

When the tanks rolled down Princes Street, one was set alight and two *kaisersoldaten* killed. The response was swift and brutal, the *Gauleiter* having no qualms about executing the troublemakers where they stood. Force was met with force. With the crowds eventually dispersed and the young and old herded into St Giles' Cathedral, the *Gauleiter*, under the command of the attending general, kept the tanks trained on the building, considering that at least one rescue attempt would be made while the gift was being delivered.

Kalpitiya, Ceylon

Angela sat at the little bar, a gin and tonic on ice resting at her elbow. The sun was low in the sky now but still beautifully warm. It glowed a satisfying orange across the sea.

She'd stopped being angry at her brother after a few days. She was resigned to the fact that he would take off suddenly, just a note left with Raj to stay he'd be back soon. He would never say where he was going—he wasn't allowed to, for a start—and Angela was left to run things until he got back.

She'd just wrapped up a meeting with an exporter with distribution channels in America. While it wasn't a country well known for its tea drinking, it was an outlet that Angela hoped would eventually prove viable. Without trying, she would never know, and Daniel wasn't here to tell her not to.

She looked at her watch. Raj would be here in less than an hour with the car to drive her back to Pilawala. She could take a stroll along the beach or head to the market before it closed for the day.

'Mrs Eades!'

Angela turned, recognising the voice. 'Raj! You're early.' She tried to hide her disappointment. She had been looking forward to some time alone but she couldn't keep Raj hanging around. But he look flustered, anxious. His dark skin was red under his eyes. 'What is it?'

'It's the boss, Mrs Eades.'

'Daniel?' She sipped her gin. She wasn't about to rush for him. If he was back, he can damn well wait.

'No, Mrs Eades. Mr Restarick.' Raj's eye looked worried, as if trying to tell her without actually telling her.

'Dad?'

Raj wobbled his head frantically. 'You must come home now.'

Angela stood, pushing her glass away, grabbing her clutch bag. 'What's happened?'

'Mrs Eades, I'm sorry, so sorry.'

'Oh my God.' Angela stood, her thoughts cascading. Father had been doing so well, recently. He was up and about, eating well, even taking an interest in the crops.

'The car is out front. I take you home now.'

She nodded, holding back tears. What was wrong with him? Had he fallen? Had a stroke? It must have been serious for Raj to come earlier than arranged.

She ignored, initially, the gasps and mutterings from the bar's other patrons. There was usually something happening on the beach that vied for peoples' attentions. But their attitudes were different somehow, more dramatic, more disbelieving.

She allowed herself a quick glance to where everyone was headed.

Out in the sea, some few hundred yards from the delicately soft sand was a shape. Grey and tinted by the setting sun, it was rectangular but curiously slightly angled at the same time. It was motionless. How long it had been there no one seemed to know, but it was there nevertheless. Further along, still in the water and at the same distance from the beach as the first, was another.

Coming from them both, towards the shore, were a handful of inflatable motorboats, dinghies carrying what looked like soldiers.

With dawning realisation at the same time as the other witnesses, Angela realised what the shapes were. They were submarines, their metal sails giving nothing away of the size of the vessels under the water line. Raj touched her arm, squinting from the orange sun.

'Who are they, Mrs Eades?'

She didn't want to answer him. She didn't want to admit that Daniel had seen this day coming.

They were soldiers and they were armed.

In a sleepy coastal village, miles away from Ceylon's bustling, financial capital of Colombo, the *Kaiser-Regel* had quietly arrived.

Mellaha, Libya

The aerodrome control tower was like an oven at the height of the day. For that reason, there were very few flights scheduled around that time and the duty watch was shared between a greater number of *sottotenente* than usual to alleviate the length of time spent in it. Nevertheless, it was necessary for the tower to always be manned to spot any enemy aircraft, especially with the looming threat of the *Kaiser-Regel* in the Mediterranean Sea.

Because no one was looking at the ground, the battered lorry with its flapping canvas tarpaulin was almost upon the airbase before the alarm was raised.

Two jeeps were sent out to meet it as it approached the wire-fence perimeter, the soldiers of the Italian air force armed and ready. The Italians had been stationed here since the outbreak of the war and with no incursions by the Central Powers had stayed. Their continued presence seemed to deter any major attempt by the Kaiser to occupy North Africa and they had proven invaluable to Room 40's need to secretly move operatives around outside of the European borders.

'This is most unusual. We had no word of your arrival,' *Tenente Colonello* Verrechia said once Mircalla had been identified and she and Restarick taken to see the airbase commander.

'This is actually Captain Restarick's operation,' she explained. 'But thank you for your hospitality. We have a colleague with us. He unfortunately did not survive an incident with an agent of the *Kaiser-Regel*.'

'We were unable to bury him in the desert,' Restarick said.

'How so?'

'His beliefs would not permit it and we couldn't disrespect that,' Mircalla explained. 'Do you have a rabbi on the base?'

Verrechia shook his head. 'This is predominantly Muslim. I think you are going to struggle to find someone to bury him correctly.'

'Will there be anyone in Cairo who could?'

Verrechia frowned at Restarick, his long Roman nose wrinkling. 'Cairo? Possibly.'

'That's where we're headed. We had assumed we could bury Kaplan before we departed.'

'I think the heat will make you decide otherwise. Cairo is a long way from here. You need a new vehicle? It looks like your transport has seen better days, no?'

Mircalla glanced at Restarick then back at the lieutenant-colonel. 'I have a request to make of you.'

An airman entered the office, carrying with him a tray of tin cups and a large jug of water. A bucket of ice cubes, water collecting on its exterior, was placed on the corner of Verrechia's desk.

'Help yourself.' Verrechia said, motioning as the young officer left. 'The water has been boiled. The local supply can sometimes play havoc with your guts. What can I do for you?'

'We were hoping to borrow one of your smaller aircraft.'

Verrechia laughed, then realised she was serious. 'By borrow, I think you mean to return it?' Mircalla nodded sipping at her refreshing iced water. 'We do not run a hire service for the British Secret Service.'

'We can fly Kaplan there.'

'Just to bury him? Then you bring the aircraft back?'

'Yes.' Restarick drank down his water.

'I cannot give you an airplane that's large enough to carry him. He will need to be packed in ice. You would draw attention to the Kaiser's boats out to sea.' Verrechia thought for a moment. He wasn't an unreasonable man. 'Is your colleague the only reason you need to fly to Cairo?'

'No.' Restarick placed the cup on the desk. 'I am instructed to return a missing agent to our HQ in London.'

'We had another of your people coming through here some weeks ago.'

'You did?'

'That's why you two arriving here is unusual. He was unannounced, also. I understand the need for discreet movements, but three operatives in as many months? Him and now you two.'

Restarick leaned forward in his chair. 'What was his name?'

Verrechia thought for a moment. 'Baker. Yes, Baker. He said his mission was of utmost urgency. He had papers to say he had authority to use a plane. We had an old Armstrong-Whitworth he was more than happy to take. We didn't want it. Always breaking down.'

Restarick felt the excitement of being closer to his goal. So Cairo wasn't just a hunch, wasn't just a raving of a fool. 'We need to get to Cairo now, Mircalla.'

'He wasn't going to Cairo,' Verrechia said.

'But...' Restarick gripped the arm of the chair. 'Are you sure? Did he say where he was going?'

Verrechia smiled through his tanned, Italian features. 'I know why you think he was. But Cairo will do you no good, unless you wish to see the Pyramids.'

'I understood he was going to the Cairo folly,' Restarick said. 'Why am I wrong?'

'This is a message Baker left you?'

Restarick sighed. 'No. I was told this by someone else. "Cairo's folly is not to be dismissed". It was a statement taken by a police officer.'

'When Baker gave us his papers, he told us he was heading for Kairos, not Cairo.'

Restarick tilted his head. 'I've not heard of that. Is it in Greece?'

'No. It's not anywhere.'

'Then where did he go?'

Verrechia stood and moved to the wall behind his desk. On it was pinned a large map of the world. He pointed to an area west of Cyprus, a blank spot in the middle of the Mediterranean Sea. 'Here.'

'What's there?' Mircalla went to look herself, peering at the map.

'Nothing.'

'So he went to a place that's nowhere and that has nothing there?' Restarick sighed. Perhaps a wild goose chase was what this really was.

'Yes, but we avoid it,' Verrechia replied, turning to face him. 'It causes interference with our radios.'

'Any reason why?'

'It's called Kairos because during the war, when the Allies had support from Greece, they were using Cyprus to home part of their air force. A number of pilots encountered difficulties flying through there. A Greek pilot, Panagiotis Kairos, made the last minute decision to not deviate. He and his aircraft were never seen again. He was experienced… *highly* experienced. Since then, we have called the area Kairos' folly.'

'So why the hell would a British agent be so desperate to get there?' Mircalla asked.

Verrechia shrugged. 'It would explain why he is missing. It also explains to you why we gave him an old plane.'

'Did you tell him before he left that aircraft have gone down around there?'

Verrechia nodded, sitting back at his desk. 'Captain, he insisted on going there precisely because of that reason. I can think of easier ways to end it all.'

'What's the bearing?'

The lieutenant-colonel rubbed his temples. 'I had a feeling you were going to ask me that. I'm sorry. I can't let you fly to your deaths.'

Mircalla leant against the wall, her shoulder touching the map. 'We're under orders from Room 40 to find Max Baker. If you refuse to help…'

Verrechia spun in his chair. 'You'll tell my superiors? These are *my* planes, *my* airbase. I'm in command here.'

'They're Allied aircraft,' Restarick said calmly. 'If Room 40 felt it necessary to bring him back, then that's what we'll do. There is the conclusion that Baker has defected, potentially with the ability to undermine our work. Taking him in could be a major step towards defeating the Kaiser.'

The lieutenant-colonel pursed his lips, leaning his elbows on the desk. A junior-grade lieutenant knocked and entered, handing his superior a typed note.

'This has just come through, coded, sir,' he said, then left.

Verrechia's eyes widened for a moment, but it was enough for Restarick to become inquisitive.

'The Kaiser has sent tanks into the cities across Europe. Reports are coming in that there are hundreds coming down with a virulent strain of influenza and that the hospitals are under orders *not* to treat anyone. Any doctor or nurse caught attempting to do so… will be executed as a traitor to the *Kaiser-Regel…*'

'Does it say who the virus has been given to?' breathed Mircalla.

Verrechia nodded and handed her the message.

'Predominantly, the Jewish populace,' he sighed. 'Occupying Europe is one thing, but this… this is *genocidio…*'

'Give us a plane, Verrechia. You can't do anything unless you're ordered to. Room 40 can,' Restarick said.

The lieutenant-colonel stared at the note for a moment, then nodded. This English captain made a good point. If this was the Kaiser's next move to continue his occupation, every opportunity had to be taken advantage of to destroy his grip.

'Very well. Your friend, Kaplan… leave him with me. I will make sure he gets the correct burial even if it means flying him to Jerusalem myself.' Verrechia buzzed his assistant. 'Pasquale, get the Levasseur ready and bring me Kairos' coordinates. Captain, it is a French fighter, two-seater. It is small and you can fly low to avoid the telescopes of the Kaiser's warships. It has Vickers and Lewis machine guns and if you need to, it will allow you to land in the sea. You can both freshen up in the officer's quarters.'

'Thank you,' Mircalla said.

Restarick said nothing as he and Mircalla showered together, his face fixed in steely determination. The news from Europe was extremely grim. He didn't believe the tale that Kairos and Baker had both disappeared in a mystery part of the open air and he was not about to baulk at the idea of following them into apparent oblivion.

Verrechia had supplied flight suits for them both, the latest design, black, with flying helmets that seem more padded than what was the norm, goggles and parachutes. The lieutenant-colonel had given Mircalla a Beretta for there was no room for the rifles they had obtained in Algiers.

The aircraft itself was, as Verrechia said, small but nevertheless impressive. Its upper wing was slightly longer than the lower, making it, Verrechia explained, more manoeuvrable; it was designed to take off from and land on naval carriers. Why it was on an Italian airbase in Libya was anyone's guess. Fitted with floats as opposed to wheels, its fuselage was designed as if it were for a boat. It carried no markings. As the pilot, Restarick would sit behind Mircalla, taking no time at all to familiarise himself with the controls. Mircalla had full governance of the weaponry, navigation (as basic as it was), binoculars and a powerful camera. As a reconnaissance aircraft, the Levasseur PL5 was certainly well-equipped. By the next morning, they were airborne, Verrechia and his little kingdom falling away, the sky above beckoning them into its arms.

Mediterranean Sea, West of Cyprus

The weather was clear and the sky cloudless, perfect for flying but not if you were potentially going to be spotted by the warships of the *Kaiser-Regel* on the horizon. So Restarick kept the aircraft low. Mircalla would tell him when to ascend to the point where it was alleged Kairos and Baker had vanished.

'What,' Mircalla began, shouting over the roar of the sesquiplane's open engine, 'if there's nothing there?'

Restarick smiled at the irony of her question. If Kairos and Baker *had* disappeared then there wouldn't be anything to see. He was hopeful they would at least see a downed plane or two in the clear waters. 'Then we head back to the airbase and start again,' he hollered back. 'If we can't spot any submerged crash site, we have to assume that Baker is still alive and that he intends to use the virus he stole to infiltrate the Allied defences somewhere. His defection is probably the most dangerous of any that have been reported.'

The plane buzzed onwards. Mircalla, holding the binoculars tight to her goggles, was able to get a relatively clear view of their surroundings. She'd also set the camera, pointing downwards, snapping photographs every few hundred feet. While the intention of reconnaissance was to take shots far above enemy territory, she hoped this low altitude would give them some good views of any murky shapes under the surface.

Around they went, circling and crossing the coordinates Verrechia had supplied. But there was nothing. No shadows under the sea, nothing to indicate Baker had flown this way.

An hour they spent, looking, peering, pointing, sighing. At one point, a pod of whales swam beneath them.

'I'm going to climb further. Perhaps we're too close to the surface.'

'What about the warships?' Mircalla reminded Restarick. 'It's such a clear day they will see us if we go any higher.'

'We will make another few passes then head back.'

Mircalla gripped the leather-edged curve of the cockpit as the Levasseur ascended, the sea dropping, leaving her stomach behind. It was even colder now, windier, too. She could see more below her, the binoculars back in her grip. But still nothing.

Restarick banked them around, then around again.

'Wait a moment…' Mircalla heard his concerned voice over the engine whine.

'What is it? Have you seen something?'

'Up ahead.'

Mircalla trained her binoculars away from the sea rushing by underneath them and saw a billowing grey cloud.

Restarick held onto the stick with both hands as the plane hit a wall of air, the cloud swooping over and around them in a flash. 'Where the bloody hell did this come from?'

'*Merde!* Can you drop back down?'

'Hold on!' Restarick yelled through gritted teeth. 'Hold on!'

He wrenched the throttle and the Levasseur tilted hard, making Mircalla drop the binoculars down at her feet. She leant in to grab them, catching them as the plane jolted.

A slice of lightning ripped across their path, buffeting them so hard Restarick feared the bolts and rivets would come loose. Worse, the stick locked itself and would not budge. They were in a spiral now, turning, descending, turning, descending. Around them the cloud thickened, growing darker, the lightning illuminating everything briefly at each passing minute then returning into blackness again every time. It was relentless, Mircalla and Restarick no longer having any sense of direction or even if they were the right way up.

'We don't have a radio! We can't even call the airbase!' she yelled.

'I think they can see this, though!'

They could feel the electricity in the air on their faces. It was as if the very atmosphere itself was charged. A great brilliance blinded them and Restarick was sure he had been knocked unconscious for a moment. He could vaguely hear Mircalla shouting for him. When he focused again, he looked around. The storm was *below* them! The sky above was clear and bright but the air was excruciatingly cold. They were levelling off, some twenty-thousand feet above sea level. That was far higher than Restarick had expected

Are you alright?' he shouted back to her, seeing her nod her head. He could feel her anxiety—and her relief. The stick had unlocked and the rudders were unaffected by the storm. 'Let's head back to the airbase. We'll stay above the storm as long we can. It should be a clear r—'

Crack!

The lower of the sesquiplane's two wings was struck by a ferocious lightning bolt and they began to plummet again, a great plume of smoke from the jagged hole swirling upwards. Mircalla was never one to scream but this time she couldn't suppress an angered cry. Restarick gasped in panic, wrestling with the stick. The rear rudder and the flaps squealed in indignation. The black clouds swallowed them up again and all was dark, save for the piercing lightning. Down they went. Spiralling, banking, shuddering. The dials before Restarick were making no sense, the pointers jerking this way and that. Had they fallen a thousand feet, five thousand, fifteen… nearly twenty? There was simply no way of telling for sure. Another crack of lightning and the tail caught alight before their descent extinguished it. Then they dropped out from underneath the storm… or had the storm dissipated at last? For there was no longer any sign of such a disturbance at all.

'Where the hell are we?' called Mircalla. Before the storm, and even during it at their highest level, it was daytime. Now it wasn't just pitch black because of the previous clouds, it was night. The stars above them twinkled quietly, giving nothing away of the nightmarish scenario moments before.

Still no time to sightsee. They were still falling.

With the holes at both ends of the plane, Restarick foresaw only one way to land. Hard and uncontrolled.

'Bail out!' he called to her.

'What? Are you serious?'

'I can't get us down safely. At least one of us will survive when this damn thing crashes.'

'In the sea? I'll drown! I can't swim that all the way to Cyprus!'

'I don't even know if we're still over the Med, Mircalla. There should be a flare gun under your seat. Use it one you've landed. You'll be seen.'

'What if it's by the *Kaiser-Regel*?'

'At least you'll still be alive! Now go!'

Mircalla fumbled under her seat and felt the pistol. Unstrapping it as well as her own buckles she thought for a split second and holstered it, shoving the Beretta behind her. 'If I get caught, they will take it from me anyway.'

Reluctantly, Restarick agreed, grabbing it. 'I'll see you soon!'

Mircalla wriggled her bottom up and gave a little salute to Restarick, throwing herself out. It wasn't even a second before she disappeared into the night sky.

'Good luck,' Restarick murmured, willing the flaps to respond.

The ground—not the sea—came rushing towards him, horrifyingly fast. Yet the angle the plane was at didn't stop him straight away. It cut a scar, some eighty feet, into the soft earth, softening his plunge *just* enough.

Checking he had no broken bones, Restarick climbed out and fell to the ground. He performed a quick visual check of the downed plane: no fuel was leaking, but the twisted propeller was smoking. The right pair of wings had disintegrated on impact, the left almost vertical to the ground when the main fuselage had tipped onto its side. With relief, he stumbled to his knees, then collapsed onto his back, groggy and exhausted.

The next few moments were blurry but Restarick was sure he wasn't alone. Was it Mircalla? Had she found him before he had found her? There were hands upon his person and he felt the Beretta slip from the holster. He groaned, shaking the haziness away.

There was a face looming at him, a man's—inquisitive, suspicious. A soldier from what Restarick could see in the gloom. Restarick lurched forward suddenly and threw his weight upon him. The unexpected assault toppled the stranger and as he fumbled for a weapon, Restarick was up and on his feet, heading towards the Levasseur's cockpit.

The soldier leapt up and went to tackle Restarick who neatly sidestepped the attempt. The man crashed to the ground, mud splattering across his face. Spitting both mud and rage he tried again but Restarick had already reached the biplane and spun back, his Luger in his grip and aimed at the man's torso.

'You're a damn *heinie*,' the man spat.

A British accent!

'No,' Restarick replied. 'You need to let me get away from here.'

'Sure thing, *heinie*.' The soldier was holding Mircalla's Beretta steady. 'There's going to be a whole squad of my chaps here at any moment.'

'I don't want to kill you.'

'You wouldn't dare. Not on a British camp.'

Restarick frowned. Where the hell had he landed? There were no British camps in the *Kaiser-Regel*. 'I'm… not a German. I work for the Allies.'

'*Work for*? That's a giveaway. None of us *work for* the Allies. We *serve*. Now drop your weapon before I kill *you*.'

***

Handcuffed, Restarick was marched to the largest of the tents, his eyes flicking left and right, absorbing every detail. There were Italian and French units amongst the British, giving every indication that this was a fully functioning *Allied* encampment. There was nothing hidden, no subversive engagement going on. No one here was of the mind-set that the *Kaiser-Regel* had complete control. Had he flown further that was possible for the small sesquiplane? Had the storm thrown them far from North Africa? By the temperature, he concluded he was in Europe but it was not possible for the Allies to have set up an operation so blatantly.

The man who had apprehended him, a captain going by his uniform, opened the canvas flap.

'The prisoner, Major Dalby, sir.'

'Thank you, Whiteacre,' said the major, a broad man, bewhiskered and straight-backed.

Restarick looked at the desk, upon which was Mircalla's Beretta (that was a point… where had *she* landed?) and his Luger.

'Anything else, sir?'

The major shook his head and dismissed the captain. As he motioned for Restarick to sit, two armed soldiers moved to stand over him. Restarick looked around the rest of the tent. The map on the free-standing frame was different, marked different. It showed information of Europe that he had not seen in ten years: the position of enemy troops, their advancements against Allied lines and vice versa… This was a map not unlike those he used to oversee himself.

'What's going on here?' he challenged. 'What's the army doing here?

Dalby looked at them with suspicion. He was not accustomed to people arriving unannounced in his camp and demanding answers.

'We are at war. What were you expecting?'

At war! In the few hours they'd been in the air, the Allies had finally begun to fight back! But this wasn't possible.

'We don't have the capacity to launch a full scale response anymore,' Restarick said.

'Anymore?' the major spat back. 'We are not done yet!'

'Who gave the order?'

'What order?'

'To attack the *Kaiser-Regel*?'

'The *Kaiser-what*?'

Restarick raised his cuffed wrists. 'Why are you treating me like this?'

The major looked at the two soldiers then back at Restarick. The anger was clear across his swarthy face. 'It is not generally considered good practice to let a prisoner wander about freely.' He motioned to the Luger. 'Was this issued to you?'

Restarick knew where this was going. A British man not in uniform caught with a Luger at an army base. There was only one thing for it. He needed to be open. Any sense of avoidance would likely mark him as spying for the *Kaiser-Regel*. This Major Dalby seemed… *Wait a minute*. Major Dalby. He knew that name. He frowned inwardly, trying to recall. But for the moment:

'I traded for it in Algiers.'

Dalby nodded. The man before him certainly looked like he'd spent some time recently in the sun. Do you have any form of identification? Name, rank, service number.'

'Captain Daniel James Restarick, retired. I hold no serial number due to my varying assignments during the war. Any identification I have was lost during my journey to Marseille.'

'Convenient. Retired?'

Restarick nodded. 'Some time ago following the surrender.'

'Who surrendered?' Dalby's question seemed genuine, if rather unbelievable.

'Ours, sir,' came the simple reply.

'Ours? Yours, you mean?' The moustache bristled.

'No, sir. The Allies.' Restarick felt like he was banging his head against a wall. '*Tenente Colonello* Verrechia gave us permission to use his aircraft for a reconnaissance mission over the Med. We left this morning. We have now returned.'

'I don't know who that is. He is not in charge here. There are no airbases for miles around.'

'I have lost my way. A storm hit, took out any ability to navigate. Taking off from Libya this morning, I crash landed and your captain found me.'

The major sat down. 'I want to know who you are and what you are doing here. If you are an enemy spy working for the Central Powers, I can assure you I have the authority to have you shot.'

'Central Powers! Good God, man! This is isn't 1918! They haven't called themselves that for ten years!'

'Are you unwell?' Dalby asked, not without sarcasm.

'Unwell? I'm… no… no, I am not!' Restarick seethed, although he was feeling less sure of his statement by the minute.

'I am on an assignment at the request of Room 40 to find and bring back a missing British agent,' Restarick responded, as exasperated as Dalby was clearly becoming. 'There is every reason to believe that his defection will undermine our attempts to overthrow the ten-year occupancy of the *Kaiser-Regel*. We would request that you contact Room 40 immediately to verify my position.'

The major leant back in his chair and lit a cigarette. He silently inhaled the smoke, letting it sit in his lungs before releasing it. 'Firstly, I concur that you crash landed. Captain Whiteacre's report was very thorough on that. Interestingly, you didn't expect to find us here. Secondly, you speak of a *"Kaiser-Regel"*. Unless the situation has changed for the worse in Europe, there is no sovereignty in the Kaiser's name. Thirdly, we are at war with the Central Powers. We have been for the last four years. There has been no occupancy for ten by this so-called *Kaiser-Regel* or anyone else.'

'Four years… That means…' Restarick's head was beginning to thump. 'Are you saying you believe this is… what… 1918?'

The major raised an eyebrow, tapping ash into a little tin dish on the desk. 'If you are not unwell, then clearly you are mad. Or perhaps your crash has given you some sort of amnesia. I shall enlighten you, Captain Restarick, if that's who you really are. You are in Padua, we are supporting the Italian Fourth and Sixth Armies—and, *of course*, it's 1918.'

Part 2: 1918

Fenile Morosina, Italy

Mircalla hadn't landed in the Med at all; she'd found herself up a tree in the dark with her parachute so tangled that she'd had to cut through the ropes with the knife in the survival pack around her waist. She wished she'd kept her Beretta rather than the flare: she had seen vague impressions of light as she had floated down.

She knew she hadn't been spotted but she'd watched anxiously as Restarick, in the plane, crashed a mile or so north. That certainly would have not gone unnoticed and, once free from the embrace of the tree, she crept stealthily through the night, keeping within the safety of the forest until she came to the bank of a river. How long it stretched, or indeed which river it actually was, she could not determine. The moon was dulled by a thickness of clouds—the remainder of the storm, she presumed—and there was a cold wind rushing along from the east. The river appeared to be quite deep and about fifty feet across. It most likely narrowed elsewhere as much as it widened, but it still didn't alter the fact that she needed to cross it. An owl hooted overhead and she saw its white plumage shine against the reflection of the water, swooping into the far bank to capture a vole minding its own business.

She put a hand in the water. It was ice cold and she would struggle to keep focused if she was to search for the downed plane whilst soaked to the skin. No. She was better off looking for a narrow part of the river, or a ford or a bridge.

Movement. Behind her, slightly off to the right.

She froze where she was, crouched by the water's edge. The blackness of her flight suit swallowed up any light, her hair tied tight in a ponytail. Breathing shallowly, she watched a shape—no, two shapes—move along close to where she was. As the moon came out from behind a heavy cloud formation, she saw it was a couple of soldiers. Their uniforms were familiar. They looked young. Relieved to be away from their superior officers if the gentle laughing and conversation between them was anything to go by. It took her a few seconds to register they were speaking English. She listened more intently, wiping her damp hand on her thigh, withdrawing the flare gun from the holster. A close range, a flare could easily fell an oncoming attacker. But the fact that they were English meant she might have found herself on friendly soil. She hoped Restarick had fared just as well.

The two soldiers were saying nothing of any use, just sweethearts back home, the rationing in the camp, how drunk one of the lieutenants had got in the night. But then they mentioned the Adige River. Was this where she was? She shifted on her haunches, crunching some twigs underfoot. The soldiers stopped talking.

'Who's there?' the bravest one said, brandishing his rifle.

Sighing, she stood, re-holstering the flare gun and raising her hands. 'Sorry, boys. Didn't mean to listen in.'

'Come forward! Identify yourself!'

'Don't shoot! I'm on your side! Olivia Duffy!' said Mircalla.

As she stepped into the small clearing, the two soldiers looked surprised, pleasantly so. They looked her up and down, less pleasantly, at the close-fitting flight suit.

'What are you doing here?'

'Oh, I got a little lost. Fell out of a tree. You know how it is. Can I?' She tilted her head and raised her palms. 'My hands?'

'Erm…' The solder with the raised gun wasn't sure if he should allow it, but what harm could she do? 'Go on, then.'

'What you doin', Pete?'

'What?'

'She might, y'know…'

'What? Shoot us? She's a bit of totty, Ed… look at her. What harm can she do?'

Mircalla watched this with vaguely-annoyed amusement, folding her arms across her chest that the smaller of the two soldiers, Peter, had been staring at intently.

'Are you boys finished?'

'Sorry, miss. We just weren't…'

'Yes, I know. A bit of 'totty', is that what you said? In the woods in the middle of the night?'

'It's dawn soon,' Pete helpfully said.

'Where are you stationed?' Mircalla accentuated her French lilt.

'We're on our way to our unit near Padua,' said Ed.

'Just the two of you?'

'Nah, our platoon is up just off the road. Ed here needed a leak… I mean he needed to… erm…'

'Yes, I understand.'

'The captain told us to go together. In case there are any *Boche* about.'

'We didn't think we'd see a French bird, though,' Pete added, suddenly finding a bit of courage as Mircalla came up to them. 'You said you were lost?'

Any Boche? That was a moniker not used for some time. For a start it was banned and more importantly what were English soldiers doing in Italy? So she asked.

'We're following orders, miss.'

Mircalla pursed her lips. 'Yes. And so you should. I need to speak to your captain.'

'Right away, miss,' Ed said. With perfect politeness, he showed Mircalla the way back to the convoy, Pete following.

Haywards Heath, England

'Is he still asleep?'

The woman nodded at her husband, raising an eyebrow as she lifted the bowl from the kitchen table to the sink. 'He came in this morning, absolutely blind drunk.'

'He'll kill himself if he keeps on like that. Two months we've put up with that! Two months!'

'Paid his rent for a whole year in advance, mind.'

'And do you really want to deal with him for another ten, Sheila? I don't. I'm going up there.'

'Leave him be. He's been through a lot.'

'Who hasn't?

Derek Fleming had seen enough action in South Africa, near forty years ago now, and was of sufficient age to be highly intolerant of those who shirked their responsibilities. Running a small boarding house in Sussex had given him a quiet retirement until war had broken out in '14 and he'd been instructed by Asquith's lot to open up rooms for soldiers passing through on their way the coast.

Pulling his braces up over his shoulders, he placed his pipe in the dish on the table and went upstairs.

He didn't wait or knock before entering, tutting at the state of the small room. Clothes strewn, bedding half on the floor, a shapeless lump on the single bed. The sound of snoring from under the sheets added to the smell of body odour and booze that permeated. Fleming pulled back the curtains and opened the window. Fresh air and daylight streamed in. Turning back to the bed:

'Mr Baker! I need a word with you!'

The groan was all Fleming got until he repeated himself.

'Oh, get out…'

The insolent drunkard… In a swift movement that defied Fleming's seventy years and his arthritic knees, the sheets were thrown to one side.

Max Baker rolled on to his back and glared up at the bearded old man standing over him. He sighed and burped and went back onto his side. No matter what way he plumped it, punched it, rolled it or folded it, the pillow under his head still felt like it was filled with rocks. The ones issue by the army were more comfortable.

'Get up, Mr Baker. Enough is enough.'

'What do you *want*?' Baker murmured, his tongue lazy in his mouth.

'You've outstayed your welcome. You need to leave now.'

Baker, in his mid-thirties but feeling as old as Fleming right now, didn't have the strength or even the inclination to argue. Instead he just ignored the man. But when he heard Mrs Fleming at the doorway, he covered himself up. Even with a raging hangover, it wasn't right to be indecently dressed with a lady present.

Mrs Fleming pretended not to notice the man's pyjamas. 'Would you like a cup of tea, love?'

Her husband glared at her. Why was she being nice to the layabout?

'Yes, that would be lovely. Thank you.'

'Come downstairs, then, and I'll fix you a nice breakfast, too,' she added.

Leaving him to it, the Flemings returned to the kitchen.

'Breakfast? It's after lunchtime,' Baker heard muttered.

He pulled himself up, head spinning and fatigue threatening to overwhelm him. Perhaps a bit of food would do him good. He knew he couldn't go on like this and Mrs Fleming was always very gracious to him. It seemed mean of him to act so atrociously towards them.

Fleming looked up over his newspaper, pipe clamped between his teeth, as Baker appeared a few minutes later, dressed but looking worse for wear.

'In my day, we wouldn't have stood for such behaviour.'

'Alright, dear, let Mr Baker sit down,' Mrs Fleming chided, sliding a teapot towards their guest.

Baker nodded and weakly smiled a thank you as Mr Fleming disappeared behind the headlines for June 20th.

The tea tasted sour. Whether that was because of the vile taste of previous night's excesses or because there was no mention on the paper's cover of the disease that was wiping out people in their thousands across the continent, Baker found it hard to swallow.

'What line of business are you in?' came Fleming's disembodied question.

'Business?' Baker put the cup back on the saucer.

'Yes, business. You must do something to be able to afford a whole year's rent. It's not unreasonable for me to ask.'

Baker rubbed his temples and sighed inwardly as a plate of bacon, egg and two sausages was slid under his nose. 'I work for the British government. War business.'

The paper lowered and Fleming's watery eyes peered over. 'I do not pay my taxes for the government to allow their staff to drink all night and sleep all day, Mr Baker. There are good men out there on the continent fighting for our freedom. And what are you doing? Nothing!'

Baker prodded at the sausages and pushed the plate away. 'I'm sorry, Mrs Fleming. I'm just not hungry.'

'You need a good meal, Mr Baker,' Sheila said, disappointed. She looked at his bony hands poking out from his cuffs. 'You can't live on whisky alone.'

Baker knew she was right but he still couldn't dismiss what he'd done. It burnt into his every thought, day and night, and being drunk was the only way it made everything more bearable.

Room 40, British Admiralty, London

'You're sure it's him?'

'Major Dalby confirmed it.'

'What the hell is he doing here? He's meant to be in France.'

'He *is* in France. At least he was yesterday when he checked in with Room 40.'

'Does Dalby know him?'

'Yes. They were stationed together in German East Africa. The odd thing, though…'

Major Chard, resplendent in his uniform, puckered his lips. 'Out with it, man.'

'Well,' Corporal Swinton began, 'Dalby said that he looks older.'

'War does that to a man.'

'You misunderstand me, sir. The mission they undertook together to German East Africa was only last month. Dalby is convinced Restarick looks damn well near ten years older. Dalby said, too, that Restarick didn't seem to recognise him.'

'An imposter?'

'Possibly, but doubtful. It took Dalby a little while to register it was the same man—but he's convinced it *is* Restarick.'

'How well do you know him?' Chard asked as an adjutant handed him a sheaf of papers.

'Not very. He was hand-picked by your predecessor a couple of years ago.' Swinton walked to a filing cabinet, opening a drawer to flick through a series of files. He pulled one out and read. 'Ah, here we are. Yes. Summer 1916 he joined us. Formerly of the Essex Regiment. His marksmanship brought him to our attention.'

'Trustworthy?'

'Never balked so far.'

Chard nodded. 'France is where he should bloody well be, though. Not turning up in Italy.'

'Unless he was following a lead?'

'Something is fishy.' Chard tapped his chin. 'Recall him.'

'If we do that, sir, it might stall our intelligence regarding the Central Powers spy.'

'Hmm. Who do we have out in the field who can investigate? Someone who knows Restarick, someone who he won't suspect is there to get to the bottom of whatever is going on?'

Swinton called for his secretary, asking her to bring him details of all operational personnel currently in Europe. The information was soon laid out before him and Chard.

'Nathaniel Richards, Claudia Apollinari... What about Thomas Callany?'

'He's on his last few days in Portugal,' said Swinton. 'Due to head to the Canaries immediately after."

"There's Julie Leander, she's on leave in Bergen, Norway. Could be available to fly out tonight."

"How about... yes. Perfect.' Swinton pushed a foolscap sheet under Chard's nose. 'Now, *this* man was stationed with Restarick. They got to know each other very well. Charlie Armstrong. He's in Rome. A bally American but all the same is succinct when it comes to working with us.'

'Surprised the Yankees haven't snatched him back if he's that good.'

'It's *because* he's that good. I wouldn't be at all shocked if he's been given *carte blanche* by his government to stay.'

'We knowingly have an American working for Room 40 who might very well be reporting back to President Wilson?'

Swinton nodded. 'But we pay him rather well and he occasionally tells *us* what *they're* up to.'

'Good God. I thought the Americans are on *our* side!'

'They are, sir. But it pays to keep an open mind.'

Chard raised an eyebrow. 'And sending him to Restarick won't alert Restarick that we're suspicious as to his movements?'

'I sincerely doubt it.'

'Then you have your orders, corporal. See to it.'

'Right away, sir.'

'And Swinton?'

Swinton turned back as he reached the door. 'Sir?'

'If Restarick does turn out to be a bad egg, tell this Armstrong chap to get rid. He can use his own discretion.'

Swinton nodded once, saluted and hurried out to pass on the major's directive.

Padua, Italy

Restarick turned over on the narrow uncomfortable bed. Facing the wall seemed a better option than facing the door with its narrow barred slit and the shadows of those outside passing by. The pattern of mould along the bricks had become familiar to him, winding away the solitary hours tracking the growth and spread of his green companions.

The evening sun crept slowly down the wall, the bars enormous in shadow above his head. It was like they were taunting him, reminding him (as if he needed to be reminded) that he was imprisoned. He was in an abandoned farmhouse, occupied and adapted for use by the Allies, only a few hundred yards from the encampment. To have places of incarceration was important, or course, so the old brick building served its purpose well, and far more secure that canvas tents.

Dalby had shown little understanding, unwilling to engage in conversation with Restarick. He was being treated as the enemy but given no opportunity to prove his allegiance.

A jangling of keys signalled the door's opening. He tensed and sat up. He hadn't been out of his cell for over a week now.

The door swung inward with a groan and in the doorway, silhouetted by the meagre lamplight in the prison guard's hand, stood a man familiar to Restarick. His stocky frame was unmistakable. Restarick tried to contain his gasp: the last time he'd seen him was in the café in La Celle-Saint-Cloud and before he'd been killed… but that would be ten years from now.

The rush of fresh air made the prisoner's nostrils twitch. A glimmer of hope crossed his mind as the door stayed open.

Charles Armstrong entered the cell, dismissing the guard.

'Charlie! Good God, man! Am I to be let out?'

Armstrong was younger than Restarick remembered, too. He looked like he did when they first met a decade ago. He still had the slight limp from his injuries when Restarick had saved him. Armstrong didn't smile at first. Restarick sighed inwardly. *This* Armstrong hadn't yet had the years of friendship with him—so what was he doing here?

'You look...' Armstrong began, his cold front suddenly thawing.

'I know,' Restarick nodded. The lines across his forehead and the flecks of grey in his hair were obvious. 'It's good to see you.'

'They thought a familiar face might help.'

Clever Room 40.

'Danny, Major Dalby thinks you've lost the plot. He told the Factory. They asked me to come have a chat with you.'

'Dalby wouldn't let me talk to him.'

A different guard brought in a chair and a tray of food and left. Armstrong sat and eyed Restarick eating. 'Slowly, bud.'

Restarick nodded, gulping down the cup of water between mouthfuls. 'I recognise Dalby from somewhere. Can't place it.'

'I'm not going to piss you around here. Room 40 is suspicious, too. They send you into France to trace the spy then you turn up in Italy.'

Restarick used the moments he was eating to try and recall the events Armstrong was referring to. 'I didn't have time to report back my movements.' Not *exactly* a lie...

'Are you close to apprehending the spy?'

This all happened ten years ago as far as Restarick was concerned! 'I've lost track of the days.'

'June 21st, Danny.'

'1918?'

Armstrong frowned then laughed. 'Yeah, sure! Damn... I thought Dalby was making it sound worse when he told the Factory you didn't know what year it is! What the hell happened to you?'

Restarick leant against the damp wall, his hunger satisfied. He breathed out slowly, looking hard at Armstrong. Could he trust him? Would the American think him delusional if he told him the truth?

'Charlie...' This was it. 'I need to say something.... something you might think is peculiar...'

'Go for it.'

'Do you trust me?'

Armstrong straightened in the chair. The look that crossed Restarick's face then indicated something big was about to be shared. 'Of course. Any man who would drag me across the battlefield so I wouldn't die alone out there? Hell, that's something I ain't forgetting in a hurry.'

'I can't explain how or why... but...' Restarick faltered. No. Armstrong would think him crazy. He couldn't tell him.

'How did you end up here? Did you find the spy?'

Restarick sagged. 'Yes. I found the spy.'

'Goddamn! Where?!'

'Saint-Mihiel.'

'France, right?'

Restarick nodded. 'I had a clear shot.'

'So you took it? Did you get the information they stole?'

'It hasn't… happened yet. At least I don't think it has.'

Armstrong stood, stretching his back. The journey from Rome had been non-stop and his war wounds were playing him up. 'Okay, you need to make sense.'

Restarick took a deep breath. 'I asked you, like I asked Major Dalby, to tell me this 1918.'

'To reassure you it was 1918. You have amnesia. I get it.'

'No… no, I don't have amnesia. At least…' Restarick put his head in his hands. 'At least I don't *think* I do… None of this makes any sense.'

Armstrong moved and sat next Restarick. 'Some of the boys out there are really suffering. This fucking war is ripping us all apart.'

'This war… it's over, as far as I'm concerned. It was over ten years ago.'

'If you're invalided out, then yeah, I get why you're struggling to accept it's over for you. Did you shoot the spy or not?'

'You don't understand!' Restarick stood, wringing his hands together. He spun to face Armstrong. 'Shit! I don't even understand it myself!'

'Danny, you have to give me something here. I have to report back to the Factory with… with…' Armstrong shrugged.

'I was on the tail of a defector.'

'The spy?'

'No. No, someone else. We were flying across the Med…'

'We?'

'A fellow Room 40 operative. We'd left the Italian airbase together in Libya. We hit a storm. She bailed. I crashed.'

'Then that's clear cut. I can't see anything untoward, although they'll want to know why you changed assignments. Do you know where your companion landed?'

'No. But, Charlie, when we took off from Libya… it was 1928.'

Armstrong fixed his stare on Restarick, looking for signs of… of *anything*.

'Okay, Danny. This really is no time for jokes. You're up to your neck if Room 40 thinks you've gone off on your own unauthorised mission. I can believe you were chasing a defector. You like to be independent, not tied down by strict rules. Damn, it's one of the reasons the Factory conscripted you. Let me piece this together for you: you were on the trail of the spy, the missing information; you were led to a defector, were hot on their tail. That I can easily understand. But all this happened—'

'In 1928,' Restarick interrupted. 'Ten years from now. Take a look at the wreckage. You'll see the plane is different. Not like anything the Allies or the Central Powers are designing and building right now!'

Armstrong shook his head. 'You really have got shell-shock. So what I am doing in 1928? Rich? A happy millionaire with a mansion in Beverly Hills?'

Restarick looked at the open door. 'I…'

'You think cooking up some cockamamie story about being from the future is going to get you out of here?'

'What do you mean? I am an operative working from Room 40. You and me… we both are!'

'Okay…' Armstrong folded his arms, feeling the wall cold upon his back. 'Indulge me. What's 1928 like? We still at war?'

'No. We lost. Everything is occupied by the Kaiser.'

'We lost? And why are you here?'

'We were following the defector.'

'Yeah, about this "we"…'

'Mircalla Richard. We were lead to believe the defector, Max Baker, had disappeared over the Med…' Restarick relaxed his shoulders. There was a dawning realisation. 'My God… He didn't disappear… He came back, too!'

Armstrong stood, circling, moving to the door. 'So there are three of you around from 1928? You're all here from the future where the Kaiser rules the world, eh? And I guess you want to go home?'

Restarick clamped a hand over his own mouth. This was overwhelming. He'd had a week to think about where he was, why and how. But every time it always came back to him believing he himself was delusional, that he was still in 1928. But he knew he wasn't! He was sure of it! From his relationship in the future with Armstrong he knew his friend wouldn't lie if this *wasn't* 1918. He had an ally here, in the past… his own past. Someone he could trust. Room 40 were right in sending Armstrong. For the first time since he'd arrived here, he smiled. Armstrong nodded at him, as if in understanding, and poked his head out of the door, clearly checking, Restarick assumed, that the way was clear.

'Okay, guys. Let's go.'

But it was with horror that Restarick realised Armstrong *wasn't* here so that he could qualify his story for Room 40 to allow his release. Armstrong was here to listen to his story to keep him here! The two guards that had appeared in the doorway were holding, respectively, a baton and a straight-jacket.

'Charlie… no… You have to believe me! I'm not mad!' Restarick stumbled back as the guards crept forward. 'Please don't let them do this! I'm telling you the truth! I'm from the future! I'm from 1928!'

'Come on lad, make it easy on yourself,' one of the men said, lifting the jacket.

'Danny-boy, go with them and they'll make you better. Then I can tell the top brass back in London that you'll be okay. I'm sure you want that, huh?'

Armstrong shook his head sadly as Restarick was wrestled into submission. He lit a cigarette and walked out, Restarick's cries of helpless anguish echoing around the makeshift cell.

Haywards Heath

Baker had asked Mrs Fleming to buy as many copies of the morning papers she could lay her hands on.

'Do you think it will get here?' Mrs Fleming asked her husband as Baker shuffled back to his room, the papers swooped up and shoved under one arm.

'Oh, I shouldn't think so,' he huffed, impatiently waiting for the day's milk delivery. He peered out of the kitchen window as if that would make the milkman speed up his rounds. 'These diseases usually stay where they start.'

If only that were true, thought Baker to himself, now at the top of the stairs, shutting his door behind him, throwing the papers to his bed, noting with great interest *The Times* surmising the sudden outbreak of flu a couple of months ago to be nothing more than a passing blot on the war effort.

Most of the papers reported much the same thing: no one could quite agree on where it had actually begun, only initially considered to be a particularly forceful variation of common influenza. It simply appeared out of nowhere with no warning. It wasn't until recently, however, that fingers started pointing at Spain. After King Alfonso XIII and many of his subjects fell victim, news began to filter out across the continent that this was something to be concerned about. Heading into a balmy summer, 'Spanish flu' became the accepted moniker, with the more romanticised 'Spanish Lady' appearing on occasion.

Baker moved over to the little sink to lean on its edge, staring at himself in the mirror before him. He looked dreadful, moustache unkempt and hair greasy. He smelt of booze and body odour. The bottle of whisky at his feet had at least three gulps left. He swigged at it, and moved back to the bed, the amount of liquid not enough to satiate him. In the distance, the bell of St Wilfrid's tolled the quarter hour. Not even 0930 and he was desperate for more drink. He sighed, the newspapers staring coldly up at him.

Death Brings Warning Of Influenza – Wear A Mask And Save Your Life!
Public Places Are Ordered Closed – Spanish Lady Strikes Without Warning!
Schools Closed – No Services In Church Sunday

What the hell had he done?

Cane Hill Hospital, Croydon, England

The large tea urn bubbled in the corner as Clive unwrapped his sandwiches. He looked at the limp lettuce hanging from between the dry bread as if it had given up all hope.

He'd arrived late for work and so his lunch would be quick. There had been an influx of new patients over the last couple month and he was concerned he'd get behind with the paperwork. The superintendent was a vicious man if he ever felt a member of staff was not pulling their weight, reminding Clive of an old bullish officer he'd had a run-in with during active service.

The staff room wasn't busy and Clive looked out to the central partially-covered courtyard, seeing a couple of attendants taking a patient for a walk in the sun. The patient seemed calm but that might have been due to the medication he'd been given and the straight-jacket wound tightly around his torso. Clive wondered if the restrains were needed while outside. But then, that wasn't his patient.

'Mind if I join you?' Art Whelvy sat opposite him before he could reply, unscrewing the lid to his flask to release the pungent smell of ox tongue soup into the room. The table wobbled slightly as he leant into Clive, his round glasses glinting in the sunshine streaming in through the windows. 'Heard the rumour?' His Scots burr matched his gruff exterior perfectly.

'No, I haven't.' Clive replied politely, smiling behind his sandwich, the lettuce suddenly more appealing than the soup his colleague proceeded to sip noisily from the cup lid.

'Old Lilly's been given the boot.'

Clive raised an eyebrow. 'The Sergeant-Major?'

Art nodded into his soup. 'Can't say I'm surprised. He's been on the ropes for a while now.'

'I don't know him too well. It's not for me to comment.'

'Oh, come on, Ricey… You've been here for a while. You know what he's like.'

Clive winced inwardly at the corruption of his surname. 'There's someone like him everywhere. Are you sure he's been fired or has he resigned? He looks like he's near retirement.'

'This place does that to a man,' Art breathed solemnly. 'He was here looking after our boys when they first started coming back home from the front.'

'Superintendent Lilly has always had the best interests of the patient at heart.'

'Apart from when that one shot himself with the homemade pistol.'

Clive Rice put his pathetic sandwich down, suddenly not hungry. 'I feel sorry those in here who aren't mad. They're locked up with the desperately insane ones.'

'If they weren't nutcases when they arrived…' Art retorted, a dribble of soup at the corner of his mouth.

Clive genuinely had concerns over the treatment of those here who simply wanted to get better, whether it be from mild shell-shock or a physical injury. He was equally empathetic to the severely unstable patients. Lilly had tried his best to accommodate the patients that he'd been sent but capacity was already extreme and there seemed to be little sign of it slowing. No wonder there were rumours he wasn't managing the hospital properly. 'Do they know when he's going?'

'How long's a piece of string, old boy?' Art slurped through his greasy lips, a couple of splashes landing on his white tunic. Clive pointed it out. Art tutted but didn't seem overly bothered. 'The worry is, whose going to replace him? Bet you hadn't thought of that, eh?'

It was as if Art was continuing a conversation that he'd started with someone else. Clive just shrugged and sipped at the tea he'd decanted earlier from the urn. Stewed and gritty.

'And I'll tell you this,' Art continued, waving a fork in Clive's bearded face after prodding it around his flask for goodness knows what, 'this place will be *Hun* before we know it.'

Clive looked at his colleague in surprise. 'What on earth makes you say that?'

'You need to be careful. They have eyes and ears everywhere. Bloody *Boche*.' The fork wobbled from side to side in demonstration, thick brown soup dripping from its prongs.

Clive frowned, not entirely convinced Art was on the right side of a cell door. But he'd known the man for a while. Harmless. Just a bit simple. And somewhat paranoid, it seemed. He did his job well, though, and hadn't overheard anything about him in idle staff gossip. Just like he hadn't heard anything about George Lilly's resignation.

As Art carried on talking, weaving a tale of how one day soon everyone might probably be talking German and how even the taps in the kitchen would be replaced if the Kaiser ever declared victory, the alarm bell sounded shrilly above the door.

'Damn!' Art dropped his fork, placing his flask heavily on the table, to rush to the door, his truncheon at his hip swinging wildly. Clive and the other wardens on their lunch breaks followed on his heels. Outside, the two with the straight-jacket patient bundled their charge back to the main building. The senior warden, Onslow, rushed down a corridor, truncheon in his grip, barking orders at his men.

The alarm ceased.

Onslow ordered the wardens back to their duties, panic over as quickly as it had begun.

Clive had finished his lunch anyway and stopped by the administration office before attending one of his patients.

'That's us going home late,' commented Patricia, one of the typists. She had always been somewhat direct in her manner and Clive found if refreshing. Her words sent a general feeling of malaise around the room. 'Mr Lilly will put everyone in lockdown now, for whatever that was all about.'

Another warden came up behind Clive. 'Bloody ridiculous,' he said, dragging on a roll-up.

'You could help the girls get things done here, Sharky, if you're hanging about,' Clive smiled.

'Don't get above your station,' Sharky replied, leaning against the door frame.

'Anything we can help you with, gentlemen?' Patricia asked, smiling at Clive.

'Looking in on patient number 1955. Has he had his meds?'

Patricia looked at the time (there was a large clock on the wall above the door) and checked a crib sheet to her left. 'Usual story. Refused them. Had to be forced down.'

'Is that your pet project fellow?' Sharky laughed. 'You have a soft spot for that one!'

Clive raised his eyebrows in mock amusement, said thank you to Patricia and hurried along the corridor, reaching a specific cell. Sharky's sarcastic observation wasn't entirely without mileage. Clive had indeed found the patient to be strangely… well, *normal*, despite his peculiar delusions.

Unlocking the thick door, he knocked before entering. He wasn't required to announce his arrival, but this man deserved some kindness.

'Hello, Daniel, how are you today?'

Restarick was sitting in the corner on his narrow bunk, knees up under his chin. Drawn and exhausted, he glanced up at Clive, and smiled. He enjoyed the time they spent together. Clive didn't treat him like a hindrance, like an idiot, not like the rest.

It was only by keeping himself to himself as best he could that he felt he could keep at bay the demons that could easily smother him in this godawful place. Yet no matter how approachable and conversant Clive was, there was one thing he could never do for Restarick: offer him a way out.

Clive could only agree with him that most of the patients here were just that: patients not inmates. How many had Restarick seen literally crumple into nothing on the battlefield? Grown men brought to their knees by mortar exploding in their ears, the constant barrage over their heads as they sank ever deeper into the freezing mud? The damn bloody war had destroyed their ability to integrate back into society—boys who never had the chance to grow up. Restarick had been one of the lucky ones: his reaction to the atrocities less intense. Admittedly, he'd been operating alone and away from the front line for the majority of the conflict but his experiences still led him to understand how a person could be broken in such a brutal way. Dead soldiers, dead friends, the enemy, too… wherever one looked. Seeing them kill and be killed… it didn't take too many days of that to start changing a man. It had been his injuries at Saint Mihiel that had forced his superiors to discharge him, though. He was glad in many ways that his memories of that day when he failed in his mission to shoot the spy were clouded. He'd rather live with that than what these poor souls here had to contend with every day.

'Have you stopped counting the days, yet?' Clive asked, remaining in the doorway, as per regulations when alone with patients.

Restarick tilted his head. 'No.' *Day sixteen.*

'You'll find it easier if you do.'

'Why did you choose this job?'

This was something Clive had not been asked by Restarick before. He considered before answering. 'I've seen conflict. Like you have. I was fortunate to only lose a finger.' He held up his right hand, indicating the space where his index finger used to be. 'Can't fire a weapon with it missing. I'm a plumber by trade. Can't even do that anymore. So I thought to myself that I can be of use looking after my mates who came off worse. I got a job as a hospital porter over at the Croydon Union Infirmary then when a position came up here as a warden, I applied and here I am three years later.'

'You're certainly one of the more agreeable here.'

Clive nodded. 'And you're one of the sanest. You just need to stop all this bally nonsense.'

'It's only nonsense if it's not true, eh? Isn't that what the quacks upstairs say?'

'You really do believe you came from 1928?'

'Yes,' Restarick replied assuredly. 'I know I did.'

'And you've lived all this before?'

'Not here, no. Right now there's a younger version of myself running around France.'

'Trying to find a spy! It's certainly one of the most entertaining delusions.'

Restarick sagged back against the wall. 'A delusion.'

'Look, I'm sorry, Daniel. If I start agreeing with you, I'm just making the whole thing worse.'

'Confirming my "delusion"? Going along with it and affecting my 'treatment'?'

'Have they discussed with you yet what treatment they're going to give you?'

'No. But I know whatever they decide will be completely unethical.'

'But they're tried and tested.'

Restarick stood, stretching his back. 'In 1928 we're only just beginning to see it's rather barbaric.'

'Yes, of course. You have all the experience of the future.' Clive tried his hardest to not sound sarcastic. 'Why don't you just accept you're not well? They'll likely just give you some pills. By the way, the office said you refused the last dosage again. You had to have them forced down you.'

Restarick held out his hand. The pills were nestled in his palm. 'You get trained on how to avoid swallowing these things, even under duress.'

'Who gets trained? In the future, yes?'

'I…' Restarick realised that bringing Room 40 into the conversation would qualify the doctors' diagnosis that he was indeed disorientated resulting from Shellshock. 'I just don't like taking them.'

Clive pursed his lips. He really should have insisted Restarick take them but the man seemed calm, measured. 'Alright. I'll pretend I don't know you haven't had them.'

'Thank you,' Restarick nodded. 'Why can't the doctors see these extreme treatments aren't working? Tavistock is in here terrified of noise, so they put him in a room by the kitchens. Rintoul has mutism so they strap him in a chair and electrocute his throat!'

'Mr Lilly and his medical team know what they're doing. You start going against that, they'll…'

'They'll what? Give me electric shock therapy, too?' Restarick looked at the pills. 'That's the answer for everything. I'm going to get it anyway, whether I play along or not.' He moved towards Clive. 'I have to get out of here. I have to tell my superiors. I know how the war ends.'

'Oh, come on now, Daniel! Keep talking like this and I will *have* to report it to Mr Lilly.'

'Then report it!'

'He'll have you wired up to the machine by the end of the day. I really don't think you want that.'

'I want someone to listen to me!'

'I *am* listening to you. But I can do *only* that. If you want to get out of here, prove to them that you're not delusional. The more you insist you're from 1928, they'll just lock you up for the rest of your life.'

Restarick considered his original idea of escape. There simply wasn't anything he could do to make anyone believe him, so either playing along or getting out without being seen were his two options. But where would he go? He'd already lived this year—and the next nine to come. 'Yes, you're right, of course.'

'Convince them you're sane and they can't keep you here.' Clive smiled. 'Are you hungry? There's some food left in the dining room.'

The dining room. Where the other patients gathered. Restarick had spent the last two weeks here trying his best to avoid everyone. Soon the doctors would diagnose his reticence to mingle to be yet another side effect of shellshock. He looked down at his ill-fitting trousers and shirt and the plain slippers: all supplied by his hosts. He sighed. He missed his home in Ceylon, the heat, the rolling hills, the physical demands of a successful plantation. Here he was in England, locked up and assumed to be mad.

***

George Lilly stared out of his open window. His office was on the third floor, purposely positioned away from any view of the rest of the asylum. The sky was blue and there was a fresh breeze coming through the fluttering net curtains. He turned back to his wide desk and the file upon it. It was open, displaying the brief profile of patient 1955, one Daniel James Restarick. If that was his real name.

When he'd been delivered here by the medical corps, he'd had no papers with him, nothing to identify him at all. All that accompanied him was a medical discharge form signed by Major Dalby and Captain Charles Armstrong. Lilly had questioned this. If this man was an unknown quantity, why wasn't he being treated as a spy? The private had indicated the signed document, confirming Restarick was delusional and deemed not a danger to the war effort.

'So his delusion extends to believing he is someone else?'

Bernie Michaels, Lilly's deputy, sitting on the other side of the desk, nodded. 'It took me a while, but I managed to find a Daniel James Restarick currently assigned to special duties. Date of birth, 2nd February 1887.'

'That makes him thirty-one. Patient 1955 I'd say looks more in his early forties. A brother, perhaps? No specific regiment?'

Michaels scratched his scalp through thinning hair. 'It's a bit odd, this. There was a reluctance to release any information.'

'A mystery patient taking on the name of a mystery soldier who appears to look ten years older than he claims to be.' Lilly shuffled through the file, a few pieces of paper compiled since Restarick's arrival. 'I think we should begin his treatment proper. He might start telling us who he really is and stop all this utter drivel about being from the future. I wonder…'

'Sir?' Michaels tilted his head.

'Did your search tell you where the real Restarick currently is, apart from on 'special duties'?'

'No. Would you like me to see if I can find out?'

'I wouldn't have asked otherwise. I'd like to get him here in front of patient 1955. That will knock the delusion out of him.'

'Right away.'

As Michaels stood to leave, Lilly waved him to stand fast for the moment. 'If you come up against any more barriers, I know a chap in Whitehall who might be able to pull some strings. Say that your superintendent is owed a favour by Dicky Chard. But only mentioned it as a last resort. That might get some rusty cogs turning.'

Haywards Heath

'Come on, big boy, you can't let a girl down, now.'

Baker could barely sit up let alone follow up on his own suggestion that the woman he'd met in a less than salubrious club on the edge of town spend the night with him. He seemed to remember her name as being Geena, but he wasn't entirely convinced. Geena had been his fiancée, some years back. She'd run off with a butcher. *This* Geena was altogether a different creature. She was blonde with a mischievous twinkle in her eye.

The club itself was breaking the law by being open—but its refusal to adhere to the lockdown rules to help curb the spread of Spanish Flu was known only to a select few. Geena had spotted Baker walking alone along Perrymount Road and tried her luck. He was eager to break the monotony of whatever it was he wasn't doing and gladly followed her to the club, the proprietor of which was an old acquaintance of hers. It appeared she had many.

A heady cocktail of absinthe, wine and whiskey later, Geena was in Baker's rented room, wrestling with his belt. He'd thrown enough money at her to pay for her services for an entire week, let alone the night, but she knew he wasn't in any fit state to keep up his end of the arrangement. Nevertheless she had them both undressed before long, doing her utmost to arouse him, with disappointing results.

The eventual sound of his snoring made her stop and roll over, staring at the ceiling rose and the green lamp shade hanging beneath it. She glanced at the paper money on the bedside table, shrugged, and scooped it into her purse. An easy session. Lighting a cigarette, she sat on the bed, feeling the draft from under the door caressing her bare feet. The clock on the wall informed her it was gone midnight. If she was quick, she could get back down to the club and pick up another client before it closed.

She was pulling up her underwear when she felt a hand at the small of her back. She didn't tense, knowing it was soft enough to indicate Baker wasn't quite awake, but aware enough to know she was dressing.

'Where are you going?' he croaked. His head felt abominable.

Geena stubbed her cigarette out on the wooden floor, turning to smile at him. 'Things to do, dear.'

He squinted at the curve of her silhouette. 'I've paid you.'

'Yes, but you couldn't push that into a sock let alone my cunt,' she replied, nodding towards his flaccid penis. She wasn't wasting her time here if he couldn't hold his drink. Baker's touch suddenly became more forceful, clawing at the swell of her buttocks. 'Leave off, mister.'

'I told you I've paid…' His hoarseness became a growl. 'Take your knickers off.'

Geena sighed. He was one of *those* customers, willing to pay, unable to perform and unwilling to accept it. Better see the contract through, she thought, and slid her underwear back down, turning to face him.

Baker looked at the mound of dark hair between her legs and shuffled toward her, still lying on the bed. His hands were clumsy and she flinched at his nails against her. Then he prodded, angrily, violently, a finger entering her. She cried out and batted his hand away.

'Gently!' she scolded, but Baker wasn't listening.

He lunged forward and knocked her to the floor. She wasn't hurt but suddenly started coughing. Baker seemed not to notice and was upon her, mouth sucking and trailing across her upper chest and breasts. His hands were everywhere, grabbing, pinching.

Geena's coughing turned into a fit and she started gagging, trying to push him away.

'What's the matter with you?' Baker growled, forcing her legs apart with his knees. 'Bloody do it, that's what I paid you for!'

'You're…' Geena couldn't say anymore. She rolled over onto her side, her lungs desperate for air. The hacking cough wouldn't subside. Her eyes widened as blackened blood, thick with mucus, spewed out from her mouth across the floor. The more she breathed out, the less she could breathe in. Clutching her chest, her temples pulsed, panic and her rising temperature shooting her blood pressure up.

Baker clambered off her, realising what was wrong.

She's got the virus! She's got the fucking virus!

In horror, he smacked at his own mouth and lips, as if that would scare away the microscopic enemy. Dazed and still somewhat inebriated, he wobbled over to his jacket, fumbling for his service revolver. He checked it was loaded and, wiping his mouth again this time with an arm, looked back towards Geena. She had passed out, blood seeping from her nose and ears, black slime oozing down her cheeks.

It was only after he'd sobered up in the police station a few hours later that he'd realised what he'd then done to her.

Pervyse, Belgium

Mircalla's arrival at the makeshift hospital was met with a mixture of relief and sadness.

Having landed in a tree in Italy, after jumping from the sesquiplane, she'd found a wounded soldier in Mons following fraught journey across the Swiss Alps, avoiding sniper fire and enemy troop movements. But it was only on reaching Pervyse that she realised that something was seriously wrong.

The enemy troops weren't *kaisersoldaten*, they appeared to be Central Powers. How was this possible? The field hospital set-up indicated that the war was still very much on. Everyone around her was convinced it was 1918. Were they all under some mass hallucination? She quickly decided that to try to explain to them that it was really 1928 and the war had actually ended ten years ago wouldn't be conducive to her wellbeing. For the moment, until she could get back to the Factory, she had to play along.

But the longer she engaged with the soldiers and the nurses, sadly, the more the misconception seemed incredible.

Elsie Chisholm, a mere twenty-two years of age, had found herself at Pervyse in the early weeks of 1915. She welcomed Mircalla's arrival with glee, eager to unburden on her the trauma of what they had all been through.

'I was a despatch rider in London at first,' she began, offering Mircalla a seat in the tiny room off to the side. Through the doorway, they had full view of the three-bed ward. 'Dr Munro—do you know him?—he found out who I was and offered me a place in Flanders.'

Mircalla recognised the name. 'And here you are. Hector was a great believer in giving us a voice.'

'Was?' Elsie frowned, cradling her tin mug as a chill wind blew through the rackety hut. Her black hair was hidden under her nurse's cap, more of a headscarf. She looked tired and exhausted, her grey eyes sunken and ringed dark.

Mircalla coughed, realising her *faux pas*. 'I meant *is*. Sorry, so much going on around here.'

'Thank goodness. I would hate to think something had happened to him. What brings you here, to this hell?'

Mircalla half smiled. 'That's a long story. But, like you, I've been given a purpose in this stupid war. I'm simply here to help.'

'That's what Dr Munro saw in me, in all of us girls, here.'

'How is the soldier I brought in?'

'Mhàiri says he's doing well. He wouldn't have survived had you not got him to us.'

Mhàiri, Elsie explained, was as another of the nursing team recruited by Munro, a leading light in forward thinking. He'd created the Flying Ambulance Corps back in 1914, saving untold numbers of lives with his proactive and dedicated approach. It was a shame, Mircalla thought, that all of them here would never get the chance to meet him. He'd died in 1925.

'I'm pleased,' Mircalla said. 'The poor boy was in a terrible state. I didn't think he'd survive the journey.'

'How long are you stationed here?'

'Just passing through,' Mircalla replied, following Elsie out of the room.

They were struggling so badly here that it seemed cruel for them to be under the impression that the war was still on. The *Kaiser-Regel* would be held accountable for this unnecessary suffering, she cursed inwardly. She needed to get to London and quick. Room 40 would know how to deal with this situation.

'That's a dreadful shame, Mircalla. We could do with another set of hands.'

Yes, you certainly could. Mircalla was led through the building that had probably once been someone's shed into the encampment. She'd not seen it from the direction she'd driven in on (in a truck she'd found abandoned by the side of a road in Switzerland). There were rows of tents within which were maimed and dead soldiers. The stench of open wounds and rotting bodies was eye-watering. Elsie spotted her grimace, even though she tried to hide it. In the thick air could be heard the distant screams of weapons firing, but it was nothing when compared to the screams of the men dying in agony all around them.

'These boys here,' Elsie pointed to seven men, all with varying degrees of missing body parts, 'were brought in a couple of days ago by Dr Van der G hist. He's been working flat out and virtually alone down in Dixmude. We had another lot in this morning. A couple of the men are really quite defiant. One fellow had a bullet in his nose and refused to let us bandage him. The blood was pouring from his face. We had to strap him down in the end—but then he started choking on his own blood. One of the doctors here eventually allowed us to give him morphine. We propped him on his side and got him all cleaned up.'

'You really are performing miracles,' breathed Mircalla, shaking her head in disbelief.

Elsie tutted. 'Not sure about that. *Les deux madones de Pervyse*, they call us. They think that if we tend to them, they have a chance to live. It's heart-breaking when we can't save them all.'

This was all terribly old news to Mircalla. "The Madonnas" had gone down in history and even the Kaiser's rewriting of the past made special mention of them. Poor Elsie. This all had to be some sort of *Kaiser-Regel* brainwashing, an experiment perhaps. But to what end? What would be the point to make these people believe it was 1918 again?

'Do you have any family?'

Elsie shook her head. 'No. I was an orphan.'

So that's it. Take kids off the streets, make them believe it's the past. No parents, no one to miss them. 'Me, too,' she lied.

Elsie's eyes sparkled then, seeing a like mind amongst the chaos. 'Dr Munro has been so good to us,' she stressed. She clearly found comfort in her role here, even though it was possibly one of the worst places Mircalla had ever been in. She'd been too young when the war had been raging but it was the efforts of people like Elise and Mhàiri, with the voice of Munro (at least in the early days) that gave Room 40 the impetus to bring operatives like Mircalla into their ranks.

'Do you keep a list of the patients?'

Elsie frowned. 'The doctors do. We know the boys by name and sight but the officers send dispatches back to HQ of all who come through here, including those who don't leave again. Why do you ask?'

Three nurses were tending to a young soldier who had lost his leg below the knee. His shin bone was all but gone and he was thrashing in agony on the narrow bed that had been set up for him in one of the tents. 'Ask one of the doctors for straps,' Elsie said as she and Mircalla passed by. 'He needs to keep still.'

'You asked me why I'm here,' Mircalla said, Elsie nodding as she checked over another lad. 'I'm looking for someone, an officer. You appear to be the nearest Allied hospital this side of Switzerland.' *The only one because you're all so damn deluded.*

'And you think he may have come through here?'

'Captain Daniel Restarick.'

Elsie paused for a moment. 'I don't recognise the name. Do you know what injuries he sustained?'

'No. We were flying across the Med towards Italy. We hit a storm. I bailed out. He surely crashed.'

'We're a bit of a trek from Italy.'

Mircalla nodded. 'A long shot, I know. I fear he may have even ditched in the sea.'

Elsie wondered what Mircalla's purpose was, flying with a captain but did not ask. 'I'll check with the girls, see if they know of him. In the meantime, you can help out if you're here for the next few hours. Idle hands, eh?'

Mircalla knew she had to get to London, knew she had to somehow trace where Restarick had gone, but she simply could not leave Elise and Mhàiri and the others to tend to these soldiers if she could help in any way. Whatever was going on here, there were still wounded and suffering men.

She found herself remaining at Pervyse for the following week, during which time she came to understand that it wasn't just a medical station, it was a last bastion of humanity in a world gone mad. Many of the men coming into the hospital were Belgians, not just British troops. She accompanied teams of nurses and able-bodied survivors out to No Man's Land almost on a daily basis, always on foot and rarely with stretchers, to bring the casualties in to safety. Mhàiri stumbled through one such journey with a soldier hanging from her neck and shoulders. When they got back to the encampment, she'd collapsed. A strained heart valve, was the diagnosis.

'You don't think of death when you're young, you know?' Mhàiri said from her sick bed during her recuperation. 'We just get on with it.'

Mircalla became determined more than ever to get to Room 40 and demand that action be taken to halt this sick charade, even if it meant a direct and blatant retaliation to the occupancy.

Cane Hill Hospital

The law courts for West Sussex were quick to absolve themselves of any responsibility as soon it became known that Max Baker was British Army. But his papers weren't traceable and the military had no option to hold him while they were attempting to resolve the issue.

Baker's insistence that he had caused the pandemic, that he had stolen a phial of the virus from a secret underground lair in Berlin, his wild stories of covert operations and mysterious activities (all of which Whitehall genuinely denied any knowledge of, stating that they had no operative of that name—at least not for another few years, of course) made the next step for the General HQ rather simple. Clearly, the man was insane. As a result, he would be incarcerated at Cane Hill until such time that his identity could be confirmed and he could be court-martialled for the murder of Geena Morelands, a prostitute of no fixed abode.

When word started sweeping around the asylum that there was a new patient saying he started the pandemic, Restarick began to engage himself with others, introducing himself to the dining hall more regularly, willing to sit amongst the other patients. All the while he was picking up snippets of information until one day Max Baker was brought into the dining hall. Restarick recognised him immediately. It was clear however that he'd been treated somewhat roughly.

Baker's temples were sore where the wires had been attached him for the electric shock therapy, his eyes sunken and black. The hair either side of his head was burnt and balding. He held his arms loosely across his chest, a sure sign, Restarick knew, that they'd kept him in a straight-jacket for an excessive amount of time. Two wardens sat him down at a table and thrust a tray of sloppy food under his nose before moving off.

Restarick waited for a while then sidled over. 'Max…' he whispered, sitting opposite. 'Max…'

Baker eventually looked up, a broken man. Pain in his expression, guilt behind his eyes.

'My name's Daniel. Call me Danny if you like.' Restarick's tone was soothing, low.

Baker's face twitched. He opened his mouth to speak then lowered his face again, staring through the plate before him.

'I've been looking for you. I was sent on a mission… by Room 40.'

Baker's eyes flicked up then down. Murmuring, shaking his head. Slight rocking motion.

This is going to take time. 'Alright, I'll leave you be, Max.'

And so Restarick did the same thing every day for a week, with Baker unwilling or unable to talk, staring at the meagre food given to him. Meanwhile, Restarick pretended to take his own medication, kept quiet, did as he was told. He still occasionally trotted out his conviction that he was from the future, just to keep the doctors wary of his apparent improvement to his mental health.

Then, on the Saturday morning, eight days after Baker's arrival, Restarick made progress.

'Why do you say you have been looking for me?'

Restarick was delighted but kept his voice calm. 'Max, this is good news. Look, I don't want to upset anything, but you need to start playing along. I know where you've come from. Have you told them that?' Restarick nodded to the pale green wall, indicating Lilly and his staff.

'I only did was I thought was right. But they don't believe me.'

'But *I* do. I was sent by Room 40 to find out why you defected.'

'Defected? I didn't defect.' Baker's voice was gravelled. He looked around warily. 'Room 40 sent me to investigate what Leo Stanley was doing.'

'Developing the virus?'

Baker nodded, his anxiety lessening slightly. 'Room 40 wanted me to bring the virus to them. They planned to drop it over Germany, on the Kaiser's bonce.'

'But what was the *Kaiser-Regel* planning? Something similar?'

Baker shrugged his shoulders. 'Stanley said they were going to cull those not loyal to the Kaiser. They were going to start with the Jews. At least that was what one of the Kaiser's right-hand men wanted to do.'

'Selective genocide.'

'I couldn't let them do that. I knew that I had to stop them somehow. Even getting a phial of the stuff to Room 40 wouldn't have made any difference to their plan.'

'But Room 40… they really wanted to retaliate that way? It would have been… just…' Restarick couldn't comprehend the devastation of *both* sides purposely releasing the virus. But… it was here now, in the past. A past that was different to the one he and Baker knew. A past created by Baker. 'Did you actually intend to bring it back here, to 1918?'

Hoek van Holland, Netherlands - 1928

Max Baker spent his afternoon in the restaurant of the Hotel Amerika waiting for the ferry to take him across the North Sea to Hull, on England's east coast. His mind was in turmoil at the thought of the terrible things the Kaiser had in store.

The country had been neutral during the war and it remained so even after the downfall of the Allied defences. As a result, it still attracted all manner of subversive operatives and agents from any number of allegiances. It also became home to many who did not want to be involved in the occupancy. There were no kaisersoldaten *here breathing down people's necks.*

The restaurant was busy this particular day and the waitress asked Baker if he had any objection to sharing his table with another customer. Baker said he didn't, moving his newspaper to his right as the old man sat down opposite. The two men both smiled at each other out of politeness.

The old man gave his order to the young girl who scribbled it down on her notepad. Baker detected a Greek accent or similar, paid it no mind, and returned to his own meal.

Soon, the old man's food arrived, steaming hot and delicately placed upon the square plate.

Baker declined dessert, instead opting for coffee.

'Do you mind?'

The old man didn't respond.

'I said,' Baker began, louder this time, 'do you mind?'

The old man looked up from his spanakopita *to shake his head as Baker indicated he wished to smoke. '*Óxi.*'*

Baker lit up and sat back, looking around the restaurant. It was small but well-spaced out, with round tables and an open log fire. The kitchen was hidden behind a slim door. He and the old man had a table by the window. Outside, the port was busy, the quayside bustling with traders and travellers alike. Baker wondered what effect the Kaiser's gift would have upon these innocent people. He tapped the end of his cigarette into the ashtray, accidentally knocking some over the checked tablecloth.

The old man looked up, looked at the spillage, looked at Baker, returned to his meal. 'Your hands shake,' he said, a mouthful if spinach tumbling over his tongue. He was a round-shouldered man, but his semi-straight sitting position spoke of a life of manual work. His back had clearly suffered over the years. His once black hair was now grey and thin, his tanned skin leathery. His English was good, even through the thick Greek accent.

'They never used to.'

'You live here or you pass through?'

The answer Baker gave would tell the old man exactly his business at the port. Instead: 'I think you know.'

The man nodded, wiping his large mouth with a napkin. 'You might live here one day. But not today.'

'Not today.'

'You seemed troubled.'

Baker blew air through his lips. 'You wouldn't believe how much.'

The old man met Baker's eyes, held his gaze for a few uncomfortable seconds. 'Living two lifetimes. Now that's hard.'

He certainly looked like he'd lived long enough, thought Baker. 'Did you serve? Baker's the name, by the way.'

'Call me Kairos. I should have retired but they still wanted pilots who were fit and healthy. I gave up being a flight instructor and returned to service. I could not turn down my country.'

'I was still a kid when the war started. I wanted to enlist but they wouldn't let me.'

'So you work for your country now, eh? It is good.'

'I want the bloody krauts *out. I just don't see any of this ending well.' There was something about this Kairos that made Baker feel like he could tell him anything. Perhaps it was the burden of the phial sitting in its padded case in the bag at his feet. 'We've got the occupancy and everything that forbids us all to do. This should be free Europe. A united Europe. Just not united in this way.'*

'What do you see as the best way to do it?'

'There is no way.'

Kairos nodded sagely, finishing his spanakopita, *the only meal he ever ate. He belched over the back of his left hand. 'There is a way.'*

'How so? My job means I know things that I shouldn't. Information that's key to our survival. But we will all be wiped out.'

'I have watched you for a long time.'

'Watched me? What do you mean?' Baker tensed.

'The comings and goings of all. See him there?' Kairos leant forward and pointed to a table by the window where there sat a man, slightly hunched, arthritic fingers. 'He comes here every day. Like me. Not like you. You come sometimes but today you seem like you need to move on, finally, yes? Anyway, that man… he sits by the window. He orders toast and coffee. Nothing else. He sits like he is waiting. He check his watch. No one ever turns up.' Kairos shifted his position and motioned to a woman sitting by the counter. 'Her. She meets a man here twice a week, they leave separately

but together, she returns alone. He is married, she a widow. They do this knowingly. We all have purpose, even if sometimes that purpose seems meaningless, pointless.'

'What has any if this got to do with me?'

'You fly?'

'I can fly, yes.'

'I have watched you. I have waited for someone like you. Perhaps it is fate not coincidence that we meet here, no?' Kairos lifted a clean napkin from a nearby trolley and wrote on it. He passed it to Baker. 'Take your information to those coordinates. You will see there is a way.' Kairos waved the waitress over. 'A drink for my friend and I here. Your finest retsina, *if you would be so kind.'*

The waitress smiled and nodded.

'Can I have my bill, please?' Baker asked.

'No. No. I pay,' Kairos said.

'I cannot allow you to do that.'

But the old man was insistent. To the waitress: 'Please, we settle up everything together when we leave.' He turned back to Baker. 'You are here to go to England with your secret knowledge. As you say it will do no good.'

'How do you know?'

'I live two lifetimes. I see it all happen again. I was given this chance for a reason. You I think are the reason. You go there instead…' He waved at the napkin. 'You will know. And you will know what to do with your secrets.'

Cane Hill Hospital

'"I live two lifetimes," he said,' breathed Baker. 'But I knew he wasn't a foolish old man, drunk on his Greek wine.'

'He travelled through the storm.' Restarick felt a burden lift. 'As did you.'

'And *you*.' Baker prodded the slop in the plate before him. 'He wrote down the place to fly through on that napkin. He must have found it by accident and lived all those years again like *we're* now doing. I didn't know that, of course. Not at first. When I crashed my plane in Italy, I began to regret my decision to disobey my orders to get to London with the phial. Then when I realised it was 1918 again, that's when what he said to me made sense. "And you will know what to do with your secrets."'

'Kairos' folly,' murmured Restarick, 'You were foolish, too. Perhaps I was for following you! He'd obviously had ten years to think about why he had found himself back here in the past.'

'But what I did next I will never be able to come to terms with. I knew exactly what to do with my secret. It seemed so clear to me. I had the phial. I thought if I could spread it amongst the Germans, on a smaller scale to what Room 40 had planned in 1928, I could perhaps slow the war machine down, give us Allies the advantage.' Baker shrank back into himself, ashamed, guilty, desperate to free himself of his demons. 'I let the virus loose on a German hospital ship… where I knew they were all too weak to fight off any infection. I fled back to Blighty, hid for as long as I was able. I sat back and watched the whole thing unfold across the continent like some living nightmare. It was low-key at first, then when it reached Spain… You see, I thought I could change the outcome of the war. Instead I've released into the world the deadliest outbreak of influenza in history. People are dying in their thousands, millions. Not just Germans. But British, American, Spanish…' Baker knocked the plate to the floor and buried his head in his hands, shaking violently.

'Now that's enough of that, patient 1985,' a warden said, dashing over as the plate smashed, spewing food across the tiles, up the wall, 'or it'll be back to the isolation cell for you.'

Baker sat upright and Restarick flinched at the look of utter hatred that quickly flashed across the man's face, gone as soon as it had appeared.

'They can do what they like to me here. I deserve everything coming to me. I deserve it. Deserve it you hear?!' he cried, voice rising with every breath.

More wardens rushed over and pulled Baker from his chair, who went without fuss, without any aggression anymore. His confession to Restarick had been all that he wanted. Someone to listen to him, to understand him, to believe him. Now that was done, Baker didn't care. He would die knowing he had killed millions. And he wanted to be punished for it.

Restarick watched with pity as patient 1985 allowed himself to be dragged away, absorbing everything that had just been said. His reverie was interrupted by one of the nurses.

'How are you today, Daniel?'

'Erm…' Restarick rubbed his forehead. 'Yes, I'm fine. Thank you.'

'Are you sure?'

'Yes, really, I am.'

'Well, Mr Lilly has arranged a special treat for you.'

Restarick was confused. 'A… treat?'

***

The sweet smell of lime trees invaded the room as Lilly opened the top half of the sash window behind his desk.

The captain standing before him was immaculate in his uniform, moustache trimmed neatly and his cap tight under his left arm.

'Look, I'm sorry to drag you all the way out here,' Lilly began, sitting back down. 'It's this patient we have here. He's a harmless sort but won't engage much with any of the others. Doesn't show any signs of shellshock apart from this bizarre idea that he's from 1928. We've got no worries he's going to harm himself or anyone else. Amicable all round, really. Most odd.'

'But he insists his name is identical to mine?' the captain responded.

'Oh, yes. Definitely.'

'Look, anything I can do to help out these poor chaps. Damned bloody awful if you ask me.'

'Seeing you for himself might knock him out of it all. Although, I have to say…' Lilly squinted at the captain.

'What it is?'

'You *do* look remarkably similar. Are you sure you don't have an older brother or a cousin?'

'No, just a younger brother and sister—neither of whom look like me. I take after our mother, they our father.'

***

When the captain sat opposite Daniel Restarick in the asylum's well-tended garden, he had to agree with Superintendent Lilly's opinion that there was a striking resemblance.

Restarick was far older, perhaps by about ten years, but it was easy to assume they were related. Perhaps there was indeed a familial link somewhere in the past. But to have exactly the same name? It was more likely that somehow this patient had discovered a doppelganger and for some unfathomable reason, adopted his identity.

The captain indicated to the accompanying wardens that he would be quite alright with the patient and the two men were left alone, albeit overseen at a distance.

'The superintendent tells me that you're doing well, that you keep yourself very much to yourself. I think I'd do the same if I were here.' The captain looked around him, taking in the activities of the other patients, how they seemed to be locked away in their own heads, or scared of the slightest thing. The sooner this war would be over, the more time could be given to those who suffered for the cause.

Restarick stared at the captain. It wasn't exactly like looking in a mirror because the captain wasn't a reflection: he was himself at this time in his life, at age twenty. He realised that Lilly's intention to bring him face to face with the 'real' Captain Restarick was to break the delusion. But of course, there was no delusion. Restarick had travelled back in time and seeing his younger self sitting across from him, in the prime of his military career, before the mistake at Saint-Mihiel, reinforced that fact. Baker's impassioned declaration an hour ago he knew he could share with no-one.

'But you are here. In me. This is what happens to you. Fighting for your sanity, fighting to be believed when there is no way in Hell that anyone could, would or even *should* believe you.'

'You really believe you've come from the future? *My* future? That you're me?'

'"Really believe…" implies it's not a fact.' Restarick looked down at his lap, at the small piece of thread hanging at the stitching of his white trousers. 'I *am* you. I *am* from 1928. If you refuse to accept that, then this is where you'll be condemning yourself for the rest of your life.'

The captain watched his older self toy with the thread. 'And how am I meant to accept what you say? They've put you in here because they think you're mad. You think you've travelled through time, for Heaven's sake! Now that *is* madness!'

'One moment we were flying over the Med, having taken off from an Italian airbase in North Africa, then I crashed in Italy. We'd gone through a storm but when I came out it was 1918.' Even Restarick understood how ridiculous that was.

'"We"… "I"… Were you alone or not in this plane?'

'There were two of us. We were on a mission to find a missing agent. Who, funnily enough, is here in this very asylum. My companion however bailed out. I kept flying.'

'So this companion might very well be in this time too, from...' The captain breathed out sharply. He was trying to make sense of this bizarre tale. 'From the future?'

'Yes. Yes! She can verify what I'm saying!' *Because you definitely won't believe Baker.*

'And where do we start to look for her?'

'She must have landed in Italy. She parachuted. She works for Room 40. Mircalla Richard. Although she does use other names.'

The captain tensed. How did this man know about Room 40? Was he a spy? Was he feigning madness under the pretence of using the Restarick name to bring the captain here? Did he know the captain was a Room 40 operative?

'Mircalla Richard, you say?' The captain didn't recognise the name.

'Yes, but I don't think she joined the Factory until the mid-1920s.'

The captain raised an eyebrow. 'Naturally.'

'So where are you now?'

'What do you mean?'

'It's June 1918. You're in France. You're trailing a spy.'

The captain swallowed hard, trying not to seem agitated that this patient knew more than he should. 'I am?'

'Yes. The Factory want to intercept some papers. Important papers.'

'Let me ask you this: if you are me... if you've come back from...'

'1928.'

'...yes, 1928, then surely you'd remember this conversation? You would know that I would have been recalled here by Whitehall. You would know exactly what we spoke about.'

Restarick frowned. 'Yes, that would...'

'Make sense?' the captain finished, scanning Restarick's expression. A gentle breeze course around the garden then, the leaves on the trees rustling, the scent of the flower beds curling into the fresh air. 'But you don't remember.'

'No. I don't.' *But I should. Why* don't *I remember?*

'Do you think that you have some form of selective amnesia? That you only *think* you're me? You saw my name on a dispatch, perhaps, and you recalled it somehow?'

Restarick shook his head. 'Lita.'

The captain tensed, now unable to hide his growing suspicion that this patient was a spy for sure. 'How do you know of her?'

'She's my... our wife.' *God rest her soul.* Something quite shocking occurred to Restarick then. He took a deep breath in; 'Is she... well?'

'Well? Yes, she is, thank you. Although that really is none of your business.' The captain felt perhaps it was time to bring this conversation to a close.

Oh my God. Lita. She was alive! It was 1918 and she was still alive! The fire that had killed her so awfully hadn't happened yet. Baker's words rang in his ears: "I thought I could change the outcome…" And what was it is sister had said? "Life goes on, Danny. It is what it is. If someone said to you that you could go back and change it all, how do you know it would be for the better?" Perhaps, he… No, he couldn't possibly.

Could he?

'I need you to get me out of here.' *I have to go to Lita. I have to take her away before the fire destroys our home. Destroys everything.* 'Will you help me?' *How can I possibly tell you she will die soon? Or perhaps* by *telling you, you'll go there yourself just to be sure I'm lying… realise I'm not… and save her! But…* I *need to see her again.* I *need to go.* I *must be the one who saves her because* I've *lived with this pain for ten years and you haven't! I can* stop *the pain here and now! I don't have to live with the guilt like Baker will!*

'I don't see how I can. You might look like me, you may know who I am, but how am I to know you're not a plant, sent here by the Central Powers to glean information about Room 40?'

'James Restarick, a retired naval merchant captain. He bought a tea plantation in Ceylon.'

'My father, yes. You can get that information if you're looking in the right place.'

'Lita…'

'I really wish you would refrain from mentioning my wife.'

'I have a photograph of her.'

'A photograph. Of *my* wife.'

Restarick nodded. 'In with my personal belongings. Speak to the staff. Perhaps they'll let you see it.'

'*This* photograph?' The captain pulled the image from his own breast pocket. Restarick's heart skipped.

'Yes.' It was the same photograph because the captain was him. So the photograph Restarick had back in the storeroom… 'I feel unwell.'

The captain frowned but tucked the sepia portrait away safely before leaning in to Restarick. 'Shall I call a warden? A nurse?'

Restarick shook his head, wiping his brow. 'No. I just need to lie down. Will you help me back to my room?'

'Of course. But I have to be on my way soon. My car is here to collect me on the hour.'

The captain helped Restarick back in from the garden, along the long corridors and back to the patient's room.

Restarick shuffled through the door and stumbled as he reached the bed. The captain's reactions were quick and he grabbed Restarick's elbows to save him from hitting the floor.

But Restarick took his younger self by surprise, twisted away from him and grabbed the tin cup that was on the little bedside cabinet. It wasn't a deadly weapon by any stretch of the imagination but Restarick had been taught well by Room 40 to use anything as a tool when needed, smashing the cup against the side of the captain's head.

The captain crashed to the floor, unconscious.

Restarick worked quickly, pushing the door to, but not closed (for that would raise suspicion). He undressed the captain and himself, changing into the uniform and putting the captain into his own pyjama-like outfit.

'Put on a bit of weight there, old chap,' he said to himself, the buttons on the shirt and jacket a little snug. A quick look down at his new clothes, which were technically at the same time also his old clothes, he put the captain in the bed, pulling up the covers over him.

Cap on to cover the greying hair around his temples and he could easily pass for the captain… if nobody looked too closely. He patted his left breast pocket, feeling the small rectangle of Lita's photograph within.

The clock on the wall outside in the corridor was just after quarter past. By the time he walked to the reception desk, picked up the captain's revolver that would have been handed in for safety and got to the main doors, the car would just about be ready. The driver wouldn't look twice. Within thirty minutes, he could be home in Thornton Heath and taking Lita to safety.

Pervyse

Mircalla dragged the soldier by his arms up the bank carved out by a mortar shell. The mud was cold and putrid, gritty in her mouth and slimy under her collar.

The soldier had been running along the edge of No Man's Land when the shell had hit, flinging him high into the air and back down the bottom of the new crater. Mircalla, on a motorbike and coming in the opposite direction, had managed to slide to a stop before being struck herself. She knew the soldier wasn't on her side but still couldn't leave him.

Once she had him flat on the ground, she soothed him with reassuring words, checking the gaping wound on his right thigh. He was shivering. Gently, she wiped his eyes clear of dirt and blood. She wasn't expecting to see the face she revealed. In fact, she had never expected to see it ever again.

'Aaron?'

Aaron Kaplan, a fresh-faced young soldier in the Austro-Hungarian army, blinked a few times, bemused to hear his own name come from this woman's lips. They were rather beautiful lips, he had to admit. 'Who… who are you?'

'It's me… It's Mircalla! How are you here? How can you be alive?'

Aaron winced as he shifted where he lay. 'If it wasn't for you…' he began, confused. Had she been struck by a shell herself and was delirious?

'But you died. I saw you. Back in Algiers. God, we left you in that desert! I'm so sorry we left you behind.'

'I don't know who you are. I have never been to Algiers.' Aaron sank back in the mud, exhausted with the conversation.

'I need to get you back to the hospital.'

'You are Allied. They will make me a prisoner of war.'

'No, no, Aaron. The war is over! Don't you remember? The Central Powers declared victory.' She grabbed some bandages from her shoulder bag, cleaning his wound as best she could. The pain was almost unbearable for him and he blacked out at least twice, but she brought him around each time. 'We're occupied now. You were helping us. Restarick and me.'

She eventually got him to his feet and looped one of his arms over her shoulders. She would come back for the motorbike. Getting to London now would have to wait now that Aaron was here. She couldn't believe it. It was incredible he'd survived the desert.

'I… am grateful you are helping me, *Fraulein*, but I do not know what you are talking about. This is my first posting since school.'

'Since school? Aaron! You left school, what, eleven years ago? We've been through hell since then! You got me pregnant twice!'

Even though he could barely stand let alone walk, Kaplan tried to pull away from her. This woman was obsessed, unhinged. Eleven years ago he would have been six! And as for getting her pregnant… He hadn't even lost his virginity yet.

'I need to return to my section. I will not say I met you. I will say I bandaged myself.'

'But you're injured, Aaron. I can't leave you in the middle of nowhere for a second time.'

Kaplan breathed in sharply and thrust against her side. He toppled to the sucking mud, his revolver out and pointing up at Mircalla. He was dressed like an infantryman but his having a sidearm, usually an officer's privilege, indicated he was a trench raider.

This charade really was sticking to detail, she mused.

'Aaron, why don't you trust me?'

'I do not know who you are,' Kaplan wheezed through the waves of pain. 'Come any closer and I will shoot you, *Fraulein*!'

Cane Hill

'You there! Wait!'

Restarick didn't turn around. He was so close to the captain's car now that he could almost touch the passenger door handle.

'I said wait!' The warden was very insistent.

The driver got out, concerned by the noise. Had a patient escaped? 'Are you alright, sir?'

'Yes, yes, get back in,' Restarick said calmly but firmly.

Ever the obedient soldier, the driver did as he was ordered,

'Driver! Driver!' came more shouting. 'That man, the captain, he is an imposter!'

Restarick could see the driver's growing confusion and concern. He wrenched open the door and dived into the back seat. 'Move! Move!'

'Sir,' the driver began, turning around.

'Just step on it!'

The driver ignited the engine and swung the vehicle towards the gates. There were wardens racing across the grass.

'Sir, they're…'

'Smash through them if you have to!'

'Yes, sir.' The driver accelerated the car on but the wardens had managed to block their exit. 'They're rather strong looking gates, sir. Are you sure we should do this?'

'Do as you are ordered, man!'

Restarick craned his neck to look out of the rear window. There were a group of wardens haring down the gravel road now, with the captain and Lilly staying behind in the arched porch.

'Sir…'

Restarick faced forward. The wardens were standing in a line before the gates. He knew it was hopeless. Those gates were wrought iron and he couldn't order the driver to mow the men down. He sighed and sat back. 'Stop. Stop the car.'

'Yes, sir,' the driver said, relieved, bringing the car to a skidding halt only a few feet from the anxious-looking wardens.

Within seconds, the wardens were upon the vehicle and had Restarick out of the captain's uniform blazer into a straight-jacket. As he was marched back up the asylum's ornate entrance, he glanced at the captain who was chewing on his bottom lip. Restarick new that expression very well. He did it when he started pondering when the facts didn't present themselves well.

The captain was insistent that Restarick was quite harmless, citing his escape attempt as impulsive and fuelled by panic. Lilly wasn't so sure but respected the officer's decision.

Restarick was back in his cell, back in the white flannel trousers and shirt. He opted to sit on the stool that was bolted to the floor. The captain stood at the door, pulling it closed.

The light was failing through the narrow slit of the high window.

'I knew that look you gave me,' Restarick said.

'It occurred to me that I would have done the same if I were you.' He raised a hand as Restarick began to reply. 'Yes, and you're about to tell me that I am you.' The captain smiled.

'I get the impression that you're starting to believe me. Why?'

'When I woke up and realised what you'd done, I called Lilly. I did think that he'd need some convincing I wasn't you, but you did that for me, thank you. When you ignored the warden, they knew something was up.'

'So you want to interrogate me? Find out why I'm pretending to be you?'

The captain shook his head and took from a pocket Restarick's worn photograph of Lita. 'I asked to see your belongings. This looks very old but it can't be, can it?' He held it up with the one from his breast pocket, clean and not yet soiled with blood and time. 'It's the same photograph.'

'Yes.'

'And whose blood is on it? Hers? Yours?'

'Mine.' Restarick sighed. 'I take her with me everywhere I go. I need to know she—'

'—is with me every day...' they both said together.

'So if I *am* to believe you, that you *are* from the future...'

Restarick straightened in the chair. 'I am.'

'...can you tell me what happens? When does the war end? How do I become you?'

Restarick wondered if knowing his own future was allowed. Would it change things? Baker had already done that, Kairos before him by telling Baker about the storm. 'I didn't try to escape to find out Room 40's secrets. I am a spy, yes, as are you... but spying on myself?' Restarick shrugged.

'I understand why you would want to get out of here.'

'I did it to save Lita.'

The captain tensed. 'Why?'

Restarick pursed his lips. 'Ten years ago for me, next week for you, Lita... dies in a fire in our home in Thornton Heath. I was told by letter when I was in Verdun.'

'I go to Verdun next week.'

Restarick nodded. 'To intercept the spy.'

The captain moved to the bed and sat down hard. 'And this is going to happen?'

'Getting that letter… my world ended. I returned home for the funeral then the Factory sent me straight back out to Verdun. I spent the next few weeks in a haze.'

'I need to go to her.'

'No.' Restarick was firm. 'You are needed in Verdun. You are so close to stopping the spy. You need to shoot. Whatever you do, you need to shoot. Kill the spy and all will be as I should be.'

'You go to Verdun! You know what to do if you've already done it!' The captain couldn't believe he was going along with the unhinged conversation.

'Max Baker knew his purpose coming here was to slow down the Central Powers war machine. He didn't realise he'd miscalculated. Kairos, who told him about being able to travel back… his purpose was to tell Baker how to do it. My purpose, I know now is to save Lita. Yours to stop the spy, no matter what. The future really does depend on it.' Restarick understood how Baker felt to unload this confession upon another, even if that other was himself. 'I've lived with the guilt for ten years.'

'But…' The captain looked exasperated. 'The idea that we can go back again and again, correcting all the mistakes we made… Paving over our failures by trying again. When would we stop? Could we stop? It's like a writer editing their own book: at some point they have to accept that any more changes will alter the story beyond any recognition—and sometimes those changes aren't always for the best.'

'I agree,' said Restarick. 'There has to be a point when one realises we should never have been given this control. This power. To actually go back and correct these mistakes. Surely that's a power worth having?'

'Time isn't something to be used and changed and altered or tweaked as we see fit.'

'Why not? Why shouldn't we use this knowledge? I can save Lita! By shooting the spy dead, you can give the Allies the victory that the future—my future—never witnessed!'

'Think about what you're implying. Tell me right here, right now as we stare down this abyss, that this world we live in isn't meant to be—that we're meant to lose?'

'I can't say that! But if we can stop whole countries entering into what is tantamount to organised slavery, then I'll be damned if I don't stand to one side and pass this opportunity by.'

'It's a futile if admirable attitude. But flawed.'

'You sound like Angela.'

'She always was the sensible one in the family.'

'She told me that what is, is what is. That we can't go back…' Restarick's voice trailed off. 'But I am here. And I can change it! We can… together!'

The captain drummed his fingers on the wall. 'I'm going to regret this, aren't I? Trusting you…'

***

Superintendent Lilly nearly pierced the form before him with the nib of his Jewel fountain pen. He growled under his breath and pushed the paper away, ruined by the swelling spread of dark blue ink.

'Will you repeat that?' he said, glancing at Michaels who coughed into his hand, as disbelieving as his superior.

'I said: I wish to sign patient 1955's release forms as I will be taking on sole responsibility for his welfare.' The captain looked straight at Lilly's round face. 'I would like to take him with me today.'

'Today?' Lilly echoed. 'You want me to release into your custody the man who is convinced is you?'

'Yes.'

'May I ask why? On whose authority are you doing this?'

'He is…' The captain licked his dry lips. 'He is my brother.'

Lilly leant back in his chair, his waistcoat stretching at his waist. 'I have to say this is most odd.'

'Most odd indeed,' added Michaels, then retreated back into silence.

'He is my older brother,' justified the captain, knowing Lilly had detected the pause when he explained who the patient was to him.

'Why did you not happen to mention this before?' The superintendent waved Michaels over. 'Get patient 1955's file.'

'My work for the War Office precludes me from the need to explain. However, I can say that when you sent the wire to my HQ, I did wonder if it was my brother that you had admitted.' He tried to keep his expression as emotionless as possible, but with Lilly looking at him intently… 'As soon as I saw him, I was relieved he was safe.'

The file before him now, Lilly flipped through to the admission form. 'He told us he had no living next of kin that we could contact. He seemed very sure.'

'That *you* could contact,' the captain pressed. 'As I say, my work—'

'Precludes you. Yes, I understand,' huffed Lilly. 'Once I sign his release, he is your responsibility. I will not accept him back here if you cannot manage the situation. If you require him to be readmitted, you will need to find somewhere else to treat him. He is not welcome at Cane Hill again.'

I think I might need locking up myself for going through with this. 'I agree with your terms. But I do hope it won't come to that.'

Greenwich Park, England

'Shouldn't you have been on the train by now?'

Lita Restarick shielded her eyes from the setting sun as her colleague from the munitions factory stopped at the bench where Lita was sitting. There was a bicycle propped up against the arm.

'Hello, Violet,' Lita replied, a smile across her pretty, olive-skinned face. 'The flowers are dying now. I wanted to see them before they disappear.'

Before them, the rose garden had lost most of its blooms, the water from the duck pond adding a chill to the late August air. Carole looked at the roses, too, agreeing with Lita.

'They are very lovely. Autumn brings its own beauty, though.' The little white dog at Violet's feet yapped at a duck flapping by. 'Enough, Milly. I thought I saw you talking to someone.'

Lita shook her head, pointing at the water. 'Just the ducks.'

Violet could have sworn blind there had been a man a few feet away from the bench as she'd approached. He'd clearly seen Violet coming along the path, pulled his large collar up around his ears and darted away. 'Well...'

Lita stood, patting down the front of her coat. 'I must be off. My train.'

'Yes, I did think you'd might be missing it. You're Croydon-way, aren't you?'

Lita nodded, her dark curls protruding from under her hat. 'Thornton Heath. My husband and I, we have a little house there. It's a by a pond. Not as big as this, though.'

'I didn't know you were married.'

'To a captain in the British Army,' Lita said, pride in her voice accentuated by her Spanish lilt. 'He is away in France on important duties.'

'Do you have any children?'

Lita shook her head. She didn't work directly with Violet but they had both arrived at the Royal Arsenal the same day following the fire at Silvertown last year. Like most of the *munitionettes*, they chatted as groups, rarely one-on-one. Lita was prone to keeping herself to herself. A few of the women didn't seem to like that she was Spanish, often over-hearing talk that all Spaniards were cowards for staying neutral during the war. Lita would ignore them for the most part, recognising their ignorance. 'If we are all cowards, why would I come here every day and do what we do?' she would sometimes say, though, smiling as their overheard gossip subsided into more mundane matters.

'Shall I walk with you?' Violet asked, her dog pulling at the lead.

'Thank you, but no,' Lita replied. 'I am going the other way, to London Bridge.'

'Goodness. That will take you well over an hour!'

'No, not long. I have my bicycle with me.'

Violet looked over at the contraption with its basket hanging from the handlebars and the chipped black paint. It had seen better days, Lita having bought it second-hand from a bakery near to where she lived, but she was perfectly happy with it.

They said their goodbyes, until tomorrow, proceeding in opposite directions. Violet looked back a couple of times, sure that man had reappeared, but Lita by then had cycled off into the distance.

Thornton Heath, England

It was dark by the time Lita's train had reached the station. She made quick work of grabbing her bicycle from the guard's van and free-wheeled all the way down Brigstock Road to the town's pond, turning off and walking the rest of the way. She rolled her bicycle along the side of her house, leaning it up against the wall. Side gate open, 'round the back, key under a plant pot and she was in her kitchen, stove lit, a pot of tea on its way.

'*Hola, corazón*.'

Lita spun, dropping to the floor the teacup she'd been holding. It smashed, flinging pieces everywhere. She looked down at it then up again at the officer standing across from her.

'Daniel?'

'My Lita, my beautiful Lita…'

He couldn't help but smile. His heart jumped, pounding in his chest. There had been no chance he would have ever seen her again, at least not in this life, but here she was, here *they* were. Together. Standing in their kitchen. Her hands were shaking. The shock, he concluded. It *had* been a long time. Ten years.

But not for her.

'What are you doing here?' she asked.

Her voice! It sent his pulse racing. 'I'm home.'

'But you left last week. You were going to France. Did they reassign you? Why are you back?'

'Let me look at you!' Restarick exclaimed, rushing towards her, sweeping her up and swinging around. 'You cannot believe how much I have dreamed for this moment again!' He smelt her hair, drank in her scent, her tanned skin, her very being.

She was rigid under his embrace.

'I do not understand, Daniel. What has happened to you?' She tried to pull away.

'Happened? Nothing!'

'Your hair. Your eyes.'

'What about them?' He didn't care that he looked older to her. He was drowning in her presence. 'Lita, I'm home! I love you!'

'You are grey… here…' she pointed to his temples, 'and here. Your eyes, you have wrinkles.'

'It's the war, my love. It ages a man.'

'It is not you.' Lita pushed him away. 'I have to clean this mess up.'

'Leave it.' He wanted to pick her up, to carry her upstairs to bed, to make love to her again like they used to. Her Latin passion wrapped around him as he sank deep inside her. 'Please… leave it…'

Was she not pleased he was home? What was the matter with her?

'I have to leave early in the morning for work. I won't have time to do it then.'

Restarick sighed, stepping back as she knelt to scoop the broken china into a tea towel. 'I have so much I want to tell you.' *I've travelled back in time. I'm here to save you. There will be no fire. We will have the rest of our lives together.* 'Come away with me.'

'Daniel… You are like you are possessed.' She didn't turn around.

He looked at the curve of her hips, saw how her back was arched slightly. 'I've missed you. It's been unbearable.'

'You have only been gone a week, Daniel.' No *corazón*, No smile. She was distant, pointedly so.

If she won't come to me… Restarick crouched next to her and picked up the larger pieces of the teacup. Their hands brushed. She paused, looking at his fingers, then at his face. He did look older. It actually suited him, made him look more distinguished. For a moment, she relaxed. Then, after a glance at the clock on the wall, her barrier was up again.

'I'm tired. I think I need to go to bed.'

Restarick knew by her tone that was not an invite.

A noise in the hallway made him tense. He'd missed this old house and was desperate to look around, to restore distant memories with reality. But the noise came again. He knew it wasn't the place settling in for the night, the pipes in the walls contracting.

'There's something out there,' he announced.

'No, there's not. Leave it.' Lita was insistent. But so was Restarick.

He moved out of the kitchen and down the hallway, feeling the raised wallpaper under his fingertips. There was a shadow falling across the floor. Restarick paused, seeing what the shadow would do next. A shape appeared at the front door, obscured by the frosted, coloured glass panes. There was a streetlamp at the end of the garden path that illuminated their hallway. Sometimes it magnified the shadows of passers-by. Tonight, it told him they had a visitor.

'There's someone at the door,' he said.

'Probably someone just going past. It's not important.'

But Restarick was thinking otherwise. He opened the door to reveal the back of a man, quite large, in a long dark coat, with the collar around his ears, a hat firmly upon his head. The image took Restarick back within seconds. He recognised the outline. It was that of the spy at Saint-Mihiel. The one he had failed to stop. The one that had given the secrets to the Central Powers to win the war.

The figure turned around, startled to see Restarick standing there. He looked beyond, to the end of the hallway, to see Restarick's wife cradling the tea towel.

Restarick whipped out his service revolver and lunged at the man. 'What the hell are you doing here? We live here! What do you want?'

The man stepped forward, not back, surprising Restarick with the unexpected assault. Immediately, Restarick slipped out from under his opponent, an elbow to the jaw. The man breathed out heavily but the contact didn't slow him down. They tumbled into the hallway, the carpet rubbing against Restarick's face. He saw a holdall, packed, at the bottom of the stairs, making a mental note to ask Lita about it as soon as he had dealt with this stranger.

He sprang up, the revolver still in his grip. But not for long. The man struck out, knocking it clean across the floor, following up with a series of swift, harsh punches. Restarick raised his hands to protect himself from the raining blows, staggering back to the kitchen. Lita had ducked out of the way, but he couldn't tell where she had gone.

A second figure stepped into the house, dressed similarly to the first man. Restarick was angry now. This invasion of their home was intolerable. He grabbed the narrow three-legged table that sat by the door to the under-stairs cupboard, throwing it at the men. It broke, the legs becoming useful clubs for whoever could pick them up first. Restarick didn't waste time bothering, instead dashing into the kitchen. He grabbed a bread knife from a drawer.

'Come on then, you fucking bastards,' he breathed, brandishing the blade, having every intention of using it. 'Are you here for me, or here for her? Either way, you can fucking forget it.'

The second man darted forward. Restarick lunged, stabbing him neatly in the gut. The man cried out and staggered into the stove, knocking the kettle off the ring of blue flames, replacing it with his own sleeve. The man roared as his coat caught alight.

The first man said something Restarick couldn't make out.

Lita suddenly appeared in the kitchen. 'Get out! Get away! Go get the police!' he yelled at her, dodging the man who by now had fallen to the floor, burning like a bonfire Guy.

The first man spun and shouted at Lita, who raced to the front door, only to be stopped by yet another visitor. Restarick raised the knife and brought it down into the first man's shoulder. The man twisted around and tripped over his roasting colleague, tumbling into Restarick. As one, they crashed through the back door and into the garden, Restarick striking his head on the flagstone path. He heard

Lita screaming amidst the sudden roar of flames as the entire kitchen caught alight, soon engulfing the whole house.

He scrambled out from under the unconscious man, the bread knife still where he had plunged it, desperate to get back into the kitchen.

The fire held him back, the heat intense and increasing.

'Lita! Lita!' he cried, seeing through the flames and in the hallway a lithe female form prone upon the burning carpet. He raced around to the front of the house, tripping over Lita's bicycle on the way.

But it was no use. His way in was blocked from the front too and all he could do was scream Lita's name over and over again as their house burnt down before his very eyes.

Cane Hill

Baker's own belief that he could end the war and wipe out the enemy by using against them the virus they that themselves created in a laboratory in the future of 1928 was for one brief moment, cemented.

When news had filtered through that the Kaiser himself had succumbed to the violent strain of influenza, it was believed that the figurehead of the destruction would end up just as dead as the millions of others around the world. But he survived. So did the virus, reaching pandemic proportions by the summer.

Baker had opened the phial in March, days after he had arrived in 1918. His choice of locale was Étaples, a vast military base south of Boulogne. He judged that the presence of port facilities, railway yards, stables, cemeteries, infantry depots, training grounds and so on would be ideal to take the disease out to the enemy. His naivety cost him his sanity and the lives of one-hundred million people, for the virus did not care if it infected German, Austro-Hungarian, British, American, Turkish troops, nor if the victims were leaders or soldiers, the old or the young.

One hundred million.

The war itself had only take thirty-eight million by the end of 1917.

Scientists across the world were desperate to find a cure. Baker had ingested the cure and destroyed any evidence it had existed. He alone could stride through an infected hospital ward, through a field of dying children, their agonising cries for an end to their tormented horror, and not succumb to the virus.

No one at the asylum believed him.

The doctors never believed any of the patients, anyway. They were all deluded, insane, every last one of them. They were only worth locking up.

The more Baker insisted he'd been the instigator of the pandemic, the more they prescribed shock treatment.

The more they prescribed shock treatment, the more Baker insisted.

They were at a loss to understand him.

When the warden did his regular tour of the asylum in the early hours of Sunday morning, peering through the peep holes in the doors, Baker in his own cell appeared to be quiet for once and staring at the ceiling on his narrow bed. His torso was entwined in the straight-jacket that was a permanent form of apparel for him. It was only when the doors were opened up at 0600 and everyone ushered out for breakfast that they realised Baker was dead.

He'd swallowed his own tongue.

Verdun, France

Second innings on the front line was not how Restarick had intended to spend his days but here he was nevertheless. It was all such a long time ago but being back made it feel like he'd never been off the battlefield. He was in a section of trench that snaked across the Western Front, used more for reconnaissance and regrouping now than defence or attack. Verdun had been the site of a furiously bloody battle in 1916, one he had never been directly involved in, but one that lingered in the memory long after the Allies had fallen.

The stillness of the land, drained of any colour, with its gaping craters and blackened, charred tree stumps seemed to send a wash of grey up into the sky that even the setting sun couldn't penetrate. The cold wind was relentless, sweeping across the scarred, still landscape, giving no respite to the wounded and dying. Yet, just a few hundred yards away there would be hundreds of men, waiting silently in their own enemy trenches for any sign of life from the Allied lines. In some places, the opposing forces could even be as little as one hundred and fifty feet apart. The dead, however, didn't care.

And neither did Restarick.

No, that wasn't entirely true.

He'd ran from his home, bewildered, lost, completely against everything he'd be trained for by Room 40 when facing impossible odds. How many times had he woken up in the middle of the night, sweat running down his face, the clarity of his nightmares of Lita's horrific death fading like sand through a sieve? It had been his imagination, soaking up the news from the letter he'd received about her death—he'd receive it again soon—but now he'd witnessed it, been a catalyst to it. To live with guilt for a decade that he hadn't been there to save Lita's life had been hell. Now he had become directly instrumental in her life ending.

Yet he did still care. Of course he did. He had to care about the world he lived in, to care about freedom and justice. It was why he agreed to join the Factory when he was a serving officer. It was why he agreed to leave Ceylon following his retirement and work for them one last time.

He had a job to do. He failed the last time. He wasn't about to fail again.

Restarick drew the handheld periscope back down and leant it against a pile of sandbags. The trench narrowed to no more than two feet wide in places, due to landslides and shelling or where the men had been simply too exhausted to dig it out any wider. Restarick's boots were sucked into the watery mud as he trudged along, his toes almost numb with the cold, heading towards the officers' dug-out (basically a hole in the ground with corrugated tin over it covered in dirt). He ducked under the twisted fuselage of a rusting, downed Nieuport 16 fighter lying across the top of the trench and into the dug-out a further hundred yards east.

Within, Corporal Richardson sat on a rickety chair, First Private Packer pacing up and down.

'Good God, sit down! You're like a floppin' caged animal.'

Packer nodded, his gold-rimmed spectacles glinting in the candlelight and positioned himself on the narrow bunk in the corner.

As Restarick entered, Richardson and Packer jumped to attention.

'As you were,' Restarick said gently, taking a place at the other end of the bunk by Packer.

Richardson was a tall man, his blonde receding hair shaved back to his scalp. One of the rugger set back home in Blighty, he filled his uniform well. 'Get the captain a drink, Packer.'

Packer obliged, pouring a tot of rum into a tin mug and handed it to Restarick.

'Thank you,' Restarick said, sipping at the tangy alcohol. 'How are your men doing?'

Richardson's section had been caught unexpectedly by a Bulgarian platoon, suffering four fatalities and severe wounds of the surviving men. Richardson and Packer had managed to find cover in this abandoned stretch of trench, sending word north that they needed urgent medical attention.

'Not too bad considering. The Pervyse lot are sending a couple of nurses down. Should be here before midnight.' Richardson stood and circled the claustrophobic area. 'How long are you staying with us, sir, if you don't mind me asking? We've limited supplies, an' all that.'

'I shall be heading out soon.'

'On your own, sir?'

Restarick nodded once. 'On my own.'

'I can spare one of the boys to accompany you if you need.'

'I'll give it some thought.'

Today was 10 September. Soon it would be the day that Restarick failed in his mission to kill the spy… the failure that led ultimately to the Central Powers being victorious and the Kaiser declaring himself emperor of Europe. Restarick knew that his younger self, the one who belonged in this time, would be on that roof and that his aim would be off. So Restarick intended to succeed in his stead.

He would get to Saint-Mihiel with enough time to settle in and wait but for now he would stay with Richardson and his men. There was some inexplicable comfort in being in the dug-out. He wondered if it was because he missed the action, that retiring on his plantation wasn't ultimately his destiny.

Room 40 had promised him a very lucrative deal to find Baker and bring him in. Well, he'd found him but bringing him in? Unless the storm worked both in directions, Restarick didn't see how that was possible. It seemed to him that this time-travel fiasco was a one-way trip, or at least travelling back to where he came from the long way around. But one thing he did know was that he wasn't prepared to see the Allies fail again. Baker said that Kairos wondered right up until Baker's own arrival what the purpose was in being flung back in time. Baker's purpose was to perhaps cause the pandemic, as unrelenting as it was. Restarick's own? Saving Lita had not been it, it would seem. Having a second chance at stopping the Central Powers was.

He realised now that if he couldn't save his wife, the next best thing would be to save his country.

As the evening progressed and the shadows lengthened, Packer and a couple of the section played cards. There wasn't much else to do.

'Been bloody awful out here,' Restarick said, Richardson agreeing.

'Lost some good men the last few days. Be glad to get out there again, more *Boche* to get rid of. Stuck in 'ere doing bugger all.'

That wasn't quite what Restarick meant, but he knew the sort of soldier Richardson was. He'd met a hundred like him in his time, eager to be on the front line, protecting his king and country. Men like him would have been culled in the world Restarick came from. The *Kaiser-Regel* would have not tolerated any anti-Kaiser sentiment, let alone from men as proud as he.

A ground under their feet rumbled slightly.

'Looks like old Fritzy has woken up,' murmured Packer. 'That were a landmine.'

'Aye,' agreed his fellow card-players. 'You got a losing hand there, Packer?'

'Looks like you'll never know,' he replied as the distant *pop* of a shell sounded.

'Right, you lot, get moving,' barked Richardson. 'Something's annoyed them.'

Packer and others sprang into motion, grabbing their rifles on the way out of the hole, to lean themselves against the freezing wet mud of the trench's parapet. Richardson and Restarick followed.

'It's the medical unit from Pervyse. They've been spotted.'

'They're bloody early!'

Another shell, followed this time by an explosion as it hit the ground close to where the ambulance was travelling. The dusk was shattered with flashes and hisses, incendiaries versus water-logged land. More shelling and great plumes of stinking mud and the remains of corpses rained down, stinging Restarick's eyes.

Packer opened fire into the gloom, shooting at ghosts.

The ambulance rumbled to a stop in the distance. Richardson clambered up the trench to across the dark wasteland, helping the nurses bring their baggage and equipment in, all around the air alive with shrapnel and heat.

A flurry of movement and efficiency and the nurses had bunks and surgical equipment laid out in another of the dug-outs, more spacious and deeper than the one used by Richardson, and where the injured were waiting.

'Mhàiri, clean these as best you can,' said Elise, rolling up her sleeves and handing the younger woman some scalpels. 'Corporal, I need boiling water.'

Richardson nodded and left to find a brazier he could easily fire up. He wasn't the kind of commanding officer who sat back and barked orders. He got stuck in, got involved, which was something Restarick found reassuring. It was his own approach, too. But he hadn't commanded a detail in years—although Angela used to say that his precision ordering of the plantation staff was more of a military campaign than a tea-picking rota.

Restarick entered the room and his nose twitched at the almighty stench of putrid wounds.

'Don't just stand there looking useless,' Elsie snapped, 'hold him down for me.'

The young lad on the bunk made from sandbags had a mass of blood and shattered bone along his left thigh down to his knee. He could have only been nineteen, if that. Restarick suspected he was much younger: many of the boys were too young to enlist and regularly lied about their ages. Holding him by his shoulders, he held fast to the boy and Elsie made quick work to amputate his leg from above his knee-cap.

The screams were sickening, the pain the poor boy must have been going through. He passed out before Elsie had the saw less than a centimetre in.

Cauterising the cut with the flat side of another saw, heated up across the brazier Richardson had found, Elsie wiped her hands and bandaged the boy's stump. 'He'll be out for a while now. Hopefully gangrene hasn't set in. Take that outside, will you?' She pointed to the leg with its boot and webbing. 'Out over the trench. Won't add much more to the poor boys laying there.'

Restarick picked it up, any sense of squeamishness long since excised from his mind and bumped straight into Mircalla who was coming through the narrow doorway. He didn't know whether to hug her or get rid of the leg first.

Her reaction, however, was far more immediate; she gasped and dropped the clean gauzes she was delivering, grabbing Restarick in a tight hug.

'Oh my God! What the hell is going here?!' she exclaimed.

'Excuse us,' Restarick said to Elsie and ushered Mircalla out into the trench. He lobbed the leg over the top.

'I thought you were surely dead! Then I landed in a bloody tree, found my way to France and fell into a ridiculous farce. All these people think the war is still going on! I thought I was going mad at one point!'

'Mircalla...'

'I had to play along. They are utterly convinced.'

'Mircalla...'

'It must be some sort of war game. I can't imagine Room 40 set this up. It has to be the *Kaiser-Regel*.'

'Mircalla...'

'But what for? What are they achiev—'

'Mircalla!'

She stopped talking. 'Don't tell me you believe it, too?'

He sat her down on a broken piece of duckboard. He was overjoyed to see her. By her outfit, she was pretending to be a nurse. 'And I thought you said you were a thoroughly modern woman?' he teased, flicking at the collar of her uniform.

She looked down and smiled, remembering their conversation on the train. 'Got to play along, *Dr Drummond*. So what's this all about?'

'I think you're going to find the notion of finding yourself in a simulated version of 1918 far more believable than the actual truth.'

'Try me.' She raised an eyebrow.

'That storm we hit? You said you landed in a tree.'

'Yes. I think I still have splinters,' Mircalla replied, shuffling briefly where she was sitting.

'The tree you landed in was in 1918, not 1928.'

'You're right. That's bollocks.'

Packer sniggered as he passed by.

'And I thought you were an educated European girl.'

'Spending too much time with you Britishers. Colloquially, I've gone native.'

'It's good to see you.'

'You, too.' Mircalla's eyes dropped to her hands, fingers dovetailed on her lap. 'I think I know we're somewhere different to where we should be. Seeing all this death and destruction around me. It's too real.'

'It's very real. Room 40 put me in a mental asylum because I insisted I'd come from the future.'

'How on earth did you get out? How did you make them believe you?'

'You know they say you're going mad if you start talking to yourself? Well, when you travel back ten years and meet your *younger* self...'

Mircalla tensed. 'Aaron...'

'Kaplan?'

She nodded. 'I met him. He looked younger, he was a kid. But it was definitely him. I couldn't explain it. He had no idea who I was. Are you saying...?'

'It *was* him. This is 1918. I can't explain how that storm got us here, but here we are all the same.'

Restarick outlined his movements from the moment he crashed the sesquiplane in Padua to his incarceration at Cane Hill, finding Baker, his eventual release and his devastating witnessing of his wife's death.

'I don't know what to say...' Mircalla breathed. They *had* to be in the past. For her to see Aaron alive again, for Restarick to see his wife alive again... Even the

Kaiser and his bizarre schemes to control the world couldn't bring people back from the dead. She'd only known Restarick for a few weeks but he'd always struck her as man focused on his past to keep his future steady. That seemed wholly ironic in light of his revelation to her this night. The glint of adventure that she first saw in him on the train had gone now that he'd experienced Lita's death twice over.

'I was foolish to think I could save her. I watched our home burn to the ground. I've never gotten over her death but I had at least accepted it. Now it's just brought it all back up.'

'I've often heard it said "you did your best". Now it seems patronising and cruel. Perhaps it was just meant to be.'

'Then why are we here?' He toyed with the mud at their feet with a heel, recounting to Mircalla Baker's attempt to understand the reason for their arrival in the past.

'Baker made a huge mistake,' she pointed out, 'but his reasoning was sound—although I can't really agree with his methods, especially as they backfired. You saw an opportunity just as he did. It didn't work. And perhaps that's for the best.'

'We can come back here but we can only be observers, is that what you mean?'

'In a way. Baker however has changed things. So maybe not. Perhaps there are rules to this.'

'Rules?'

'Like we can't do certain things. Killing our mothers before we're born, that kind of thing.'

'That's rather disturbing.'

'Think about it. If this ability is open to anyone, what can stop someone from going back in time and murdering their enemy's parents? The Kaiser could go back and alter the outcome of Franz Ferdinand's assassination.'

'But surely that couldn't work? If that happened, then they might not be a war and so the Kaiser wouldn't need to go back and change things, because the war would never have occurred.'

'Exactly my point. There has to be rules.' Mircalla held Restarick's hand. 'And so you trying to save Lita from an accident that has already happened, that is part of your experience, cannot succeed.'

'That still doesn't explain how Baker was able to change the past.'

'No, it doesn't. But it does indicate why this Kairos man lived out the last ten years in relative obscurity. Why didn't he announce to the world that he had come from our time?'

'Because he'd be locked away.'

'Like you were, yes.' Mircalla looked up into the black sky. The stars had broken through the clouds. It was the most peaceful night she'd had in a long time—which was odd seeing as how they were in the middle of the biggest war known to mankind. She let go of Restarick's hand, conscious she'd held it for longer than she should. 'Looks like the bad guys have gone back into their holes.'

'Won't take them much to rear up again. You know, it's strange being here again, reliving this.'

'I was too young to experience it. Reading about it and being taught about it by the Factory… they didn't hold back.'

'To think, some of the lads in 1914 were eager to enlist, to get out here and kill the *Boche*. It was like a game for a few of them, a scouting trip with a hint of added danger. They didn't know what was in store for them. When it all started, it was all cavalry charges and swords. The speed at which technology advanced—from both sides—was terrifying. If there is one thing that came out positive from the Kaiser declaring victory is that he suppressed any further developments—unless it was signed off by his senior staff.'

'But we *need* to progress, to make sure that there will never be a *second* world war. Can you imagine all this happening again?'

'Oh, I agree. The stunting of progress will take us back to the Dark Ages. The quicker we can change the outcome of the war, the better.'

Mircalla widened her eyes at that. 'Pardon me, what did you say?'

'That we will be back in the Dar—'

'No, not that. You said we need to change the outcome of the war! Didn't we just agree that doing something like that is impossible? We know it happened, so we can't change it.'

Restarick was still clinging on to the fact the Max Baker had brought the virus back with him. 'We know of *our* past. We know of *this* past. They are different.'

'But it's *impossible*!'

'If someone had told you last week they could travel back ten years, what would you have said to them?

Mircalla breathed out sharply. 'That it would be impossible,' she said slowly, quietly.

'So is it worth trying?'

Mircalla looked at him, his face steely and determined. 'I don't know.'

'Then I'll try on my own.' Restarick turned to leave.

'No, that's not what I meant.' She wasn't used to chasing after anyone, let alone men, but Restarick was subdued, verging almost on despair, she felt. Could she let him do this alone, no matter how futile his attempts would ultimately prove to be? 'Of course I'll come with you.'

He smiled weakly. 'Thank you.'

A cry from the dug-out and Mircalla pushed past Restarick into the gloom. He followed hot on her heels.

It was the young soldier who'd had his leg amputated. He was awake and wailing in agony.

Elsie was attending to him. 'I don't know how he's awake! He should have been out for hours. Mircalla, grab me some morphine. There isn't much but it should be enough to numb the pain a little. Quickly!'

Restarick grabbed the boy's hand and held it tight. 'Come, lad, you'll be alright.'

Mircalla was back within seconds and before the solider knew it, he had the drug pumping into his thigh. He sagged back, tension easing, into the bed. 'Am I… going to die?'

'What's your name?' Restarick asked.

'Harker, sir. Private Quincey Harker.'

'Let me tell you something, Harker… no, you're not going to die.'

'My leg don't half hurt, sir.'

Restarick's eyes flicked towards Harker's stump. 'It will ease.'

'My father's going to be awful cross, he is.'

'Why would that be?'

'He didn't approve of me joining up.'

'I'm sure he'll be very proud of all you've done for your king and your country.'

'He wanted me to follow in the family business. He's a…' Harker winced as the morphine worked its way around back to his thigh. 'He's a solicitor.'

Restarick noticed the wedding band on the young man's left hand. 'You married?'

'Yes, sir. Was meant to be home on leave in two days.'

'Soon be your turn.'

Harker struggled to open the flap of his bag that was still over his shoulder and hanging down by his right hip. Restarick assisted, pulling out a small, framed portrait of Harker and a pretty young lady standing next to a proud-looking Alsatian.

'That your wife?'

'Yes, sir,' wheezed Harker.

'You're a lucky man.'

'The photograph doesn't do her justice, sir.'

'Oh, no, not at all. She's lovely. You must be very proud.'

'I am, sir.'

'And that's your dog, is it?'

'Yes, sir, she's a bitch.'

'She's a stunner, Private Harker. I'm rather fond of dogs.'

'Are you, sir?'

'Indeed. When I was your age before the war, I had a Labrador. Lovely boy, he was. Lived to a ripe old age—for a dog, that is.'

'This will all be over soon, won't it?' Harker looked up at Restarick, brown eyes filling with tears. He had the light shadow of a young man's early stubble around his chin and above his top lip. His face was splattered with dried blood and dirt.

'Yes, it will. Don't you worry about that.' Restarick patted him on the shoulder as he let go of Harker's trembling hand. 'You'll be back with Mrs Harker soon enough.'

Restarick moved away from Harker as the young soldier sank into a morphine-induced sleep. It was the effect on the next generation that would be this war's true legacy. Old soldiers like he would step back one day and let those younger than he pave the future. But with the Allies doomed to failure, the brutality of combat all seemed for nothing. The Central Powers would claim victory, the oppression would begin and Harker and others like him… their vain attempts would be simple footnotes in history. And history, of course, was always documented by the winners, not the losers.

Outside, in the distance, the shelling began again. It wouldn't be safe to leave for Saint-Mihiel now. He would wait a couple more days and help Mircalla with Richardson's wounded men.

Outside, he saw Mircalla smoking with one of the nurses. He left them alone and walked along the trench, ducking instinctively whenever a mortar whistled overhead. The black night was pierced occasionally by distant gunfire flashing into the sky.

For the first time in his experience of trench life, there were no rats. They were usually fat things, nibbling away at the food stores or gnawing on numb toes as soldiers slept awkwardly in the mud. With this trench being empty, abandoned almost, they had gone elsewhere to find nourishment. They were most likely in the German trench or out up top burying their sharp teeth into the rotting dead.

As he rounded a sharp corner—the trenches were designed in zig-zags so that an encroaching enemy couldn't fire in a straight line down their lengths—he stumbled upon a young private asleep at his post.

'Wake up, lad!' he hissed, kicking the boy's ankles. 'You're on duty!'

The private shook himself into motion, straightening his helmet while picking up his rifle from the foul-smelling mud. 'Sir, sorry, sir…'

'Where's your NCO?'

'Haven't seen him, sir.'

'And he clearly hasn't seen you either. Snap to it!' Restarick spun on his booted heels and slopped back the way he had come, to the officers' dug-out. The mud was ice-cold, his toes beginning to go numb. He hadn't missed that feeling. On arrival, he reprimanded Richardson.

'Packer should be out there regularly checking on the men. So should you. I do not expect to find them asleep!'

Richardson was about to object but thought better of it. Four years into the conflict and the action was moving away from trench warfare. The grey skies were now spotted with bombers and fighters as the new tanks thundered across the tired landscape below them, where the roots of blackened tree stumps still desperately clutched. Nevertheless, it was of course vital that any manned trench, no matter if a small stretch and by a tiny handful of weary soldiers, still be guarded properly.

'Right away, Captain Restarick,' Richardson saluted. He dashed off.

'It's not your responsibility anymore, Daniel. You know that.'

Restarick turned to see Mircalla sitting in the corner, her feet up on a crate, enjoying a Murad before she returned to dress more wounds of Richardson's other men.

'Maybe not.'

'I've been thinking about what you said. About trying to change things.'

'And?' Restarick took the cigarette she offered from the soft pack and joined her. The Turkish blend was coarse at the back of his throat, but it warmed him inside and the smoke went some way to disguise the smell of death that permeated everywhere.

'The war ended for us. We're just observers here, helping out where we can until our own time catches up with us.'

'I'm still going to Saint-Mihiel.'

'Yes,' she said, tapping the ash to the floor. 'I thought you might. I won't be coming with you.'

'You're going to hide here until it's all over?' Restarick never had her down as a coward. He knew she wasn't one, even now, but she'd not lost everything she'd held dear—twice over. He had no need to remain here any longer if she wasn't leaving with him. He'd avoid the shelling better alone.

'*Va te faire foutre*,' she said calmly. 'I'm sorry. I didn't mean that.'

'Neither did I. I'm sorry, too.'

They looked at each other for a moment. He wanted to hold her, to bury his face in her hair, to feel that closeness with someone again. Mircalla squinted slightly. She trod her Mircad out in the mud and moved to him, pulling him to her.

She said nothing. Neither did he. They were both tired, filthy with blood and mud, but for a moment, the trench faded away. He felt hair across his face, her breasts under her uniform pushing into his chest. She felt wonderful. Strong. Comforting. Secure. Her embrace was what he needed and he began to weep softly into her neck.

She held him tight until he released himself from her, wiping his eyes with his sleeves, leaving dirty smudges across his face.

'Thank you,' she said.

'What for?'

'Doesn't matter. Go to Saint-Mihiel. Do what you need to do. I'm going to stay here, help Elsie and get these men back home. Richardson will see you right with weapons.'

'I'll pull rank on him if he objects,' Restarick retorted lightly. 'Where shall I meet you?'

'You're intending on coming back for me?' she smiled. 'Take me to dinner.'

'I know a great restaurant in Karachi.'

Mircalla laughed. 'No. Paris. *Le Procope*.'

'I'll meet you there. Eight o'clock sharp on the fourteenth.'

'It's a date.'

Restarick swallowed hard, threw his cigarette down and kissed her once, firmly, on the lips, his right hand clutching the back of her neck. There was no true passion, no longing for her. He just had the urge to kiss her, was all. He stepped back and looked straight into her eyes. 'Keep out of trouble.'

'You, too. But… what if you're wrong?'

'Wrong?'

'You said you thought the spy you'd seen at Saint-Mihiel was there at your home.'

'There were three men there, dressed the same. I killed one, injured another. I guess the third fled. I never saw the spy's face when I missed the shot.'

'Then go. Bring all this hell to an end. Make Barnabas and the others proud.'

'If this changes things as I pray it will, they'll never even know.'

Restarick left the dug-out. Mircalla sat back down. She considered all that had happened to them since they'd first met. Something told her that one of them wouldn't be keeping their dinner engagement.

Saint-Mihiel

Restarick came upon Saint-Mihiel and his memories came flooding back. His younger self, the captain, would be on his way, arriving in the early hours to take up his sniper position on the roof opposite the church having spent the last few months obtaining intelligence, tracing the spy's path from England into France. Restarick would not let himself be known to the captain, their interaction at Cane Hill more than enough. Instead, he would lie in wait and intercept the person who had caused the captain to miss his target, allowing the captain to succeed, the spy to be killed, the information to be retrieved and the war won.

The town was starting to settle now that German offensive had been pushed back towards Metz, the sound of rifle shots ringing out sporadically as the US Army picked off any enemy soldiers that had been left behind. Smoking ruins and shattered walls gave intermittent cover, Restarick having to navigate carefully through the town. The night was illuminated by the brightest moon he had ever seen.

Finding an old shop storeroom, well away from the open air, he settled down under a window, checking over the weapon Richardson had given him. For the first time in a decade he missed his Mosin-Nagant but the rifle he had instead would be adequate. Standard army issue. Weighted correctly and with a kick to stop a rhinoceros. He checked his watch. 2200 hours. He was hungry but had no food with him, so instead made sure he couldn't be ambushed and tried to sleep.

Restarick rolled over onto his side, the wall beneath the window cold on his back.

Scrape.

Thud.

'Why did you let me die again, *corazón*?'

His eyes snapped open, heart in his throat, pounding, thumping, aching. The tension in his body eased as Lita's dark eyes met his, and she wriggled into his embrace. He held her gently, drinking in her beauty, her hair cascading over her shoulders, obscuring with alluring flows the delicacy of her breasts. She never liked wearing anything in bed, even here in this godforsaken bombed-out room.

Restarick shuddered with contentment, then growing alacrity as her hands began to trace the outline of his chest, abdomen, the swelling in his groin.

'Do you still love me, *corazón*?'

Scrape.

Thud.

He gasped awake, squinting in the gloom, rifle ready. Lita had gone from his mind and he could feel the vestiges of tears in his eyes. A quick look at his watch again. 0220 hours. *Four hours. Damn! That was stupid.*

The scrape that had roused him came again, followed by the thud. It was close by. Restarick held his breath. The moon had moved across the sky, casting long shadows, obscuring most of his vision. There were shafts of silver on the wall, across the floor. When no more peculiar sounds repeated, he breathed out, flexing his fingers around the rif—

Thud!

That was closer. The scraping sound followed.

Restarick kept deathly still, his eyes moving to his right, towards the door frame.

There was a soldier on his side, dragging himself into the room. He was burdened with something heavy. A large bag. No… it was another soldier. By their uniforms, they were British!

The soldier shuffled again, his companion groaning deliriously.

It was only when they painfully reached the centre of the room did Restarick realise the terrible shape they were in. The groaning one of the pair most devastatingly, for he was missing his legs from the thighs down, his uniform black with blood.

Restarick lowered his rifle and leant out of the shadows.

'Private…' he whispered to the more able soldier, who was so exhausted he didn't have the strength to be startled by Restarick's unexpected appearance. Instead he sagged to the floor, his companion resting against his belly.

'Oh, thank God.'

Restarick crawled over to them. 'You're safe here. What's your name?'

'Private Saye, sir,' the Tommy responded, attempting to salute. 'This is Private Ingram.'

'Where is your unit?'

'Lost them, sir. The Yankees arrived. Bombed the whole place, they did. Stinking Fritz didn't know what hit them. We were caught in the crossfire.'

Restarick nodded. 'I've not seen any other British troops. They must have left. The Americans are busy cleaning up.'

'Good job too, sir,' Saye replied. 'You haven't got a drink, have you, sir? Bloody parched. Ingram probably needs a bit, too. Might come straight out his stumps, though.'

Restarick smiled gently at the Tommy humour, passing Saye his canteen. 'Not much left, I'm afraid.'

'I'll give some to Ingram. I'll go without until we get rescued.'

'I don't think there's much chance of that, lad,' Restarick said, his knowledge of this battle reminding him that by dawn, the only inhabitants in the town would be mongrel dogs and fearless rats. 'But I'll get us out, don't you worry.'

'Where's your unit, then, sir?' Saye eased some of the water between Ingram's cracked lips.

'I'm here alone on special duties, private.'

'Oh.' Saye handed the canteen back, but Restarick shook his head. 'Thank you, sir.'

Restarick gave Ingram a cursory glance. It was all he needed to tell him that the soldier wouldn't survive much longer. 'You're a brave lad, risking your own life to help Ingram.'

'He didn't want to die alone out in the cold, sir. He would have done the same for me.'

'I understand.'

Ingram groaned, his mouth opening and closing like a beached fish.

'I think his lungs are shot, too.'

'Were you able to cauterise his legs?' Restarick motioned to Saye to give more water to Ingram.

'Didn't get the chance, sir. He's done for, isn't he?'

Restarick nodded. 'Yes, I believe he is. Not long now, poor chap.'

Silence fell upon them for a while, broken only by Ingram's laboured breathing.

Then: 'Do you think we're going to win, sir? The war, I mean.'

'Of course, Private Saye. The odds are against Kaiser Bill's stormtroopers.' An element of a lie.

'That's what I think too, sir. The boys, they thought so.' A grasping of hope.

'That's the spirit, lad. With that attitude, the *Boche* don't stand a chance. You and Ingram serve together long?'

'Not long, sir. He joined our regiment at the Somme. Known him since school, though. Nice to see a familiar face after weeks out here. Damned rotten luck about his legs, sir. Still, bloody good show that we got to serve together in the end. Most of the lads don't make six weeks out here.'

That was the average—and savage—life expectancy, Restarick mused. Most survived only a month or so. Some, like he and Saye here, were fortunate. Although living through it all again didn't seem much like fortune from where Restarick saw it.

A crack of gunshot, some shouting in the distance, a little in German, a few exchanges in English. The weapons firing continued, growing closer. Restarick put his fingers to his lips, Saye nodding, and peered over the window ledge. There was some movement, some running, some stumbling.

Are you armed? Restarick mouthed. Saye pointed to his hip where a rifle lay. Restarick motioned to move Ingram as gently as possible to the far corner. The private did as he was ordered then returned to under the window.

'There are two Germans right below us,' Restarick whispered. 'They are pinned down by our chaps across the street, but I don't think they can get to them.'

'What shall we do?'

'Aim at something down the road. Draw the Allied aim. That will make the Germans run. Then we can pick them off ourselves.'

'What if we miss, sir?'

Restarick raised an eyebrow. 'I'm a trained marksman, Private Saye. I won't miss.'

'Yes, sir. Sorry, sir,' Saye replied sheepishly.

'Ready?'

'Ready, sir.'

Restarick rested his rifle on the ledge, ready to swing it around depending on which way the Germans headed. 'Now…'

Saye fired his own rifle, hitting an upturned lorry some distance away. The hiss of escaping air from one of its tires alerted the Allied soldiers who immediately opened fire in its direction. The trick worked and the two Germans launched themselves from their hiding place and away from the gunfire.

Restarick was upon them. In an instant he fired, downing one of the Germans in the small of the back. The other, gripping a holdall, long trench coat flapping bat-like in the motion, spun around instinctively to see what had happened. That very motion told Restarick this person was not a properly trained soldier.

He shifted his sights to look at the fleeing enemy's face.

And almost reeled in utter shock.

He immediately released the pressure on the rifle's trigger but otherwise remained glued to the spot, transfixed by the image before him. This wasn't a dream. This wasn't some sick, twisted, subconscious thought. Or was it? Could it be anything *but* his waking imagination? Was he so torn apart by what had happened? There was no other explanation.

With hands shaking he lowered down from leaning on the window ledge, rifle cradled on his lap.

'What it is, sir? Did you get them?' Saye asked.

Restarick looked at the young soldier as if he'd appeared out of thin air.

'Yes,' Restarick lied, 'yes, I got them.'

'Well done, sir! That'll teach them, the bloody Fritz!'

The bloody Fritz.

That had been no German soldier running away to god-knows-where.

That had been Lita.

***

Watching someone of a senior rank sobbing quietly was something Saye could honestly admit to never having experienced before. As he sat cradling the dying Ingram, he didn't know whether to say something to Restarick or not. He deferred to the easier option and talked gentle nothings to his injured friend who was unconscious.

Outside, the gunfire had stopped. There was calm and the day progressed into the afternoon. The air was heavy with despondency and rain, the town deserted. Ingram had stopped breathing some time ago, his eventual death painless and without any more drama. Saye laid the man's head softly on the damp concrete and said a silent prayer.

'What time is it?'

'Sir?'

Restarick who had been silent for most of the day repeated the question.

'Nearly five o'clock, sir.'

'Five!' Restarick jumped to his feet, grabbing his rifle, checking it was loaded.

'Is there anything I can do for you, sir? Are you alright?'

'What?' Restarick was annoyed by Saye's presence. 'I'm fine. Look after your friend.'

'Ingram? He's dead, sir. Popped off some time ago.'

'Well,' Restarick inwardly shrugged, 'then return to your unit.'

'My unit?' What was wrong with him? Didn't he remember their conversation last night? 'It's just me here, sir.'

Restarick never replied, striding through the doorway, stepping around the door half off its hinges.

'Goodbye then, sir,' Private Saye said to his retreating form.

***

Outside, the stench of rotting bodies and dog faeces stung Restarick's nose as he raced to a higher vantage point, and to the end of town where the church was. He was in a daze, his head filled with whirling thoughts, confused emotions and an overwhelming feeling of betrayal. Yet he realised that if it was Lita, then his younger self would be on that roof ready to shoot her dead.

Never before was a moment in his life so defined as he ascended an open staircase, two steps at a time, diving down to the soaking flat roof next to the church—and opposite to where he knew he was *at the same time aiming at the church door.*

He scanned the street again. All was quiet.

He nodded to himself and aimed his sights for the roof opposite.

The church bell tolled deep.

A few moments later, Lita appeared from without the church, with the holdall still tightly held in such a way that the information had to have still been within.

And Restarick's sights were focused back on the Mosin-Nagant that the captain was aiming at Lita.

He pulled the rifle into his shoulder, the weapon tight in his arms, and squeezed the trigger.

Crack!

He saw the Mosin-Nagant shatter and heard his own distant voice cry out, lingering in the air.

Restarick looked down at the scar on his own left arm, realising with dawning, spinning, realisation that it had been *he* that had shot his own rifle out of his own hands ten years ago, an event that was happening again here and now. That it had been *him* that had caused the spy to run free and spill the secrets to the Central Powers. The spy… Lita!

He hared back down the stairs and threw himself into the empty street, caring little now that he was out in the open and potentially a sitting duck for any remaining Germans. He'd also left his rifle behind. Up on the roof he knew the captain would be dazed from the unexpected shooting and he himself had no memory of hearing any shouting coming from below. So:

'Lita! Stop! I know it's you! Stop! I just need to talk to you!'

He leant against the church wall, breathing hard.

Casually, with an arrogance that he had never witnessed before, Lita strode up to him, a Maschinengewehr 08 in her grip, pointing straight at him. The holdall was over her shoulder. She was looking keenly around.

'Daniel.'

'There's no one else here to harm you. I made sure of that.' He didn't want to explain how. 'What are you doing?'

'Fighting for freedom,' she said. She removed her hat and wiped her brow with it. Her hair was tied back tight behind her head. 'I take it you were sent here to stop me.'

Restarick stared at her in disbelief. Her expression was stone. 'I did. I came the long way around admittedly, but yes, I was sent to intercept the spy. Not you!'

'I am the spy, *corazón*.'

'No. You're not. This is all some ridiculous charade.'

Lita lowered her weapon, her hands covered in blood. 'Come. Let me show you something.'

She led him into the church, the great doors stiff with the bomb-damaged masonry.

It was cold inside and a flock of pigeons, startled by their entry, fluttered up into the rafters, near to where the vaulted ceiling had collapsed. Rubble was strewn everywhere, pews upturned or smashed to splinters. At the end, the altar was cracked in two, the stained glass to which it stood penitent amazingly undamaged.

Behind the altar itself, where Lita stopped, was a body.

She turned it over, pointing. It was a man dressed in black, his throat slit from ear to ear.

'Why are you showing me this? Who is he?'

'I killed him. We were working together.'

'You… killed him? Why?'

'He no longer served any purpose. I am showing you so that you understand how much more I am than your little wife.'

Restarick flopped down onto the steps, leaning against the altar. 'But I watched you die. Our home. It burnt. I watched you fall into the flames.' His disbelief was gradually turning sour.

Thornton Heath, England

It was dark by the time Lita's train reached the station. She made quick work of grabbing her bicycle from the guard's van and free-wheeled all the way down Brigstock Road to the town's pond, turning off and walking the rest of the way. She rolled her bicycle along the side of her house, leaning it up against the wall. Side gate open, 'round the back, key under a plant pot and she was in her kitchen, stove lit, a pot of tea on its way. The English climate was forever cold and the tea would warm her up. She looked at the tin sitting by the sink: "Pilawala. Direct from Ceylon. Imported fresh."

'Hola, corazón.'

Lita spun, dropping to the floor the teacup she'd been holding. It smashed, flinging pieces everywhere. She looked down at it then up again at the officer standing across from her. He was framed by the table lamp, but he looked different somehow.

But more importantly what the hell was he doing back?

'Daniel?'

'My Lita, my beautiful Lita...'

She saw him smile, like it was the first time he had ever seen her. They'd slept together only a week ago, the night before he went. He wouldn't divulge his destination.

'What are you doing here?' she asked.

'I'm home.'

'But you left last week. You were going to France. Did they reassign you? Why are you back?'

'Let me look at you!' Restarick exclaimed, rushing towards her, sweeping her up and swinging around. 'You cannot believe how much I have dreamed for this moment again!' He smelt her hair, drank in her scent, her tanned skin, her very being.

She was rigid under his embrace. She wanted to get away from him but he'd always been physically stronger than her. She recognised his grip as impassioned, not forceful.

'I do not understand, Daniel. What has happened to you?' She tried to pull away.

'Happened? Nothing!'

'Your hair. Your eyes.'

'What about them? Lita, I'm home! I love you!'

'You are grey… here,' she pointed to his temples, 'and here. Your eyes, you have wrinkles.'

'It's the war, my love. It ages a man, so.'

'It is not you.' Lita pushed him away, glancing down at the smashed teacup. 'I have to clean this mess up.'

'Leave it. Please… leave it…'

She couldn't find the energy to pretend. She wasn't pleased he was home. His expression alone asked her what the matter was.

'I have to leave early in the morning for work. I won't have time to do it then.'

Restarick sighed, stepping back as she knelt to scoop the broken china into a tea towel. 'I have so much I want to tell you. Come away with me.'

They would be here any minute. He'd see them. He'd demand to know who they were. He had to leave. 'Daniel… You are like you are possessed.' She didn't turn around.

'I've missed you. It's been unbearable.'

'You have only been gone a week, Daniel.' She always called him corazón, but not now. Probably not ever again. She refused to smile. She remained distant, pointedly so.

She breathed through pursed lips as he husband next to her, picking up the larger pieces of the teacup. Their hands brushed. She paused, looking at his fingers, then at his face. He did look older. It actually suited him, made him look more distinguished. For a moment, she relaxed. Then, after a glance at the clock on the wall, she knew she had to get him out.

'I'm tired. I think I need to go to bed.'

A noise in the hallway made him tense.

'There's something out there,' he announced.

'No, there's not. Leave it.' Lita was insistent. But so was Restarick. She always hated his stubbornness.

She watched him move out of the kitchen and down the hallway, feeling the raised wallpaper under his fingertips. There was a shadow falling across the floor. Restarick paused. A shape appeared at the front door, obscured by the frosted, coloured glass panes. There was a streetlamp at the end of the garden path that illuminated their hallway. Sometimes it magnified the shadows of passers-by. Tonight, it told him they had a visitor.

'There's someone at the door,' he said.

'Probably someone just going past. It's not important.'

But she knew Restarick was thinking otherwise. He opened the door to reveal the back of a man, quite large, in a long dark coat, with the collar around his ears, a hat firmly upon his head. The figure turned around, startled to see Restarick standing there. He looked beyond, to the end of the hallway, to see Lita cradling the tea towel. The broken pieces of crockery felt uncomfortable under her grip within the cloth.

Her expression told the newcomer, who she knew went by the name of Blake, he was concerned for her safety. She shook her head imperceptibly, indicating she was alright, but Restarick whipped out his service revolver and lunged at the man.

'What the hell are you doing here? We live here! What do you want?'

Blake stepped forward, not back, surprising Restarick with the unexpected assault. Immediately, Restarick slipped out from under him, an elbow to the jaw. Blake breathed out heavily but the contact didn't slow him down. They tumbled into the hallway, the carpet rubbing against Restarick's face, but sprang up, the revolver still in his grip. But not for long. Blake struck out, knocking it clean across the floor, following up with a series of swift and harsh punches. Restarick raised his hands to protect himself from the raining blows, staggering back to the kitchen.

Lita ducked out of the way, to the living room. She dashed to the fireplace, pulling out a loose brick. In the little alcove was shoved a manila file, held together with string. She pulled it out and stuffed it under her blouse. In the hallway, she heard another man enter the house. He reached the living room doorway. It was Gunther, Blake's lieutenant. The sound of splitting wood and she glanced back out to see the hallway table go flying by. Restarick dashed into the kitchen.

'Come on then, you fucking bastards,' Lita heard him say. 'Are you here for me, or here for her? Either way, you can fucking forget it.'

Gunther darted forward. Restarick lunged, stabbing him neatly in the gut with a bread knife. The man cried out and staggered into the stove, knocking the kettle off the ring of blue flames, replacing it with his own sleeve. Gunther roared as his coat caught alight.

'Carajo,' *Lita cursed. As soon as Blake had gone for her husband, she had known this wasn't going to end well. Now Gunther was alight and likely going to take the whole house with him. She never liked it anyway, pokey little English hovel.*

'Leave now. Take the file with you,' Blake said to Lita in Catalan. 'Go to the rendezvous.'

Lita nodded, moving to the kitchen to grab her shoes.

'Get out! Get away! Go get the police!' her husband yelled at her, dodging the man who by now had fallen to the floor, burning like a bonfire Guy.

Blake spun, shouting at Lita again, who raced to the front door, only to be confronted by yet another visitor. Restarick raised the knife and brought it down into the first man's shoulder. Blake twisted around and tripped over Gunther, tumbling into Restarick. As one, they crashed through the back door and into the garden, Restarick striking his head on the flagstone path.

The third arrival was their neighbour, Sally from number 73. But behind her was Steine, another of Blake's men.

'Are you alright, Lita?' Sally asked, eyes widening in horror as she saw the kitchen alight. 'Oh my goodness!'

'I'm fine. Having some problems. Nothing I can't deal with.'

'Lita, we need to go… now,' Steine, growled, making Sandy jump.

'Goodness, I didn't hear you come up behind me. Are you the fire brigade?'

Steine ignored the neighbour. 'Lita… come on.'

'Daniel can't know I've gone. He'll come looking.'

Steine considered for a moment, looking at Sally. In a flash, he had knocked the neighbour unconscious to throw her into the hallway, the flames licking around her prone form. He grabbed Lita's hand. They ran into the night. As the house was consumed in flames, she could hear her husband crying out in anguish for her.

'Lita! Lita!'

Saint-Mihiel

'I know that look,' Lita said.

Restarick glared at her, anger swelling. 'It seems I know you far less well than I thought. I deserve an explanation.'

'Do you?' Lita turned a pew upright and sat on it, checking first for shards. 'Does it matter?'

'Does it matter? Yes, it fucking matters!'

'So we're going to sit here and have a little talk? You sound like your sister.'

There was a peculiar sense of disassociation about all of this. He'd spent ten years missing her, mourning her, so being with her again and trying to comprehend the notion she had been the spy he'd been sent to kill was almost as if this was all happening to someone else. Did it make the situation easier? No. Did it give him the courage to confront her? Yes.

As far as she was concerned, this was her husband of last week, albeit a little greyer, a little more grizzled. Let it stay that way. That would be his advantage: experience of remorse and time, not saddled with a fresh wound. As for old wounds, they remained dangerous.

'Did you use me for our entire marriage? Did you?'

'When I left Spain, I had nothing. My people had nothing.'

'You remained neutral in the war. Your country still is.'

'We did not have the luxury of taking sides.'

'So you opted to stay out of it. So why are you involved?' Restarick stood and circled the body. 'Was this Steine you mentioned?'

'Yes.'

'A German.'

'Yes.'

'And what did he promise you?'

'A better life than the Allies could.'

'But who was he to commit you to that? You had everything you ever wanted. Our plantation in Ceylon, a family. You wanted for *nothing*.'

Lita shrugged. 'He promised me.'

'Did you love him?'

'No.'

'Did he love you?'

'Yes. But not at first.'

'Did he know about me?'

'You are Room 40. Special operations. He was *very* interested in you.'

'He used you.'

Lita nodded.

'And that's why you killed him.'

'I was in too deep. When he told me that he needed me to get information out of you, I killed him.'

'But by then you'd obtained secrets from my superiors. How?'

'A neutral Spanish girl. Husband to a decorated British army captain. I was the last person they would suspect.'

'But you killed Steine because he wanted you to betray me.' So she *did* still care.

'And I used him to get these.' She patted the holdall.

'What's in it?'

Lita shook her head. 'No, my *corazón*. I will never tell you that. But what I will say is that when the Central Powers win the war, they will ensure Spain is relieved of all debts. We will be a world player. We will be *alive*. Truly alive.'

'You're doing this for your country?'

'What are you fighting this war for?' Lita looked at her MG08, then looked at Restarick. She answered for him: 'For *your* country.'

'Give me the bag.'

'No.'

'Give it to me or I'll…'

'You'll what? Kill me for it? For King and Country, *corazón*.'

'Why are you doing this?'

'I never expected it to be you sent to stop me. The war would soon be over, you'd come home and we'd be together. You would have known none of this. Why did you come home when you did? Why didn't you stay away?'

'I came back because I knew you were in danger.' I never imagined it would be from me! Me! Who started the fire that I thought had killed you!

'I do love you, Daniel. And no, I never used you for our entire marriage. Steine, he introduced me to the others. Blake and Gunther. There were more, too. They told me I could help my country. That you never needed to know. Had you not come home when you did…'

'Nothing will change.'

'What do you mean?'

'If you help the Central Powers win the war with whatever is in that bag, it won't make any difference.'

'Of course it will.'

'The Kaiser will declare himself Emperor and forge the *Kaiser-Regel*. Europe will come under his tyranny. There will be curfews, executions, closed borders. Spain will remain neutral, remain outside the control of the Kaiser and outside the sphere of any protection from Room 40 if the Kaiser ever decides to expand his empire.'

'That's not true. It's just propaganda! The Kaiser has said that's what the Allies will do! We need to be free!'

'You are free! We will all be free if the Allies succeed in overthrowing the Central Powers. If they don't, none of us will be free ever again—and that includes Spain.'

'Do you love me, Daniel?'

'Yes…' Restarick knew what she was about to say.

'Then let me do this.'

'If I say no?' Restarick's mouth began to dry.

'Then this will be the last time you ever see me.'

'But I can't let you betray the Allies. Don't tell me that you're not invested in this. You chose to be with me.'

'I chose to help my country.'

'Over me?'

'You do the same. You leave me for weeks at a time on your "special duties". Why is my cause less deserving than yours? What we fight for is bigger than what we had.'

'But you're going against everything we believe in. Freedom, helping the oppressed. By giving up that bag to the Central Powers you're condemning the world. And no matter how much I love you, no matter how long I've dreamt of us growing old together, of shutting away the world, I cannot—I will not—let you leave here with that bag. I am taking you home.'

Lita's nostrils flared. Restarick understood her passion to do what she felt was right, but he had seen the future. He knew what would happen. And what he did next did he ever think he could, or even ever needed to.

He took out his service revolver, cocked it, and pointed at her. He mustered all his courage to stop his hands from shaking, but she could see the tremor.

'Will you really shoot me, *corazón*?'

The single gunshot rang out and Lita clutched at her chest.

Legs folding, Restarick crumpled to the floor.

Panicked, she glanced up, around, spinning on her boots.

'¡*Corre, Lita! ¡Correr*!' came a voice, echoing around.

She needed no further prompting and ran from the church, the holdall held tight, her mission continuing.

***

Restarick hadn't been shot that many times in his military career but he remembered each time with furious clarity.

The stinging at his shoulder, followed by the waves of pain shooting down his right arm; he realised it was a single bullet, aimed true. No major arteries had been severed but his nerve endings in his hand had been compromised. Whoever had shot him knew he would be unable to pick up a gun and shoot back.

He found himself lying on the floor, legs folded under his backside, the cold stone church floor adding to his discomfort. He craned his neck to see who it was who was padding slowly towards him, for a moment thinking it was his younger self in some bizarre act of paradoxical vengeance.

He had to laugh when the face appeared above his, smiling sweetly, thick black hair tied back in a ponytail. She looked older, mature, stunningly beautiful. Laughter lines around the corners of her mouth and gentle crows' feet by her eyes.

'*Hola, corazón*,' Lita said. 'It has been a very long time. I have missed you.'

'You have a funny way of showing it, my darling,' Restarick replied, caressing her face with his shaking left hand.

'How else was I going to convince you?'

'But I've seen what happens, Lita. I couldn't tell you that, but I think you understand.'

'Yes, I understand.' She moved him to make him more comfortable. 'I have friends on their way. They will tend to your wound. It is clean. Came out the other side, see?'

Restarick looked down and saw the bullet's exit point above his right nipple, blood soaking out into his jacket. 'Who taught you to shoot like that?'

'I did,' replied Mircalla. 'A few years from now.'

'A few years from now? Mircalla… you found a way back?'

'Yes. It just took me a few years to get there,' she smiled. 'Now we have a faster method.'

Restarick sank back. 'What were you trying to convince me of, Lita?'

Lita sat on her knees next to him as Mircalla sat him up, tending to his bullet wound. 'You were right about the future. *Your* future that is. When you came back, you and Mircalla, you changed things, simply by being here. My younger self needed to deliver the holdall because her future—my future—was set.'

'Set, how?'

'In the time that Mircalla and I have just come from, there is a war.'

'There is always a war,' sighed Restarick.

'We have a part to play in it. So do you. That's why we came back for you.'

'The same war as now? Did it ever stop?' Restarick winced as Mircalla cleansed his wound.

'Sorry. I always was a bad nurse…' Lita said, mopping up the blood coursing down his front. She continued: 'A different one, a different war. Another world war.'

'World war?' Restarick breathed. 'When?'

Coda

The walls either side, they might as well be mountains
Rising high beyond any soldier's reach
The narrow canyons giving an elongated view of the sky
All we have to remind us that the world still turns

The trenches are all we know now
Our home where we will surely die
Not even going over the top offers an escape
Because we all know that the end there is painful

Fireworks around, the noise of hell
Make us cower in our uniforms
Like shrunken corpses, living but already dead
With no hope of ever finding a peaceful end

We stay here until we are told not to
Among the rats and the lice and the disease
Our wet feet rotting in our boots and pissing blood in the rain
Our guns so thick with mud and sand that they no longer fire

Yet we are expected to stand fast
To defend the honour and the lives
Of those who shelter safely back in the bunkers
Warm and safe and fed and healthy

We feel the futility, our innocence ripped out
By a war that was thrust upon us
Forced to be men when we are but children
Our mothers weeping into their aprons

Their sons have gone and so too have their hearts
Lamenting the visions of their offspring in their uniforms they now wear
Yet our fathers burst with unalloyed pride
Seeing them as badges of courage in a world gone mad

Our cold, empty bedrooms that used to burst with colour
Are grey now, the curtains always drawn
As if to shut out the knowledge that war is upon us
Or to shut in the memories of who we once were

Over by Christmas, that was what we were told
But we believe nothing anymore
Nothing to make us think our mothers' boys will be back home soon
As if this had been some hideous dream

We hear of victories but never of losses
Even though we see the scythe of death every day
We know the news is tainted
To make us keep going and to never give up

But whose son will go home
And whose family will receive the apology from the King
His commiserations undersigned by a simple rubber stamp
For the loss of a soldier, brave and committed?

We all wait, all here and all at home
We all know, we all fear, we all foresee the worst
And when news comes, it is neither good nor bad
It is what it is and there is nothing we can do to change it

About the Author

Elliot Thorpe is a freelance writer, having previously worked for *Starlog* and written for the sites *Den of Geek, Shadowlocked, Doctor Who TV, Red Shirts Always Die* and *TrekThis,* as well as for *Encore*, the magazine for the theatre professional.

He scripted the full cast audio drama *Doctor Who: Cryptobiosis* for Big Finish in 2005 and in 2013, his first novel *Cold Runs the Blood* was published.

He also has contributions in *Seasons of War: Tales from a Time War* (2015), *Grave Matters* (2015), *Doctor Who: A Time Lord for Change* (2016), *The Librarian* (2017), *The Wretched Man* (2020) and *Sherlock Holmes and the Woman Who Wasn't* (2021).

For many years he enjoyed a working relationship with the West End production of *The Definitive Rat Pack* and in 2017 co-wrote *Just Dino: A Recollection of Dean Martin* with Bernard H Thorpe, which was expanded and re-released the following year as *Dean Martin: Recollections*. To date, three further volumes have followed – *Dean Martin's Movie Moments, Dean Martin: A Discography* and *For the Good Times: The Dean Martin Compendium.*

He has written a number of official *Robin of Sherwood* continuation novellas for Spiteful Puppet/Chinbeard Books and is a long-term regular columnist for the San Francisco-based magazine *Search*. He also writes for the site *The Doctor Who Companion.*

deanmartinassociation.com

worldwarwhen.co.uk

searchmagazine.net

You may also enjoy…

Lightning Source UK Ltd.
Milton Keynes UK
UKHW012018240122
397652UK00002B/54

9 781789 828429